Under the
Black Flag –

Piracy Is *Not* a Victimless Crime

Jim Guigli

a
Bart Lasiter
mystery

Praise for this Author

This Novel: *Under the Black Flag – Piracy Is Not a Victimless Crime*
"This was a superb noir mystery, with all the necessary elements, great
characters, excellent dialogue, great descriptions of settings."
PSWA Contest Judges.

Short Story: *Looking for Mishka*
"Great story. Pitch perfect characterizations. Well done."
Roger Johns, Author of the Wallace Hartman Mysteries.

Short Story: *Blood on the Stairs*
"Throw a clueless PI in the middle of a Crime Conference and watch
pencils fly. Jim Guigli's tongue-in-cheek humor is a delight:
'Writer groupies. They call them readers.'"
M.E. Proctor, author of *Love You Till Tuesday,* a Declan Shaw mystery.

Short Story: *Just a Dream*
"Haunted Vietnam vet John Moss searches the drug-addled streets of
Bicentennial San Francisco for his missing sister while battling reoccurring
nightmares from his Laos combat experience. Guigli handles the transitions
from the compelling story to the savage dream sequences with the aplomb of
an expert writer. The man knows his craft."
Michael A. Black, author of the Military Thriller *Trackdown* Series.

Short Story: *Just a Dream*
"Jim Guigli's tale melds elements of a Dragnet style with heart-breaking
loss and even a touch of the surreal, as his John Moss is haunted by
memories of war. A compelling mystery with a strong sense of humanity
that exists very firmly in the time and place it occurs (mid-seventies San
Francisco). A gem of a story that fits in with its fellows in this anthology."
Frank Zafiro, award-winning author of the River City series.

Short Story: *Always Rings Twice*
PSWA Contest Judges Unpublished Short Fiction Contest, First Place 2018.

Novelette: *Bad News for a Ghost* –and– *Bart's First Arrest*
"If you enjoy private eye tales, particularly of shorter duration, you will love
Bad News for a Ghost. It truly is a pleasurable read."
Lee Ashford, Readers' Favorite Five Star Review.

Bulwer-Lytton Fiction Contest
Grand Prize Winner 2006 "The judges were impressed by his appalling
powers of invention."
Professor Scott Rice, San Jose State University.

Copyrights & Credits

This novel is a work of fiction, entirely the product of the author's imagination. Where the names of real people, real organizations, real places, real incidents, and real products appear in this novel, they are used fictitiously. Any resemblance of the fictitious people, businesses, incidents, and places to real people, businesses, incidents, and places is unintentional.

Permissions to reprint song lyrics:

Back cover photo '54 Chris-Craft Corvette (*Countess*)
credit to 2015 Chris-Craft Rendezvous

Cover photography, artwork, editing, and book layout by the author.
Author assisted by EditPros LLC Davis, CA.

First Edition, 2024, Labrador Publishing (through IngramSpark)
ISBN 979-8-9893337-1-4

Dedication

To my wife, Fran. Besides tolerating a writer's usual defects, she offered good advice (usually taken) and editing help.

Acknowledgements

Throughout the years of my writing struggles, I have received and appreciated much help and advice. Earlier, I was a member of The Mystery Writers of America (MWA) and Sisters in Crime (SinC). I am currently a member of the Private Eye Writers of America (PWA), The Short Mystery Fiction Society (SMFS), the Public Service Writers Association (PSWA), and the Sacramento branch of the California Writers Club (CWC). Friends and advisors in each organization have helped me.

A great source of trial and encouragement has been the annual PSWA Writing Contest. The many PSWA awards for my unpublished work kept me going.

I am very grateful for the people who have published my short fiction, especially John Connor at Murderous Ink Press, the editors at Rock and a Hard Place Magazine and Pulp Modern Flash, Brandon Barrows's Guilty Crime Story Magazine, and Scott Rice, father of the Bulwer-Lytton Fiction Contest. The Sacramento FBI, Sacramento Police department, Sacramento County Sheriff, and Berkeley Police department have also provided help. However, any errors the reader may find are entirely my own. www. jimguigli.com

PWA   SMFS   PSWA

Persons this *Mystery* is about —

BART LASITER,

former Berkeley, California Police Officer, now honest, impoverished Sacramento private detective who isn't confident around women. No Spenser, he's hardly a lover and rarely a fighter. He doesn't sport shiny loafers with tassels, nor is he a gourmet cook. And no three-beer lunches for Bart. The closest thing he has to a muscled sidekick is his orange cat, Aggie. Bart's live-in office is where the semi-humorous collides with the semi-serious.

AGAMEMNON (AGGIE),

adopted partner, a tough, no-holds-barred, fixed male orange tabby who loves whiskey and calls Bart's Old Town office home.

MRS. DRAKE CONCANNON,

wealthy, attractive, middle-aged blonde who loves the color black and fast boats. From a modest, challenging childhood, she's advanced to become a woman of the world, but few know who she really is. Her husband has been kidnapped, and she will pay Bart handsomely to aid in her husband's safe return.

MR. DRAKE CONCANNON,

wealthy, multi-degreed MIT postgraduate, successful engineer and inventor who specializes in gambling equipment and owns acres of Nevada Lake Tahoe waterfront.

FRED CLIFFORD,

Bart's landlord, advisor, friend, and retired Berkeley Police training officer, now a Sacramento River waterfront resident and investor.

HOOK,

ex-convict, Viet Nam vet, now aging, one-handed, outlaw biker with an unquenchable thirst for pirate lore and criminal adventure.

Persons this *Mystery* is about —

SCAR,

ex-convict, now aging, fire-damaged, outlaw biker and faithful, long-time Hook follower and enabler.

STUMPY,

ex-convict, now aging, peg-legged, outlaw biker and faithful, long-time friend and assistant to Hook and Scar.

ISABEL,

middle-aged woman who left Mexico in her teens for restaurant work in Reno, where she met young Drake Concannon and became his Lake Tahoe live-in cook and housekeeper.

SID,

veteran employee and customer of Lake Tahoe North Shore casinos, repository of Concannon and Sinatra North Shore history, now aged bartender at the Crystal Bay Yacht Club.

AL WEXLER,

veteran Nevada newspaper reporter with decades-old underworld sources, and Bart's friend.

ANGELO (ANGIE) STANGETTI,

mysterious Reno businessman and Mob watchdog with long-time ties to Drake Concannon.

MARTY BROOKS,

former Bart Lasiter Berkeley Police Department partner when they were rookies, and current Placer County Deputy Sheriff.

PETE & PHIL, and DALE EINHORN,

Eastern Region FBI Special Agents reassigned to Lake Tahoe and the Concannon Estate investigation.

Under the
Black Flag—
Piracy Is *Not* a Victimless Crime

Jim Guigli

Prologue

Why?

Lake Tahoe, 12:30 AM, Sunday, August 12, 2007:

He knew he was still alive.

He could breathe the cool air.

He could see the stars above him.

He could feel the cold water soaking through his clothes.

Why was he floating in the lake?

Part One

The Dream

1

The Black Spot

Dream

Sacramento, 10:30 AM, Wednesday, four days prior:

Detective Bart Lasiter was in his office studying the light from his one small window falling on his super burrito when the door swung open to reveal a woman whose body said, You've had your last burrito for a while, whose face said angels did exist, and whose eyes said she could make you dig your own grave and lick the shovel clean.

He thought she was perfect.

A black sleeveless dress, long black gloves, a black straw hat with a flat brim and thin black veil hanging down to her red lips, black nylons that matched the veil, black high heels, and a modest black purse — a flood of black that was merely background, like the velvet in a jeweler's case, for her tanned, flawless skin and shoulder-length blond hair. It was the kind of blond that appeared as a matter of course when certain women reached a certain age, as if scheduled by Nature.

He sat dumbstruck while she closed the door behind her.

"Mr. Lasiter?"

The detective smiled and nodded, struggling to swallow his mouthful. His anxious fingers fumbled closing the aluminum foil wrapper around the burrito, while his feet resting on the desk greeted her with the worn soles of his Nike Air lowcuts.

He dropped his feet to the floor and jammed the burrito into a drawer. Under the desk, he quickly wiped his hands clean on his jeans, too late to hide the fresh salsa and guacamole stains spotting the front of his Old Sacramento T-shirt.

Her deep blue eyes watched. She waited.

After forcing down a resistant sprig of cilantro, he stood and opened his mouth.

"Please sit down. How can I help you . . . miss?"

"Mrs. — Mrs. Drake Concannon."

Her eyes scanned quickly from Bart to the corners of his office, and then back to him. When she turned her head, her hair brushed across the top of her shoulders and parted, exposing a flash of black earring.

The shape of the earring, he thought, was —

"Mr. Lasiter?"

"Yes. Pleased to meet you, Mrs. Concannon. How can I help you?"

"I do need help. It's my husband, Drake." She took a deep breath. "They've kidnapped him." She clenched her purse. "He took his boat . . . out . . . out on the lake, and . . . he never came back!"

"Please, sit and tell me."

She eased her tall, slender body into his client chair. Like his chair and desk, hard use since the forties had humbled the blond oak. Time had stolen the chair's finish from its broad arms and contoured seat. The steel rollers and tilting swivel base, like those of the detective's chair, had endured decades without oil.

"Let me try to help you." He sat.

She was older than his thirty-nine years. But how old? Had he been expecting a visitor like her, instead of daydreaming, he'd have already rehearsed sounding confident and nonchalant, as if a woman who looked like she looked walked into his office every week.

He saw her long, thin nose flinch. He'd seen that before. The building had an odor he'd grown accustomed to. Old wood, old plaster, old paint. Old. He hoped it wasn't that he lived in the office. But today her perfume ruled.

She ignored the arms of her chair and held her purse in her lap, her elbows pressed against her body. She was trembling.

This August morning the desk thermometer was already at the eighty-degree mark. Not cold, she was afraid. She needed help.

"You're certain he's been kidnapped? Not boat trouble?"

"That was my hope. Until I received the ransom demand."

Her eyes took another restless tour of his office.

"Ransom? You've told the police?"

Her eyes came back, fixed on him. "They warned me not to contact any law enforcement, or they would ki . . . *kill* him. We, I . . . we could pay the specified sum." Her eyes darkened. "No. *No* police."

Bart didn't want to turn away a new client, but he wasn't in the detective business just to make money. He wanted to help people, correct wrongs, and do right.

"I want to help, but you should report this to the police."

"No! I don't *want* to report it to the police. I don't *want* to tell law enforcement. *Listen* to me. The police, the Sheriff, whoever — they'll surely make a mistake and he . . . he might be . . . *hurt.* He's all I have in life. I desperately want him back, and I would do *anything* to get him back — except tell the police.

"My husband has warned me many times: '*Never* trust the police.' He would never forgive me. Surely, *you* can help me."

Don't call me Shirley entered his mind and was quickly pushed aside by *The Dream.* Like any of hundreds of bored PIs living day-to-day, Bart had dreamed *The Dream*: A beautiful woman enters his office and asks for his help. Now the woman from the dream was here in his office, sitting in front of him. But the reality felt strange, more troubling than thrilling.

The heat from her eyes behind the veil made him sweat. She was the type of woman who had always been a problem for him. A *woman*-woman.

How could he help? She should go straight to the law.

Her eyes held him. Those eyes — the blue.

He turned away, leaned back, and fought to think while his black-iron ceiling fan offered a flickering slideshow of the water stains coloring the plaster above.

Now resolved, he would politely explain why she should pass on Lasiter Investigations and contact law enforcement.

He turned to speak, but she spoke first.

"Mr. Lasiter, I'll pay triple your normal fee."

Her words were fingers clamped over his mouth. He wanted to say that money wasn't the issue, but sums whispered in his ear, past-due sums like his rent and telephone bill.

"Please, tell me more."

"Yes."

"How did they contact you?"

"This arrived at our home." She removed a manila business envelope from her purse.

He swiveled in his chair and held the envelope up into the light. A red ink rubber-stamped date of Monday, two days ago, stained the envelope near the printed return address of a Reno commercial messenger service. Scrawled in felt-tip pen, the delivery address read:

PERSONAL   To:

Mrs. Drake Concannon

One Eagle Cove Road

Eagle Cove, Nevada

"You came from Nevada to Sacramento for a detective?"

"I approached several agencies, first in Reno and then here in Sacramento. Drake keeps an office here. No one offered to help. No one. Then I saw your Yellow Pages ad. With your picture."

She gazed beyond him.

Bart guessed she was seeing his ad again, not the back of his office. She raised her hand to run black-gloved fingers through her blond hair.

"Mr. Lasiter, in your ad, you looked honest. And kind."

"Thank you." It was one of the few times the ad had done anything but lower his checkbook balance.

She looked down at her hands.

"Oh . . . there was some trouble with your telephone. So, I came without an appointment. Is that all right?"

"Certainly. I encourage people in need to contact me at any hour."

She smiled.

He opened the manila envelope. Inside, a white letter envelope with the same address typewritten contained a single sheet of thick paper, folded into thirds. The typewritten note began:

WE   HAVE   YOUR   HUSBAND!

HE IS OK BUT YOU MUST COOPERATE.

NO   SHERIFF   OR   FBI!

IF YOU WILL PAY FIVE MILLION DOLLARS IN

USED HUNDREDS

SHINE A RED LIGHT IN YOUR WINDOW

MIDNIGHT FRIDAY NIGHT.

YOU WILL BE CONTACTED.

PAY   OR   HE   DIES!

"Five million? Wow. Your window?"

"From the water, they would be able to see the red light. We live on the lakefront."

"Oh. Which lake?"

"Lake Tahoe."

"Oh . . . ." Bart began to believe.

A distinct thud rattled the glass in the top half of his office door. She turned to the door as the latch snapped. No shadow appeared behind the frosted glass, yet the door opened. At the bottom, a muscular orange cat pushed his way into the office. She leaned back as the cat jumped onto the desk.

Bart smiled. "Sorry. He's my cat."

Bart rose to close the door. Tall and thin, he moved without precision. His brown hair fell over his ears.

"I'm not used to animals. Drake has dogs, but they're not allowed inside our home."

"Hi, Aggie. Say hello to Mrs. Concannon." The cat looked up at her.

"You called him 'Aggie?'"

"Short for Agamemnon. I didn't name him."

Bart stroked the cat's ears and head. "He's discovered he can defeat the latch by ramming his shoulder into the door."

Bart returned to his chair and the note while his prospective client watched from behind her veil. He sat studying the note, oblivious to the unbalanced whisper of the fan turning above their heads and the squeaking of his chair, as he slowly swiveled back and forth.

She waited while the orange cat curled up on the green desk blotter. The cat stared at her before closing his eyes.

Bart's swiveling stopped mid-swivel.

"What?" He had just unfolded the note completely. He saw a dense, doubloon-sized spot of black ink, a blotch soaked into the paper above a crude ink drawing of a black flag displaying crossed white bones beneath a white skull.

Bart looked up and out through his small window, past the golden tip of the State Capitol dome, toward Lake Tahoe.

"PIRATES?"

* * *

2

Trust

Out Beyond the Window

She watched him squint to look out past the spotlight that was his little round window.

He was out beyond the window now, watching the sky's blue turn to black and white. He heard the music. The film began. His lips moved as familiar words filled the screen:

The Maltese Falcon . . . Pirates —

"Mr. Lasiter?"

Fate . . . Mystery —

"Mr. Lasiter?"

"Oh . . . yes. Sorry, I was thinking."

"I thought that part — the black spot and flag — was truly strange. But safely bringing Drake home is my sole interest, not decoding the note. Under the best of circumstances, I have never been good with puzzles or details. And now, when my precious Drake is taken . . . *help* me."

"I will. Please tell me about your husband. What does he do for a living?"

She looked down to her lap and purse. "Well, Drake is retired now, but he is an accomplished, much-respected, brilliant engineer with many patents." She touched her hair again and watched Bart's eyes. "He was a consultant in the gaming industry for years. He's made a good living helping people."

"Casinos?"

"Sometimes." She looked back down to her lap and purse.

"Do you have a recent photo of him?"

"Yes, I do." She retrieved from her purse a four-by-six color print. Pausing a moment to look at the image, she smiled. The smile collapsed. She looked away and handed the photo to Bart.

Drake Concannon was heavyset, balding, maybe seventies, standing on a pier next to a stone boathouse. He was holding a fishing pole and tackle box. Bart flipped the photo over and saw their address and telephone number.

"Please keep the photo."

"Thank you. When was this taken?"

"Just a few weeks ago, at our home."

"Do you think your husband could have any enemies from his work?" Casinos, the honey pot for every mean ant within a hundred miles.

"I wouldn't know. He never talked to me about his work. He never mentioned trouble. He never mentioned enemies. There was no warning." Her eyes flared, her jaw tightened, and crimson darkened the tan of her throat and face. "This ransom note — it, it just happened!" Her long fingers, squeezing her purse, came up to the desk. She stood, ignoring his cat, and leaned forward on the purse, staring into Bart's eyes. "Without Drake, why, I just . . . I feel so vulnerable and alone! That is why I must have your help. Please be generous, Mr. Lasiter — *Please!*" She lowered her head and slid back into the chair.

Did he see tears beneath the veil? He barely controlled an urge to reach across the desk for her hand.

"Try not to worry. Please. We'll get him back."

"Thank you," she whispered, taking a black handkerchief from her purse and dabbing at her eyes. Then, as if to turn attention away from her eyes, she removed her gloves. She turned her head away from him, blushing.

It hit him then, a hard fist to the gut. Again, he was having trouble controlling his emotions around a woman. But she was so special, so different from any woman he'd known before. Every time she looked at him, it unnerved him. Hers wasn't an everyday look — it was total, unblinking, locked-in eye contact.

It made Bart feel she was reaching deep inside him. He

resolved to manage her hold on him by concentrating on logic and the details of the kidnapping.

"What about you, Mrs. Concannon? Has anyone threatened you? Have you fired anyone?"

She reached up to wipe her eyes again. Light from his window haloed her blond hair and flashed off the diamonds in her engagement and wedding rings, brighter than it had from the aluminum foil around his burrito.

"Threatened? Me? No, no. I am only a housewife. Drake supervised the help. They've been with him for decades."

"Well, you're a *wealthy* housewife, and I can tell you from experience, money draws trouble like honey draws ants."

"Yes, I suppose that you are right. But it is all a blank, a dark, terrible puzzle to me. Drake and I have few contacts with other people. I have been content to stay in our home by the lake, and my husband has restricted his social activity to the Yacht Club for years, recently only attending the Club's Spring and Fall Galas."

"Which yacht club?"

"The Crystal Bay Yacht Club. Do you think there could be a connection?"

"Possibly. Please, leave the investigative details to me — it's what I do. And try not to worry."

"Yes. You know best."

"How long have you been married?"

"Four, almost five years. Since August two thousand two." She paused, and then her voice broke. "Sunday will be our wedding anniversary."

"Sorry, but I have to ask — your husband was single when you met?"

"Oh, yes. He was married for a short time when he was a young man, in the fifties, and then divorced."

"And you?"

"I was single, too."

Bart raised his eyebrows and waited.

"Oh . . . I've . . . been married before."

"So, there would not be an angry husband from your past?"

"Oh, no. My first husband, he . . . I was a widow when I met Drake. No, there would be no problems from the past."

"What about the money — the five million dollars in used hundreds?"

"I can imagine some would consider it unusual, perhaps even incautious, but we can pay the ransom with money we have at our home. Drake has never trusted banks."

Bart took a minute to imagine having five million in cash to spare, and then keeping it under the mattress.

"Then I'd better be at your place Friday night, for the red light."

"Oh, thank you!" She sat up and smiled behind the veil. "I hoped you would agree. I was afraid you might change your mind, that no one would help me."

"I'll be helping you."

She opened her purse and withdrew five one-thousand-dollar bills. "Expenses."

Bart stared. He'd never seen a thousand-dollar bill but once, in Bogie's hand in *The Maltese Falcon*.

"When you require more, please ask. When my husband returns, you will receive a fifty-thousand-dollar bonus."

Nearly paralyzed by the bonus, Bart focused on her red fingernails, trying to control the tremor in his hand while he accepted the bills. When the bills were safely in his hand, he smiled. "You're very generous, Mrs. Concannon."

"He is my husband."

Bart put the money into a desk drawer and pulled a blank contract form out from under the burrito.

Her smile disappeared. "Oh . . . no." She leaned forward. "Please. No written contract is necessary."

He stopped. After a few seconds, he returned the form to the drawer.

She smiled and pulled on her gloves. "I *trust* you, Mr. Lasiter."

* * *

3

It's Poetry

From the Bottom to the Top

They descended the two flights of stairs carefully, with Mrs. Concannon's gloved hand holding Bart's bare arm to steady herself on her high heels. She trusted him. The wooden treads creaked and flexed under him and his new, his only, client. He guarded her, his priceless china doll.

They stepped from the dark staircase and lobby onto the sunlit wooden sidewalk. She took large designer sunglasses from her purse, slipped them on under her veil, and looked past the building's flaking white paint up to the window that illuminated Bart's office.

They rested on the west side of Second Street, near L Street, eight blocks from the Capitol. Against a fence on the east side of the street, a thin stand of trees shaded a stone and bronze monument commemorating Theodore Dehone Judah, the father of the Transcontinental Railroad. The few dusty trees protected Judah's backside from the traffic on Interstate 5, roaring by a few feet beyond the fence. Bart didn't notice any of it.

With her right hand bracing her black hat against a light breeze, Mrs. Concannon turned to Bart. She was tall but, even in her high heels, had to look up to Bart.

"Thank you, Mr. Lasiter. I'm feeling much better now."

Her throat reddened. "Mr. Lasiter, you . . . you are my hero. You know I am depending on you now, depending on you to carry me through this terrible thing and return my beloved husband safely back to me and our lakeside home."

"That's why I'm here."

She let go of her hat and offered her hand to Bart. Her eyes hid behind the sunglasses in the shadows of her hat and veil, but Bart felt their heat. A breeze stirred her veil and carried her perfume to him. When her hand touched his, he felt a pulse of electricity pass through her glove to somewhere deep inside him. She let him stare a moment before turning away and walking to the corner, and then west on L Street.

Nailed to the sidewalk boards, Bart's feet didn't move. Stone-still as Teddy Judah, Bart watched her walk away. After she had disappeared around the corner, minutes passed before Bart relaxed.

He finally snapped to and returned to his building, slowly climbing the front steps to the entrance lobby, wondering if this morning was only a dream. *The Dream.* With the lobby door closed behind him, he heard tires chirp and turned in time to see, through the door's century-old glass, ripples of black Mercedes coupe rush by.

Climbing the stairs to his office, Bart weighed his two conflicting challenges: his covenant to follow the law and his calling to help a woman. As in the past, he would risk being accused of skirting the law, usually to pay the rent, now to help a woman.

This case appeared to be a genuine kidnapping. Helping Mrs. Concannon avoid law enforcement might put his license at risk, or worse, depending on what story he could spin, if caught. Did he have to report it? He wasn't sure. He'd never had a kidnapping case before, except for Mrs. Tereshkova's cat. It was academic, because he would be working in Nevada, too, and he knew that wouldn't be lawful.

An earlier skip-trace job taught him Nevada didn't have a reciprocity agreement with California for private investigators.

A reciprocity agreement between the two states would have allowed Bart the freedom to treat Nevada as part of California. Without the reciprocity agreement, he was required to request permission to investigate in Nevada, and then request a Nevada-licensed private investigator to supervise him, but only after he had presented a written contract signed by his client.

All Bart had on a contract was his very own Jackson Pollock, a painting combining drizzles of red hot sauce, smears of green guacamole, and splashes of brown beef juice. His real paper contract was the five portraits of Grover Cleveland, now safe in his desk drawer.

This was a cross-your-fingers-and-hope case, working in the gray. Long ago, Bart had learned the law was seldom like his former Berkeley patrol car, black and white. You mix black and white and you see gray.

His gut told him Mrs. Concannon was a good woman who needed help.

Rule One.

His desire to help her outweighed any legal issues. Also, she was a *woman*-woman, with a lot of cash.

This case and his new client had also forced Bart to alter his attitude. When circumstances allowed, he liked to joke with his clients, keep things light. His father always told him you had to laugh, or life was just too hard. But jokes and laughs were just a sideshow compared to paying the rent. Or saving a life.

Until this blonde with the black purse full of cash walked into his office, his detective career was in constant jeopardy. Several times he'd concluded that someone would soon scrape *Lasiter Investigations* off the frosted glass of his office door. Then an unexpected little job in Old Town would carry him a few weeks more.

But Bart had never had a case this lucrative, or mortal before, nor had he a client as special as Mrs. Concannon. This case changed everything.

His thinking had used up all the stairs and put him on the third floor. He entered his office and opened the desk drawer. Before he suffered a sticky mess again, he removed the burrito and pocketed his expense cash.

Aggie woke and stretched across the blotter.

Bart sat in his chair, rolled toward the back of his office, and bent down to store the burrito in his mini refrigerator.

Bart felt rusty. Since moving to Sacramento, he had used his police skills infrequently. Mrs. Concannon was so afraid of the police, yet he hadn't mentioned to her he had once been a police officer, answering to daily assignments, never waiting for work to walk into his office.

July 2002 — "Are you sure, Lasiter? You're giving up a nice salary and benefits. Steady paycheck?"

"Twelve years. It's time, Sarge."

Bart was on his last stop returning Berkeley city property. He'd turned in his gun, Sam Browne belt and its attachments, body armor, riot helmet, and gas mask. He dropped his badge, keys, and other items onto the property clerk's table. After one last look at his badge, he slid it across the table.

The Sergeant took the badge and checked the number. "Not a job for a sane person, Berzerkeley. A decade or two and you begin to lose your sense of humor." He recorded each item on a three-ply form.

Bart didn't understand. "After a decade or two . . .?"

"Irony, Lasiter, or maybe understatement for effect — you should know. You were one of the jokesters here."

"Ah, of course. Yup. Good one, Sarge."

"Heard you're leaving town. I'll miss those football games on your big TV, and your movies, too. I still have two of your tapes I borrowed a few months back."

"Thanks. Bring them here and I'll stop by to see you before I leave Berkeley."

The Sergeant completed the form and slid it across the table to Bart. "Your John Hancock, Lasiter. A lot of you guys don't stay until retirement."

Bart leaned against the table and stared at his receipt, thinking about his years of service to the City of Berkeley.

"It was okay, most of the time. But things get old. Things change. You know Marty Brooks left. And Sergeant Clifford retired. Then my wife took off. My dog died."

"Lonely, huh?"

"Restless. I want to leave all this behind. I want to be on my own. I want to do something different."

"So, you're going to move to Oregon or Idaho and fish?"

Bart laughed. "No. I want to continue the job. But private."

"Lots-a-luck, Lasiter. Many have tried before you. They usually wind up back in uniform somewhere. Cop again, or security guard. Then there's motel management, or bartender school. Eventually they miss the bennies and steady paycheck."

"I know, but I'm optimistic."

"You always were. Pleasure knowing you. Where to now?"

They shook hands.

"Up north, Sacramento. A new beginning in the Capital."

Cleaning out his apartment that night, Bart stopped and did something he hadn't done in years. He sat with pencil and paper and marveled at his bold decision to change careers.

<u>Haiku</u>

by Bart Lasiter

Deep water all 'round

Man swims to find his island

Optimism rules

* * *

4

A New Beginning

Watertown

Bart could feel the five bills burning a new hole in his jeans while he enjoyed a short walk, east through the K Street pedestrian-only tunnel under Interstate 5, to his bank in the mall.

In his bank, a savings and loan in one of the mall's small side branches, Bart approached a teller. He intended to deposit three of his five one-thousand-dollar bills to join the fourteen dollars in his checking account and exchange the remaining two bills for hundreds, fifties, and twenties. He removed the bills and a deposit slip from his nylon wallet and set them down on the counter.

A young lady, Tiffani, looked closely at Bart's currency and tapped a painted and bejeweled fingernail on the counter.

"Sir, I'll be right back."

She left the window to speak with an older woman behind a low partition. The woman looked at Bart and said something to Tiffani. They came back together to the teller window, where the older woman looked at each bill.

Bart shifted his weight from one foot to the other. "Aren't they good?"

"Yes, they are. It's just so unusual. We don't see many like these because the one-thousand-dollar bill hasn't been produced since 1945, and the government has been taking them out of circulation since, I think, 1969. These bills look almost new.

A collector might pay you more than face value for them."

Tiffany nodded in support and waited for Bart's answer.

"Maybe . . . but I can't wait. Face value please. Thank you."

"Certainly, Sir." The older woman smiled and left.

Tiffani counted the bills and handed them to Bart. "Have a nice day."

Outside his bank, Bart walked from the dark branch corridor into the mall's open-roofed center and blazing sunshine. He looked up into the light. $3014 in his checking account, his pockets packed with currency, and a wealthy client — leaving Berkeley was finally paying off.

On Second Street, walking back to his office, Bart started feeling twitchy. While the money was great, the responsibility was greater. Instead of his typical Old Town cases, stolen T-shirts, a life was at stake. He needed to, as his mother used to say, center himself. Bart didn't live in a trailer on the beach like Jim Rockford, but he did live near water. When he reached his building, he passed by and kept walking south to L Street, then turned west toward his river, the Sacramento River.

From the library, Bart had learned the Sacramento River begins two hundred miles to the north, near Mount Shasta, and draws water from the Feather River in the northeast. Another source, the American River — mother of the 1848 gold strike at Sutter's Mill — flows from the Sierra Nevada near Lake Tahoe down through the foothills into the Sacramento River just north of Bart's office.

After crossing Firehouse Alley, Front Street, and then the old railroad tracks set into the heavy-timber boardwalk, Bart arrived at the edge of the river. He sat and didn't say or think anything. He watched the water slowly flow by the way people before him had a hundred or five hundred years ago. His mother had tried everything, including Zen and meditation. Sitting quietly at the river's edge was as close as Bart would get to meditation. After a while, he felt better and started back to his office.

Bart turned into Firehouse Alley, looked up, and waved to Aggie, sunning himself on a table set on their slight balcony, an extension of the second floor of their building's backside. The wooden gate in the fence fought him as usual. When he had it beaten, Bart sprinted down the narrow gravel path, ignoring the encroaching dry grass and weeds clawing at his legs, until he reached the back staircase. A new sense of purpose hurled him up the stairs, two at a time, to his office. He needed the keys to his garage and car, and he had to find his checkbook. Bart was anxious to pay the back and current rent he owed his landlord, Fred Clifford.

* * *

5

Home

I Got Plenty of Nothing

When Bart was a naïve rookie in the Berkeley Police Department, Fred Clifford was his principal training officer. Fred was near retirement when his father died and willed him real estate in Sacramento. Now a landlord in the Capital, Fred settled into what had been his father's home, an old cottage on a half-acre of Sacramento River frontage north of downtown.

Several of Fred's properties were in Old Town. Old Town, Old Sacramento, and Old Sac are all the same place, a compact area fronting the Sacramento River between the I Street Bridge in the north and the Tower Bridge in the south. Second Street, Firehouse Alley, and Front Street occupy a narrow strip between the modern Interstate 5 on the east and the ancient river on the west.

When Bart decided to leave Berkeley behind to start his own detective business, Fred offered him an economy office in Old Town. Thinking of that day in 2002 made Bart smile.

Bart borrowed a cop-friend's car for the drive from Berkeley to Old Town, where Fred would show him the office.

Finishing the 85-mile drive early that morning, Bart put his detective's observational skills to work while he drove several laps in each direction around Second Street and Front Street, and through Firehouse Alley. Each time he passed Fred's building, he studied its wood and stucco façade, its neighbors, and the nearby attractions.

Old Town, almost a separate village isolated from the city of Sacramento, surprised Bart. Bohemian, not wealthy, yet not like the sketchier areas of Berkeley, overrun with street people or drug dealers. Many people walking the streets of Old Town were obviously tourists, peering through the front doors of gift shops, candy stores, bars, fast-food shops, and restaurants. Most of the buildings were very old, or looked old after being totally restored, like the old firehouse converted into a restaurant, *The Firehouse*. Others, like the original Wells Fargo building and California's first Supreme Court were serious history.

After Berkeley, Bart needed to downsize. Old Town looked like a place he could wrap his arms around, a place he could enjoy calling his home. Old Town felt like his kind of town.

On Bart's last pass sight-seeing down Second Street, he saw Fred, standing tall, still thin and muscular, waiting out front. After smiles and handshakes, Fred led him to the third-floor door marked $301^{1/2}$.

"This office is so small I have trouble renting it. A former owner split this room off from 301, to rent storage space to a tenant. I was told walls were often torn down and replaced to suit new tenants."

The door's stained wood was the color of coffee grounds and didn't match its frame. Frosted glass filled the top half and rattled when Fred opened the door.

"He replaced the original solid door when he converted the space back to an office."

Bart followed Fred in, looked around, and then up to the ceiling. It was high, at least ten feet. A black-iron fan hung from its plaster. He found the switch on the wall and tried it. The fan turned.

Fred pointed to the one window high on the front wall. "The light from that small window is all you get, Bart, except for what comes through the door from the hallway. This office, it's not much, Bart, but it's the cheapest I have. You have to watch your budget when you're starting a business."

Bart moved to the center of the empty room and stepped into an ellipse of light on the floor. His hand shaded his eyes as he followed the bright light up to its source. The window was a disappointment. Sam Spade, Lew Archer, and most of his favorite detectives from the forties had venetian blinds covering rectangular windows, casting noir shadows into their offices. This round window wouldn't work with venetian blinds and was too small for his name. His business name would have to be on the glass in the door. With little competition, the high window's light was intense.

Fred watched Bart bounce on his toes, testing the unpainted pine boards in the floor, then step to a wall, painted white in a previous decade, and put his finger into a hole in the water-stained plaster. After examining his finger, he wiped it off on his jeans.

Fred nodded toward the ceiling. "Roof's been replaced."

Bart stood again in the ellipse of light and turned full circle for a last look. When he moved about, he saw his shadow run from his feet and climb up the back wall. He saw a taller version of himself.

"Cool."

"Bart, you could, if you want, live here, too. It'd be good to have someone in the building at night. There's a toilet and shower at the back end of the hall."

"Okay."

Back in Berkeley, Bart borrowed another cop's pickup truck. He loaded it with his remaining personal possessions, what his ex-wife, Sonja, hadn't taken, plus surplus office items from the University's furniture outlet.

Bart left behind his old computer, a Windows 98 PC clone, cobbled together in a one-man shop off Telegraph near the campus. He had never liked paying for computer upgrades and security problems. Spam bewildered him.

A typical spam would be a friendly email from a stranger: "Hi, I'm Jane," followed by the pitch. The subject line of the last spam he received, from "Marsha," read, "Pleasure All Women with the Size of Your Instrument." Bart donated the computer to a passing student.

Fred helped Bart lug the furniture up the stairs. After nearly killing themselves carrying and sliding the heavy wooden desk up to the office, they both were grateful Bart had chosen older, light-weight, wooden file cabinets, instead of the modern, heavy steel examples. The dark green wooden cabinets had working locks. They reminded Bart of old detective movies. He thanked Fred and set about arranging his new office.

The desk with two chairs, and a hat-and-coat tree were all University blond oak. He positioned them and the two file cabinets at the front of the room, near the door. At the back of the room, he arranged the remaining things he'd brought from Berkeley, along with his new purchases.

He had found a used, Yugoslavian, waist-high apartment refrigerator, and placed it at the head of his single bed, set across the office back wall. On top of the refrigerator, he stacked his microwave, a one-burner hot plate, and a twisty goose-neck desk lamp. The lamp would allow him to read in bed.

On a bookcase against the wall at the foot of his bed, Bart balanced his TV, Goodwill VHS player, and rabbit-ears antenna. His appliances, and another lamp on the desk, all plugged into a complex network of multi-socket adapters and long extension cords, which then plugged into the one outlet at the back of the room.

Sonja had taken his 32" Sony XBR TV, his Sony VHS recorder-player, and his movie tapes when she left, while he was still at work. She took his car, too, but Bart could walk to the station. When he told a few cops about Sonja and his TV, a divorced cop took pity and gave Bart his daughter's old 13" TV.

The bookcase's lower shelves were packed with paperback true crime stories and mysteries: Raymond Chandler, Robert B. Parker, Ross MacDonald, Charles Willeford, James M. Cain, Joseph Wambaugh, and others. Videotapes and a well-worn copy of Dashiell Hammett's *The Maltese Falcon* filled an upper shelf under the TV.

One drawer of one of his file cabinets held his dishes. The combination of a few cardboard boxes under his bed and nails in the wall became his wardrobe. To shield his sleeping area from the office area, he found a matched pair of thrift-store folding screens. They were tall enough to prevent visitors from seeing his bed and offered impressions of oriental waterfalls.

Bart spent most of a morning moving the desk around and changing its angle relative to the door. He settled on a placement where the light from his high window would fall on the desk in the morning.

Worried about spending too much time arranging his office, instead of finding work, Bart rationalized that a comfortable base and home was worth the effort. It would be a retreat and anchor in troubled times.

The telephone man arrived and connected Bart's black dial phone, another thrift-store find. Later, Bart placed ads in the local free papers and ordered a photo-ad in the Yellow Pages. That done, he filled his thrift-store Italian aluminum coffee pot and set it on his hot plate.

When the coffee had finished perking, he poured a cup, sat at his desk, and surveyed his domain. He felt for the first time his career change was real. He'd have *Lasiter Investigations* painted on the frosted glass in the door, right below the $301^{1/2}$. Bart Lasiter — *Detective*. Wow. Dreams *can* come true.

Rules and *Goals* — now was the time to set them, before unforeseen difficulties might cloud his vision.

Rule One, he was in business to help people, good people the police had failed to help. Chandler's Knight.

Rule Two, he would avoid any shady deals, or clients who thought money could buy him to do or be anything they wanted. Bart Lasiter would not be a Blunt Instrument.

He was sure there would be other rules in time, but these two would be a good start.

Bart's mind stalled at *Goals*. He decided, for now, paying his bills and being comfortable would be sufficient.

Fred came by a week later.

"You've done a lot, Bart."

"I'm happy. My office works and it feels like home. Fred, where can I find a car cheap, almost free?"

* * *

6

The Klimo

Available

Fred leaned against a file cabinet and thought. He looked at the Oriental screens and adjusted his pants.

"How bad do you want a car? I've got one you could have for, say . . . a hundred seventy-eight bucks. It's in one of my buildings in Firehouse Alley, right behind us."

Bart swiveled in his chair.

"I need a car. I would ask why only a hundred seventy-eight bucks, but it doesn't matter because I'm down to fifty bucks. You remember, she left me with all those bills."

"Sonja, your dream girl?"

"The world needs dreamers."

"All that time busting crime, Bart, and here you are, mid-thirties and broke. You never should have married her."

"Water under."

"Okay. But, except for women, you developed good cop instincts. You were dependable and a skilled shooter, too. I hope you figure out women before —"

"I liked shooting, but just on the practice range." Bart stood and sat on the edge of the desk. "More, I liked investigating and interviewing. I really liked talking to people. As for women — what about the car?"

Fred nodded and shrugged. "Okay, okay, the car. What it is, a tenant skipped on me. His car. He looked iffy when he wanted to rent, so I made him sign the release on the car's title and let me hold it as a security deposit. He owed me a hundred and seventy-eight when he skipped and left the car. We'll add five bucks a month to your rent until it's paid off. You can keep it where it is, rent-free."

"Deal. Absolutely."

"Don't you want to see it first?"

"I'm sure I can't find a better deal. Where is it?"

"Follow me."

At the bottom of the wooden back staircase, Fred and Bart walked through the weedy yard and back fence gate to Firehouse Alley, and across to Fred's compact brick warehouse. Next to the wooden garage doors, a padlocked entry door sat under a painted-over glass transom. Fred removed the padlock and pushed the door open. It was dark inside, until Fred removed a long board that barred the accordion garage doors and folded them open to the Alley and sunlight. In the light, Bart could now see sheets concealing a vehicle-sized lump. Fred pushed boxes aside and removed the sheets, filling the air with dust.

Sunlight fighting through the dust helped define the lump. Bart, waving his hands and coughing, moved closer. "Wow." The big silver thing Bart saw neither disappointed nor pleased him, because he'd never seen anything like it.

"It's a K-car."

Mouth open, Bart stared.

"The Limo model. Like Nixon had. After he left the White House."

"Don't remember when Nixon left the White House. I must have been young."

Fred got in and released the parking brake and moved the gear selector to neutral. They grunted together, pushing the silver limo out into the alley.

Seeing it out in the sun, Bart nodded. "Okay, that's a car."

Fred used his cell phone to call a towing service.

When the truck arrived, Fred told the driver, "Take it to Tony's, at the end of the Alley near the Railroad Museum."

"Yup, I know."

Fred turned to Bart. "Tony's another tenant. I'll see he tunes it up and makes it right. He owes me a favor."

Bart smiled. A home, an office, and now he had a car, too.

After Tony returned the car, Bart was in heaven, driving it anytime he wished, if he had gas. Bart called his new car the "K-Limo," until one day, with a mouth full of burrito, he said, "*Klimo.*" Later, Bart got the Klimo a new twenty-nine-dollar paint job, silver-gray over the blotchy original Radiant Silver. The new paint almost matched the duct tape he used to repair rips in the padded vinyl top.

The paint also covered the Klimo doors and their advertising from the previous owners, *Old Town Limousine.* When he could afford to register it in his own name, he'd see how expensive it would be to replace the black and gold personalized plates from the previous owner. They read SAC LIMO. Maybe Bart's new plates would say SAC PI

People who saw the SAC LIMO had been stopping Bart in Old Town to hire him. He made the rent a few times by giving people rides for cash, but he didn't have a limo license and was risking a bust.

But now, today, Bart had a real job. For the first time in months, he folded open the doors, once again washing the garage interior with the sun and fresh air from Firehouse Alley. He removed the sheets and slid in behind the wheel, settling into the pillow-top velour seat cushion. He'd forgotten how right it felt. He'd forgotten how cushy the Klimo was, that it really was a limo, if only a K-car version.

First, he would wake the Klimo from months of sleep. He raised the hood. After securely connecting his portable charger cables to the battery, Bart dove into the big back seat to nap for a while. Inexplicably, he dreamed a *Gulliver's Travels* kind of dream. He felt powerless, while tiny creatures surrounded him, tugging at his shoelaces, and pulling loose threads from his jeans and T-shirt.

After an hour, Bart woke. He set the charger controls to BOOST, and then sat behind the wheel. After his version of a prayer, he closed his eyes and turned the key.

His prayer wasn't answered. The four-cylinder engine was turning over, but it wasn't starting. No spark? No fuel? A real man's loneliest moment. Just as Bart was losing patience, after applying all the tricks he knew, including pounding the steering wheel, the Klimo spared Bart additional threats to his manhood by coughing back to life.

Relieved and joyous, Bart apologized and high-fived the steering wheel with both hands. He shouted into the drooping headliner, "It's A-*LIVE!*"

Bart jumped out, removed the cables, closed the hood, and jumped back in just in time to keep the engine from dying. Bart played the throttle like the pedal of an organ while the Klimo sang a song, off-key, accompanied by coughs, backfires, and clouds of foul smoke. Choking, Bart held his breath until he could ease Klimo out of the garage without killing the engine. The engine remained running in the alley at rough idle long enough for him to get out and lock the garage.

Fingers crossed, Bart coaxed the Klimo out of Old Town, north along the river, to the home of his landlord, Fred Clifford.

* * *

7

Fred's Cottage

River, Stay 'Way from My Door

Fred's cottage hid out among tall trees on the Garden Highway, an uneven blacktop strip barely two lanes wide riding the crown of the earth levee built long ago to hold back the east side of the Sacramento River at flood stage.

Bart always loved this drive and seeing the old trees between the levee and the river. Under the trees, an eclectic selection of old and new homes faced the river. Piers led from lawns into the river. To the east, the flat prairie farmland below the levee was filling with clusters of new, stucco, McMansions on tiny, treeless lots. Like the older riverfront houses, Bart preferred the older apartment buildings and houses of midtown Sacramento, all resting safe under a cool canopy of towering mature trees. "Sacramento, City of Trees."

Bart's sight-seeing was punctuated by Klimo backfires, each a threat spiking his anxiety. He regretted his decision to drive to Fred's instead of simply mailing the rent check, afraid he would return to Old Town riding in the cab of a truck towing the Klimo.

Bart turned on the radio to block out the Klimo's backfires. He scanned the local stations until he found news. There was a to-do about bikers creating a ruckus at one of the restaurants in the huge Galleria Mall in Roseville, east up Interstate 80 from Sacramento. The news reporter said the bikers were ordering everything on the menu, refusing to pay, and then running wild through the mall. Bart thought many bikers were like rogue mastodons, unaware that their glory days were numbered.

When Bart saw Fred's cottage, he killed the radio. He let the Klimo roll down off the levee into Fred's driveway. After he'd removed the ignition key, the engine continued to cough and rattle. When it stopped, he could hear birds singing in the trees, and the engines and muted exhausts of pleasure boats down on the river. Bart saw Fred sitting alone at his barbecue pit, set at the edge of a tree-lined bluff overlooking the river.

Walking down the path to Fred, Bart disturbed yellow-billed magpies poking in the lawn. They chortled in mild annoyance at his approach, fanned their black and white wings, and escaped into the trees. Flying close above, a Boeing 737, displaying Jack London's face on its tail, cast a shadow over the river while circling the nearby Sacramento Airport.

"Bart, my handsome Lad! Plant your butt in a chair and gobble up some fresh air." Fred waved his beer at Bart. "Can I get you something?"

"No, thanks." Bart settled into one of Fred's white plastic chairs. He noticed Fred had less hair now, more of it was gray, and he had gained weight.

"You need money today?"

"No, Fred, thank you. Today I've brought money."

"Atta-boy. I knew you could do it."

"Here's a check. It's everything, the back rent, and the rest of what I owed you for the Klimo, and the other things."

Fred looked at the check and smiled.

"Ah, the Klimo. Was that you, backfiring up on the levee?"

"Yeah, sorry. I'm taking the Klimo straight to Tony when I leave here."

"Good. Say hello for me."

Bart looked back toward Fred's cottage. "What's different about your house. Something's changed."

"Oh, yeah. Since you were here last, I had a contractor raise the cottage and add another bedroom suite. Now it has a new, taller, concrete-block foundation with a drive-in basement, all sealed and water-proofed. I can park my cars in the basement.

"But, better, if the river rises over the bluff, I just have to evacuate the basement. If the river ever tops the levee, my main floor will now be above the water. Gives me peace when the river rises."

"Cool."

"Bart, the money's great. Where?"

"I have a new, wealthy client. You know I can't tell you much about it, a private investigation, but if I handle this job successfully, I'll be in good financial shape for a year."

"You deserve it, Bart. Finally — before you hit forty."

"Next July."

"Ah, yes. I remember those 4th-of-July birthday parties we'd throw for you in Berkeley, trying to get you drunk. What was the place we'd go to . . . on San Pablo?"

"The *Albatross*. I remember it, too, not fondly. You guys weren't cool, sometimes. Marty Brooks hit me with a dart."

"We were just trying to toughen you up a little. We liked you, and you survived. Look at you."

Bart's face curled with skepticism.

"Hey, remember your first bust, where you and Marty saved Berkeley from nuclear weapons?"

Bart wondered how many beers had passed Fred's lips this morning.

"Of course, and you know we really didn't save Berkeley. Just look at it."

"Just teasing you." Fred moved in his plastic chair, shifting his weight from one hip to the other. "Ow! Sonofabitch."

Bart had forgotten about Fred's cursing.

"You okay, Fred?"

"My hip's getting worse."

"What's wrong?"

"The doctor says arthritis. I think it was training you pups. Too many obstacle courses and hill runs, trying to prove I could still do it."

"I remember. Of course, you can still do it."

"Maybe. Bart, speaking of toughness and survival, listen to me — you be careful, okay? I don't want to lose a good tenant. Remember what I taught you back in Berkeley — and Bart?"

"Yeah?"

"If your client is a woman, please be extra careful — you know your history with women."

Bart frowned. Another lecture.

"Remember, Bart, not all women are like Snow White, or Glinda, the Good Witch of the North, swinging a magic wand sprinkling protective fairy dust around you. Some women are more like Sharon Stone, swinging a big ice pick."

"I know. I watch movies. I'm smart."

"Bart, I'm not saying you're not smart. I know you're smart. It's just, sometimes, when a woman comes in the door, your smarts go out the door. Temporarily, of course."

Bart listened, but he'd always had difficulty accepting a woman could be really bad. He knew they could go astray or be difficult, like his wife, or mother, but he was sure men had a near monopoly on really bad things.

"You like the PI business?"

"Yes, I do. I like it better than what I did for the Berkeley PD, except for missing you and Marty Brooks and the other guys. I like being on my own, free. I like helping people and solving problems. And mysteries."

"Then, no regrets about leaving school and poetry behind to go to the academy?"

"No. I don't think I was much of a poet."

"How about your arm? No lasting effects?"

Bart held his left arm out to Fred. A shaft of sunlight through the trees spotlighted the pea-sized scar on his forearm, white against his tanned skin. He opened and closed his fist, moving the muscles under the scar.

"Just like new."

"Good."

Fred adjusted himself in his chair again, took a long pull at his beer, and looked up into the trees.

The lecture continues.

"Bart, I want to tell you something about the PI business. All police work, public or private, is similar, give or take the amount of bureaucracy bearing down on you. Call me a cynic, but rather than solving or fixing anything, with best intentions and all — sometimes you just can't avoid making things worse. There's *always* something you don't know. All those crime movies you watched — you saw *Chinatown*, didn't you?"

Bart nodded.

"All my experience says police work is one continuous wade up to your balls through the dark, swampy, waters of the Human Condition. You're born, you live, and you die — we're all equal there. The rest? People are complicated, and the details can be troubling."

"Fred, I know you're trying to help me."

"I am. I hope the work is better for you. Me, I'm done with law enforcement now. I'm just trying to enjoy my retirement. But you're young. I'm glad you're happy."

"Thanks for covering me on what I owed."

"You're welcome."

"Oh. My phone is working . . . will be, tomorrow. I should go now — the new job."

Bart rose from his chair and shook hands with Fred.

"Come back soon," Fred waved his now-empty bottle at the cold barbecue pit. "We'll grill some steaks."

"Okay, that I'd like. I promise."

Another 737 passed over.

"Fly me to the moon, da-da, da-da, da-da . . . ," sang Fred, shading his eyes from the sun while following the jet overhead.

Bart smiled and turned uphill. When he looked back, he saw a retired cop and six empty chairs around a cold barbecue pit.

Again, the Klimo resisted starting. When it consented to run, he coaxed it back up Fred's driveway and toward Old Town.

It was nice of Fred, thinking Bart was smart. Bart wasn't sure. Occasionally, his smarts seemed to randomly come and go like the weather. On this case, he'd need his smarts full time.

Visiting Fred had been a detour from his to-do list, but he was back on Number One again. The to-do list, as he'd planned, began with Fix the Klimo, then:

Number Two — Library research.

Number Three —Drake Concannon's Sacramento office.

Number Four — Drive to Lake Tahoe.

Number Five — Search for pirates.

Number Six — Visit Mrs. Concannon.

Number Seven — Deliver the ransom money.

Bart had penciled the list into his spiral notebook. The small notebook was made of waterproof paper — *be prepared.* Pencil and *eraser,* because he knew future events might alter his list.

Back in Old Town, Bart pointed the grumbling Klimo down Firehouse alley, toward Tony's.

"Come on, Klimo, just a little further — you can *do* it!"

Bart slipped the transmission into neutral and let the Klimo coast the last twenty feet into Tony's five-car parking lot.

Upon hearing the engine backfiring, Tony came out from the garage with his hands on his hips, scowling. Before Tony could say anything, Bart stuck his arm out the window and waved a check.

Tony approached, took a rag from his coveralls, and wiped his big hands before touching the check.

"This check feels hot. Burning. How fast do I have to cash this, Lasiter? Where'd you get the money? Drive more old ladies to the airport?"

"No. It's okay. The money's there. Call the bank. It's what I owe you, plus extra toward the new work I want, if it's okay with you."

"What do you want?"

"After you've cashed the check, do a complete tune-up, and mount new front tires. Please. I have some driving to do on a new job."

"The new tires — white walls?"

"You're kidding."

"No. It's what this thing wore, originally."

"Jeeez. Okay, Tony. They won't match the rear tires."

Tony bent down to look at a rear tire tread. "Soon they will, Lasiter. You should replace the rears, too."

Bart got out and looked at the rear tire. "Not today."

"When do you need it back?"

"Tomorrow? Too soon?"

"I had planned on waxing my wrenches tonight, but . . . okay. You'll pay off anything left for the extra work when you pick it up tomorrow?"

"Yes. Call me when you're done."

"Your phone works now? The last time I called —"

"Yes, yes, Mr. Tony. Anyway, tomorrow it will work. The bill's paid."

"Okay, Lasiter. Let's keep on keeping up from now on. Fred seems to have a soft spot for you. You know, the only reason I carried you for so long was that Fred's my landlord, too.

"Fred and I go way back. Thanks again. And Tony, Fred says hello."

Bart turned up the alley. "See you tomorrow."

* * *

8

The Three Barts

Three Barts in the Fountain

Bart wanted to get moving on this case, but nothing would happen before Friday, when he'd drive to Lake Tahoe, and then not until Friday night, at Mrs. Concannon's home in Nevada. Still, he wanted to move down his to-do list while he waited for Tony to fix the Klimo.

Number Two on the list was Library research.

The Sacramento Library flagship was anchored on I Street at Eighth Street, a tolerable walk from Old Town. Today, flush-with-cash Bart took a cab.

Bart looked through the library stacks, rolled through film reels of *The Sacramento Bee* back-issues, and sat at a computer, trying to add to what he already knew about Drake Concannon and the Nevada gaming industry. He turned up nothing on the Concannons, and nothing new about the gaming industry: Big money attracted the players on either side of the table, and few were Boy Scouts.

Both modern and historical books celebrated a Lake Tahoe known for its beauty, not pirates. Bart paged through dozens of books, including *The Complete Idiot's Guide to Pirates*. He reviewed the nautical terminology used by seafaring types and their various pirate flags. Captain Edward England's flag, a skull over two crossed bones. was like the one sketched on the ransom note. The Johnny Depp pirate books were numerous and useless. But Bart found something surprising: There was yet another historical Bart.

Bart was a namesake. When Bart's teenage mother was pregnant, she found a California history book in the donation box outside the Haight-Ashbury Free Clinic. She liked a story about Black Bart, the 1880's Wells Fargo stagecoach bandit. She'd already decided her first child would be male, and now she would name him Bart. He'd often wondered if he'd been led to the Berkeley PD by a subconscious desire to resist his bandit name. Lucky for Bart, he was ultimately born male, or he'd also be suffering gender-identity issues. Mom never backed down.

The new, additional historical Black Bart was a very famous pirate. Bartholomew Roberts drank tea instead of alcohol and never wanted to be a pirate. His unfortunate capture by pirates, the death of their captain, and his nautical skills made him a reluctant captain. Once he'd accepted his role, he became the most successful pirate known, capturing four hundred ships over four years. Fascinated with Black Bart Roberts, Bart Lasiter read it all.

Besides Bart Lasiter, the former Berkeley cop and current Old Town detective, there was his eponym, Black Bart Two, the legendary Wells Fargo Bandit, and now Black Bart Three, the famous pirate. Three Barts — could knowing this help him?

Back in his office, Bart retrieved his cold burrito from the refrigerator, removed the aluminum foil, and pulled a few pieces of beef loose to put in Aggie's dish. His dish was shaped like a cat's face, with ears for handles, and a metal fish token attached, like a little bell. Any jiggling of the dish would ring the bell and bring Aggie running.

While Aggie purred and chewed his beef, Bart watched the leftover burrito spin on a paper plate in the microwave and took his last Coke from the refrigerator. Detective and cat ate quietly.

After he'd finished dinner, Bart wanted a shower before getting into bed. He undressed and gathered his thrift-store robe and towel from their nails in the wall. After slipping into his robe, graying white terrycloth with an embroidered purple Sacramento Kings logo, Bart started down the hall to the bathroom.

The building was empty now, and the only sounds in the hallway were the muffled I-5 traffic noises from across Second Street, and his flip-flops playing a backbeat to the music of his toiletries bouncing around in the plastic bucket swinging from his hand. Agamemnon was already asleep on the bed when Bart returned. He hung his damp towel and robe back on their nails and made a mental note-to-self to find rust-proof nails.

From a box under his bed, Bart retrieved his lucky pajamas. They were polka dot, like the ones Ricardo Cortez wore playing Sam Spade opposite Bebe Daniels as Miss Wonderly in the 1931 version of *The Maltese Falcon*. In Dashiell Hammett's book, Sam Spade went to bed in green and white *checked* pajamas. Bogart's Spade wore polka dot pajamas, too. Maybe checked pajamas were only available when Hammett wrote the book. Because the movies were black and white, Bart didn't know what color pajamas any of the film Spades wore. The red thrift store pajamas Bart found had white dots and they fit.

Bart turned out the lamp on his desk. Behind the Oriental screens, by the light from the lamp next to his hot plate, he moved Aggie enough to slip into bed. He found the correct remote for his 19" TV, a Disney Princess model, pink plastic with grand purple scrolls decorating its top. Two pink remotes controlled the TV and the base containing separate VCR-DVD players, gifts from the same cop in Berkeley who'd provided Bart's old 13" TV. When his daughter abandoned the 19" to attend U.C. Santa Cruz, it became Bart's. Waiting for the TV to warm up, Bart set his alarm clock, adjusted his pillow, and turned off the light.

Bart considered Mrs. Concannon replacing Bebe Daniels in the role of Miss Wonderly. Mrs. Concannon was taller, much better looking, and slender. He couldn't place her accent, a mix of several American regions, unlike the barely suppressed New York accent of Bebe Daniels. He didn't waste time thinking about Mary Astor's Miss Wonderly, a casting mistake.

Bart tried to imagine himself as Sam Spade, opposite Mrs. Concannon, but he couldn't think of himself as Sam Spade. He was neither as silly as the 1931 Ricardo Cortez Spade, nor as tough or cynical as the 1941 Humphrey Bogart Spade. And he knew he couldn't talk or think as fast as Bogie's Spade.

Unlike the action themes of his favorite detective stories, Bart thought people should talk more and try to get along. He wouldn't use his mother's favorite warning, Bad Karma, but he didn't enjoy pointless displays of machismo, what Fred called pissing contests. This was part of his hippie upbringing. His mother was a starry-eyed Summer of Love teenage free spirit who hitchhiked everywhere, dragging him along behind. She trusted anyone who would give her a ride, money, or a joint, and a place for her and her son to crash for the night.

As a cop, Bart knew he had to change. He forced himself to be less trusting, more cautious, and more reluctant to accept people at face value. The '60s hippie in him resisted these changes, but as time passed, he embraced them as essential tools required for street survival.

If there could be a Bart personal style, it would be similar to his eponym's. Describing Black Bart, the chivalrous stagecoach bandit, Wells Fargo detective James Hume had said Black Bart was a polite person of wit who avoided profanity, and a poet. And Black Bart, the Wells Fargo bandit, didn't take money from women.

Old Town's Bart Lasiter was also a polite person of wit who avoided profanity, and a poet, too. And Old Town's Bart was not a bandit, but he did accept money from Mrs. Concannon.

The real reason he wasn't comfortable in his Spade fantasy, he concluded, wasn't the Black Barts, or money. It was because Mrs. Concannon could not be Miss Wonderly.

True, like each Miss Wonderly, Mrs. Concannon offered more money than was required to hire the detective, but the $50,000 bonus was only one percent of the ransom money. It didn't seem excessive when you looked at it that way. And Mrs. Concannon didn't appear deceptive — she really needed Bart. She was wealthy, and her money was only a tool to get the help she needed. Bart believed her.

"Hey, Aggie. We've got a real paying customer. Things are going to be better around here now."

Aggie turned toward Bart and opened his eyes.

"What do you think, Aggie? Mrs. Concannon is all right, isn't she?"

The cat closed his eyes and began to snore.

Among the few channels his rabbit-ears antenna captured, Bart landed on an old black-and-white movie, *Captain Blood*, starring Errol Flynn as Dr. Peter Blood, and Olivia de Havilland as the wealthy Miss Bishop. Good, a pirate movie. Bart was half-asleep when Dr. Peter Blood, now a convicted rebel, was sentenced to be hanged.

The King was advised that his West Indies colonies needed slaves, and that it was a waste of money to hang men when he could sell them as slaves. The king suddenly had an original idea. He would have convicted rebels sold as slaves.

Bart dozed. He woke to see a commercial with speed skaters in multi-colored Lycra body suits racing across ice against a background of killer whales breaching the surface of a pristine Alaskan bay, while a mesmerizing female voice recommended investment products.

Bart's eyelids fluttered as he listened. Jolted awake again when the remote slipped from his hand and bounced off the floor, he fought to keep his eyes open and follow *Captain Blood*.

Miss Bishop, in a long frilly dress and big hat, worried as she watched the slave auction of the rebels. Would Dixon's Mines buy Dr. Peter Blood?

Miss Bishop jumped in and outbid Mr. Dixon. Now she owned Peter Blood. What was she going to do with him?

Bart's eyes closed for the night. He fell into a restless sleep where he dreamed his own movie, *Captain Lasiter*. While the words *convicted* and *not yet hanged* rolled past his eyes, he saw Mrs. Concannon dressed like Miss Bishop.

"What am I bid for the detective? A healthy compliant Lasiter can be reckoned worth five thousand dollars."

"His debt is his ticket to Concannon's Mines!"

"Sold to Mrs. Concannon for five thousand dollars!"

"What would you like done with him, Mrs. Concannon?"

* * *

9

Concannon Services, Inc.

I Like Sacramento in August, How About You?

8 AM, Thursday

Aggie was walking across Bart's chest, purring. Bart heard the TV and rubbed his eyes awake with one hand while he groped around for the TV remote with the other, spilling his mug of laundromat quarters from the microwave to the floor. He found the remote among the quarters and turned off the TV, squelching the weather reporter's prediction of a nice day in the low nineties.

Bart retrieved a can of cat food from his file cabinet and showed it to Aggie, bending down so the hungry cat could see. "This flavor's okay?"

Aggie stood on his hind legs and rubbed his cheek across the can.

"Good." Bart opened the can and began spooning Salmon & Beef into Aggie's cat-face dish, while Aggie wound himself between and around Bart's legs.

"Aggie, you never give me any rest when you're hungry, do you?"

Aggie looked up.

"I know. I understand. Had trouble getting steady meals so long now you want ten squares a day. You're just an orphalyn, aren't you?"

Aggie had rammed against the office door one day until it popped open, and he adopted Bart. Ever since Bart's little dog, Bullets, had died in Berkeley, he was afraid to have another pet. But then this cat pushed right in and jumped onto Bart's desk. He looked at Bart for a few seconds, then curled up on the blotter and went to sleep, an orange fur ball at peace.

Fred Clifford explained how the cat, cruising the building for three years, belonged to former tenants who named him Agamemnon, and then abandoned him one night when they skipped on the back rent.

"He's been pestering people, eating what they'll give him. He's a determined scrounger. Bart, he's a fixed orange tabby. You couldn't ask for a better cat. If you like cats. And he's tough. I've seen him deal with other cats who wandered into his building. Brutal. Looks like he's found a home with you."

Bart prepared breakfast, Blueberry Pop-Tarts, and coffee. He made the coffee in his Italian aluminum pot on his hot plate and warmed the Pop Tarts in the microwave, pulling them out when they were hot but before they got too hard. When he'd finished his second cup of coffee, he shed his lucky pajamas, folded them neatly, and returned them to the box under his bed. After push-ups and sit-ups, he put on clean white briefs and socks, a fresh white T-shirt, blue jeans, and his old Nikes.

The T-shirt said Old Sacramento, like most of his T-shirts, and came from an Old Town T-shirt shop. After he knew the managers by name, he'd get a shirt at cost, or free, depending on what Bart could do for them, like catching grab-and-run thieves or solving minor burglaries. A mostly white hundred-percent cotton T-shirt washed fifty times was hard to beat for comfort.

After cleaning the coffeepot down the hall and returning it to the file cabinet, he called his insurance agent to tell him a check was in the mail. Then he wrote other checks, one to renew his lapsed subscription to *The Sacramento Bee*. The check for the telephone bill he would hand-deliver to beat the final cancellation date and keep his number.

Investigating the phone book, Bart found the address he wanted, Drake Concannon's office. Number Three on his to-do list. He hailed a cab cruising Second Street, outside the store that sold Matryoshkas, nesting Russian dolls. He'd deliver the telephone payment, and then visit Concannon's office. Because he'd neglected to ask Mrs. Concannon for a key, he'd have to improvise.

Drake Concannon's office building was near the Capitol in an area of once-prime real estate, now patiently waiting its turn for revival. The tree-lined street was busy with car and bus traffic passing by a mix of stores and offices. Businesspeople, shoppers, and a few street people pushing shopping carts shared the sidewalk shade under the trees.

Bart paid the double-parked cabbie and entered the lobby. From the cab, the building appeared unremarkable, blending easily into its surroundings, but inside it was quiet and cool, all twenties Art Deco brass and marble.

The minimal lobby had just enough room for an unmanned marble reception desk and two elevator doors. On a directory list on the wall, he found *Concannon Services, Inc . . . . . . 529.*

Approaching the elevators, Bart pressed the UP button. One of the brass sunburst-covered elevator doors split open. He entered and pressed FIVE, the top floor. The doors clanked shut, sealing him inside a softly lit booth of brass and walnut. When the doors opened, he stepped out into the hall.

A man was polishing the waxed marble floor with an electric buffer. The buffer's steady whirring was the only sound in the hall.

Bart followed the numbers over the dark oak and glass doors until he found 529. The letters on the glass read,

CONCANNON SERVICES, Inc.
By Appointment

With one eye on the buffer man, Bart tried the brass knob. Locked. He heard the buffer stop.

"Hey, you. What you do?" The man walked toward Bart.

"The manager said this office was for rent."

The buffer man examined Bart from head to toe. "I don't think so. Manager don't tell *me*."

"I just talked to him on the phone. This morning."

The man wasn't buying it. Bart changed the subject. "What kind of accent is that? Are you Russian?"

"*Not* Russian. Ukraine. I come from Ukraine."

"Wow. Must be quite a change for you."

"Why manager send you this office? It never for rent. Plenty other office to rent. Every floor has office for rent. All empty."

"I was told this office was furnished. Better to look at this one than an empty one."

"Yes, furnished. Because not for rent."

"Okay . . . what did you say your name is?"

"Not say. Anatoly. You say, Anton."

"Not Tony?"

Anton looked at Bart like he was a scuff mark on his floor.

"Okay . . . my name is Bart. Pleased to meet you, Anton."

"Not meet. You doing funny stuff with Mister Concannon office. What name, manager talk to you?"

"You know Mr. Concannon?"

"Hah! You interested Mr. Concannon — not rent office."

"Well, I am an investigator. I'm interested in finding out what I can about him, but I mean him no harm."

Bart showed Anton his PI license and gave him one of his cards.

"I tell you only this. I lightly see him. He come only once a month, maybe less. I clean office when manager say. Only then. Mr. Concannon fuzzy . . . fussy. Fussy man. One time he get mad. 'Anton, dust the pictures, too!'"

"Any chance I could look inside the office?"

"Hey. I tell you something. I think Mr. Concannon owns whole building. I let you in he could fire me. Why I do?"

"I could give you a little money. For your risk."

"How much you give Anton?"

"Twenty dollars?"

Anton shook his head. "I get fired, I lose plenty."

"All right. I could give you a hundred dollars."

"Oh. So, now you bribe Anton?"

"No, just for your risk."

"Bribe. Anton no take bribe. You have car?"

"Yes?"

"What kind car?"

"An '86 K-car. The limo model."

"Kay car? Kay? Oh! I know. You mean Khechkt-car!

Like Khechkt-mart store. I know car. Is like Moskvich car. We have in Ukraine."

"Yes, K-car, like Kmart."

"No bribe, work. You give hundred-fifty dollar, Anton give Khechkt-car tune-up."

"It's already getting a tune-up this morning."

"No matter. Give Anton money now, get tune-up later. Brakes, starter, whatever."

Bart wanted to keep Anton talking. He hoped Anton would eventually say something useful or let him into the office.

"Where did you learn to work on cars, Anton?"

"Whole family in Ukraine fix car. We liv near Myla. We never have new car. Must fix old car. Fix car good. When I was tin-ager, I have own car I fix good from junk. Bitch-boyz on tape, play loud, windowz roll down, drive to Kiev, pick up gurlz. Here Chick-ki, Chick-ki."

"Bitch-boys . . . ?"

"I gehdt around?"

"Oh, the Beach Boys!"

"I weesh the gurlz be Cal-li-forn-nya gurlz! Guhdt, guhdt, plenny why-bray-shuns, she make on me plenny Ecks-aye-Tay-shuns! Very heaf-vy stuff, no?"

"Of course, Anton. Back to the car —"

"Ah! Brothers and Anton have business here. We rent space in boatyard, North Highlands, fix many cars there. Man say, you brothers go, too many peoples here, too many cars. Now we work, save money for our own auto car garage."

Bart nodded. He had worked for the storage yards north of Sacramento, tracking people who'd skipped on their rent. He stopped because it didn't pay for the gas he used. One owner complained about "Russians," who sublet their storage spaces to other "Russians," who sublet again to new immigrants. "I threw them all out. After a few months I couldn't find the people I rented to, but there was dozens of people I didn't know coming and going with all these junk cars."

"So, Anton, where would you work on my car?"

"My apartment. Par-khing lot. No problem. Iz guhdt."

Pointing to the door, Bart said, "What about the office?"

"I can't let you in. Show money."

Bart hesitated and then pulled three fifty-dollar bills from his wallet.

Anton took the bills from Bart's hand and stuffed them into his pocket. Smiling at Bart, Anton took a key attached to a lanyard and extended it from the reel on his belt. He slipped the key into the lock and opened the door to Drake Concannon's office.

"Oh! Look! Ooop-sy-daisy — door open by self."

Bart waited.

Anton pointed at the hallway wall clock. "Look! Lunch time. I bet when Anton come back, door closed and lock by self. Bye-bye, Mr. Bart. You find Anton when ready for Khechkt-car fix."

Anton abandoned his floor buffer resting where it sat and disappeared around the corner.

When Bart heard Anton whistling his way down the stairs, he pushed Concannon's office door open, entered, and closed the door. With his hand still on the doorknob, he leaned back against the door and looked.

What Bart most expected wasn't there: chaos. Everything was neat as Sunday church, at least what Bart thought church was like. If the kidnapping had involved papers or wall safes, they'd have tossed the office.

Concannon's office was much larger than Bart had expected, like an old club or private library. The thick carpet was gray, and the picture windows at the back wall had heavy curtains, dark greens, and grays. Quiet and comfortable, it looked like it had been this way for years.

Near the windows, a sitting area comprised a deeply padded couch and matching brown leather chairs surrounding a glass coffee table. The table held stacks of casino trade magazines. From the windows, you could see part of the Capitol building. Away from the windows there was a mahogany desk and a bank of steel file cabinets.

The file cabinets were locked, but Bart found the key in a crystal dish filled with casino coins. The file cabinets contained purchase agreements, design-and-installation contracts, and invoices for services rendered to hundreds of casinos in Nevada, California, and other states where gambling was now legal.

There were income and business tax records going back to the fifties. Besides American Express and Diners Club invoices, Bart found bills showing Drake Concannon, like Chief Justice Earl Warren and Justice Anthony Kennedy, was a member of Sacramento's Sutter Club. Bart leafed through the records without finding anything unusual.

The only real decoration in the office was an arrangement of framed photographs on the walls. They began with three black and white cap-and-gown pictures of young Drake Concannon. A close-up of Drake holding his diploma hung next to a formal picture of his M.I.T. 1950 bachelor graduating class. A little arrow applied to the class picture identified Drake. In the third photo, Drake stood next to an older couple — his parents, Bart guessed. Drake smiled broadly in each photo. Neither of the parents displayed any emotion. Then his framed Bachelor of Science Mechanical Engineering diploma, and a similar set of graduation-day photos next to his M.S. Mechanical/Electrical Engineering diploma, dated 1952. No parents for the Master's.

The next was a candid snap of Drake on a stool at a tall wooden drafting board. Drake was leaning over a drawing and T-Square, holding a mechanical pencil in one hand and a plastic triangle in the other. He wore a white shirt, dark tie, and a big smile. The label read Reno Engineering Service, 1953.

Two photos showed young Drake with a wooden runabout. In the first, dated July 1954, Drake stood on the pier of a boat dealer shaking hands with a smiling man. The boat floated just below their feet. Signs hung above their heads, O'Hara's and Chris-Craft. Drake was taking delivery of his new runabout.

The next shot, dated 1960, showed a still-young Drake with the same boat at a wooden pier. Bart was sure it was the same pier shown in the photo Mrs. Concannon had given him but before the construction of the stone boathouse. The boat sat tied to the pier and pointed out to Lake Tahoe's center.

The runabout was handsome, with sleek lines made for speed. One cockpit for the controls and operator sat in front of the engine compartment, with a smaller cockpit behind the engine for extra passengers. It looked like a boat to be driven by one man, alongside one or two women in bathing suits. Drake stood on the pier, smiling, and pointing down to the runabout's transom and the boat's gold foil name, *Em-Eye-Tee*.

The Concannon pier appeared in another photo, with Drake smiling on the pier, now with the stone boathouse, holding a magnificent fish. The photo's caption read,

Mackinaw   29 lbs-3oz   June 3, 1963

The photos pleased Bart, but he hadn't found any of Concannon's written history. Except for those early photos, most of the remaining shots were business related, with Drake Concannon posing with groups to commemorate an event, usually in, or in front of a casino, sometimes cutting a ribbon, with the name of the casino and date noted below. As the photos went from black and white to color, Concannon looked older, gained weight, and smiled less. Bart kept looking. One photo might show the real kidnappers, if he knew what they looked like.

One of the few newer photos, this one showing a smiling Drake Concannon, hung near, but apart from the casino photos. This black-and-white photo was un-posed, a candid action shot. Concannon and three laughing men in suits were grabbing and hugging each other. The camera had recorded their frolic in front of another casino. Bart couldn't see a casino name, just part of a tall metal sign shaped like a cactus, outlined with neon tubes surrounding rows of light bulbs. A fifth man at the side of the photo wore a serious suit and expression. The man pulled Drake Concannon's arm with one hand while he tried to block the camera lens with his other. This young man with a full head of dark curly hair would have been handsome after the bandages encircling his neck were removed. The caption below read, G.C. 1962.

Positioned away from the others, an eight-by-ten photograph showed a young Drake Concannon with a much older man. The older man looked like he warranted everyone's attention. He had that steady, fearless look — straight into the camera lens — that often comes from a lifetime of easy access to gross sums of money, and a straight spine stiffened by the determination to keep as much of it as possible. They stood on a long pier in a private cove, admiring a huge wooden boat, styled in stained and varnished wood, polished metal, and shaped like a streamlined wingless airplane from the thirties. The photo was dated 1954 and autographed:

Drake — Thanks for all your help,
your friend,
George.

On the desk sat a Rolodex file packed tight with hundreds of cards, categorized by state and casino name, and dated. Nevada cards went back to the fifties. The Rolodex rested near a flat screen computer monitor. Bart found the keyboard and mouse in an upper drawer and the CPU and a printer out of sight in the desk's lower areas. He tried the computer, but everything was password-protected. Other desk drawers held a high-end HP calculator, miscellaneous pens, stamps, and envelopes, and letterhead paper marked *Concannon Services, Inc.*

In a bottom drawer he finally found several framed color photographs of Mr. and Mrs. Concannon, piled one on the other. A Concannon wedding photo, she in white satin and lace and he in a gray suit, showed them smiling, arm-in-arm, standing on their boathouse pier.

Bart went back to the wall of photographs. He took from his jeans Mrs. Concannon's picture of Drake. When he compared it to the other photos, he now noticed Drake Concannon looked surprised, even startled, in Mrs. Concannon's picture. What did that mean?

Bart decided he had spent enough time this morning in Drake Concannon's building and office, learning something about the man but not much. Now he had more questions than answers. This is the way of investigating. You look and look but only sometimes find or see. He set the office door latch to lock and pulled the door shut behind him.

The hallway was quiet, with no sign of Anton. Bart rode the elevator down to the lobby. When he opened the door to the street, the day's heat and noise hit him.

Bart wondered if he might need his gun. There was little reason to think he would need a gun, and it would be a detour from his to-do list, but you never know.

* * *

10

Six Shots, Three Tenors, & Mice

A Man Alone

Buy and Sell. Loans. We Buy Old Gold.

Bart always felt happy, looking past the painted invitations through Capital Pawn's front window. He knew he might see musical instruments, watches and rings, unusual cameras, stereo components, swords, and guns. What else he might find was unpredictable, except it all had been handed over by someone like Bart, someone trying to get by.

A bell in the back room announced Bart opening the door. Waiting for a response, he looked through a glass countertop, investigating a dark blue .45 automatic with exotic carved bone grips. The tiny scrawl on the price tag attached to the gun's blue-velvet-lined wooden case challenged Bart's detective powers. He gave up when he heard the owner, Mr. Branford, come out of the shop's back room. Mr. Branford was another ex-cop. He treated Bart like one of his personal cop-squad members.

"Hey, Bart."

"Hey, Mister Branford. I need it again."

Without another word, Mister Branson returned to the back room. When he emerged, he was carrying a brown paper bag with a tag stapled to it.

"Here it is." Mr. Branford removed the blued-steel revolver from the bag and set it down on a foam rubber pad protecting the countertop. "Smith-n-Wesson, three-inch barrel, round butt

Model Thirteen, .357 magnum. It's been back here so many times since I sold it to you, it's like I'm just storing it for you."

"Well, my income hasn't stabilized yet, Mr. Branford." He counted out the required cash on the counter.

Mr. Branford picked up the cash. "What would I do without customers?"

"I don't know. I just expect you'll always be here."

"Someday I won't be." Mr. Branford attacked the cardboard tag with a staple remover. "Didn't you tell me Smith made this model for the FBI?"

Bart picked up the revolver and felt its weight. "They did, at the FBI's request. The Feds wanted a magnum with the heavy three-inch barrel and round butt — until they switched to autos. I still like it though. I'm used to it, and it's a good size — not too big and not too small. It's got enough barrel to give you a decent sight radius. And you gave me a good deal when I bought it."

"Yes, I remember. It's a wheel gun. I have trouble selling revolvers. Only six shots before you reload. Today everybody wants autos — thirteen, sixteen, nineteen shots — I can't keep up with it. You'd think every day it's the OK Corral."

Bart pushed the cylinder latch forward and let the cylinder flop out. He squinted through the empty chambers and barrel. "I think, if you can't solve your problem with one or two well-placed shots, you need more than a gun to help you. Are we going to do the paperwork this time?"

"A cop is a cop is a cop. Not going to shoot anybody, are you, Bart?" He impaled the cardboard tag on a steel spike.

"Hope not."

"Ammo?"

"I still have some in my office."

Mr. Branford handed Bart a receipt and closed the cash register.

"Thanks, Mr. Branford."

"Until next time. Stay frosty."

Bart kept the gun in the paper bag and walked back to his office. His holster, still in his desk, fit inside the waistband of his jeans at the back of his right hip, and strapped to his belt. On his left side rode a pouch holding twelve extra rounds in two speed loaders. You never know. During the hot months, Bart rarely wore his gun, even if he had detective work. Much of the year in Sacramento was T-shirt-and-jeans weather, even shorts, except he didn't like shorts. Though he could cover the holster with his T-shirt, the bulge was too obvious, especially if he had to bend over.

He still remembered the shock of being thrown straight to the sidewalk downtown, his lip cut, and his cheek abraded by the weathered concrete, and his arm sore from being twisted behind his back. Someone had seen the suspicious bulge under his T-shirt and pointed him out to a large policeman. Everything was cool after the officer emptied Bart's nylon wallet onto the sidewalk and found his PI license and CCW permit. Afterwards, the cop always recognized Bart and said hello.

Back in his office, Bart put his gun into its holster and locked them into a lower file-cabinet drawer under his T-shirts.

At his desk, sorting his mail, separating the bills from the ads and offers, Bart called out to Aggie.

"How about these offers, Aggie? Do you want a hearing aid, or a course in managing real estate, double-paned windows, or even a free sit-down restaurant pancake breakfast to learn about retirement opportunities? It is hot in here. We sure could use a double-paned window.

"What did you say, Aggie? You say you want the pancake retirement breakfast? You're already retired."

Bart balled up the breakfast-flyer and threw it on the floor toward Aggie near the oriental screens. Aggie launched himself into the air and landed on the paper ball, pulled it against his belly with four paws, rolled onto his back and wounded the ball severely by biting and slashing it with his claws, then rolled and spun in circles. He spun like an orange, furry break-dancer, and then batted the paper ball off the wall, behind the screens, and onto the floor. Aggie raced behind the screens after it.

Bart grinned and turned back to his bills. He was listening to Aggie bat the paper ball around the floor when the black dial phone on his desk jumped to life.

"Aggie, it must be Tony, and just in time." He picked up the receiver. "Tony!"

"Oh . . . oh . . . you have Sesame Street . . . Poirot . . . Inspector Lynley —" Aggie came back to the desk and listened. "The Three Tenors . . . the Three Sopranos — how about the Three Stooges? I'll join when you have the Three Stooges."

He hung up and turned to Aggie.

"It wasn't Tony."

It rang again. Bart frowned and grabbed the phone.

"I told you, not until you have the Three Stooges."

There was silence at the other end — then a different voice.

"Lasiter? It's Tony. The Klimo is ready. Are you okay?"

"Yes, thanks, Tony. I'll be right over."

"Wait, Lasiter — one more thing. I added twenty bucks to the total, beyond what you asked me to do."

"For what?"

"I had José spend a half-hour vacuuming your back seat. Did you know you had mice back there?"

"No."

"They were building a nest under the seat. José thinks he chased them all out."

"Thanks, I guess."

"Well, *detective*, keep it running and on the road and you're less likely to have a problem in the future. With those tinted windows, it's nice and dark back there. And pillow-top velour upholstery — mice love velour."

"Know any talented mechanics?"

"Ha, freaking, ha. I'm here 'til six.

* * *

11

Free Spirits

Three Kerns in the Fountain

The Klimo, now sharply tuned, safely rested back in its garage, while Bart climbed the wooden back steps of his building. He felt happy and bounded up the steps, until he heard a telephone ringing in the hallway. Couldn't be his. When his phone was working, he didn't get many calls, except from the people looking for his check. In time, he tempered his rush to answer the telephone. But, as he neared his office, he could tell this was his phone. Bart fumbled with his key. Frustrated, he gave the door an Aggie shoulder bump. The door popped open in time for him to grab the phone.

"Lasiter Investigations."

"Bart? Help!"

He recognized Mr. Bocco's voice, owner of the Ristorante Positano, around the corner on Front Street. Amalfi Coast style, the restaurant included a working fountain in its inner open-air courtyard.

"What's up, Mr. Bocco?"

"You *know*, Bart — again, it's happened!"

"Somebody didn't pay?"

"Come right away. Maybe they haven't gone far. Hurry, Bart!"

"Okay, Mr. Bocco. I'll run right over."

Bart speed-walked north up Second Street and turned west

on K Street, toward the river. This part of Old Town had once been home to Sacramento's brothels, 150-plus years ago. Now it was an ever-changing mix of novelty shops, restaurants, and bars.

Halfway to the Positano Bart froze mid-step on the wooden sidewalk. Across K Street, in front of Donegan's Bar, he saw a dozen parked motorcycles. All but three were backed in, with their front wheels toward the street. That's normal. What froze Bart was the sight of the three choppers parked nose-in. Each of their skinny rear fenders held an identical chromed license plate frame topped with a pirate's skull and crossed bones. The skulls grinned, mocking Bart.

Bart's heart raced. He stepped into the street, headed for the skulls. In the middle of the street, he stopped. Wait. Pirates on the brain! There must be thousands of bikers in California with pirate decoration on their jackets or motorcycles. Even boaters on the river flew pirate flags. And Oakland Raiders fans.

He turned back toward Front Street and continued to the Positano. When he had barely put one foot into the restaurant, he heard Mr. Bocco.

"Bart — you *have* to find them. This eating and not paying is killing me. These motorcycle bums eat without paying, then tell their friends, and *they'll* do it, too."

"Okay, Mr. Bocco. What did they look like?"

"Like motorcycle bums, three of them. What do I know? They all look alike."

"Did you see which direction they went?"

"They rode around the corner, to K Street — I couldn't leave my restaurant to chase them."

"You're sure they didn't intend to pay? Maybe they lost a wallet?"

"The last thing they said — the big one says, 'Pirates don't pay!' and they jumped into my fountain, laughing. After they splashed water all over, they ran out to their motorcycles, fast, even the crippled one."

"I'll get back to you, Mr. Bocco."

Bart was already running to K Street when Mr. Bocco yelled after him, "Find them, Bart. Find them!"

On K Street, Bart's eyes zeroed in on the row of motorcycles in front of Donegan's. There was a three-motorcycle gap where the grinning skulls had mocked him. A deep roar jerked his head to the east. Across Second Street, where K Street transitions into a dark, pedestrian-only tunnel dipping under Interstate 5, three motorcyclists were scattering people in their path while enjoying an illegal shortcut through the tunnel. Their red taillights were visible while they dipped below the freeway, followed by the deep echo of their engines' exhausts, and shrieking shoppers holding their ears.

The motorcyclists disappeared up to street level, to several more pedestrian-only blocks of K Street and the shopping mall, the Westfield Downtown Plaza. They're gone. Too many paths from restricted K Street back to city streets for Bart to know which way they turned.

Frustrated, Bart crossed K Street and entered Donegan's. It was dark inside, and Bart had to let his eyes adjust before he could find Nicki Donegan, halfway down the long mahogany bar.

"Hi Bart. You want a Coke today?"

"No, thanks, Nicki. Some information."

He told her about the three bikers, repeating what Mr. Bocco had said.

Nicki wore a black leather vest over a green Donegan's T-shirt and continued her bar work while she listened.

"They skipped on Mr. Bocco, huh? Yeah, I think I know the ones. Wish I'd known. Never seen 'em before. In a hurry. In and out in a minute."

"Did they have the bikes with the skull-and-crossed-bones license plate frames?"

"I didn't look. After a while, they all look the same."

"Where were they going — did they say?"

"Nope. Got what they wanted and left."

"What did they want?

"Real characters, they were. The big one says he wants me to mix 'em some major-league rum drinks in Slurpee-sized takeout cups, with lids and straws, please — fortification against highway danger, he said. And put it on their tab, thank you."

"So, did you?"

"Sure — lose my liquor license, and on credit, to three hard cases I never seen before. Not gonna happen.”

“What did happen?”

“I said put your cash right on the bar, and no hooch for the highway. Pissed, they was, but they dug into their jeans and pooled all their cash. Pathetic. Including coins, they came up with enough for three plastic two-liter bottles of Squirt and a fifth of Captain Morgan’s Rum. I felt a little sorry for them, so I threw in the straws.”

“What did they look like?”

“Just old bikers but kind of piratey. Soaked wet, too.”

“They didn’t say anything?”

“Yeah, they did, if I can remember it. The big one, in the doorway, he stopped to pose, like he’d rehearsed it, and said something like, ‘Drink, battle, murder, shipwreck,’ and, uh, ‘Hellfire to kern an’ the Lawr.’ Right on, they now being plum out of coin — or ‘kern,’ as he called it. A poet, he was. And he wore an eye patch.”

Bart yelled, running out the door, “Thanks, Nicki — I’ve got work to do!”

“Mr. Bocco? Bart Lasiter here,” he said into his phone three hours later. “Sorry, but I’ve had no luck finding the guys who skipped on you. I got a description from Nicki at Donegan’s. Never seen them before. I drove around to all the city’s biker hangouts I know, but I couldn’t find them.

“Right, Mr. Bocco, it’s all I can do for you today. A dead end until I spot them somewhere. My advice is, if in the future you feed any suspicious diners, get their license numbers *before* they leave. Sorry. Good night, Mr. Bocco.” Bart hung up and prepared for bed.

In bed, Bart checked the late news on his pink TV. Among the local stories, one stood out. It was a breathless, on-the-scene report from a younger female.

Standing near the giant guitar outside the Hard Rock Cafe at Seventh and K, Marti Planker held up her microphone, faced the camera, and said, “A ga-lor-ious summer afternoon was spoiled for some of our Sacramento shoppers today. Here, live to you from the Hard Rock Café, I’ll tell you how it all went down.”

She reported the Sacramento Police had received multiple

complaints that afternoon about three outlaw motorcyclists who recklessly drove down K Street through the pedestrian-only freeway underpass and into other pedestrian-only areas of the Downtown Plaza, menacing innocent shoppers and tourists.

"They literally grabbed cash, burgers, and fries from the outdoor tables of Hard Rock Cafe diners, and then fled south on Seventh Street to L Street, where they were last seen racing west to the Interstate 5 North on-ramp."

Marti caught her breath and continued, "And witnesses said the motorcyclists" — she paused and made her eyes big — "actually, were-*ent,* wear-*ing,* hel-*mets!*"

Bart frowned. Not only were the three perps still hungry when they left the Positano, but these "pirates" obviously didn't care about California's motorcycle helmet law.

There *was* trouble in River City.

* * *

12

Road Warrior

On the Road to Mandalay

10 AM, Friday

Driving to Lake Tahoe was next, Number Four on Bart's to-do list. Tony had done a great job fixing the Klimo, especially the tune-up. The Klimo's four-cylinder engine was purring, pulling Bart up Interstate 80 towards the Sierras and Lake Tahoe. The new whitewall tires were rolling true, without the usual whine and thumping from the tires they replaced. All the Klimo's dashboard instruments that worked were indicating everything in order. For the first time ever since he'd owned the Klimo, the fuel gauge showed full. And Bart's gun was where he liked it, in its holster in the console between the front seats.

In heavy traffic near Roseville, motorists who saw the Klimo would smile with two thumbs-up, or scowl with two thumbs-down. Past Roseville, I-80 traffic thinned until Auburn. After Auburn there were so few cars sharing the road with the Klimo, the occupants could kill time observing each other and their vehicles. Bart noticed an abundance of old cars and hot rods. Some were pulling trailers carrying other old cars.

When many of the old-car people saw the Klimo, their facial expressions showed shock, then recognition: *Ah, yes, of course.* Then they smiled and waved, or gave a big thumbs-up, or an okay sign.

Because the air conditioning didn't work yet, Bart kept the Klimo's windows lowered. He listened to the other cars and the air passing his window, instead of the radio. Besides the CB radio previous owners had installed, the Klimo had *two* standard equipment radios. The one in the dashboard was one of the first with electronic tuning, and the one in the rear seat was the same, *plus* a cassette tape deck. Someday he would have the CB and back seat radio fixed.

A few people yelled to Bart across the lanes as they passed him. "Going to Reno? For sale?" Bart just smiled.

Bart had heard, "Is it for sale?" before, when he worked for the storage yards north of Sacramento off Elkhorn Boulevard, tracking people who had skipped on their rent. A homeless man saw the Klimo and asked Bart if he'd take twenty dollars for it. The man said he knew where he could park it and live in it. Bart, horrified at first, politely declined. Bart always tried to be polite, maintaining his theory that anyone could be a future source of information, if not a customer.

It had been a while since Bart had driven any distance, and the time allowed him to ponder. The skull and crossed-bones symbol, he mused, was definitely intended to be scary. Just ask any Raiders football fan.

Maybe that's why the Raiders weren't very good in recent years — they weren't scary, Bart would argue. According to Bart's theory, symbology had finally caught up with the Raiders. Raiders players and coaches who looked closely at the Raiders logo suffered crippling doubt.

The Raiders logo is a player wearing a silver helmet and an eye patch— *already* he can't see the field of play as well as two-eyed players. Instead of crossed bones, the logo has crossed cutlasses, but not *below* the skull/helmeted head. The blades are *behind* the head — at least that's what Bart assumed the logo artist intended. "Take a good look," Bart would say to Berkeley cops who were Raiders fans.

"The cutlass blades enter the helmet's ear holes! How can you expect a Raider to succeed on the field of play when he has a patch over one eye, and he's skewered through both ears? I rest my case," Bart would say, thinking he had settled the issue. And then the Raiders fans would —

VARRRRR — *ROOOOOOM!* A motorcycle at full throttle, screaming through open exhausts, passed by two feet off Bart's window, assaulting his ears with throbbing Harley-Davidson.

Bart jerked his head and the Klimo's steering wheel away in reaction to the sudden noise. He recovered when he saw the motorcycle's chromed license plate frame sporting a grinning skull and crossed bones.

VARRRRR — *ROOOOOOM!*

"Yow!" yelled Bart.

VARRRRR — *ROOOOOOM!* Two more motorcycles blew past Bart's open window. They, too, were displaying the same grinning, skull-and-crossed-bones license plate frames. They flew by and ahead so fast Bart couldn't look at both the license plate frames and the riders. These last two riders were fighting to catch up to the first one.

Bart didn't have time to see if these riders were "kind of piratey," but the last one threw an empty plastic Squirt bottle over his head. It bounced off the Klimo's windshield. A clue.

Surely, these were the same three motorcycles he had seen at Donegan's in Old Town. He floored the Klimo and said, "Don't call me Shirley!"

While the Klimo was running well, he didn't expect to catch the bikers unless they slowed. They were already above 4000 feet and climbing. The thinner air was robbing the Klimo of its turbo-charged four-cylinder power. The speedometer said 80, but the Klimo resisted going faster. The bikers were pulling away like he was parked.

Before Bart lost sight of them, Mr. Bocco's bikers passed the cars ahead on both the right and left, weaving back and forth with abandon, fighter pilots banking their machines to swing through the air.

Mr. Bocco, do you want the good news first, or the bad news first?

* * *

13

Triple Trouble

Send in the Clowns

Bart reached Truckee without seeing his three motorcyclists again. He turned onto Highway 89, south to Lake Tahoe. He'd been through Truckee before, on the way to Reno, but this would be Bart's first visit to Lake Tahoe.

Bart left I-80 thinking Highway 89 led *downhill* to the lake, but the Truckee River, which originates as overflow from Lake Tahoe, and then spills through downtown Reno, would have to be flowing *uphill* on its way to Truckee. His disorientation matched the bizarre nature of this case. Maybe water *could* flow uphill if there could be pirates on Lake Tahoe.

The river wound a snake's path through canyons and forest alongside Highway 89. Resorts renting cabins peppered the spaces separating the highway and river. Enthusiasts sharing rubber rafts alongside solo kayakers appeared at nearly every turn of the river, fighting their way through rapids, then resting in the quiet pools between. The resorts welcomed rafters, their parking lots full of SUVs with roof-rack-mounted watercraft. Bart came to the end and beginning of the river at Tahoe City.

There, in all its grand splendor, lived the source of the Truckee River, the vast natural jewel some called The Lake of the Sky. Bart parked and sat by the water, enjoying the stunning lake view, and thinking about the task at hand.

Where to begin Bart's search for pirates, Number Five on

his to-do list? He might as well start in Tahoe City and follow the lakeshore north and east, around to Nevada on his way to the Concannon residence. Steadfastly optimistic, he hoped to find something helpful.

Where do you find pirates in modern society? Bart had heard of Florida pirates, who stole shipments of cocaine or boarded the yachts of the wealthy to take their jewels and cut their throats, but they didn't sail under the Black Flag. Those pirates were more likely to be wearing casual sporting clothes than tatters of weathered sail cloth.

Lake Tahoe, summer playground of San Francisco's fogged-in wealthy, was not a place where you would expect to find a Wet Criminal. Wet Criminals — not un-papered immigrants wading the Rio Grande — were outlaws doing the work normal Americans wouldn't do, the work normal Americans had never considered, taking prisoners and loot from boats on the open water.

This question gave Bart a headache only food would cure. Where in Tahoe City could he find a good burrito?

He drove up North Lake Boulevard slowly, looking for an independent taqueria where the owner cooks, and the parking lot is full. While an impatient driver behind him crowded his bumper, Bart dodged jaywalkers wrapped in beach towels.

Ahead on the left he saw an old fast-food place, flat roofed, with the usual aluminum-framed windows and ceramic-tiled facade. Familiar, except this one had two recycled telephone poles pretending to be the masts of an old ship. A cable strung between the poles supported sails and a ten-foot-wide black metal sign shaped like a pirate's eye patch. The restaurant's name, *Captain Jack's Pirate Fish Grotto,* flashed in red and gold neon across the eye patch. At each corner of the parking lot, shorter poles flew the Jolly Roger. The parking lot was nearly empty, and they probably didn't sell burritos, but Bart pulled in.

Too piratey to ignore.

Bart locked the Klimo and walked toward the entrance. As he passed near one of the "masts," he looked up at its sail and saw a Martha Stewart label. A sign filled one of the windows:

WE LOVE PIRATES!

Captain Jack himself guarded the entrance. Manspreading on one boot and a wooden leg, he wore a pirate hat, headscarf, gold earring, eye patch, frilly shirt, sash, and satin pants — all painted fiberglass. Captain Jack wasn't going anywhere soon because his boot and peg-leg were fixed in a block of cast concrete chained and padlocked to a ring in the sidewalk. An electronic voice from Captain Jack's belly interrupted Bart's study of the Styrofoam "Grotto" rocks glued to the door frame.

"Arrrrgh, Maight-tey! Come ta eat,'ave ya? Wel-come a-board! This week the gal-ley is ser-vin' a spesh-shal fur-ya — a bowl o' Sea Boun-ty with Pirate Fish Sand-wich, only a dollar nine-ty-nine cents!"

Bart didn't really expect the Captain's fiberglass lips and marker pen whiskers to move, though the Captain's arms and sword were wobbling around. The arms moving reminded Bart of a mechanical Santa he saw at the mall last Christmas.

Bart entered and stood at the counter. The place looked like a pizza joint on the road to bankruptcy via Disneyland's Pirates of the Caribbean. Bart had enjoyed Disneyland many times, but never returned after the PC-Nazis banned the wench-chasing.

A young woman wearing a black T-shirt greeted him. The front of her shirt read, in scary script, ***Pirate's Wench***, and carried a plastic name tag — AMBER — shaped like an old ship's cannon.

Pen poised above a pad, she said, "Sir, are you ready to order?"

Bart looked above the counter at the menu: Grog (draft beer), Nuggets-o'-Gold (miscellaneous species fish chunks, breaded and deep fried), Cannon Balls (quarter-pound burgers), Sea Bounty (fish soup), Dreaded Ice Bergs (frosty cone), and more.

"No burritos?"

She frowned. "No, sorry."

"What's the closest?"

"Well, you could have a Pirate's Wrap. Last week's special? We still have some."

"Okay, and a cola. Classic Coke if you've got it." He put a twenty on the counter.

"Classic it is." She wrote a ticket and passed it through a window to the kitchen, then gave Bart his change.

While Bart waited, he questioned Amber. She'd worked at Captain Jack's full-time for two summers but didn't plan to return next summer.

"Why not?"

"I hate wearing a uniform."

Besides the Pirate's Wench T-shirt, she wore a black polyester headscarf and white plastic skull-and-crossed-bones earrings.

"How did you come to work here?"

"Mom wanted me to get a job. She told me there was a Help Wanted sign here, only she messed up what the place is."

"How so?"

"Mom thought it was a health club, that the sign said WE LOVE PILATES! After I took the job, I told her, 'Mom, it's PIRATES, not PILATES.' She should wear her glasses."

Bart nodded in sympathy. "Who likes the pirate stuff?"

"Mostly kids and family. The kids are wearing parts of a pirate outfit with a movie logo. They're having fun and they're no trouble."

"Trouble?"

"The ones who've been coming here way before the Johnny Depp movies, they're trouble. They say they really hate the new movies because they say" — she deepened her voice — "'they're not Real, Maaaan!' They're always loud, trying to scare the kids and families away."

"Scare people?"

"Like, one time, this old guy came late, just before closing, from a costume party. He was wearing this stuff he got from a website in the back of *Pirates Magazine*. He spent *waaay* too much dressing like a pirate. Hook sees him — Hook's already finished three pitchers of beer — and one-punches the guy half-unconscious to the floor. Then stands over him and says, 'Well, don't you look store-bought?'"

Bart remembered an article in *The Sacramento Bee* about a thirty-eight-year-old programmer from San Jose, assaulted in a Tahoe City restaurant after a pirate costume party.

Amber's face twisted. "I mean, they shouldn't attack an old guy for dressing like somebody he's not."

"Right, Amber. How many people who buy barn coats from

L.L. Bean actually have barns?"

"Huh?"

"These guys, they don't sound tolerant."

"Hook and his friends — they act like pirates, but they're more like outlaw bikers. I heard the first time they ate here they tried to run without paying."

"What happened?"

"Red, the cook — he's been here forever — he hit Hook in the butt with an iron frying pan. He told Hook he could come back and eat if he paid, or he could have the frying pan and the law — Hook's choice. Only Red would do that. Andrew, the manager, a total wimp, is mostly never here — just to count the cash and do the books. After Red used the frying pan, they always pay. I think Hook's afraid of Red."

"Good. Where's your restroom?"

"Follow the sign behind me."

"Thanks. Back in a minute."

Bart had just zipped up his jeans when the restroom window rattled from Harley-Davidson thunder in the parking lot. When he left the restroom, he saw Amber nod toward the front door.

"They're here." She rolled her eyes.

"Who?"

"Hook, and the other two losers."

Bart looked through the front window in time to see three parked motorcycles, and their riders heading for the entrance. His eyes zoomed to the rear fenders and license-plate frames. Three grinning chromed skulls mocked him again.

* * *

14

The Earff Moved

We'll Meet Again

The Grotto's front door flew open, making way for the three strange men stomping in. The first was a big man, at least six-four and 250, with a rough, mean face under stringy gray hair and an eye patch. A metal hook shined from where his right hand should be. The second man was smaller and had burn scars covering most of his face and arms. Scattered patches of hair remained above a purple bandana. The last one, the smallest, wore a red bandana encircling his head below the hairline. He limped in on a wooden peg-leg. They ignored Bart and sailed toward a table in the corner.

The big man with the hook was all attitude, strutting and posing, the group's obvious leader. He called out to the kitchen.

"Hey, Red! Our usual. Be quick. We'll be on the fo'c'sle."

He raised his right arm high and clicked his hook open and shut, like he was playing castanets. "Hey, Amber! When ya gonna let me take ya for a ride, huh?"

"When you can walk across the lake, Hook." Leaning closer to Bart, she lowered her voice. "See what I mean? Losers."

"Yeah. Where'd they get their injuries, the hook, peg leg, and scars.

"I overheard Hook talk about that old war. 'The Nam, in the shit, behind the lines.' Excuse my French."

Red passed Bart's steaming order to Amber, who added a

complimentary cardboard pirate hat and eye patch.

Bart picked up his tray. "Do you have hot sauce?"

Amber hesitated and looked behind her. "Not officially. I keep a bottle of tabasco under the counter. Here, take it. Some of this pirate food needs it. That's what the customers say. I never eat it myself."

"Thanks, Amber."

Bart took his tray to a table away from the few customers, but within earshot of the three bikers, hopefully not near enough to draw their attention. They were on the fo'c'sle, which Bart knew from his library pirate studies was the *forecastle*, the front or bow deck of a ship. In Captain Jack's, the fo'c'sle was a wooden platform raised a foot above the tile floor, for a non-existent band.

Sipping his Coke, Bart examined his Pirate's Wrap. It did not look good, and it did not taste good. It reminded him of a burrito he ate at the State Fair. Amber's tabasco helped.

While he nibbled at his Pirate's Wrap, Bart concentrated on trying to hear what the three pirates were saying. Between bites, he tried to sneak a look without being noticed.

Red delivered a platter of Pirate Nachos and three pitchers of beer to the fo'c'sle. He accepted their money with a nod and smile.

Bart observed they'd found more cash. The Hard Rock Café and Roseville?

The three odd men dug into their food. Bart listened to Hook dominate and control the conversation, alternately reassuring and bullying the other two. Hook followed his statements with self-applauding grunts and loud clicks from his hook.

As a patrol cop in Berkeley, Bart had his fill of tough guys like Hook, bored bikers who'd visit the campus and hang out on Telegraph for a day, trolling for sheltered ingenues from Beverly Hills, Palos Verdes, or Woodside, who might want to try a walk on the wild side. He felt comfortable around these bad boys, at least more comfortable than he felt around women.

The three men talked while Bart sipped his Coke and poked at his wrap. Their rambling conversation turned to stories of the motorcycles they had owned and the women they had met on each machine. Each of the three appeared to be on the golden side of fifty and most of their stories were decades old. Because they hadn't said anything interesting, Bart decided these pirates were not likely *his* pirates. A waste of his time.

Then the peg-legged man blurted out something Bart didn't understand. Hook reacted immediately. He bent his head down near the table-top and got the other two to do the same with a few growled words. They talked with their faces near touching. Now Bart was too far away to hear their whispering, and he couldn't see their lips.

Sliding his table and chair a few inches at a time, Bart tried to move closer to the fo'c'sle. His table leg caught on gum stuck to the tile floor. He pushed, and the leg screeched when it broke free.

"Yikes!"

The three pirates turned to look at him.

To escape their gaze, Bart dropped a plastic fork to the floor and bent down to retrieve it. If the pirates suspected anything, he didn't see it. He recovered and went back to his wrap. Now he was close enough to hear.

The man with all the scars was gesturing with his fork. "First thing, I'm goin' ta Vegas."

Hook quickly countered. "Nah, Scar, you lissen. We're all goin' to the Carry-Be-In, where there's no snow, an' pirates ruled for hun-nerts a years. An', we're gonna stick ta-gether, keep a eye on each other, an' lay low fur a cup-la years," he said, swinging his hook through the air.

The wooden pegleg man said, "But Hook, with all that money, I wanna go back home to Seattle. There's cool bars near the airport where —"

"Shut yur face, Stumpy! No Mutant County 'til I say." The big pirate's body tensed as he slammed his shiny hook into the polyurethane coated hatch-cover tabletop. "Stumpy, I tol' ya a'fore. I'm not letting yu or Scar out-ta my sight more than's necessary, now or after, 'til we're clear o'er the horizon."

Hook, Scar, and Stumpy, names confirmed.

"All right, Hook. You're in charge, like always. You know Scar n me are always with you, but we're not confident like you," Stumpy said, using two hands to lift his peg leg up onto an empty chair. "Be real, Hook. This thing's a lot bigger than we're used ta."

"We're taking orders. An' it ain't finished yet," said Scar.

"In due time, Bucs, in due time."

Now, *that's* interesting. What are they up to? But Bart had let down his guard.

Hook looked up and caught Bart staring at him. He turned to the others. "Buccaneers, time ta abandon ship. Lively now!"

Bart quickly faked interest in his Pirate's Wrap.

Passing Bart's table, Stumpy said to Scar, "Maybe we should go to Tortuga, like in *Captain Blood.*"

Bart expected they would pass without notice, until Hook stopped at Bart's table and stared down at him.

"What werya lookin' at, Citizen?"

Surprised, Bart said, "Nothing. Oh . . . you mean when I was looking at you for a second?"

"A-course."

"You're just such righteous pirates. It's hard not to stare."

Hook grabbed Bart's T-shirt sleeve with his metal hook and pulled.

"Did we have an Earff-quake here, an Earff-quake like what destroyed Port Royal? Yur table slid might-ty close, in-vay-din' ar pry-va-cy."

"I hadn't noticed. Sorry." Bart looked down at his table. "Say, look, it did move. Not an earthquake . . . maybe a storm? Maybe the deck tilted in the storm."

Hook cocked his head to one side. "You ain't bein' a smart-ass, are ya?"

"Me?"

"Just in case, I wanna show ya somethin', Citizen. See this hook here? Look real close."

Bart obeyed. He turned his head to look at the hook pulling his sleeve.

"See, see? There used-ta be a good hand there, once. Then in nine-teen six-ty-nine, a dirty, rotten, sneaky, little Vee Cee bugger blowed it clean off, with a Arr-Pee-Gee. But a'fore that, my hands was tattooed serious, on the knuckles. One letter for each knuckle. Two hands, four letters each hand, see?"

Bart hoped this wasn't going to be a really long story or require any more math. His arm was sore from Hook jerking on his T-shirt sleeve with each word he spit out. And it was one of Bart's best shirts, washed enough to tear if Hook didn't let up.

"I got a *man's* tattoos, Citizen, not like those pansies what got drunk and run off base ta get a tattoo says MOM, or their virgin high school sweetie's name. Or even the ones with LOVE an' HATE tattooed on their knuckles. I *knew* about all-out war!"

Bart listened, growing impatient.

"See, see?" He let go of Bart's sleeve and waved the hook in Bart's face. "See? See where the hook is now? That's where my right hand, my righteous strong hand, use-ta be, an' it use-ta say, **L - I - F - E** — LIFE. Now that hand — an' LIFE — are gone!"

Hook whipped his hooked arm back and straight out behind him. *Gone.* He swung his left arm forward and straight ahead. Bart visualized Hook cross-country skiing.

"See? Now, all's left, is the hand what's left — the *LEFT* hand. See?"

"Want some of my Pirate's Wrap? I don't think I can eat it all."

"Pay a-ten-shun, Citizen!"

Hook brushed strings of gray hair back off his eye patch and formed his left hand into a fist. He put the knuckles right up to Bart's face.

"See what *that* says, Citizen!"

"Sorry, I can't. It's too close to my face — it's out of focus."

"Oh." Hook pulled his hand back a few inches.

Now Bart could see. Each knuckle on Hook's left hand had a faded-blue tattooed letter: **D - E - T - H.**

Bart smiled. "D-E-T-H. I get it — DEATH. Hey, scary."

Hook's face turned red and angry.

"Just like them hun-nerts a Vee Cee I faced an' sent to see their weird little buddy, Boo-duh, down in Davy Jones's locker, death is what yur — gonna — get! Don't mess with us, bilge rat!"

"I have no reason to mess with you."

"You better not," said Hook, calming down.

"Have you considered putting the L-I-F-E — LIFE letters back onto your hook, maybe chromed metal ones, or varnished walnut?"

Hook's face froze, and then he gave Bart a fierce staring. His eye was huge, ready to pop out, and his face turned beet red.

"Are-ya *MAKIN' FUN* a the handy-capped?"

"No, no — just trying to help."

Hook brought his hook up to his un-patched eye and — click-click — snapped the hook open and shut. "I'm gonna be keeping my eye on *you*."

"You ever play for the Raiders?"

"No. I'd be too tuff fur 'em. What's yur name anyway, tuff guy?"

"My friends call me Biff."

"Biff? Biff?" Hook's face formed a quizzical frown. "Biff what?"

"Biff Jerky."

"Oh! Oh! There's just always *got* to be a smart-ass, ain't there?" Hook, spewing toxic beer-and-nacho breath, leaned into Bart's face. "Ya just don't belong here, un-salty dude. Go back to dry land an' Burger King a'fore I soaks-ya so's-ya never dry out."

After he had stared into Bart's eyes long enough to let the message burn in, Hook turned and stomped out after the others.

As the three cleared the door, Bart shouted after them.

"*Biff.* With *two* Fs!"

* * *

15

Bad Boys

Bad, Bad, Pirate Clowns

Bart waited until he'd heard them blast out of the parking lot. He threw a tip onto his tray and waved goodbye to Amber as he left.

Outside, Captain Jack was still pitching while Bart looked for the three pirates. He heard them roaring north. He jumped into the Klimo and caught up with them between Lake Forest and Carnelian Bay.

Bart still worried about wasting time with this bunch, but he would follow them for Mr. Bocco — at least to get their license numbers — and, who knows, they might lead him to other "pirates," and eventually to the pirates who had taken Drake Concannon. And they were going in the right direction for his next to-do list item, Number Six, visiting Mrs. Concannon.

Bart's assignment was just delivering the ransom money, but what might be his reward if he could find the kidnappers and free Drake Concannon before paying the ransom?

Soon, Hook and his friends stopped at a motorcycle shop:

BILL MEYER & SON
SHORELINE MOTORCYCLES — SINCE 1951

Bart parked across the road up a side street. He watched and waited. After a while, they came out of the shop carrying a few boxes, straddled their motorcycles, and again drove north. Bart followed.

As they neared Carnelian Bay, traffic slowed, and the road curved to the east. Signs tacked to trees and posts advertised a classic boat show for the weekend.

Trying to stay a safe distance behind his bikers, Bart let a truck turn in front of him, blocking his view. When he could see the traffic ahead again, they were gone. Bart's head swiveled in all directions as the Klimo crawled past a boat sales shop and marina, advertising that they would host the boat show.

Just past the boat shop, he found his bikers. They had turned off the road at the east side of the boat shop and headed toward two buildings near the water.

Bart found a place to park and walked back, just in time to see them pushing their motorcycles into a compact metal shed. They padlocked the shed door and entered a rusty, single-wide trailer near the shed and fifty feet back from the water's edge.

This side of the boat shop looked like a two-story blank wall, except for a door near the shed. Beyond the trailer, a low-slung boat under tarps floated tied to a pier. Bart estimated the boat to be thirty feet long. He found a place to sit and observe.

As the sky faded toward dusk, lights came on in the trailer. Bart supposed these pirates were settling in with grog from aluminum cans. After a while, a beater Toyota arrived. The driver got out carrying an insulated package. When the trailer door opened, hands exchanged cash and pizzas. The driver slammed the Toyota's door and sprayed gravel. Pirates don't tip.

Bart bet they wouldn't move until they'd finished the beer and pizza. In the Klimo on the way back toward Bill Meyer's, he looked at the front of the boat shop. The name on the window was O'Hara's, the place he had seen in Drake Concannon's office photos.

At Bill Meyer's, a thin, muscled man with a gray crewcut and wearing a Harley-Davidson T-shirt, rotated the OPEN sign to the CLOSED side. Bart waved and knocked on the door. The man opened the door. "We're closed."

"Are you Bill?"

"Bill junior. My dad passed in eighty-three. But we're still closed."

Bart showed him his PI license and asked, "How about a minute for a few questions."

"Okay, but we've got to walk and talk because I want to close up and go home. My old lady gets pissed if I'm late for dinner."

Bart followed as Bill closed and latched windows.

"Bill, I'm interested in three guys I saw come into your shop this afternoon, fake pirates. Hook for a hand, peg leg —"

"Those morons. Let me guess. What are you investigating? Stolen motorcycles?"

"Maybe. What's their story?

"It's a long, dull, bad story, what I know of it. These days my business with those guys is cash-only. Today they bought parts. Years ago, before I knew them, they offered me some Harley parts. Some were new, and some were good used parts — all at a good price. I bought from them, and sure as the lake is deep, the parts turned out to be stolen. The Sheriff had been watching them for weeks. I was going to be a witness instead of an accessory. They pled guilty for a reduced sentence, and I didn't have to testify. They never knew I was part of their case, and I still sell them what they can pay for, as much to keep on their good side as anything."

"So, they've done time."

"Does the Pope shit in the woods?"

"You think they could be involved in more serious crimes?"

"As far as I know, they're small time, but you never know. There are clowns like them on death row because someone died over three dollars. They never have much money to spend — real one-per-centers."

They had walked and talked their way to the service area at the back of the shop. While Bill turned off lights, Bart asked another question.

"I heard they got those injuries in the service . . . maybe Special Forces, behind the lines in Viet Nam."

A warm smile spread across Bill's face. He closed his eyes and looked like he might roll on the oil-stained concrete floor laughing.

"For sure they were in the service. The laundry service at

Folsom, the food service at Susanville, the library service at Mule Creek. You name the facility — they've been there." He shook his head and looked at Bart. "Behind the lines, you say? You want me to die laughing? Behind lines of coke maybe — certainly behind in their rent."

"So, no Viet Nam?"

"Okay, I don't know for sure. Maybe, maybe not Nam. They probably got their injuries the way most hard-case bikers get them — falling off their bikes. As old as they are, you'd think they'd learn. They would've had too much booze, weed, or meth. Or maybe some half-blind geezer made an unexpected left turn in front of them. The sure thing with that bunch is they will occasionally disappear, in the hospital or lock-up. There used to be four of them, but I haven't seen the other guy for months. Who knows where he is?"

"What about — who are their friends?"

"Friends? None that I've seen."

"Anything else you could tell me? How do they operate their bikes with those injuries?"

"The only times they've ever appeared grateful is when I modified their bikes to work with their handicaps. Each time they wrecked one, I'd have to fab and install the special controls again. You know about Hook and Stumpy, but Scar wanted special controls, same as Hook, because scar tissue knotted up one of his hands."

"Thanks, Bill. I'll let you go home. But I might come back another day for more questions. Okay?"

"You got it, if you promise to tip me about anything illegal these counterfeit pirates might do that affects me."

Bart promised and left his card and drove back to O'Hara's and around the east side to where he could see the trailer. The trailer was dark now. The only light visible in the area was on a pole, splashing yellow green over a pile of canvas tarps on the end of the old pier. The boat was gone.

Bart waited as long as he could for them to return and then left for the Concannons' place.

* * *

Part Two

The Setting

16

Another World

The Nearness of You

Afraid of being late to his new employer's home, Bart paid little attention to roadside attractions as the Klimo cut through the night toward the Nevada side of Lake Tahoe. It was cooler, making it practical to keep the Klimo's windows closed. He enjoyed the solemn quiet provided by the limo-quality sound insulation. It made it easier to think.

It was past nine when Bart turned right off Highway 28 at the Eagle Cove Road sign. The narrow, dark, asphalt-paved road wound through trees until it ended in a cul-de-sac, where his headlights illuminated a high stone arch capped by a weathered dark bronze eagle. Yellow bulbs in black-iron lanterns at each side illuminated a bronze number **1** clutched in the eagle's talons.

A tall chain-link fence extended from each side of the arch, beyond what Bart could see. Under the arch, a chain-link gate was open. A sign on the side of the stone arch said:

PRIVATE — NO ADMITTANCE
BEWARE!
PATROLLED BY DOGS WHEN GATE CLOSED

Bart drove through. He couldn't help feeling that he was someone the fence was meant to keep out. If Drake Concannon kept millions in cash at home, Bart understood the security.

Several hundred yards down the road, Bart saw lights at a stone gatehouse. The gatehouse supported one side of another high stone arch, which was the only break in a tall stone wall extending far into the darkness on both sides. Light from his headlights flashed off coils of concertina razor wire fastened to the top of the stone walls. Within the archway, a gate of heavy black-iron bars blocked the road. A gravel and sand turnaround area at one side told Bart the unwelcome were sent back to the highway.

Blinded by a floodlight above the gate, Bart shaded his eyes with his hand and honked twice. A short muscular man near Bart's age came out of the gatehouse and approached the Klimo. Bart lowered his window and held up his driver's license. The man compared Bart to the photo on the license and went back inside.

The iron gate parted in the center and swung in. Bart started forward and switched on his headlights. When Bart passed, the man in the gatehouse was using a telephone.

The drive to the house took Bart downhill over more paved road, around groups of tall sugar pines and boulders, terminating at an asphalt turnaround enclosed by low stone walls attached to a stone garage, fronted by six arched openings filled by wooden folding doors. To the right of the garage, a driveway, probably a service road, led off into the trees and out of sight. More wrought iron lanterns, attached to the garage and walls, emitted circles of warm light from their yellow bulbs.

Bart parked off to one side and stepped out. The size of the garage complex made him feel small. He followed the lights downstairs through a cut in the low wall at the left of the garage. The stairs led to a stone path which passed several lesser stone structures and ended at the main house. The house had many wings and levels, built to follow the profile of the land. Sections of the foundation flowed over and incorporated giant, centuries-old boulders. As he approached the house, he could see Mrs. Concannon holding open a heavy wooden door.

"Good evening, Mr. Lasiter. Come in. I've been holding dinner until you arrived."

"Sorry to delay you. Thank you, Mrs. Concannon."

She stood to the side as he entered the foyer. Bart thought

the light sweater and slacks she wore fit with the rustic lakeside setting, though he didn't have much experience with people who lived on a lakefront. After closing the door, she walked ahead into a hallway.

"I hope your drive here was pleasant. Did you have any trouble finding us?"

"Very pleasant, and no, no problem."

"Good."

They entered an immense room with walls of stone, cut and mortared into one. The floor was also stone, smooth, irregular flats precisely joined and mortared. The walls supported a high, vaulted ceiling with exposed timbers. To the left, a cavernous fireplace built into the stone wall had an opening as tall as Mrs. Concannon. Bookcases covered the wall on the right. In front of the bookcases, a mahogany bar sat on a stone base.

A picture window divided the wall facing the lake. It was the biggest single piece of glass Bart had ever seen in a private residence, and he had seen a few in the Berkeley hills. Through the picture window, Bart could see below a boat house next to a lighted wooden pier, the dock in the photographs.

"Welcome to our home, Mr. Lasiter. I sincerely hope when Drake is home safe again, and this unpleasantness has passed, you will visit and be our guest."

"That . . . that would be nice, Mrs. Concannon. Thank you."

Bart knew there was too much to do and worry about until Drake Concannon was home safe again, and little time for filling in the social calendar, but he appreciated the gesture. None of the owners of expensive old homes in the Berkeley hills had invited him to come around after the burglars he caught for them were tried and convicted.

Bart observed her demeanor. He tried to keep in mind how a kidnapping could tear the victim's relatives apart emotionally. Mrs. Concannon was coping very well, and he wanted to do whatever he could to keep her on even keel.

"You must be hungry, Mr. Lasiter. Come with me to the kitchen. I want to select a wine for dinner." Mrs. Concannon left the big room and started down a hallway, looking back to confirm that Bart was following. Upon entering the kitchen, she pushed a button on a brass wall panel near the door.

The kitchen was a sizeable room with more stone and high ceiling. It looked like the kitchen of an old restaurant or hotel, with stainless steel counters and sinks, an oversize double-door refrigerator, and, under a big metal vent hood, professional gas burners and ovens. Ivory painted cabinets with doors fitted with chromed hinges and latches covered the walls. Bart didn't see any wine.

"What are your tastes in wine, Mr. Lasiter?"

"Oh, I don't drink much wine. Red, I guess."

An older woman came into the kitchen. "You rang, Missus Cee?"

"Yes, Isabel. This is Mr. Bart Lasiter. He will be helping me." She turned to Bart. "The staff know what's happened.

"Isabel, now that Mr. Lasiter is here, you can make supper for us. You know what to do."

"Pronto, Missus Cee."

"This way, Mr. Lasiter." Mrs. Concannon led him toward a door at the opposite end of the kitchen. They crossed a floor of waxed and polished magenta linoleum sheet. She opened the door and flipped a switch. The harsh light from bare bulbs on the ceiling revealed wide wooden steps.

The air became cool and dry as they descended, and Bart detected mixed odors of wood and spices. At the bottom of the stairs, he saw a cavernous underground storage room containing a commercial freezer and many wooden shelves. Cooking supplies in cans, bottles, and tall glass apothecary jars, full of what Bart assumed were whole spices, filled the shelves. Wine racks holding hundreds of bottles spread across an entire wall. The redwood racks extended from the simple concrete floor to the twelve-foot-high wood-beamed ceiling supporting the kitchen above.

"I can assure you, Isabel is a wonderful cook. She's been cooking and keeping house for Drake since she was a teenager. But I've found that she doesn't read well, and she doesn't know wine. I don't fault her for that because Drake didn't help her further her education, and he was never interested in wine. I try to help her, and I do like wine. I had these racks installed soon after we were married."

Mrs. Concannon scanned the bottles of wine before walking

to the end of the wall near a rolling ladder attached to a rail at the top of the racks.

"What do we want?" She rolled the ladder to one row and climbed to the top.

"Hold the ladder for me, would you please, Mr. Lasiter? It can start rolling on its own."

Bart stepped to the ladder and held it steady.

After a brief search, she retrieved a bottle and started down the ladder. Near the bottom, she let out a cry as her foot slipped through a rung. She fell into Bart's arms. He could feel the weight of her body against him, and their faces were inches apart. Her face flushed red, and she looked away from him.

"Oh, I'm so sorry, so embarrassed, Mr. Lasiter! I don't know what happened — I guess I slipped. Did I hurt you?"

"It's okay. I'm okay. You're okay. Ha, ha — that's a joke."

"Thank you for catching me."

She still held the bottle of wine and didn't move to leave his arms. She turned and looked into his eyes.

Those blue eyes. Her perfume. He felt the room closing in. He hadn't noticed any sounds there before. Now, the freezer's compressor hummed like a train, but his heart was louder. He could hear it beating, louder and faster. And now the room felt warmer than before. He was sweating.

He blushed and froze, not knowing what to say. Then he set her down, feet to the floor, and took a half step back.

She smiled, then said, "This bottle will do," and led him back upstairs.

* * *

17

Ships in the Night

In the Wee Small Hours of the Morning

When they returned to the kitchen, Bart saw flames under a grill in the cook top, and Isabel removing two steaks from a shallow glass dish of liquid. She wiped each steak dry with a towel, and then coated them with gray mustard and cracked black pepper.

"How do you like your steak, Mr. Lasiter?" asked Mrs. Concannon.

Isabel turned toward Bart, waiting for the answer.

"Well done, please." Did Isabel roll her eyes for Mrs. Concannon?

"Let's go to the dining room." Carrying the bottle of wine, she turned away from Bart and left. Bart followed.

Directly across the hallway from the kitchen, they entered a rectangular room featuring a heavy wooden table sized for ten. Mrs. Concannon invited Bart to sit at one end of the table, where he could see another view of the lake through tall windows.

A mounted fish, over three feet long, glared down at him from the interior wall. Bart's first reaction was, *Hey, I didn't do it.* Then he stood for a closer look. An engraved brass plate on the wooden mount confirmed it was the same Mackinaw he'd seen in the photo at Drake Concannon's Sacramento office.

"Drake caught that poor fellow years ago. Please sit down."
Bart sat and watched.

Mrs. Concannon sat at the opposite end of the table, already set for two, with a folding corkscrew at her place.

She opened the bottle, deftly using a blade in the corkscrew to cut the foil in one turn, and then inserted the screw and removed the cork with speed and a minimum of motion, as if she had done so thousands of times before. After pouring an inch into her glass, she swirled the wine around and put her nose into the glass. "Hmmmm." Then a sip and pause. "Good." She came around to Bart, put one hand on his shoulder, and filled his glass.

"What is it?"

"A California central coast Petite Sirah. I bought two cases of it last year at a wine tasting."

"Mrs. Concannon, tell me about your husband and his yacht club, if you wouldn't mind."

She returned to her end of the table and filled her own glass.

"Yes, the Crystal Bay Yacht Club. You can almost see it from here. It's directly across Crystal Bay near the California-Nevada border. Drake joined when he was a young man full of energy. Since we married, he spends more time here, with me. We're very happy together and don't need to travel or socialize. But I think Drake is still a member."

Isabel arrived with two plates of grilled steak and salad. She placed them and left.

Mrs. Concannon smiled. "Well, you're working hard for us. You need some good beef for energy."

Bart started cutting his steak. He noticed Mrs. Concannon's steak was very rare. His meat was very good, well done without a trace of pink, but the salad was strange to him. He was used to the iceberg lettuce from his burritos and combo-plates. There was a purple crunchy leaf he was eating, but not enjoying.

Mrs. Concannon noticed his hesitation. "It's radicchio. You don't have to eat it."

Bart used his fork to rake the purple stuff to the side.

She cut some meat, ate a piece, but then set her knife and fork down. "I thought I was hungry. Since Drake's been gone, I'm afraid I don't have much appetite."

After Bart had finished his dinner, she led him back to the living room, bringing her wine glass after refilling it. He resisted drinking more than that first glass. The wine was stronger than what he was used to, infrequent wine coolers and well-diluted fruit punch made with cheap wines, all served at Berkeley PD after-hours parties for those who didn't like beer, or hard liquor.

"Let me show you the red light." She stopped at a mahogany end table centered in front of the picture window. A brass lantern with red glass lenses sat alone on the table. A cord ran from the lantern to a wall socket under the window.

"It's an old ship's navigation light that Drake wired to work in the house. It should be easy to see."

Bart switched the light on and off. "Good. Now we just wait until it's time."

The bookcase caught Bart's attention. "Mind if I look at your books, Mrs. Concannon?"

"Of course not. Please do."

He saw rows of Tahoe books, new and old nautical books, volumes cataloging classic wood boats, and blue binders of *Classic Boating* magazine. Other shelves held a decade's worth of thick annual membership directories from the *Antique and Classic Boat Society,* travel books on Europe, ports of the world, major cities, older volumes of *Who's Who*, and books on food, wine, and art. Impressed, Bart went back to the boating books.

"Wow, Mrs. Concannon. If you've read all these boating books, you could answer just about any question someone might ask you about boats."

"Oh, really, Mr. Lasiter. My, who would have thought of that?"

He noticed the absence of any video tapes or DVDs. He realized he had not seen a TV, either.

"Do you like movies, Mrs. Concannon?"

"Not really, Mr. Lasiter. Drake doesn't like them. My father liked them. He and I had different . . . tastes."

"I like movies." He stood back and scanned the width of the shelves. "You have a lot of books. I'm surprised there aren't any engineering books here."

"Drake keeps most of his books down in his workshop. He's adamant that I and the staff stay clear while he putters the hours away. Brilliant men must be allowed their quirks. Some of these books are mine, and some are Drake's. Do you read?"

"When I have the time." He moved further along the shelves and kneeled to see the lower shelves. "Oh, look at all these mysteries." He ran his fingers over the book spines. "So, you like mysteries, Mrs. Concannon?"

"Mr. Lasiter, all of life is a mystery. But, as I've told you, I'm not good with puzzles. I can never see ahead and solve the riddle."

"Being a detective, I like mysteries. I've read a few, and I have my favorites. Some really are a bit much. Maybe like this one." He held up an older hardback, Nancy Drew's *The Hidden Staircase*. "The things these writers think of. No offense to Nancy Drew fans, Mrs. Concannon, but how many times have you ever heard of a *real* hidden staircase? Other than the Winchester house in San Jose, *I* don't know of any."

"Perhaps you would like to borrow a volume or two?"

He returned the book to the bookcase. "Thank you. I don't have much time to read when I'm on a case. At most I'll read at night, just enough to help me fall asleep."

So casually that Bart had barely noticed, Mrs. Concannon removed the Nancy Drew he had shelved. "Really? That's interesting." She checked the spines of some books and re-shelved *The Hidden Staircase*, back where Bart had found it. She ran her fingers over the spines as if they were piano keys. "There."

She looked to the bar at a clock encased in brass, like a ship's compass. "Is it time, Mr. Lasiter?"

Bart checked his plastic-strapped Casio. "Okay. It's past eleven-thirty. We should turn the red light on now."

When Mrs. Concannon switched on the lamp, the window reflected red light back into the living room. She went behind the bar and switched off the other lights in the living room. The room glowed red. In the red light, she looked like someone else, someone he didn't know.

"Come upstairs. We'll watch from Drake's photo room."

She led him up stone stairs, down a hallway, and into a room. The room had another picture window facing the lake. Instead of a sofa or chairs, tripods faced the window. Each tripod supported a different still or motion picture camera, including video tape. The length of each camera lens varied, and the video camera had both an extreme telescopic lens and a night vision booster.

"Drake used this room for his photo projects. You can see the lake well from here, sometimes even at night."

Bart pointed to some lenses on the shelves in the room. "Wow."

"It's true that most of Drake's work has been with gaming devices, but he has patents in other areas, too. Photo lenses and cameras, for example."

"It's near midnight." Bart pointed at the tripods. "Can I use one of these things to find them out there?"

"Oh, yes."

"What about the night vision one?"

Mrs. Concannon looked away to the lake. "I don't know how to work that one. I just know still photography."

"Okay. This still camera with the long lens should work."

Through the viewfinder Bart saw bits of light from a narrow sliver of moon and the stars reflected off the peaks of slight waves. The effect of the telescopic lens was to stack the waves closer to each other and bring the lights of the distant shoreline nearer. He slowly swept the lens back and forth, searching. He checked his watch again. It was midnight.

Bart thought he saw something. After refocusing the lens, he could see a dark shape interrupting the pattern of waves and light. It was moving slowly, traveling parallel to the shoreline.

"I think I see something, maybe a black boat. It could be the kidnappers looking for the red light."

"Can you see what they look like?"

He carefully adjusted the lens focus. "No . . . uh — oh-oh."

"What happened?"

"They're leaving." He watched the sleek, black boat turn and accelerate toward the west shore, whipping the water behind into a broad white wake. "They're gone."

"I think we've done what they have asked, Mr. Lasiter. Now all we can do is wait and hope for the best."

Her eyes were not as confident as her voice. Bart worried again about her state of mind. She'd been strong so far, but how long could a wife endure her husband's kidnapping?

"I don't think you'll have to wait long, Mrs. Concannon.

They want the money."

"Yes, I suppose so. I have faith in you, your talent, and your knowledge of these terrible, ugly things, but I do worry. Now, Mr. Lasiter, I think it's too late for you to go back to Sacramento, or to a motel tonight. Why don't you stay here this evening, in our home?"

He decided Aggie would be all right. "Okay. Thank you."

Mrs. Concannon left the photo room and turned down the hallway. He followed.

She stopped at an open door, her outstretched arm inviting Bart into the room. It was a suite with its own bath. What Bart thought was a Navajo rug covered the stone floor. The walls had framed oil paintings of older Lake Tahoe scenes. The paintings looked original. One was signed, A. Bierstadt.

"I hope you will be comfortable here. In the bath cabinets you'll find extra blankets and towels. If you need anything, my room is at the far end of the hall. Good night, Mr. Lasiter." She closed the door.

The room was more than what Bart was used to, with a bed twice the size of his own back in Old Town. Removing his clothes, he remembered he didn't have his lucky pajamas.

He laughed. What could hurt him in this house?

* * *

18

Breakfast in Paradise

The Good Life

Morning light from the lakeside windows advanced across the Navajo rug and up onto Bart's bed, warming his face.

Bart remembered where he was. He eased out of bed and went to the windows. Below, as far as he could see, the lake was mirror-glass smooth, a magnificent body of water resting at peace beneath a bright and clear blue sky.

While he showered, he remembered hearing voices during the night from the hallway. He thought he'd heard Mrs. Concannon shush someone. A dream? He dressed and went downstairs, where he found Isabel in the living room.

"Missus Cee outside, in gazebo. She wait for you, Meester. Bart." Isabel pointed to a door adjacent to the picture window. "Follow the path."

The path of mortared flat stone, bordered by a low stone wall along the lakeside, faithfully paralleled the lakeshore, curving gently and stepping up and down as it followed the hillside and detoured between sugar pines and heavy boulders.

Down at the water's edge, a large grouping of huge, smooth, gray boulders lay against each other, elephants sunbathing at the beach on a fine August day. Scanning the lake as he followed the path, Bart thought he had never enjoyed a more beautiful scene, nor breathed fresher air. This was the way to live. If you could.

Through an opening in the trees, he saw the gazebo. Shaped like a short silo, with rough timber posts supporting a conical roof of wooden beams and shingles, it sat alone on a promontory of boulders rising from the water, a stone and wood period at the end of a long sentence written by the stone path.

Though set lower than the path, close to the water's surface, the gazebo offered an unobstructed view of the lake and the shoreline in any direction. The water was so crystal clear that Bart, looking down, had to stare to see where the atmosphere ended, and the water began. It was as if the gazebo and its pedestal of more elephantine boulders sat in a white sand bowl filled with the clearest gelatin, run through with flecks of gold light. As the bowl tilted toward the lake's center, its turquoise bottom shaded to darker colors of blue as the water deepened.

Mrs. Concannon sat at a round table under the gazebo's roof. She was wearing a white blouse and designer blue jeans, leaning back in her chair. A pair of sandals lay on the stone floor beneath her. Her legs and slender bare feet rested across another chair, with her red-painted toenails pointed out to the lake. Through sunglasses, she read a newspaper while sipping coffee from a white china cup.

She had not heard him. Bart paused and treasured the vision.

She looked as exciting to him this morning as on that first day she'd stepped into his office, only now she was yet another version of herself. A goddess. The shape of her face and head and blond hair made her a twenty-first-century version of the mythical Sirens, carved wooden women who, when jutting from the prows of sailing ships, lead men out to sea. Or something. There was more to the myths. Bart remembered only bits and pieces of what he'd read in the library.

When Bart entered the gazebo, he saw his own place setting on a blue linen tablecloth, blue that matched the lake's deeper water. White china bowls held black grapes, brown and purple figs, and apricots, next to white china cream and sugar servers.

"Good morning, Mrs. Concannon. You have a beautiful setting here."

She looked up from her newspaper out to the lake.

"*La Superba.*"

She seemed somewhere else, then composed herself and

turned to him.

"Forgive me. For a moment, I was in Genoa. The lake, it's beautiful, isn't it?"

"Absolutely, yes. Wait. I have a quote, if I can remember it."

She smiled. "Please, sit down and tell me."

He slid his chair out and sat as he tried to remember.

"Mark Twain. I read in the library he called Lake Tahoe a 'noble sheet of water.' And some more I can't remember about it being, 'the best he ever saw.'"

"Yes, I've heard that. I have traveled and lived in many places, Mr. Lasiter, and I couldn't disagree with him."

"It is wonderful."

"Please relax, enjoy the lakeview, and Isabel will bring your breakfast." She pressed a button on a panel in the gazebo wall.

She sighed and seemed to settle into the present.

Bart saw a change in her face, returning to the reality of the kidnapping.

"Did you sleep well?" asked Bart.

"I haven't been sleeping well since . . . you know. You were comfortable, Mr. Lasiter?"

"Oh, yes."

"Another note from the kidnappers arrived, while you were asleep. I've tried hard as I could not to worry about it, but I have failed. Please, tell me what you think."

She took an envelope from the table and placed it at his setting.

Bart saw the same label as before, Bailey's Reno Messenger Service. The note inside read:

PUT THE CASH IN PLASTIC BAGS.

SEAL AND WRAP EACH BAG WITH TAPE.

AT MIDNIGHT A WHITE BOAT WILL BE DRIFTING

THREE MILES DUE WEST FROM YOUR DOCK.

SEND ONE PERSON ONLY IN A SMALL OPEN BOAT.

NO LIGHTS! NO FLASHLIGHTS!

PUT THE BAGS INTO THE WHITE BOAT.

RETURN TO SHORE.

HE WILL BE SET FREE IN THE MORNING.

The same black spot and hand-sketched Jolly Roger as before stained the bottom of the page. Bart had to visit Bailey's as soon as he could.

"I'm worried, Mr. Lasiter, and yet, at the same time, very excited. To think that my Drake might be home tomorrow!

"Yet, I am afraid to believe it's possible. Where everything in our life here before was so secure and predictable, now nothing is sure."

"Keep your hope and spirit up, Mrs. Concannon. We'll know soon. The best thing to do now is to just concentrate on the steps we have to take to gain your husband's safe release. Do you have everything required in the note?"

"Oh, yes. I think so. You could use a small boat we have, and we have plastic bags and tape."

Isabel arrived with a tray for Bart. She'd made an omelet with Monterey Jack, green chilies, bacon, and avocado. There were also thick, buttered English muffins, home-fried potatoes, watermelon slices, and a fresh pot of coffee.

Bart thanked her and ate. After he'd finished his breakfast and coffee, he said, "Okay, Mrs. Concannon. Can you have the money bagged and the boat ready?"

"Yes."

"Good. Then I'll be back here by ten-thirty tonight. I have some errands to run. Will you be okay until I return?"

"Yes, I will. You know best, Mr. Lasiter."

* * *

19

Deliveries

I'm Gonna Sit Right Down

and Write Myself a Letter

As Bart was leaving the compound, the same man as before opened the gate and nodded to him. This level of security — walls, wire, and gates — had forced the kidnappers to take Drake Concannon from the water.

Bart turned left and drove north on highway 28 toward Incline Village. With Number Six on his to-do list finished, he felt confident about what he had to do next, but still worried something might have escaped his attention. He needed more information.

The kidnapping could be over tomorrow because the ransom money was available, and no police were involved. Still, Bart knew all kidnappings are dangerous and potentially murderous. Just the wife's willingness to pay up quickly would encourage some kidnappers to take the payment and then stall for more money. Others, once they had the money in their hands, would lose interest in leaving their best witness, the victim, alive. Bart was afraid of what he didn't know.

Highway 28 became Tahoe Boulevard in Incline Village, where he pulled into the first gas station he saw, filled up the Klimo's tank, and went to a pay phone.

Bart hadn't been able to afford a cell phone. Maybe, after this job, he would buy one, and a newer car, too.

He called his friend in Reno, Al Wexler, a reporter he knew

who had spent decades covering the Nevada gambling scene. Al had spent time, however briefly, at every major newspaper in Nevada. Bart mentioned he would be in Reno for some supplies and offered to buy lunch.

"Bart, how about tomorrow? I have to finish something."

"Okay, Al. The extra day will give you a little time to dig. How about that great little Mexican place near your office.

"Rosalita's? Virginia Street? Bart — the parade."

"What parade?"

"It's Hot August Nights week. The parade of old cars and hot rods fills Virginia Street tomorrow. Wait, I know a place, further south. Remember the Juarez?"

"Oh, yeah. Near . . . Holcomb and?"

"No. On West Plum near South Arlington. Remember?"

"Okay. Now I do."

"And make it about three. Bart, hey — you said, 'dig.' Dig for what?"

"Be prepared to tell me about Drake Concannon."

When Bart left the phone booth, he saw a young man filling the gas tank of a compact pickup truck. The man stepped away from the truck to return the fuel hose to the pump. Now Bart could see a white plastic sign held by magnets to the truck's faded red door. Bingo. The sign read:

Bailey's Reno Messenger Service
775-555-3333

Bart approached and asked, "Kid, are you on your way to make a delivery?"

"No. You got something to deliver? Dude, I'll make you a deal if you got cash."

"No, no. I have a few questions for you."

The young man turned back to his truck and opened the door.

"If you don't have a delivery for me, I have to get back to Reno to wait for another delivery, or I don't get paid, man." He sat down in the truck and put his key into the ignition switch.

"Wait, it's like pizza delivery?"

The young man let go of the key and turned to Bart.

"Yeah, but sometimes businesspeople don't tip too good, especially if you bring something they don't want. People are always happy to get their pizza. I might go back to pies."

"What's your name?"

"Tyler."

"Mine's Bart. Tyler, if you're not scheduled for something, I could pay you to talk to me here for a few minutes."

"How much?"

"Twenty bucks."

"Dude, what about my gas?"

"What gas?"

"The gas I just pumped. Who's gonna pay for my gas?"

Bart rolled his eyes. "Okay. How about twenty bucks for questions and ten for gas? Thirty bucks?"

"I can count. Bailey told me to never answer questions about the messenger service or customers."

"Fifty bucks?"

"Let's see it."

Bart pulled out his wallet and showed the kid a new fifty-dollar bill. "See?"

Tyler got out of his truck, stood up, and dropped his wrap-around sunglasses from his face. They hung against his T-shirt, which said *Chill Out & Relax*, from a foam rubber loop around his neck. He held the fifty-dollar bill up to the sky and squinted, turning the bill at different angles.

"It's good currency," said Bart.

"Awesome, but a fifty could be tough to break. Give me three twenties instead."

Bart sighed, pulled three twenties from his wallet, and took back the fifty. He had to pull it from Tyler's grip. If he'd let him, this kid would empty Bart's wallet. But any information about whoever gave Bailey's the kidnapper's notes was critical. Mrs. Concannon could afford it, and Mr. Concannon's safety was at stake.

"Tyler, you ever deliver to the lakeshore on the Nevada side?"

He put the bills into his pocket. "Sure."

"How about Eagle Cove?"

"Yeah, some."

"I'm interested in deliveries to One Eagle Cove Road."

"Maybe . . . ." Tyler leaned back against his truck.

"What do you mean, 'Maybe,' Tyler? That's why I just gave you sixty dollars."

"I'm like — like I didn't know you were gonna ask that kinda question."

"What did you think? I was going to ask you about the best places to snowboard?"

Tyler sprung back to standing and threw both hands into the air.

"Oh! Dude! I'm all about boardin'. I know some awesome, extreme —"

"Focus, Tyler. One Eagle Cove Road." Bart handed the kid another twenty.

Tyler stuffed the twenty into his jeans, slouched, and folded his arms. "Yeah. I did two there myself. Nice tips."

"When?"

"This week."

"Okay." Bart leaned toward Tyler. "The customer? Did you see the customer, the one who ordered the first delivery?"

"Whoa!" Tyler fell back to leaning on the truck. "Dude, now you're asking tough questions."

Bart handed him another twenty.

"I remember now. I don't normally see customers, but I saw this dude *both* times because it was early in the morning and no one else was around. I'm like waiting for a delivery job, sitting in my truck in Bailey's lot, listening to some tunes. You dig heavy metal?"

"Focus, Tyler."

"Anyway, Monday this chopped Harley pulls in. A dope machine. Old dude gets off, takes a envelope into the office, all serious lookin', you know? Five minutes later he comes out, gets on his machine, and goes."

"See the license number?"

Tyler gave Bart his best *What-Planet-Are-You-From* look.

"Okay, did you see the license plate frame? Anything unusual?"

"Nope — didn't notice it."

"Go on. What happened next?"

"A minute later, Bailey comes out and gives me a delivery. One Eagle Cove Road."

"When was the other one?"

"Today, early this morning."

"You work seven days a week?"

"Dude! Like just the days I'm not out rafting the Truckee. River's too crowded Saturdays. Or I'm —"

"Who was the customer this morning?"

"— on the lake in my kayak."

"Who?"

"I told you — same dude."

"Okay, Tyler. Now describe him."

Tyler put his sunglasses back on, threw his head back onto his truck's roof, and surveyed the dusty underside of the pump shelter. "Oh. I don't know if I can remember."

Bart poked him with another twenty.

"Remembering."

"Good. What do you see?"

"I see like . . . he looked like a old biker. You know?"

"Tyler, you already *told* me he was old — and rode in on a chopper!"

"Hold on. A kind of outlaw biker, like I said, you know, but like, *different*."

"Different how?"

"You know, like, some of the bikers are all into wearing weird stuff. They wear a thing covering their head, a bandana cloth thing? And gold earrings, thick belt, tall boots?"

"Yeah?"

"Yeah, only *different*. He looked like a old-time pirate."

"Good, good. What else?"

"What else? Nothing. Uh, unless you mean . . . like, under his purple bandana, he had scars, scars all over?"

* * *

20

In Over His Head

Yesterdays

The customer Tyler had described sounded like Scar. But how could Bart be certain? He would keep going until he found real proof.

Because he wouldn't meet Al Wexler in Reno until Sunday, Bart adjusted his plan and schedule. A good detective must be flexible and anticipate surprises. Bart decided he would return to Carnelian Bay. Given Drake Concannon's history with the lake and his classic runabout, the boat show could be worth the time.

The drive west was uneventful until he neared Carnelian Bay, where the traffic on North Lake Boulevard thickened and slowed. Closer to O'Hara's, Bart's Klimo crept along following the Boat Show Parking sign's arrows. He was grateful Tony's tune-up let the Klimo idle smoothly in traffic.

The last Boat Show Parking sign directed him away from the lake and up Carnelian Woods Avenue. He drove up the hill past a lot marked VIP Parking, protecting a group of classic Ferraris. The avenue became a narrow road, lined solid on either dirt shoulder with parked cars. A quarter mile up the hill he found a spot for the Klimo. He parked and walked back down toward the lake. At the VIP parking lot, a boy hawking plastic bottles of water from a Styrofoam ice chest noticed him and offered, "Cold, only a dollar."

Bart joined several people waiting at the edge of North Lake Boulevard. When the cop in the crosswalk stopped traffic, Bart walked across toward the ticket table in O'Hara's parking lot.

After paying for his boat show ticket, he passed tables where people in summer attire were selling T-shirts, show posters, and memberships in boating clubs and charitable foundations. A young woman checked his ticket and let him pass. Bart walked past O'Hara's showroom and on to the marina. O'Hara's had carved out from the shoreline a harbor filled with dozens of piers. Metal bulkheads held back the surrounding soil and sand, right up to the edge of North Lake Boulevard. Booths shaded by white canvas canopies fluttering in the breeze filled the space between the harbor and boulevard, and around the harbor's west side.

What Bart saw in the harbor impressed him. What little he knew about boats came from one summer as a teenager spent with his mother at Clear Lake in northern California, and it didn't involve classic wooden boats. Tied to the piers, at least a hundred wood boats floated proudly, each one show-quality.

Leaning against a railing above the piers, Bart took in the scene below. The piers sagged and rolled under the weight of ticket holders, both children and adults. They walked along the piers, stopping at each boat, pointing, and taking pictures. Some of the boat owners were standing by, answering questions, and accepting compliments. Other owners were on the piers or in their boats, adjusting and polishing. Segregated by type and size, each boat had a sign displaying the boat's name, make, model, and year of production.

Near Bart, just down the ramp from his railing, a group of runabouts waited for the judges. Far across the harbor, on the opposite side, floated larger boats, including cabin cruisers. Another area grouped some old, unique boats. Something about the runabouts looked familiar. He went down the ramp to see.

When he was at the pier level, he saw runabouts like the one in Drake Concannon's office pictures. A few were painted white, with red or blue or turquoise trim. Others were stained and varnished mahogany. He moved closer to one of the stained boats and read the display card:

FAST TIMES
1949 19' Chris-Craft Racing Runabout
George Hartwell owner

The boat's engine compartment hatch doors were folded open, revealing a powder blue, flat-head, straight six-cylinder engine. The driver's position ahead of the engine compartment featured chromed instruments and burgundy leather upholstery. The cream-colored steering wheel looked like it belonged on a fifties convertible. Behind the engine compartment, another upholstered cockpit provided a cramped fit for two.

Bart walked out onto the narrow pier between two of the runabouts. The pier moved under his feet with each step, slowly tilting and floating up and down. It moved when he moved, and it moved when other people moved on nearby piers. This was something he wasn't used to, and it disturbed him. He tried to adjust, but couldn't, and just ignored it by focusing on the boats.

Up close, these constructs of wood, cast iron, and chromed bronze impressed even land-lover Bart, someone who'd enjoyed a minimum of youthful carefree summers at the lake. He could see why the young Drake Concannon in the photos was so proud of his new boat.

On a pier near the open lake, a crowd had formed around a giant boat. From where Bart stood, he could see the waterside of the boat. It was huge, a long cigar-shaped mass of stained and varnished mahogany, topped with a dramatic, long, smooth-metal cabin. Among the polished metal cabin attachments were chromed searchlights, horn trumpets, and railings. Along the cabin side, chromed air scoops provided interior ventilation, and arrow-shaped chromed rub-strips protected the mahogany hull. This boat sat there as if it owned the lake and had for decades.

Bart followed the labyrinth of piers to the crowd admiring the big boat, carefully accounting for every tilt and undulation of the pier under his feet. His pier-walking skills were growing.

People were lining up for free lake rides in a classic boat. A thirties-era three-cockpit runabout was offering twenty-minute rides around Carnelian Bay, alternating trips with a similar boat.

Tied to a pier near the huge boat was a fast aluminum boat, labeled Placer County Sheriff Patrol Rescue. An odd boat for a classic boat show. Bart guessed it might be there because of the people taking free classic boat rides, except it was un-manned.

Once through the crowd, Bart found an open spot on the pier where he could examine the big boat. He realized it was the same boat he had seen in one of Drake Concannon's office photos. The cabin roof wasn't the same, but it was the same boat. Maybe now he could learn something.

Metal letters screwed to the front side, and a pennant on a wood mast on the cabin roof, declared this was the *Thunderbird*. Edging along the pier toward the aft end of the boat, Bart saw a break in the boat's metal railing, a place where you could board the boat. Where a person would step on the round edge of the hull side, there was an oval ring of chromed metal, a foot plate filled with black rubber and chromed metal letters spelling out *Hacker Craft.* "What's that?" Bart mumbled.

"Hacker Craft, from the great pre-war naval architect, John Hacker," a voice replied. "You don't know the *Thunderbird*'s history?"

Bart turned to see a man about Drake Concannon's age.

"No, I don't. What can you tell me?"

"First, it's a Tahoe boat. Built for Tahoe, and it's never left the lake except for maintenance."

"Where would you buy a boat like this?"

"Not buy. *Commission.* A boat like this is commissioned. A man with money and vision hires someone to design and build the boat. A man with a *lot* of money. It took really big-dollar horsepower to commission and build something like this."

"So, a man with money hires Hacker?"

"Yes. Hacker was like a renaissance sculptor, waiting for a patron with money and vision. Or someone who would give Hacker a rough specification and blank check, and then stay out of the way. He made production boats, too, but he was at his best when he worked unencumbered on a special order."

"I thought I saw this boat in an old photo, but the cabin looked different. There was a man in the photo who looked like he might be the owner."

"You mean The Captain, George Whittell. The man with the money. And the vision. Whittell once owned most of Tahoe's Nevada shoreline. Flew Hacker out here, told him what he wanted, and flew him back east with a check. The boat arrived from Michigan by rail the following summer. A subsequent owner, a casino owner, added the upper windshield to the cabin, and made other changes, as you see it now. The Nevada side of Tahoe has been a summer home to many casino people."

Bart took another long look, sweeping his eyes from one end of the boat to the other. "It's something, isn't it?"

"It certainly is."

"Do you have a wood boat?"

"Did, when I lived here by the lake. I moved away. When you are older, the winters here are hard. And the boats require maintenance and off-season storage. What I liked most in the past I get now by coming to this show every year."

"What?"

"Memories."

"From boats?"

"Certain boats, seeing them just like when they were new, or standing close enough to smell the upholstery, fresh varnish, the engine compartment, or the exhaust. Sometimes it's seeing a chromed detail I've forgotten. Or listening to an engine turning over and catch, like it was the first run of the spring — any of these things might instantly take me back, fifty years."

The man looked away from the *Thunderbird* and pointed to runabouts at another pier.

"See the boat at the end of that pier, the nineteen-foot Gar Wood?" He pointed across the harbor to a sleek runabout with a slanted V-shaped windshield framed in chromed metal. "We had one. As I age, it gets harder to remember my father. Just put me up close to a classic boat like that Gar Wood, and we're together again, toweling down the upholstery and varnish after a fast, exhilarating run along the shoreline. Another beautiful, timeless summer together."

The man was quiet, staring at the Gar Wood.

"Just once a year. No more."

Bart sensed the man had left for the past. "Thanks."

Turning away from the *Thunderbird,* Bart worked his way toward the cabin cruisers tied up at the far-side piers. Pleased with his new pier-walking skills, Bart was not as nervous now when the narrow piers moved, and even could manage some balancing near the pier's edge when he had to pass other people walking in the opposite direction.

He passed an all-stained-mahogany Chris-Craft cruiser from the thirties, and a restored Gar Wood cruiser from the forties, both big enough to go on comfortable sleep-over cruises.

These larger boats were more dramatic in chromed detail than the runabouts. Looking in their windows at their interior appointments, Bart wondered about all the money involved in owning one of these boats. Thinking about money made him melancholy. He put money out of his mind and looked farther down the pier.

"Wow." Bart saw another cruiser, one with a mean stance and black hull sides. It had to be well over thirty feet long. It seemed to stare at him, like it knew him. Silly, of course.

As Bart approached this black boat, the first detail he noticed was the shape of the prow or nose of the boat. It was sleek, yet bulged aggressively, and the black paint rolled up from the sides over the deck near the nose. Just floating there, tied to the pier, the black boat still looked fast and powerful. And mysterious. Without understanding why, he felt like it might run him down.

He dismissed his irrational fear and walked alongside to see into the boat's cabin. Though the blinds in the cabin windows were slanted open, all Bart could see through the tinted glass was dark upholstery. The cabin windows ended at a chromed air scoop. After the scoop he saw a small, white, life-saving ring, and more cabin windows, ending with a flowing, chromed-metal script, *Chris-Craft*. The second set of windows belonged to an extra, aft cabin. Its roof, like the main cabin's roof, was gently curved and coated with canvas painted white. Most of the cabin sides were stained and varnished mahogany, and each of the chromed items appeared flawless.

Without warning, melancholy again stabbed Bart. The big black Chris-Craft proved someone had a lot of money, more than Bart had ever imagined seeing in his life. But he didn't want this mood swing to interfere with learning what he could.

To jog his mind, Bart reflected on some of the boat names he had seen today. Naming a boat was apparently a special thing, an opportunity for the boat owner to be both clever and sentimental at the same time, and then display his choice for all to see in gold leaf foil on stained wood. There was, of course, the *Thunderbird*, and *Fast Times, Duckers, Wampum, Steinway, Mountain Lyon, Miss Lu Lu II,* and more — too many to remember.

But there were no pennants or flags on this black boat to suggest a name or theme. Some of the other boats had pennants honoring the Tahoe Yacht Club, or the Crystal Bay Yacht Club. None here. And he didn't see an informational show card on the black boat, like the other boats displayed. What would be the name painted on this substantial Chris-Craft?

Bart was holding onto a pier post, leaning around the back of the Chris-Craft to see its transom and name when four boys came running down the pier, causing the pier to undulate and tilt. Bart held on to the pole and was skillfully riding out the worst of the pier movement, until the last boy passing slipped and fell against Bart's back.

"Yikes!" His grip on the post failed and his feet slid from the wet pier into the air. He was turning in space above the water. Just before his face hit the water, he glimpsed on the Chris-Craft's transom, part of the boat's name:

Coe ....

He saw no more — it was dark and wet now.

* * *

21

Dollars for History

Best of Everything

Big hands dragged Bart back onto the pier, where he struggled to clear his throat and eyes.

"I'm very sorry about this, Sir. Ted, take this gentleman back to the shops, and help him dry out. See to his needs."

"Sir, I'll take care of it."

Before Bart could see clearly, Ted was helping him down the piers toward O'Hara's main building.

"Thanks. Guess I slipped."

"Sure you're okay?"

Bart nodded while he squeezed water from his hair. "I'm Bart, by the way."

"I'm Ted, Ted Watson. Don't worry about falling in — it's nothing. Let's dry you out."

Ted Watson led Bart back into the shop areas of O'Hara's. Bart's Nikes squished with every step, leaving puddles on the gray epoxied and waxed concrete floor.

"Sorry, Ted. I'm getting your clean floor all wet."

"It's okay, Bart. Getting wet is part of boating. I've fallen in twice this year. My record is four. It happens. In the end, it's just part of what we do — it's all about the water."

"Thanks for pulling me out."

"Wasn't me. It was Mr. O'Hara himself. During the show, he's always walking the piers, checking to see if the exhibitors and ticket holders are happy."

Inside, on low-wheeled steel support frames, rested boats of many different types and lengths, in different states of repair or restoration, but all were wood and inboard powered.

Ted showed Bart the O'Hara laundry room. "You can take your clothes off here and use one of the dryers. Wear one of our shop jumpsuits from the lockers until your clothes are dry. Put your tennis shoes in, too. There are some sandals there."

Bart stripped and wiggled into a jumpsuit, zipped it up, and chose a pair of sandals. After emptying his jeans pockets, he put his wet clothes into a dryer and watched them tumble.

"I wouldn't expect to find a laundry in a boat shop."

"Besides our shop clothes, we wash and dry hundreds of towels each month. The towels are used to dry the boats after test runs, the shop floor, us — anything wet."

"You're sure I'm not keeping you from work?"

"It's okay. Everything is pretty much under control out there now, and I was about to go on lunch break anyway. You can put your wallet and other things on the table here between some towels. You were in the water just a few seconds, probably not enough to soak your papers." Ted sat and opened his lunch.

Bart spread out his pocket and wallet contents between the towels and sat down.

"Ted, you mind if I ask you some questions?"

"If you don't mind talking while I eat. Shoot."

"The boats are so beautiful and well-maintained. I wonder about the costs. It looks like keeping a wood boat takes a lot of money."

Ted swallowed a bite of his sandwich. "So, you don't own a boat yourself?"

"No. I just came to see the show."

"Yes. Most people with wood boats have extra money. It's a luxury, or expensive hobby. You spend money to keep them dry and running. They're just like classic cars. Some of the owners showing their boats here today collect and enjoy both. A few own collectible aircraft, too."

"What was the boat where I fell in?"

"You mean the Bullnose Chris with the black sides? The Corvette?"

"Corvette? Like the car?"

"No. Like a World War Two British destroyer — compact and fast."

"I remember the black sides."

"Yes, the Bullnose."

"Bullnose?"

"Oh. The Bullnose is a name for the bow shape, a phase of Chris-Craft styling from the mid-fifties. It only appears on some of those models. See, the prow of those boats where it meets the deck is special." Ted set his sandwich down on the table and moved his hands in the air, trying to describe the shape. "It's built up with blocks of solid mahogany and then shaped into a bulge with compound curves running in several directions — *that's* a Bullnose." Ted returned to his sandwich.

"It's really different from the other boats I saw today," Bart said, adjusting his jumpsuit, moving the wet spots around.

"Very different from most other wood boats, cool, but labor intensive. It added cost to the boats when they were built and will add cost to them again when they are restored. Over time, the mahogany blocks may have dried out or rotted and will have to be replaced completely."

"I think, after the black sides, I most noticed the Bullnose. Dramatic. So, what about the rest? It did look special."

"You could say any of the boats out there today is a special boat, but that Bullnose is a special version of a special Chris-Craft, just to begin. And I was lucky enough to work on it."

"What do you mean?"

"It's a thirty-six-foot Corvette, which was a rare model by itself. I think they made only thirty-three of them. And only for 1954 — no more just like it after those thirty-three. After fifty years, only a few of the thirty-three remain."

"What happened to the others?"

"The occasional collision or fire took some, but it's usually neglect. Once a wood boat, especially a bigger boat, reaches a certain state, it takes a lot of labor and money to bring it back.

"Decades ago, when these larger boats weren't prized and collected, some were scrapped out. They became firewood, if you can believe it, because the owners ran out of the desire and money required to maintain them."

"To survive more than fifty years, that's special."

Ted nodded and poured from a thermos. "Coffee?"

"No, thanks."

"It's different now, the business of wood boats. No one who knows would scrap out a classic — at least the smaller boats. Gray-wood skeletons of classic boats are sitting in warehouses — we have many here — waiting for that special customer, someone willing to pay for a keel-up restoration. Hundred-point owners — their passion feeds my family."

"Hundred-point?"

"The hundred points is the show judge's score for a one hundred percent original and perfectly maintained or restored boat."

"So, the Bullnose is a hundred-point boat?"

"No, the Bullnose is not, for good reason. Hundred-point boats don't have improvements or updates except for safety, at least as far as a show judge can detect."

"So, what's been improved on this boat?"

"Wait, there's more, *before* the improvements. The Corvette is a double-cabin model. A boat only thirty-six feet long usually didn't have the luxury of separate cabins. Normally, all the living area is forward of the helm, and shared with the galley. This boat has another, more private, cabin aft."

"Now I'm sorry I didn't have a chance to look inside."

"The Corvette is not really part of the show, officially. It's just in for service. But Mr. O'Hara is so proud of our restoration work he put it out there for everyone to see. When your clothes are dry, I could take you back there, to see inside."

"Thanks, Ted. Maybe. I have a tight schedule today."

Bart was spooked, afraid of falling into the water again. It's why he refused the coffee and wasn't eager to walk on those piers again.

"What else is different?"

"As you saw, its sides are painted black. Most Chris cruisers have white sides. This boat, even among the Corvettes, is rare, one of a handful. Check your clothes, and I'll tell you more."

Bart opened the dryer door and sorted through his clothes.

"They're almost done."

Ted finished some sliced peaches from a plastic container

and continued. "What I've told you about the Bullnose so far is just the foundation, the blank canvas. The rest of the story is a solid-gold, patient owner who paid for the keel-up restoration. If a piece of wood wasn't just right, it got replaced. If there was any iffy chrome on a piece of hardware, we sent the part out to be stripped to the bare bronze, polished, re-plated, and polished again. We ignored nothing."

"Sounds like a lot of work."

"It was — hard, expensive work. But, as I said, it wasn't just restored, it was restored and *improved*. The problem for me working on hundred-point boats is, it can get monotonous. It's good to save another classic boat from salvage, to bring a hulk of gray wood back to its original glory. But after you've done a dozen or fifteen Chris-Craft Riviera runabouts, they all blend into one. It's monotonous repetition except for the owner and my paycheck. The Bullnose was an exception and pure joy."

"Well, what was *improved* . . . and why?"

"To start, the hull sides were a dull black, for two reasons. There wasn't any good glossy black marine paint in'54, and glossy black will show all the defects and planking flaws. The modern glossy paint is excellent, and — after we finished — there are no planking flaws on this boat. Gray paint covered the original cabin roof canvas. This boat has new white canvas roof coating — owner's choice."

"It looked great, what I saw of it before I slipped."

"Also, this boat has a new interior to suit the owner's taste. Where some of the wood inside was painted white originally, and the original upholstery was a sturdy green material, now the wood is all stained and varnished mahogany, and the upholstery is all water-resistant black leather. And all the glazing is now UV-resistant tinted glass, to shield the new interior from the sun. We improved the seating, bunks, and galley space as much as we could. Throughout the boat, we added small drawers and cabinets, wherever they could fit, and the galley and bath fittings are all modern."

"Bath?"

"As in the original, each cabin has its own shower and head. And now, compact air conditioners, too. The aft cabin is very luxurious, like nothing I've ever seen before in a Chris-Craft smaller than a fifty-footer."

"Wow."

"And then the boat has all new electronics — radar, depth gages, weather, charting, and navigation, things not available in fifty-four, some not even a decade ago."

"This sounds really expensive."

"We would rather not talk about money in this business. Most of our customers avoid discussing money openly. They consider it to be . . . uh, bad manners. Some families who own waterfront property have been here for two or three generations. No matter how many millions they have, they like to wear old casual clothes here. They avoid any open discussion or show of money."

Another man wearing an O'Hara's jumpsuit entered the room.

"Hi Hank. I was telling Bart here about the black Chris."

"Oh yeah? Did Ted tell you about the new engines?"

"You tell him, Hank. Bart, this is Hank Delaney. Over a year, Hank and I worked together restoring the Corvette."

"Good times, Bart. Ted's woodwork is masterful. For me, the fun part is my specialty, the engines." Hank sat down at the table. "The original in-line six-cylinder gasoline engines would push the boat to 26, maybe 28 knots, fast for its size and age. We replaced them with larger diesel V-8s. The owner wanted the boat to be faster while using less fuel, and to travel long distances without refueling. Why long distance? I don't know, but why complain when you're being paid to have fun? We found a matched, opposite-rotation pair of new marine engines crated in a warehouse."

"How big?" asked Bart.

"About 570 cubic inches and 425 horsepower each — almost double the displacement and three times the horsepower of the original engines. They're both supercharged and turbo-charged, with intercoolers."

"My car is turbo-charged, but the rest, whatever that means, it sounds impressive."

"The design of these engines included every feature that would increase their power and strength. And, though they are very compact for their power and have a low profile, finding room for the new engines below deck required enlarging the engine bays and raising the amidships deck several inches, something most people would never notice.

"There were other changes, like strengthening the boat's frame to handle the increased weight and power, new props and shafts to match the engines, and additional fuel tanks, too. The original fuel capacity was 150 gallons. We've doubled that, with the secondary tanks positioned to maintain the boat's balance. Again, I don't know why so much fuel, but that's what the owner wanted."

"So, it's faster now?"

"Yup. See, big old cruisers are usually too heavy and under-powered to get up on plane — get up on top of the water, like runabouts. Cruisers as big as the Bullnose often can't plane. They plow through, not on top of, the water. That's why they call them cruisers. But this boat can cruise, and then, when you push those throttle levers forward, it can almost fly. It's got torque you wouldn't believe — she jumps on plane like a runabout. And though heavier now, it can cruise — on plane — at a much higher speed and use no more fuel than the original gasoline-powered straight sixes did at a lower speed. If you wanted, these engines could run flat out at top speed for weeks without suffering. And, the engines are two-cycle, firing twice as often compared to the original four-cycle gas engines, and eight cylinders versus the former six. It all adds up to the smoothest ride imaginable. Sometimes, if it weren't for the instruments and exhaust sound, you'd have to move the throttle levers to be sure the engines are running."

Ted leaned forward. "Go on. Say it, Hank."

"Okay, Ted. Bart, these engines — they're the engines God would want in this boat."

"And he's absolutely right, Bart. The switch in engines, a really difficult undertaking, turned out so well, even we were surprised. I have been on test rides at the helm of the Corvette that just left me amazed. It's hard to imagine a better ride. This was without question my best rebuild in the twenty years I have worked here."

"Ditto," said Hank.

"Wow," said Bart.

"Of all the big wood boats on the lake, only the *Thunderbird* is faster," said Hank.

"*Thunderbird* — the big boat out there with the metal roof?"

"Right."

"Give me a fast ship for I intend to go in harm's way."

Ted and Hank stared at Bart.

"John Paul Jones said that. American Revolutionary War. I read that in the library."

"No sea battles here, we hope." Hank's pocket radio came to life. "Ooops. My boss needs me. Nice talking to you, Bart."

Hank left, and Bart checked the dryer again.

"A little more. Hey, Ted, your Bullnose owner sounded special."

"Very. Maybe a little strange, too."

"How?"

"The owner was understanding and patient, but very detail oriented, specific, and insistent about the boat. Like the extra storage throughout, and the luxuries in the aft cabin. — all well organized and considered before we started work. Then, it's a Tahoe boat — why the long-distance fuel capacity? Why the open-water nav-gear? Why prep it for saltwater? Strange, but I was not going to question an owner who's kept me employed doing what I love for more than a year."

"Hmmm." Bart opened the dryer and felt his clothes. "Hey, they're done." Pulling on his clothes, Bart paused, holding his T-shirt. "Ted, do you know anything about those buildings on the back side of this shop, the shed and trailer?"

"Yes. They belong to O'Hara's. The pier, too."

"Are they rented out?"

"Not exactly. It's . . . see, the men there are security for O'Hara's."

Bart smirked. "They don't look like security guards."

"It's a difficult subject for me. I love our boss, but don't like those people being there."

"How did they get there?" Bart finished dressing and sat.

"Back, maybe a year ago, we had a series of minor break-ins and some random vandalism. At that time, the trailer and shed were temporary storage. The present tenants came into the shop asking if the buildings were for rent. And, by the way, they suggested, if people like them lived in the trailer, it would be good for our security. Most of us connected the break-ins and the offer to rent. They claimed they were Viet Nam vets and could use a break. That got to the boss. His boy died over there. Next thing we know, those three are not only living in the trailer, but they don't pay any rent and they draw a salary."

"Do they do any actual security work?"

"Depends. As soon as they moved in, the break-ins and vandalism stopped. But they are often not around, even at night. I guess their occasional presence terrifies would-be thieves."

"Anything go missing?"

"Not obviously, but we've all noticed a tool gone here and there. It's hard to pin down. But the break-ins stopped, so the boss is happy."

"So, what do you *really* think about them?"

"Ha! Don't quote me, but they're at least hustlers, if not crooks. Worse, they're taking advantage of the boss."

Bart stood. "I think it's time I let you go back to work."

"Stop by again. And when you're ready for your own boat, we're here to take care of you."

"Thanks, Ted." He shook Ted's hand and found his way outside.

Bart remembered he needed some things for the ransom delivery, things he had planned to buy in Reno. Maybe he could grab them in O'Hara's ship's store. In the store, Bart found hand-held compasses with good glow-in-the-dark markings. He chose a suitable, inexpensive model. In one of the booths along the west side of the harbor, he bought a dark blue sweatshirt to keep him warm on the water at night. The *Thunderbird,* in the form of a multi-colored illustration, threatened to leap from its front.

Shopping done, Bart crossed the road and started the climb up Carnelian Woods Avenue to the Klimo.

After Bart had closed the Klimo's door, he realized he'd forgotten to ask Ted something about the black Bullnose.

What was the rest of the name on the transom?

* * *

22

The Yacht Club

Let's Get Away from It All

Bart followed Highway 28 around Lake Tahoe to Nevada, in daylight this time. Near the California-Nevada border, the highway curved left toward the northeast. When he looked back toward the lake, he could see the Cal-Neva Lodge, straddling the state line and commanding the view south and east across Crystal Bay. He'd read you could see the state borderline marked across the bottom of the Cal-Neva's swimming pool.

Bart remembered Frank Sinatra both performed at the Cal-Neva and, from 1960 to 1963, was one of the owners. This he knew because his father was a big Sinatra fan.

After Bart's mother and father got back together, Dad tried to teach Bart everything he knew about Sinatra, using his nearly all-Sinatra record collection. Bart had heard the music so often he needed to hear just a few bars to identify the song and album. It was his father's music, but Bart had become a passive Sinatra fan.

Frank's music always brought Bart pleasant memories of his father, someone he admired, and other memories. His father had been just an occasional presence until Bart's mid-teens, and the reconciliation between his parents was an unfinished project.

His father would play certain albums only on nights when Bart's mother would suddenly leave, refusing to say where she was going, only, "Out!"

His father assigned Bart to play the albums. Pouring a drink, his father would say, "Bart, you know the ones to play now."

They knew she wouldn't return for a day or more. His father would sip from his drink, the first of a few, and hold and study the worn cardboard slipcases from those special Sinatra albums. After some time and drink, he'd call to Bart again.

"Now. You know the one. Hand me the cover and play it."

Seeing the Crystal Bay Yacht Club sign snapped Bart back to the present. Blue letters on a white wooden arch announced,

CRYSTAL BAY YACHT CLUB
ESTABLISHED 1946

Another sign said,

DINER & BAR
OPEN TO THE PUBLIC

Bart forced the Klimo off the paved highway through the arch into the Yacht Club's gravel parking lot. The bulk of the Yacht Club sat balanced on piers over the Crystal Bay shoreline below. The Club's cedar-shingled walls were painted white and accented by deep blue canvas awnings shading the windows.

Bart parked the Klimo, stepped into the gravel, and ascended the Yacht Club's wooden steps to the entrance. Up close, he saw both the blue canvas and white paint were fading.

He pushed through the door into a sunny room. Couples and families filled the booths to his left. To his right he saw a bar, and then a portal, which warned,

CLUB MEMBERS ONLY

Through the portal he could see tables covered by white linen, and another bar.

Bart approached the public bar. A tall thin man with white hair and mustache, well into his golden years, was steering a white cloth around the mahogany bar surface.

Bart chose a stool close to the man. "Say, old timer. How's it going?" Bart was the only customer at the bar.

"I'm still standing, still working. And you, Sir?

"Fine, just fine."

"What'll you have?"

"How about a cola — got a Coke? Classic?"

"Coming right up. Two-fifty."

Bart put a twenty on the bar. "Keep the change. I feel like talking."

The man looked at the twenty and then scanned the room. "Talk away, Sir."

"You ever work on the members-only side?"

"I've been working for this club over forty years. Worked both the public and the members-only sides. I have been here longer than half the members."

"You must like it then?"

"It's all right. No complaints. Who would listen if I did complain? Where at my age am I going to find another job in Crystal Bay? I don't like casino work."

"They pay you well?"

The bartender looked around. "Not big, but they treat me okay. I'm in good shape, financially. I rent a little room with a TV in the motel across the street. Don't need a car. And what they pay me plus my Social Security takes care of my rent and some spending money, so long as I stay away from the casinos. And I get a good discount on eating here, on the public side. The food is good. I eat here a lot. Are you staying for dinner? They have an excellent steak dinner here."

"I haven't decided. I've got some things to do today. Was this always open to the public?"

"No. Time was this was all private — members only. Then the other yacht clubs got bigger, and some got cheaper. Too many of our wealthy founding members passed. The original members who aren't dead yet don't come to the Club much now. Maybe just at Christmas, or for the Spring Gala, at the start of the boating season. Even then, they might be in a wheelchair, pushed by some precious young thing."

Bart listened and sipped his Coke.

"Anyway, the originals, they spent their own money to keep it nice. Then money got tight, so the newer members opened the public side to bring in some extra. Nowadays people want a bargain — even if they're rich."

"What's your name?"

"Sid. Just Sid."

"Sid, I'm Bart, Bart Lasiter."

"Want another Coke, Mr. Lasiter?"

"Not yet, Sid. Just some talk. And you can call me Bart."

Sid picked up the twenty.

"Funny thing, Bart. You said you wanted to talk, but I'm doing most of the talking."

"Fine, Sid. I like to listen, too."

"See, now that's the difference. Bartenders are supposed to listen, not talk. You can get in trouble talking. Say I listen to a member complaining about his wife for hours? I'm supposed to keep pouring and listening and seem interested. Let him ask, 'What do I do, Sid?' and I want to say, like the kids say today, 'Duh-uuh! She's robbing you blind and playing hide-the-sausage with the pool boy. Get a *DEE*-VORCE!' The bartender I replaced forty years ago did just that. Turned out his opinion wasn't appreciated. He went from bartending here to a J.C. to study counseling. Probably rich now. So, dangerous, or not, I enjoy talking at least as much as listening."

"You like to talk? Tell me about Drake Concannon."

Sid looked at Bart and then stared at the bar where a twenty had recently rested.

"Oh." Bart put another twenty on the bar.

Sid paused a few seconds and looked around again. "Why not?" Then he picked up the second twenty. "Oh, he's a member all right. Long-time member. Well, to be accurate, as far as I know, *if* he's still alive, he's still a member, but I haven't seen him for several years."

"What can you tell me about him?"

"Concannon was a member long before I started here, way back. When he was young, they say he bought a flashy new boat, a Chris-Craft runabout, sleek and very fast. They say every Sunday morning he used to take his boat, fast as it would go, across Crystal Bay from his place somewhere on the east shore, straight to the Club here. He'd tie up at the Club's piers down below, come up for breakfast, then spend the day in the bar and restaurant, maybe play some cards, have lunch and a drink, and then head back across the bay just before the sun set.

"By the time I started here, his boat looked tired. He didn't keep it up."

Sid started polishing some stemware.

"See him with guests?" Bart put another twenty on the bar.

"Yes, but rarely. And, when I saw him with guests, he came by car, not boat."

"What kind of people?"

"Vegans."

"Vegetarians?"

"No. Las Vegans. Nevada vampires. They'd say, *'vita notturna'* — not boating people."

"Vampires?"

"The night people who frequent the casinos and avoid the light of day. No tan. And sometimes his guests looked like heavy types. You know, casino managers and muscle."

"How did he get along with the other club members?"

"I think people didn't like him much."

"What do you mean?"

"Mister, yacht club people are sociable and friendly, and maybe a tad snooty. Concannon had cash, but he didn't fit in."

"This is good, Sid. Keep talking. If you don't mind."

Six men came in and sat at the other end of the bar. One motioned for Sid.

Bart stood up. "It's okay, Sid. Thanks, I'll come back later."

Bart made a pit stop before leaving the Yacht Club. Back in the parking lot, just sitting in the Klimo, he checked his to-do list. Only one item remaining, Number Seven: Deliver the ransom money across the lake to the white boat at midnight.

The sun was just setting, and he had nothing else to do until evening. He wasn't hungry, as he would have been by now on a normal day. There was only one feeling in his stomach, a deep, unsettling ache about what he had to do that night.

He got out and crawled into the rear seat. A few hours of sleep now would help him later delivering the ransom. After setting his Casio wristwatch alarm to ten, he stretched across the seat and fell asleep. Sleeping was easier than he expected, and he was soon dreaming.

He dreamed he was floating in the lake at night, all alone. It was dark. Blackness filled every direction. He heard a deep roar, like a lion. No, it was a machine. The roar got louder. He could hear it clearly now. He looked to the sound. At first, he couldn't see anything, just the blackness. Then something black was fighting its way out of the blackness. It was growing, a big black shape. He could see it clearly. It was coming straight at him, hard and fast. It was going to run over him and cut him to pieces. He twisted and turned, trying to move out of the way. It was a big black boat.

* * *

23

The Whiteness of the Boat

Strangers in the Night

Bart's chest smothered the beeping of his wrist alarm. He'd slept on his watch and through the alarm. When he finally woke from his backseat nap, it was ten-thirty. Yikes! Was he late for the ransom delivery? He didn't want to blow the biggest job he'd ever had, and he didn't want to fail Mrs. Concannon.

Bart jumped out, kicked the back door shut, and yanked open the Klimo's driver door. After donning his new *Thunderbird* sweatshirt, he slid back in behind the wheel, simultaneously pulling the door shut and jabbing the key into the ignition. Racing the engine, he put the spurs to the Klimo, spraying gravel as he left the Yacht Club behind.

Ignoring the speed limits, Bart raced along Highway 28. By the time he saw the stone wall, it was already eleven. When he stopped under the light at the gatehouse, the man inside nodded through the window to Bart while the gate opened. Bart returned the nod, and the man motioned him through. After parking at the garage, he grabbed his compass and hurried to the house. Mrs. Concannon waited at the door.

"Good evening, Mr. Lasiter. I was beginning to worry about you. Everything is ready for you."

They stood looking at each other for a few seconds without speaking, until she broke the silence.

"Would you like some hot coffee? It can be cold on the lake

at night." She gave him a strange, concerned look he didn't understand.

"No, no thank you. I'll be okay." He couldn't tell her he'd been too nervous to eat anything. He feared coffee on an empty stomach might push him over the edge. "Maybe some carrots, so I can see in the dark."

She just stared.

He wished he could make her smile. "A joke, ha, ha."

"I'm sorry. I'm so worried. I wasn't expecting a joke. You were trying to lighten my mood, weren't you?"

"Yes, if you like."

"Thank you. You're always looking out for me."

"Why don't you show me the boat, Mrs. Concannon?"

"Yes. Come with me down to the dock, and I will show you everything I have prepared."

They left the house and followed the stone steps and path down to the boathouse. Next to the boathouse, the wooden pier was lit by gooseneck lamps on poles. Tied to the pier under one lamp floated a 12-foot aluminum fishing boat with flat bench seats. Bart saw a small outboard motor mounted to the transom.

"Drake used to take this boat out to fish. I would sit in the living room, or outside on the patio, and watch him motor out on the lake. He didn't catch much but it made him happy. The motor is old, but Ramon always takes care of it."

Bart nodded his approval. "I've used a similar boat before." He hesitated, and then asked, "Was this the boat he was in when he was . . . ?"

"Oh, no. He was in his old wooden boat, the runabout. I worried about him when he used the runabout because it wasn't well maintained. It leaked a lot."

"How do you know it was the runabout?"

"I didn't at first. I had been in Reno shopping. When the ransom note arrived, I thought it had to be a hoax. I could not believe he was gone. I got the staff together, and we looked all over the property. His car was still in the garage. When we went to the boathouse, his runabout was gone. We took this boat out, searching the shoreline. The next day we saw the runabout on the bottom, just past the cove."

Bart worried she was about to cry.

She gasped. "They took Drake, and they sank his boat!"

A man Bart recognized as the gate guard opened a door in a lower level of the main house. The man backed out of the door, pulling a full wheelbarrow. Once completely outside, he turned the wheelbarrow and guided it down to the dock.

Mrs. Concannon nodded. "Thank you, Ramon. That will be all."

The money. A half-dozen fat cubes formed of black plastic bags tightly bound in duct tape. Bart had never seen five million dollars before, let alone transported it. He carefully transferred the packages to the boat and stepped in.

"Mr. Lasiter, you must wear a life preserver." She held out an orange nylon-covered foam vest.

"I'll be okay, Mrs. Concannon. It looks too bulky."

"Okay. Then wait." She went into the boathouse. When she emerged, she was carrying a set of thick, padded suspenders. She handed it down to him. "Put this on. I insist. Please."

"What is it?"

She smiled. "Mr. Lasiter, it's a life preserver, only easier to wear."

He slipped it on and fastened the straps. "How does it work?"

"It's automatic. Nothing happens unless you fall into the water. When it gets wet, it inflates itself."

"All right, if you say so." He looked at his watch. "It's time to go, Mrs. Concannon."

"You promise me that you'll be careful out there? I'm afraid for you."

"I promise. Don't worry. They want the money, and we're giving it to them. There should be no trouble." He turned away from her to the outboard motor.

One good yank of the cord started the old motor. Bart gave it a minute to warm up, untied the line from the pier, and looked back up at Mrs. Concannon. She smiled yet looked worried. He smiled back, trying to look confident for her sake.

Bart pulled the gear lever forward and gently twisted the throttle. Mrs. Concannon waved as he eased the boat away from the pier and increased speed. He smiled back and saw her saying something. He barely heard her.

"Goodbye, Mr. Lasiter."

He waved. He thought that was a strange look on her face, when she'd said goodbye.

After Bart had the motor giving its best without straining, he turned his attention to maintaining the direction specified by the kidnappers, due west, confirmed by the fluorescent face of the new compass in his hand.

The night was fresh and cool, with only starlight above. The moon, completely gone, would not help. He could see little but water and darkness in front of him, and when he looked back, Mrs. Concannon had left the pier. The main house was well lit and would be a good landmark for his return.

To do list Number Seven: Deliver the ransom money. He visualized his successful return from the delivery. Maybe she would be waiting on the pier. Then he might be hungry, and want a sandwich, even another steak, and finally a pot of coffee.

The idyllic return he visualized didn't seem unreasonable. Finding the white boat would be the first and bigger challenge, like looking for a paper napkin in a darkened coal mine.

Though his thick cotton *Thunderbird* sweatshirt helped, clothes alone couldn't keep out the cold and damp, or loneliness. He tried to ignore his discomfort and concentrate on moving ahead toward the white boat. If it were out there, and if he could find it. He settled into a comfortable but discount version of a Zen state, meditating on the steady pulse of the outboard motor while watching his compass and the bow of his boat plowing through the darkness.

Bart had never embraced Zen, despite his mother's sixties whirlwind tour of the world's greater and lesser religions. One of the many lesser faiths she sampled, when they lived in Marin County, was Breatharianism, a practice where a person replaced eating food with just breathing fresh air. His mother had heard about this practice in radio interviews with a local guru. She had already gone without food for four days when she heard on the radio the Breatharian guru had fled the County. His girlfriend had revealed to reporters the guru's secret: enormous bags of potato chips eaten daily. Bart smiled and shook his head. Mom.

What good fortune. Fifty-thousand dollars to deliver a few bundles. Could it get any better? Of course, the job was the safe return of Mr. Concannon, not the bundle delivery. But Bart's delivery of the money would safely return Mr. Concannon.

Bart knew something could always go wrong, but he chose to remain optimistic. This was exactly the type of job — low risk, high dollar — he needed to solidify his detective business. *Nice Work if You Can Get It*.

Calculating the dollars-per-minute-of-boating he would earn for this delivery vexed Bart. He almost had a number in mind when he realized he had drifted out of his meditative state and there remained a lot of water to cover.

He began laughing, picturing pirates on the high seas of Lake Tahoe, big cutlasses and shiny knives clamped between their teeth, swinging on ropes to his twelve-foot aluminum ship. You had to laugh and not take it all too seriously. He could almost see the fifty-thousand-dollar bonus.

When he was, he guessed, about halfway there and his eyes had fully acclimated to the darkness, he could see ahead a hole in the black. Maybe his eyes were tricking him. He aimed his boat straight at the tiny hole and watched as the hole in the black grew and became a white boat. It was all working out.

As he was getting closer, he became cautious. Looking in every direction, he throttled back. Just water and darkness, and the white boat. He didn't know why, but he was getting a bad feeling.

Killing the motor, Bart let his boat slowly float up against the side of the white boat.

Abandoned without windshield or motor, it was a seventies tri-hulled eighteen-foot fiberglass outboard runabout, neglected for years. Abandoned, probably not on the water, but in the tall grass of some empty lot, where its hull baked and cracked in the summer sun, then filled with the winter's rain, snow, and ice. Bart guessed it had been towed out to where it floated now. He peeked in over the side. Empty.

While holding onto the side of the white boat, Bart searched the surrounding darkness. The kidnappers had to be watching. He assumed there wouldn't be trouble if they got their money. Bart slowly turned his head, listening. He heard only the sound of slight waves licking against the two boats, floating alone in miles of water. Bart stood in his boat and held a bundle above his head. They would see he had brought their money and was following their instructions. Saying to himself, "Oh well, here we go," Bart tossed the heavy bundles of cash over into the white boat, one at a time, singing in rhythm with each bundle toss, his favorite lines from *Luck Be a Lady.*

Each bundle hit the white boat's warped floorboards with a loud thud. After Bart had transferred the last bundle, he pushed himself and his boat away from the ransom boat. He again stood in his boat and took one last look around. Nothing. He sat and started his motor, picked up his compass, and slowly turned his boat back toward the Nevada shore and the Concannon dock.

Watching the compass, Bart thought about tomorrow. Drake Concannon would be back with his wife and Bart would collect a fat paycheck, the biggest of his career as a private detective, the biggest paycheck of his life. He smiled.

The first bullet passed by his head an inch from his ear. He jumped up and jerked his head around in pain. "Yikes!" By the time he had finished yelling, he'd lost his balance and heard a second shot. Then, while falling back out of his boat, a third shot was fired.

The third bullet hit the back of his skull. Then he was unconscious and couldn't feel anything, not even the cold water as he sank beneath the lake's surface.

* * *

24

Call Me Lasiter

Lost in the Stars

Why was he cold?

He had to find someplace warm.

It felt like an oven. He was so warm, and so hungry. He looked down and saw it in front of him, on a paper plate on a round table. With the sun flaring off the aluminum foil wrapper, a plump, warm, beef super burrito waited for him. He was sitting in the summer's dry heat on the balcony at the back of his building. Agamemnon lay below in a patch of sun in Firehouse Alley. The cat rolled on his back over the warm concrete, stretched, and lifted his nose into the air.

"Aggie," Bart yelled. "Burrito! Aggie, come and get some beef!"

Then Aggie and the sun were gone, and Bart was cold again, and wet. He was floating on his back in the dark, coughing and spitting up gulps of Lake Tahoe while the stars watched. Mrs. Concannon's fancy life vest had inflated underwater and carried him back to the surface. She had saved him.

As soon as he was breathing freely, he froze at what he saw. It wasn't the miles of dark water around him. It was the stars! Billions and billions, as someone used to say. His near fatal shooting and drowning had sharpened all his senses. He saw the stars — really saw them — for the first time. They were so clear and distinct he felt he could reach out and touch them. He was elated.

Then Bart's elation collapsed into fear. There was nothing between him and whatever was out there, in billions of miles of space. There was no shield between him and meteors, the most distant planets, or the unknown. Now he felt fear and loneliness like he had never felt before. Who would help him here?

Snap out of it! Get your act together! Survive! Fight back! At least there was one thing he was sure of: Getting shot was not something he had ever enjoyed.

Now both his head and ear hurt. The shots must have been rifle bullets. The supersonic shock wave from the first bullet might have broken his eardrum. It left behind a sharp, stabbing pain. But when he touched the back of his head where the third shot had hit him, it felt rough and raw. He flinched each time he touched it. He rolled around full circle searching. His boat was not in sight, but he saw the white ransom boat a short swim away.

The sudden noise of engines startled him. Big V-8's. While Bart visualized being shot again, or run over, the engines went to wide-open throttle, and something long, low, black, and shiny jumped on plane beyond the white boat, racing toward the west shore.

At the boat's helm, Bart saw some instrument lights, but not who was at the wheel. He might have seen a black pennant or flag with white detail at the transom. In seconds, the black boat was gone, leaving only the smell of engine exhaust, white foam, and heavy swells pushing the empty white boat toward him.

Bart backstroked toward the white boat until he hit his head. "Ow!" He rubbed his head, got a grip on the transom, and pulled himself over and in. The absence of an outboard motor clamped to the transom made hauling himself in easier. But no motor meant no go, and his compass was on the way to the bottom.

There was just enough starlight to see the money bundles were gone, replaced by six inches of rising water. Using his hands, he found water squirting in from a line of bullet holes near the bow at the waterline. He relaxed when he remembered many of these old fiberglass boats had flotation installed at the factory, either foam blocks or sealed air spaces built into the hull. They would float even when full of water. But if this boat didn't have the built-in floatation, it might sink during the night. He still wore Mrs. Concannon's life vest, just in case.

He groped around in the dark and found no paddle, flares, or anything else useful, like hot coffee or dry clothes. With nothing to do but wait for morning daylight and help, Bart curled up on a seat. Shivering from wet and cold, his head and ear aching, Bart closed his eyes. He'd block out his discomfort by thinking.

Bart remembered his dad, who, in times of trouble, would quote Lloyd Bridges playing Mike Nelson on *Sea Hunt*, an old TV program about scuba diving. Nelson always attracted trouble, on or under the water. In another hopeless fix, Nelson would think aloud for the TV viewers, "If I'd only known then, what I know now."

What did Bart know?

Why did they try to kill him?

Bart hadn't seen them. Therefore, he could not identify them.

He gave them the money. How did killing him help them?

Did they intend to release Drake Concannon? Was Drake Concannon even still alive?

Now that they have the money, why would they want to keep Drake Concannon alive?

Bart couldn't believe the words. Kill. Kidnapping. Murder. These were words he hadn't in mind while he was watching the man paint *Lasiter Investigations* on the glass of his office door. He had just wanted to make a living — as Mrs. Concannon had said about her husband's work — *helping* people.

Homicide. Another word. When he was a cop in Berkeley, Bart had avoided the Homicide unit and its detectives, people who were alien to him. Even though the San Francisco Bay Area suffered multiple homicides each week, Bart had always resisted accepting homicide as a part of normal life. For the homicide detectives, it *was* part of normal life.

One afternoon, Bart was called to Homicide to talk to two detectives who wanted background information on someone he knew from his beat. The detectives thought the man might have information about one of their cases.

When Bart entered their area, all the homicide detectives turned and looked at him. For a few seconds, no one spoke. Bart felt their looks like arrows, like he was in that dream where he has no clothes. He felt like they were examining him, he hadn't studied, and he was flunking the test. He gave the detectives the information they requested and didn't linger.

Whenever Bart encountered these homicide detectives their demeanor and their coarse language repelled him. Fred Clifford had tried to explain. He told Bart the detectives used their public persona of indifference like a shield, to protect themselves from what the job forced them to learn.

When Bart had started his police work, he wanted to know everything there was to know about the job and life. He listened to every cop's war stories until, eventually, he understood there could be things you were better off not knowing.

In time he understood, viscerally, what Fred had meant about the homicide detectives' shield. Without this shield, they wouldn't be able to function and do their job. The detectives wanted to protect themselves from the past, from things they had already seen and wanted to forget. And more, they wanted to protect themselves from the future, from things they knew were yet to be seen, and never forgotten. Most of all, they wanted to protect themselves from the ideas, the ideas they had not yet experienced, or even imagined. Ideas of what one human could do to another.

"Bart, they're hunters of men. They can never rest."

"But —"

"Bart, someone has to do it."

Bart believed Homicide was an exclusive club. Bart was not a member and didn't think he wanted to join. Even if they let him in, he didn't know if he could, or would want to, pay the dues.

Homicide — California Penal Code 187.

T-Shirt: *187 — Our day begins when yours ends.*

It was all too much for him now. The day's events had done him in. He curled up across a bench seat and fell asleep.

Sun. Bart was dreaming the wet and cold were leaving him, and were being replaced by dry warmth, warmth from a new day's sun.

"Señor? Hola? Señor . . . wake up?"

Bart's eyes fluttered open, and then slammed shut when the sun burned into them.

"Señor?"

"I'm okay, I'm okay. I'm getting up." He sat up on the seat and his legs went into cold water to his kneecaps. "Yikes!"

"Señor, I think your boat, she is sinking. Get out now, right away."

"It's not my boat." He saw the water level in the boat near the lowest area of the transom. "Ooops. I guess it is sinking."

Bart's rescuer, an older man with curly silver hair, sat in an aluminum fishing boat, like the one Bart had just lost. The man used a paddle to move his boat toward Bart's. Pushing some fishing poles to one side, the man said, "Get in my boat, Señor. Hurry."

Bart stepped from the white boat's bench seat over the side into the man's aluminum boat and sat down.

"I go into Tahoe City. Okay?"

"Yes, thank you."

"I could tow your boat —"

"No, thank you. Let it go."

The man started the motor and pointed them toward the west shore.

Bart turned to see water rush over the white boat's transom. As it sank, beginning a journey of sixteen hundred feet to the bottom, Bart saw on the transom, *Linda Lou,* in mottled, faded turquoise script.

You deserved better, *Linda Lou.*

And you could have been me.

* * *

25

Tahoe Style

My Kind of Town, Tahoe City Is

With dry land under his feet, Bart thanked his rescuer again, and offered the man some money for gas. He'd noticed Bart's blood during the trip to shore and didn't want money, or further involvement.

"It is the rule of the water, Señor. You always help."

The man waved goodbye to Bart and quickly returned to taking care of his boat.

After a short walk from the dock, Bart found a pay phone and, with wet coins, called Mrs. Concannon.

"Oh, my goodness, Mr. Lasiter. I'm so relieved to hear your voice. I didn't know what to think when you didn't return last night. I was up all night with worry. Are you all right?"

"From the tone of your voice, I'm afraid Mr. Concannon hasn't returned home yet."

"No, no, he didn't. What happened?"

"I'm not sure. They didn't act like they were glad to see me, but they took the money."

"When will I see you? You say they took the money — what will happen to Drake? What do we do?"

"They *should* release your husband, Mrs. Concannon. They have the money now. But I'll admit, I'm uncertain. They didn't do what we expected. I'm going to think things over and do some checking. I'll be at your home this evening. Try not to worry. Let's assume they will release Mr. Concannon."

"I hope you are right, Mr. Lasiter. But how will you get here? You left your car here."

"Oh . . . yes, I did. Don't you worry about the details, Mrs. Concannon. I'll see you tonight. Good luck."

"I'll be waiting, Mr. Lasiter."

"Duuh!" said Bart, after hanging up. "She's right, I'll need transportation." And he had to go to Reno to see Al Wexler.

When Al Wexler said he couldn't see Bart before the ransom delivery, Bart had concluded whatever Al found about Drake Concannon would be academic. Mr. Concannon would already be back home. Now, what Al learned could be important.

Bart was still soaked wet and needed something dry to wear. He took off the life vest and *Thunderbird* sweatshirt. Maybe his T-shirt would dry out while he wore it. Parts of the sweatshirt were still heavy with water. He gulped when he saw the back soaked with his blood as he squeezed out red-tinted water. He walked to North Lake Boulevard, with his Nikes squishing and his jeans dripping and sticking to his legs.

Approaching a trash can, Bart considered discarding the life vest. No, it belonged to Mrs. Concannon. He would return it.

He looked up the street for a clothing store.

On the west side of the street, about a block north, a group of buildings fashioned as log cabins or ski lodges sat in the sun. As he got closer, he saw they were conventional wood-framed buildings with fake-log siding. A few had dropped the log-cabin pretense and painted their logs gray or blue over the original varnish. On one building he could see part of a sign saying Second Hand. He hoped it was Clothes, and not Furniture. He crossed the street.

On his way to the second-hand store, Bart passed a parking lot where a man was washing a sports car.

"Hey Buddy!"

Bart turned back to the man. "Yes?"

"You know you've been bleeding? Kinda bad?"

"Yes. I mean, I got hit on my head last night, in the dark. I haven't had a chance to look at it yet."

"Come over here. I work nights on the County Paramedics'

team. Let me look at it."

"Okay."

"Your T-shirt is a goner — bloodstained and torn in the back. Lift your arms up straight."

Bart obeyed, and the man carefully slid the shirt over Bart's head.

Taking a clean white towel from inside his car, the man covered Bart's neck and told him to hold the towel in place. Then he took his garden hose and let some cool water trickle over Bart's head. The water stung when it first hit the back of Bart's head but soon felt soothing.

"Wow. You've got an open gash back there. It looks mostly skin deep, but, sorry, I can see bone, and there's a groove in the bone. It's ugly. What happened?"

"Nothing worth talking about, thanks."

"You should have a Doc clean it out and put in some stitches, real soon, and you should be on antibiotics right away. Any infection around your head is dangerous. Believe me, I know what I'm talking about."

"Thanks."

When the man took the towel away from his neck, Bart saw blood on it.

"Here — hold still." The man dried Bart's head and neck and washed the dried blood from his back. He wrapped Bart's head in another towel. "That'll do until you can see someone about it. There's Dr. Gupta a block up the street. He's open Sundays and has his own pharmacy. Above the tattoo shop."

"Thank you, very much. Can I pay you for the towels?"

"No. Just promise me you'll have your head looked at soon. Good luck."

Bart nodded his towel-wrapped head and continued along the side of the road toward the second-hand store. He could see now it was a clothes store. When he stopped in front of the store's display window, he saw blue letters on the glass:

Deep Waters Experienced Clothing
Buy or Sell

A selection of clothing covered the floor of the display

window, arranged on top of old surfboards and beach towels. Odd shirts and shorts clothed a few mannequins positioned in awkward poses on the surfboards. All the beach towels and clothes had been in the window long enough to be sun-faded and dusty.

When Bart opened the door, a buzzer sounded at the back of the store. After he'd closed the door and the buzzer stopped, it was quiet. He was alone in the store. When he approached the counter near the cash register, he heard what sounded like a toilet flushing, and then a door open and close.

A man's bare arm spread the curtains covering a doorway. The arm's owner yawned, and his other arm set a magazine, *Tahoe World*, down on the counter. Without bothering to look up, he said, "How can I help you?"

Then he looked at Bart and noticed the bare chest, wet jeans, the bloody sweatshirt and life vest in his hand, and the turban-like towel encircling his head. "In town for vacation?" He tucked his T-shirt into his shorts. The sudden twist in the tanned wrinkles surrounding the man's eyes said he'd wanted to ask a different question.

"No. A mishap. I fell into the lake, and I want to buy some dry clothes. And I'm sure glad to find you open on Sunday."

The man noticed water dripping from Bart to his wooden floor.

"In the summer here, everybody's open on Sunday. Glad to help a visitor. Look around. There's a fitting room there. We're low on stock right now. One of our lakefront summer residents came in last week and bought most of our inventory. She takes the clothes back with her to San Francisco and gives them to the homeless. I won't have new stock for a few days."

The man eased himself down into a chair behind the cash register and brought his tanned, muscled legs and bare feet up onto the counter. Picking up the magazine, he said, "Go ahead, look around. Make yourself at home."

Bart wanted a dry T-shirt, but even an XXL would never slide over his head towel. After rejecting many undersized button-up shirts, he found a roomy, mostly tan, polyester shirt-jacket with button-down collars and deep, red pockets at the sides. Red dice were embroidered over each chest pocket flap.

The big, reinforced side pockets closed with zippers, probably to hold casino chips. More important, the shirt fit and buttoned down the front — it didn't have to fit over his head.

The pants were mostly too big or too small. He settled for a nice pair of pleated brown wool suit pants. At least they looked like they would fit.

Bart decided not to bother asking about socks or underwear. Even as frugal as he was, secondhand underwear was below his standards. He'd go Commando.

Shoes? His Nikes were soaked through. Maybe a nice pair of wingtips to match the pants.

The shelves labeled Shoes should have been labeled Empty. Five shelves, each at least twelve feet long, held nothing save one lonely pair of boots. Cowboy boots. Not a Bart favorite. Silver, not a Bart favorite.

He took off his wet shoes and socks, rolled his wet jeans up to his knees, rubbed his feet with the dry part of his sweatshirt, and tried the boots on. They felt soft and well broken-in. They fit perfectly. He walked up and down the aisles and couldn't find a flaw. He left them on and went to the man at the counter, carrying the shirt and pants in one hand, and his wet clothes and the life vest in his other hand.

"How much?"

The man looked at Bart's selections, then up to the dusty ceiling, consulting the great calculator in the sky.

"Let's see . . . the shirt — oh, a casino collector's item —*I'm a stranger with a pair of dice,* eleven ninety-five, the pants, Brooks Brothers, sixteen ninety-five. And the boots?" His gaze came down from the ceiling and he gave Bart a bored-but-hungry look, like Aggie sneaking up on a mouse.

"I've been saving those boots for just the right customer. I wouldn't let that lady — good customer that she is — take those boots to the homeless. Those boots look like they were custom made for you."

"How much?"

"See, they belonged to a famous artist. Don't remember his name right off, but they were for years his favorite, faithful pair.

"Then he got painter's block and couldn't paint. They say he was ready to give up and kill himself when he got the idea to paint these boots silver. Friend, did you know Nevada is the Siver State? Anyway, it changed his life. Every day he wore these boots after he painted them silver, that was a better day for him. He made and sold many paintings after that."

"What happened to him?"

"He died. But not with his boots on. His girlfriend brought them in, to trade."

"Some story. So, how much?"

"Well, you look like a fella in need. I'll give you a break. Fifty-nine ninety-five."

"Ouch!"

"Okay, okay. It's Sunday. I'll throw in a nice belt — no charge. You're gonna need a belt for those classy trousers. Take any belt."

Bart looked at the five-belt display. He chose the only one that would fit, hand tooled leather, with *Tom – 1969* carved into its surface. It had a big brass metal buckle shaped like a '57 Chevy grill.

Bart waved his choice at the man. He nodded and offered Bart a Macy's plastic shopping bag for his wet things.

Bart took it all into the fitting room. Shortly, he returned happy. His new clothes were dry and comfortable. His old wet clothes and life vest were in the plastic bag.

The man saw him in his new outfit.

"Wow. A gay cowboy on his way to Reno!"

Bart winced, gave the man some damp currency, and left.

* * *

26

Medical Care

I've Got You Under My Skin

Bart decided to see the doctor first, then look for a car rental. With places to go, he couldn't depend on cabs.

After another block, Bart found Dr. Gupta's building. The Doctor's offices were on the second floor with an entrance to a staircase at the left of the street-level tattoo shop:

Lake of the Sky Body Works

Reaching for the Doctor's doorknob, Bart paused to study the window display of tattoo designs. He rested his plastic bag of wet things and one knee on the sidewalk bench beneath the tattoo shop window. A metal ashtray, overflowing with butts, was attached to an arm of the bench.

Scanning the tattoo designs in the window, Bart concluded some were like those he'd seen on the three pirates.

Something moved behind the window. The tattoo shop door flew open. A mid-thirties long-haired man wearing a T-shirt and shorts came out. His exposed skin was covered with tattoos. He looked Bart over, from towel-covered head to silver boots.

"Wassup, Swami? Dude — you're a true gesso-white blank canvas. You seriously need some tats — today!"

Bart stood. "Oh, no thanks."

"Dude, a few minutes and a few dollars will change your

life. Don't even need dollars. A credit card works fine, and for
special jobs, we can do monthly installments — after a friendly
down payment. Got some serious art on sale today. Whattaya
say?" The man struck a match, touched it to his cigarette,
inhaled, and held the pack out to Bart. He waited for Bart to
respond and then exhaled a cloud of smoke toward Bart.
"Wanna smoke?"

Bart coughed.

"Sorry. Can't smoke inside. Ain't allowed."

Bart pointed up. "I'm going to the doctor, and I don't smoke.
Thanks anyway."

"You're a clean-liver-kinda-guy, huh?"

"Sort of."

"Hey, cool. I know lotsa clean-liver veggies — don't smoke
or drink. But they still love body art and piercings."

"Thanks again. Not today."

"Cool. Say hello to Doc for me. He don't care for tats and
piercings himself, but Doc 'll vouch for my work on maintaining
healthy procedures. Stop by after. We'll talk. Peace out."

Dr. Deepak Gupta, M.D.
7-6 Closed Wednesdays

The doctor's glass door led to a stairwell full of odd smells,
probably from mold in the thick carpet on the stairs, and the odor
of disinfectant and medicine, growing stronger as he climbed.

At the top of the stairs, a young Indian woman commanded
an open reception area. Patients waited in chairs near her desk.

"I'd like to see the doctor. I want him to look at my head
wound. And my ear."

"What is your insurance, Sir?" She barely looked up from a
college textbook.

"I don't have insurance."

Now she looked up. "You have no insurance?" With quick,
economical eye movement, she took in Bart's new clothes, his
bag of wet clothes, and his head towel. "No insurance?"

"No insurance. But I can pay cash."

Her eyes brightened.

"Excuse me, Sir. Please, sit down and wait a moment here."

She smiled. "I'll be right back."

She left her desk and went through a door marked Private at the far end of the reception area. After a minute, she opened the door and guided a bandaged patient back to the waiting area. Then she led Bart through the same door. He felt the eyes of the waiting patients on his back until the door closed.

A man in a white coat closed a folder and rose from his desk. "Welcome, welcome, Sir! I am Doctor Gupta."

"I'm Lasiter, Bart. Are there forms to fill out, Doctor?"

"Oh, no, Mr. Lasiter, not cash customers." Dr. Gupta stared at Bart's bare chest and the towel on his head. "Ah, a turban."

"Turban? Oh, no. Are you from India, Doctor?"

"No, Mr. Lasiter, I grew up in London. I have never worn a turban. Did you think a turban would get you a discount?"

"No, Doctor. It's just a towel to cover the wound. And my ear — is my eardrum okay?"

"Sit in this chair. We'll have a look."

"Aren't those other people out there in front of me?

"No, Sir. You are number one today. Cash is king here."

Bart held still while Dr. Gupta removed the towel, examined his ear, and probed around his head wound.

"Your eardrum is not punctured, but your head wound will need stitches. We should shave some of your hair around the wound. We've got to get under your skin and clean out the bad things. Okay?"

"Okay, Doctor."

Twenty minutes later, Bart started back down the stairs, pleased to have avoided the word *gunshot* and a police report. Now the detective had a tetanus shot and a dozen stitches under a new white bandage held in place by multiple turns of white tape around his head. In exchange for this treatment, and a supply of antibiotics and painkillers, Dr. Gupta had performed a walletectomy on Bart.

When Bart stepped from Dr. Gupta's stairwell to the sunny sidewalk, he saw the tattoo man on the bench, smoking.

"Did Doc tell you? You need a tattoo, Dude."

"No, thank you."

"What about removing a tattoo? I do removals, too."

"No. *Thank* you."

Bart was impatient to find a rental car and continue his work. He'd been more than polite to the man while trying to convince him, bodywork for Bart was no sale.

"So, you have tats you want to keep? Where? On your butt? On your Johnson?"

"I don't *HAVE or WANT* any tattoos!"

"Chill, Dude. It's bad to be angry. Bad Karma. Just tryin' to help. It's tough getting' my business goin' up here at the lake. I did better down in Sacramento, when I was *Big River Ink*."

"Then why did you leave? Wait. Your place was in Old Town, right?"

"That's an affirmative."

"Up the stairs, above the Chinese ribs place, right?"

"Buck's. Buck Choy, the Chinese cowboy. *Ribs are my game, sauce is my name.*"

"No more. Buck's gone."

"I heard. Grass Valley now. Lotta turnover in Old Town."

"Like a shark, Old Town has to keep moving to stay alive. But I was in *Big River* last year. I talked to some other guy."

"My partner. He left to go mobile. I couldn't carry the rent by myself, so I came up here."

"When I talked to him, I was trying to help this old lady. She thought someone kidnapped her cat."

"Mishka? The Russian lady? She was always bugging us about her cat. A real nut-bag."

"Yes, she was. Go mobile?"

"My partner, he hated being indoors. He bought a new van, painted the sides with his designs. *Ink on the Road*. No more office. He'd drive to client's houses." He took a long draw on his cigarette and smiled while he exhaled. "The rich ladies in Fair Oaks or Granite Bay wanted their tats done in the privacy of their homes. 'Specially when they wanted ink in their sweet areas."

"Looks like the tattoo business is expanding."

"Yup, but Old Town, like, tourists don't want tattoos so much. And Sacramento? Man, stand in the street, throw a rock o'r your shoulder an' you'll take out the front window of a new tattoo shop. More shops every day. Way too many — worse than Starbucks."

"So, you miss Old Town?"

"Some. I miss Buck. Buck, he was a philosopher. Once I was in Buck's for some ribs and he started this whole rap about movie stars, how Jim Carey and Jeff Daniels — you know, in *Dumb and Dumber* — were carrying on the work and tradition of The Three Stooges, and all."

"I guess. But there were only two of them."

"You've got a point there. But like which one was the dumb one, and which was dumber, you know?"

"Sorry. That *is* a philosophical question. I can't help you, but you could help me. Do you know where I could rent a car?"

The tattoo artist sat back down on the bench and thought about it.

"No. Not around here. You probably have to go to Truckee, or even Reno. There's a used car lot up the street, though. Maybe they'd rent you one."

"Thanks. I've got to go now."

"Glad to help. Stay real, man."

A thirties Ford roadster with no hood or fenders rumbled by, its impatient, chromed V-8 restrained by a smiling bikini-clad female driver. A third of the roadster's shiny black finish had been painted over with orange and yellow flames.

"Awesome," said the tattoo man.

In the distance, Bart could see the car lot. He was zipping his bottles of drugs into his big shirt pockets, when he heard the tattoo artist calling behind him.

"Hey, Bro — how about a piercing?"

* * *

27

King for a Day

Come Blow Your Horn

Bart stewed as he approached the used car lot. Losing his cool with the tattoo artist was uncool. If his mother were here, like the tattoo artist, she would have warned him that his impatience would create Bad Karma. He also knew, if true, she would have died from Bad Karma long ago.

The tattoo man's T-shirt had his business name on it and was artsy, yet tasteful for a tattoo business. Maybe, when this case was over, Bart would have some *Lasiter Investigations* T-shirts printed, with his address and phone number.

He still had to find a rental car. With so many places to go and so little time, cabs wouldn't work. He hoped this car lot would rent.

A compact one-room building set at a corner of the car lot supported a billboard-sized sign:

DEEP BLUE DEALS

A man inside holding a coffee mug watched Bart through the top half of a window over a growling air-conditioning unit. Air-conditioning at eighty degrees? Sacramento Bart smirked. He approached a car for sale, confident this would bring the man outside.

"You're looking at a fine vehicle there, Sir, and it's on sale today, too." The salesman ran his hands slowly over a paunch scheduled to increase in size as he turned forty. The paunch pushed his white shirt and dark blue tie out over his belt and blue jeans. The jeans kissed the toes of powder blue cowboy boots.

Bart nodded.

"My name is Larry King, Sir. You're probably thinking the TV-star Larry King, but no, I'm not that guy. Larry is my real name, but King is my adopted name." The man smiled while he examined Bart.

His melon-shaped, permed, dark, frizzy hair dwarfed his white face, and moved up and down as he took in Bart's clothes and head bandage. He frowned when he saw the plastic bag of wet clothes, as if Bart were carrying a dead cat, but smiled again when he saw Bart's silver boots. He offered Bart a hand heavy with silver and turquoise rings and bracelets.

Bart shook his hand. "You were adopted?"

"No, no Sir. I adopted the *name* King, because my goal is to be King — the King of Sales in the Lake Tahoe auto sales world. And when you buy a car from me today, Sir, *you* will be a King."

"I can't see myself as king of anything, but I have heard it's good to have goals, and achieve them."

Larry King's smile slid off his face, replaced with a troubled twitching while his hair bobbed up and down again as he searched the blue sky.

"My goal is real, *and* achievable, but it's harder now, with all these women." His eyes turned hard, and he abandoned his salesman's voice. "There was too many of 'em in real estate, and then they spread out, to appliances and what-all, and to . . . auto sales." He began to talk faster. "It's not fair. They can do things I can't. Even though they *say*, 'No tail before the sale,' I don't —"

Larry King saw Bart staring at him and found his smile.

"I haven't seen you here before, Sir. From around here?"

"No. Sacramento."

"Oh, yeah. You're smart to come up to Tahoe to buy a car. I always have better deals than those guys down in Sacramento."

"Actually, I'm not interested in buying a car. I heard you might rent one."

"Oh." Disappointment rushed across Larry's face. "Well, I

don't know of a place in Tahoe City, no Sir. Truckee maybe, certainly Reno. Yeah, in Reno you can rent a car. Give 'em your credit card and take your pick — no problem."

"Credit card? I only have cash."

"Oh?" Larry's face brightened. Then he looked down at his powder blue cowboy boots and casually kicked a few stones in the dirt.

"You can't rent a car with cash, Sir. Unless you put down a huge deposit. You *always* have to have a credit card to rent."

"Oh."

Larry King's eyes came back up to Bart.

"Sir, *rent* a car? Why *rent*, when you can . . . *own?* What kind of car do you want?"

"I just need it for a day or two. You won't rent one to me?"

"No — can — do." His hair jerked side-to-side, trying to follow his head. "Company policy."

Bart frowned. "How much is your cheapest car?"

Larry looked off into the distance. "You're on a budget, Sir? How much do you have to spend?"

"Just show me your cheap cars, please."

"Yes, Sir. All right. Follow me. They're in the back row. Just remember, they're not really *cheap.* We only sell the finest vehicles. Our customers demand a high standard."

Bart followed the salesman but became alarmed as he saw the prices painted on windshields. Yikes.

He had money in his checking account, but, in his haste to hit the road, he'd left his checkbook behind. With so much cash, who would've thought he'd soon run short? In the future, to be a successful private investigator, Bart would have to improve his financial management skills.

Larry King stopped when they reached the back row. "Here we are, Sir. Our value collection."

Larry's "value" cars were not cheap. Some were almost fifteen hundred dollars. If he had to pay that much, he would be flat broke until he got more expense cash from Mrs. Concannon.

Bart walked along the row, looking for a windshield marked with an acceptable price.

Larry stayed close, studying the attention Bart paid to each car. Bart wanted to give up halfway down the row.

"This is it? Is this all there is?"

"You're a fan of Peggy Lee, Sir? All the great entertainers come to Tahoe."

"Yes, but what about the cars?"

"This is our entire value collection. Maybe tomorrow we might . . . ."

Bart looked again at the long row of unaffordable cars. Now he saw something down at the end of the row. Hidden behind the last car was something red he hadn't noticed before.

"Is there another one down at the end?"

"Oh! The red BMW. Sir, you've got really good taste and car sense to spot that one, our least expensive car. Look, it's on special sale today."

Bart didn't ask which of the cars *weren't* on sale and walked down the row for a closer look. He pointed at the strange little red car. "That's a BMW?"

Larry King caught up. "I almost forgot about this one, Sir. We just got it in. It's a little jewel straight from a collection."

Bart frowned and shook his head. The car was tiny with little tires and only one seat and one door — across the front. He circled the little car, surprised to see it had four wheels. The two at the rear were closer together, making it look like a three-wheeler. Attached at each corner, a curved chrome bumper tube protruded. Except for having wheels, it looked more like an egg than a car.

Larry King ignored Bart's disappointment and kept pitching.

"We found a group of Classics in a Truckee barn. The man died, and his wife wanted to sell the entire collection. Porsches, Ferraris, Jaguars — our affiliate dealer in Reno bought them all. We were lucky they sent this one down to us. You get first crack at it."

"Crack — at an EGG! Good one, Larry. But a BMW?"

Larry looked hurt.

"Look, Sir. It's a BMW, really. See the blue and white BMW badge on . . . ah, the front door?"

"Oh."

"It's a BMW *Isetta*. The 300 model. And look, Sir. It has a sunroof, and even a luggage rack, too."

"I don't know."

Larry King swung open the Isetta's only door, a door that spread full width across the front of the car.

Inside, the steering wheel column was attached to the back of the door, and its base hinged to the floor, allowing the steering wheel to move out of the way when the door swung open. The pedals mounted at the base of the steering column looked like soupspoons. Small clutch and brake pedals sat next to a tiny accelerator pedal. The gearshift was on the left side, where a door should have been. A padded bench and back was the only seat. Above the seat there was a package shelf under the rear window. No trunk.

Bart stepped in to sit and check a tear in the bench seat's plastic cover. Backing himself out, he inadvertently leaned on the center of the steering wheel.

BEEEEP!

"Yow!"

"See, Sir, the horn works, too. Can't you picture yourself driving around the Lake with the sunroof rolled open, honking at the ladies?"

"Not if it hurts my ears."

"It would be different out on the road with the wind and an open sunroof."

"I bet the sunroof leaks the first day it rains."

"No Sir. And it comes with a thirty-day limited warranty."

Bart opened and closed the big door three times, watching how the steering wheel and column moved with the door.

"It's a 1959 model. Very rare. And Sir? That red paint isn't just any red, it's *Ferrari* red."

"Larry, at the boat show, I saw Ferraris parked there. Not one of the red ones had paint this faded. Or rust spots."

Dragging his finger through a snowdrift of dust around the tiny speedometer, Bart said, "He collected it? Looks like he collected dust, too."

"One moment, Sir." Larry King turned toward the sales shack. "Harold! HAROLD!"

A short older man in a gray cotton mechanic's jumpsuit came out from the shack.

"Yes, Sir?"

Watching Bart closely, Larry King barked, "Harold! Why

isn't this BMW detailed? It needs a polish and wax, and there's dust inside."

"Mr. Lepkowitz, you told me not to bother with —"

"King, *King*, Harold — it's *KING!*"

"Yes, Mr. King. Right away."

"Wait." Bart counted some hundreds and fifties from his wallet. "I've got to get to Reno, and I don't have a lot of time."

He tossed his bag of wet clothes in onto the package shelf and turned back to Larry King.

"If the battery is charged, and it starts, I'll take it the way it is."

* * *

28

Who Is He?

Who?

The Egg Car Isetta made it to the outskirts of Reno without incident, though the engine's loud thumping noise hurt Bart's ears. He didn't know if the noise was normal, if there was a hole in the tiny muffler, or if the one-cylinder engine or motor mounts needed work. What was an Isetta like this supposed to sound like? The engine was right behind him under the package shelf, making a sound that made his head throb. Sliding back the side windows didn't help. The noise was both inside and outside, hammering Bart's sore head.

Did the engine need work? No time for that. Because he needed the Egg Car, Bart decided he would call it "the Isetta." Maybe it would appreciate the respect. "BMW" was too much, at least for now.

Near Reno, traffic began to crawl. Bart left the highway south of the Reno-Tahoe airport and avoided Reno's busier streets, already filled with Hot-August-Nights-drivers. He tried to stick to back and side streets on his way to the *Juarez.*

Even the back streets Bart tried had many Hot August Nights celebrants. Some pointed at the Isetta and waved. Bart waved back and kept going.

He made it to the *Juarez* early. When Al walked in, Bart was seated in a booth, reading a menu, and sucking through a straw from a tall plastic glass of Classic Coke. Bart reached across the table to shake hands.

"Hi, Al. Thanks for doing this. Good to see you again. How are you?"

"Busy, but I'm getting closer to retirement — or death. Sometimes it's hard to tell which will be first. Hurt your head?" Al slid into the booth.

"It's okay. So, what did you find?"

"Wait. Bart, you *are* picking up the check today, right?"

"Of course."

"Just asking. Few get rich in the news business."

"Maybe later I can get some money for you, like a consulting fee."

"That would be nice."

"I'll try."

"Now, Bart, you threw me a curve with Drake Concannon. I had trouble placing him until I went to my archives. Just one article, from forty-five years ago, brought his story back like yesterday." He stared at Bart. "You're going to tell me what you're working on?"

Before Bart could answer, a waitress arrived to take their order.

"I'll have a number three combo plate and a Dos Equis," said Al.

"And, I'll have the Chiles Rellenos combo, uh, with black beans, and a re-fill on my Coke, please."

"Diet?"

"Classic, no ice, please."

The waitress finished scratching on her order pad and left.

"I can't tell you more right now, Al. Maybe later. Call it research for now, and we didn't have this conversation. Okay?"

"Okay, but you'll owe me more than lunch. Questions about Mob business are worth more than lunch."

"Mob business?"

A young man came to their booth with bowls of white corn chips, fresh chunky salsa, and guacamole.

Bart, who hadn't eaten breakfast, grabbed a chip and stabbed it into the guacamole. "When life hands you avocadoes, don't complain, just make guacamole!"

Al scooped up a chip's worth of salsa. "Hmmmmm."

Sliding forward in the booth, Bart put his elbows on the table. "So, what have you found? What did you mean, 'Mob business?'"

"You'll see. Have some more chips and listen while I tell you Drake Concannon's story."

"You're in charge." Bart coated a chip with salsa.

"Remember, Bart, the article from my archives was only a reminder. The best of what I'm going to be telling you came from my sources going back decades, and they weren't too eager to talk about it then, or when I asked again yesterday."

"Wow. Long-time history. Understood. Go on."

"What I mean is, Bart, watch out. My asking these questions might make other people ask questions about why I'm asking questions. And who-for I'm asking questions. Watch your back."

"Will do." Bart spun his finger over the table. "Lift off."

"Consider yourself warned." Al inhaled and started. "Drake Concannon was always different. Drake insisted on attending a local public high school near his home in Philadelphia instead of going away to the exclusive prep school his parents chose for him. In the public high school, he was considered an annoying, math-science nerd, and got picked on a lot. Instead of 'Drake,' his classmates chanted 'Ducky, Ducky, shot out of a cannon!'

"He didn't like his parents, both children of poor immigrants who'd achieved wealth and status in Pennsylvania. Distancing themselves from their old-country parents, Drake's mom and dad became proud, tight-ass Philadelphia Mainliners. Drake's mother was a wannabe debutante, and his father became a hot-shot surgeon. They wanted Drake to be a doctor, too, or at least a lawyer or banker — not an engineer. They wanted him to stay near Philadelphia, go to Penn like dad, marry a Bryn Mawr girl just like mom, and give them many grand-kiddies —"

"Bryn Mawr — Sonja went there, a few years."

"Sonja?"

"My ex."

"Oh, yeah."

"Sorry. Wait. What's a Mainliner?"

"It's someone who lives on the commuter train line running from the wealthy suburbs east to downtown Philly."

"Okay. Please continue."

"Sure. Young Drake knew what he wanted. Adventure and new things, engineering, inventions — not medicine, or law, or finance. He accepted a scholarship from M.I.T.

"After Concannon graduated with high honors and a double Master's in electrical and mechanical engineering, he defied his parents again by moving out west. The casino Italians would say he dumped *la via vecchia* for *la via nuova*."

Bart gave Al a blank stare.

Al sighed. "It means he rejected the old ways of the past for the new ways of the future."

"Oh."

The waitress arrived with their food. Al paused his story while they tried a few bites.

"Wow!" Bart smiled.

"What?"

"My Chiles Rellenos. I love this dish. Wow, that's good."

"Bart, you're foaming at the mouth with egg white. The Juarez is good — maybe not as good as Rosalita's, but we would have been stuck in the car-nut crowd on Virginia Street. I do enjoy a good meal — anywhere, anytime."

Al had another mouthful of Enchiladas Verdes and resumed his Drake Concannon story.

"After Concannon left Philly, he found an intern position in a five-man contract-engineering office near the airport here in Reno. Besides their regular, conventional customers, they also supported gambling equipment suppliers.

"He liked the work, and his employers found him innovative and reliable. Soon they sent him out on his own to consult with both equipment manufacturers and the casinos directly. After a while, he'd developed enough contacts to open his own contract design office in Reno. When California allowed gambling at Indian casinos, he opened another office in Sacramento. The Reno office is closed now, but I heard the Sacramento office is still open."

"Yes, it is."

"Eventually, after visiting every casino in Las Vegas, Reno, and the Nevada side of Lake Tahoe, Concannon knew almost everyone important in the business. He met top movie stars, performers, and Howard Hughes. He got to know most of the casino owners — the owners of record, and a few of the actual owners."

"What do you mean?"

"Eat your chiles and listen.

"Eventually, he met The Captain, old George Whittell, the guy who owned twenty-seven miles of Nevada-side Lake Tahoe shoreline. They —"

"The guy who owned that huge wooden boat, too?"

"That's the one."

"I just saw it at the boat show in Carnelian Bay. The wooden boats, they're so beautiful, and they take you back in time."

"Haven't had the pleasure. I only like water when it's in my bourbon. I don't get out of Reno much these days, but if I want to see water, we've got the Truckee River right downtown. I do know what you mean, Bart, about old boats, or cars, or old whatever, taking you back in time. My advanced years say it's something to be careful of — going back in time. Sometimes the old days aren't as good as you remembered. Sometimes people get stuck back there, and they don't know how to get back."

"Maybe . . . ."

"So, George Whittell and Concannon hit it off right away. Whittell was a futurist. He saw something similar and special in young Concannon and invited Drake to his home. They were both interested in gadgets and machines of all kinds, and The Captain thought Drake was a genius. Drake helped Whittell with dozens of projects at Whittell's lakeside home, a castle-like house built of stone and filled with advanced technology. He called it the Thunderbird Lodge. It's a museum now — you can go see."

"Maybe."

"Old Whittell, a man who never gave anything away without weighing what he might gain in return, offered Concannon a piece of the lakeshore near his own place, during a land split in 1959. It was choice waterfront acreage at a very favorable price, with easy terms. Whittell, now disabled and using a wheelchair, wanted young Drake close and obligated.

"Drake Concannon was so grateful for the land deal that, as

a tribute to The Captain, he used Whittell's architect, carpenters, and native-American stone masons to construct his own house in the same style. But, after Concannon started his hidden casino work, he quickly paid off the note in full, well before Whittell died in 1969."

"Wait. What do you mean, hidden casino work?"

* * *

29

Mechanic

Mr. Success

Al held his fork up. "Hold on, Bart. I'm telling the story."

Bart was feeling unsettled about the story's direction. He pushed some egg white to one side of his plate, away from the black beans. He decided the cloud of foamy whipped egg white represented Drake Concannon's innocence. And then the black beans the other.

Al swallowed another mouthful of enchilada and continued.

"After Whittell died, Concannon expanded his own house and improved his property. He'd intended to develop some of his land for profit but he lost interest when privacy became more important to him than the money he could make in real estate. After selling just a few lots near the highway, he stopped. He called it all Eagle Cove."

"There were eagles there?"

"You betcha. Bart, if you keep interrupting, this is gonna take a long time."

"Sorry."

"They say Drake was a real Boy Scout when he first came to Nevada. Something changed him, maybe his marriage and divorce."

"Divorce. A bummer."

Al nodded. "Been there, done that." He scooped some

refried beans and rice onto a homemade white corn tortilla.

Bart looked straight at Al. "Come on, Al. Cut to the chase. What exactly does he do?"

"He's a mechanic."

"A mechanic? A hit man?"

Bart changed his mind. Now he saw his cloud of egg white as both a symbol of Drake Concannon's innocence and his own ignorance regarding Drake Concannon.

"No, no, Bart. A mechanic-mechanic. He fixes gambling machines."

"Oh."

"He fixes them when they break, and he fixes them when they don't pay enough, or when they pay too much. Better yet, he designs gambling machines. Slots, wheels, you name it. And money machines, too. Money-handling, money-sorting, and best of all, money-counting machines."

"So?"

"Genius Concannon has so many patents you couldn't count them, and most of them are for gaming equipment. It's public knowledge, but not widely known."

"So?"

"The real story, Bart, is the nerdy kid from Philly went over to the Dark Side."

Bart pushed a few black beans into the cloud of egg white.

"You're telling me he's involved with the Mob? I thought he's a straight arrow."

"Bart, Bart." Al smiled, sighed, and sipped more Dos Equis. "He's invented hundreds of clever things he could never patent."

"So? What's that mean? He's clever and successful. Wait. Why can't he patent them?"

"Well, they were special things. For special customers. Or, you could say, the Mob holds the patents. Owners of record, versus actual owners?"

"Oh."

Bart pushed more black beans into the egg white.

"Isn't Vegas supposed to be Mob-free now? All kiddie rides and G-rated entertainment?"

"Yeah, pirate ships and everything." Al rolled his eyes. "All good they tell you."

"Al, sometimes, when you cut down a tree, the roots are still deep, where you can't see them — right?"

"Trees? No, Bart. Creosote."

"Creosote?"

"Larrea tridentata — creosote. Pretty yellow flowers. The desert around Las Vegas is full of the creosote bush, a tough, tough plant. When it dies, it doesn't. The roots make new plants. Like the Mob, it inhibits the growth of other plants by hogging their water.

"Whatever-den-ta-ta. Mmm . . . ." Bart exhaled a breath of puzzlement while he stared at his darkening cloud of egg white and thought about creosote. And pirate ships in Las Vegas's desert. Pirates on Lake Tahoe seemed almost reasonable once you accepted the existence of pirate ships in Las Vegas.

"May I go on?"

"Sorry, Al. What was the newspaper story you found?"

"Golden Cactus." Al rolled the tortilla to fit into his mouth.

"What?"

Al pulled a folded paper from his pocket and handed it to Bart. It was a copy of a front-page newspaper clipping from the *Nevada Sun*, dated July 22, 1962.

Federal Agents Raid The Golden Cactus Casino
Employees and others detained during the raid not identified

"What's that mean?"

"Good question, Bart. Back then, I didn't know. I dug hard for those *others detained, not identified*, names. One turned out to be Drake Concannon, of Concannon Services, Inc. So, who is he? Everything I learned came from under the table. He never made the papers again. Learned to keep a low profile, I guess."

"What was this raid all about?"

"Bart, my young friend, for the Feds, it was supposed to be Apalachin Two."

Bart wrinkled his brow.

"Don't you know, Bart?"

"Remind me."

"Back in November 1957, major Mob bosses from across the country went to a mobster's farmhouse in Apalachin, New York for a big meet to sort out leadership issues and realign the details of their heroin smuggling routes, a supposedly secret meeting."

"Supposedly?"

"Supposedly very secret, until a nosy, smart-ass state trooper noticed all these Cadillacs arriving full of gumbas. Once they realized they were going to be identified, the boys scattered in all directions, like roaches after the kitchen ceiling light is switched on, some into the nearby woods. They didn't want to get caught assembling as a group. Remember, the Mafia didn't exist, Hoover claimed. Hoover's non-existent merry band of Good Fellas elite looked ridiculous, flopping around in mud and cow shit, ruining their hand-made silk suits and custom shoes, tearing their camelhair overcoats on barbed wire fences. A PR disaster for the Mob."

"I think I read about it, maybe. In the Appalachians?"

"Ap-a-LAKE-in. It's a little town, central New York, just north of the Pennsylvania border."

"Oh."

"New AG Bobby Kennedy didn't agree with Hoover on the Mob. In response, the Golden Cactus raid was supposed to be part of Bobby Kennedy's *'Operation Big Squeeze'* — an all-out effort to prevent similar Mob get-togethers and arrest mobsters. Apalachin Two, the Feds hoped, without all the chasing through the woods. Not even chasing through the desert, because they had the Golden Cactus surrounded. Remember, Nancy Hoover had been trying to sell the idea that the Mob didn't exist. Reality stepped on his dick in Apalachin. Golden Cactus was supposed to heal his sore dick."

"You have a way with words, Al."

"I know. Golden Cactus? Surprise! It didn't turn out the way they expected."

"What happened?"

"The Feds had an informant."

"Informant?" Bart's fork stopped mid-air.

* * *

30

Dark and Stormy

Witchcraft

"Yeah, an *unwilling* informant. He was just a low-level soldier, an average mobster, a driver, a *gofer,* except he was first cousin to a west coast boss. He traveled with the bosses and heard a lot. And he was careless.

"The cousin had accumulated a series of minor outstanding California warrants, and the gun he bought in a bar had been stolen from an ATF agent's car in L.A. When the cousin's car was T-boned near Las Vegas, unknown to his bosses, the cops found the gun and ran the serial number. They called the FBI who offered him the standard choice: You talk and work for us, or go down on the federal gun charge, and then to California for more charges, all to be served consecutively. Many mobsters would have laughed, but he was a Fredo. Weak. Instead of slow walking his cooperation, he offered big news. Let him off, and he'd tell them about an important meet at the Golden Cactus. Mob bosses would be there to see a skimming demo. The feds were thrilled and made plans for Fredo. Here was their chance to re-hab Hoover's lance. They made the cooperative cousin wear a miniature recorder. For two weeks, they enjoyed hearing the Mob's inner secrets. Then, 'Clunk.'"

"Clunk?" Bart was getting a tad impatient with Al's details.

"Clunk. The cousin was not one of the sharper knives in the drawer, a few fruit short of a nickel jackpot. Two weeks after he agreed to help, long before the demo-meeting, he dropped his tape recorder on the tile floor in the crapper. 'Clunk.' Another soldier saw it and quietly told the boss. The boss decided to use the cousin and didn't let him know he was now a sure dead-man-walking. They staged fake conversations for the Feds whenever he was near."

"Wait. Okay, I understand about this cousin, but I didn't know skimming was so complicated."

"Didn't used to be. It was easy to skim. They took currency from the under-table cash boxes before the boxes went to the count-room. They'd divert coins and play tricks with play slips and receipts. A Mob guy would just walk into the count-room at a certain time and walk out with a briefcase full of uncounted cash. The Feds and IRS suspected and started to pay attention. The Mob had to find better methods and put law enforcement to sleep.

"And these skims were all performed by human methods. Humans can make mistakes. Humans will steal. Concannon's genius was removing the human element. His latest skimming methods were machine-based witchcraft."

"Wait. What do you mean, 'methods?'"

"Okay. In the beginning, coins from the slots went from buckets to the count-room, and currency would be hand-carried, counted, and bundled. Labor-intensive. Concannon gave them machines to move the cash, count it, and weigh it automatically. Every method upgrade he provided used more electronics and automation. Concannon's counters and scales looked legit but allowed the bosses to fudge the count whenever they wanted."

"Can't someone see the extra cash? How do they get it out?"

"The conveyers moving the cash passed through walls and under floors, going from the casino to the count-room. Some cash went in one side but never came out the other. Out of sight, some cash would be machine-diverted and stored, waiting for pick-up."

"Yikes."

"Wait. It gets better. To test Drake Concannon's latest and greatest, they'd already picked the Golden Cactus, a small, Mob-run casino with a hundred hotel rooms. It had been built in the early fifties, old and way overdue for a total makeover and more hotel rooms. The plan was to build a new annex in the back-parking lot. The boys wanted normal activity to continue in the Golden Cactus casino areas during the new construction. Using the cousin's recorder, they scammed the Feds. The Feds heard that the new equipment would be installed in the old count-room and the new multi-level annex in the parking lot would be just more hotel and new banquet rooms, food service, laundry, and maintenance shops.

"Bart, count-room access is restricted now, and mobsters aren't allowed in the casinos. Supposedly. The annex fixed both problems. Until the annex was state-certified and approved for operation, it wasn't a casino, or a count-room.

"Contrary to what the Feds had heard, the annex basement level would hold the new count-room. When it was ready, the old count-room would now be only cashier operations. The cash from the casino would move on conveyers through passages in the walls of a new, connecting service tunnel under the parking lot. Other, secret, underground passages led through a tunnel to a mob-owned drycleaning business across the street. There were many jokes exchanged about taking the IRS to the cleaners. The Concannon-designed annex was built by a local Mob-owned construction company, so the plans they filed for construction permits neglected to show the tunnel to the drycleaners. A few bosses did get a private demo of the new annex count-room, days before the state gaming people could see it.

"The Feds waited for the very perfect moment, based on the cousin's tapes, and then sent in an army of agents with search warrants straight into the original Golden Cactus count-room. They were hoping to find not only cash skimming in progress but as many Mob guys at one time as they could — they'd bust skimming for good. But they found no mobsters and no new equipment. The few casino employees there, trying to help, told the Feds maybe they were looking for the new machines in the annex. The Feds were pissed and arrested them anyway.

"Now confused, the Feds forced one of the old count-room employees to lead them to the new annex and basement count-room. There they found Drake Concannon and several Golden Cactus employees schmoozing with Nevada Gaming Control Board people, who knew Concannon from his many previous legit installations. Concannon was proudly demonstrating all the new equipment features that addressed the many State and IRS concerns. The newly-arrived Feds, now totally confused and angry, arrested everyone.

"Of course, by the end of the day they had to let everyone go, with apologies. It was highly embarrassing for the Feds. They'd invited some press to stand by as witnesses, but now they didn't want any follow-up stories."

Bart slurped the bottom of his Coke. "Well, what happened to Drake Concannon?"

Al smiled. "Nothing. And *everything*. The new machines were so good the State and Feds couldn't see the skim. Standing right there, they couldn't see it. No proof, no case — to be a model for the future.

"Gee, couldn't they find it, eventually?"

"They probably could, if they'd had a few weeks to tear the place apart, but when the initial search warrants turned up nothing, Mob-friendly politicians went to work and pressured the Feds to pull out."

"The cousin?"

"Don't know. If he's not in WITSEC, he's studying creosote roots, up close."

Bart frowned and pushed his fork around the plate, gathering the last of his black beans.

"Now, after the raid, Drake Concannon was a god to the Mob. They paid him even more from then on. The downside for Concannon was he was forever one of theirs, and he could do other work only with their okay. But he really didn't need extra work because he was already receiving royalty checks every month from all his legit patents. The big royalty checks gave him good cover with the IRS for the under-the-table cash from his real employers. He became a cash-wealthy man."

Bart thought the story was both interesting and sounded authentic. And he trusted Al Wexler. But he wasn't ready to call Drake Concannon a criminal. There must be an explanation. Why would Mrs. Concannon marry a criminal?

"Anything else?" Bart asked.

"The news photos of the Golden Cactus raid were missing from the newspaper microfilm, and ditto at the libraries. Funny, but not unheard-of. Maybe the Mob disappeared them. Or the Feds."

The photo with the men laughing and the neon and metal sign shaped like a cactus fought its way back from Concannon's office wall to the front of Bart's memory bank.

"Hmmm."

"And there were announcements of his marriage in 1957, and his divorce a year later."

Bart finished his Coke. "Do you think he might have gotten into trouble with the Mob? Would they want to hurt him?"

"I haven't heard anything new about him since the Golden Cactus raid, except for one thing. It's the sort of thing you'd expect would put him in good light, but some people like to shoot the messenger."

"What?"

"One source said Drake tried to anticipate problems, always be ahead of the game and help the boys out. He told them the more they used those metal tokens they had coined for the slot machines, especially those in the high-dollar denominations, eventually someone would counterfeit them. Common sense says it would be too tempting.

"Concannon couldn't help them with Blackjack players who counted cards or roulette players who palmed chips, but he *could* show them how to fool-proof the slot machine coins, with a miniature insert he'd invented. A chip would be installed in each coin automatically during manufacturing. A counterfeiter would have to destroy the token to find the insert — foolproof. When a counterfeit coin, one without the insert, passed through the slot machine, a device in the machine would sense the insert was missing from the counterfeit and instantly signal the surveillance staff above the casino floor.

"It added cost to the tokens and machines, and the boys couldn't see anyone bothering to counterfeit them. They already had subtle marks on the tokens, and the metal alloy was special. If a slot machine detected the marks were off, or if the alloy wasn't kosher, the machine rejected the counterfeit coin. *But it didn't tell anybody!* So, the counterfeiters kept trying until they got it right, without anyone noticing.

"When successful counterfeit tokens did begin to show up in

quantity, starting in the nineties on the east coast, the boys were unhappy. Some suspected their Drake Concannon. Others were pissed he'd warned them, they'd ignored the warning, and now they looked like schmucks.

"Here's the bottom-line answer to your question, Bart. These people are the most suspicious people alive — wouldn't trust their own mothers. If for any reason, any reason at all, they didn't trust Concannon, he's gone. They'd hate doing it, but he knows way too much."

"So, is the Golden Cactus still there? I can go visit?"

"No, sorry. It was torn down in 1972. If anything remains, it's buried under a newer casino. That's Vegas."

Bart looked at his darkened cloud of whipped egg white and paused. Then he shoved the rest of his black beans into the formerly white cloud. Now it was all dark and stormy. He ate the evidence.

"Thanks, Al. All this helps. I owe you."

Bart grabbed the check and stood to leave.

"One more question, Al. What about his second marriage?"

Al looked up at Bart. "He got married again?"

"Yeah. Would you try again on the second marriage? I'll call you."

"Okay, Bart, if you need it."

"Please."

* * *

31

Traffic Problems

Accidents Will Happen

As before, Bart avoided the Reno Hot August Nights traffic by finding a path through the back streets, now to return to Lake Tahoe. His traffic Good Karma ran out when he turned onto a two-lane residential street. He fought the Isetta to a stop an inch short of the rear bumper of the last car in a long line of motionless cars.

Bart heard honking up ahead. He grabbed the handle above his head and rolled back the Isetta's sunroof. Dust from another decade swirled above his head. He waved his hands to clear the dust, poked his head up through the opening, and stood on the bench seat to see ahead. Leaning forward with his hands resting on the top of the door frame, he saw the source of the traffic tie-up, a collision a dozen cars ahead.

It was just a fender-bender, except two custom cars had locked beautifully painted sheet metal. The owners stood in the street near the cars. Bart could tell they were the owners because they were approaching hysteria, holding their heads, and then bending down close to the tangled fenders, then jumping back up and circling the cars, as if that might undo the damage.

The owners' wives or girlfriends stood clear and waited. Bart could tell they were the women who belonged to the owners because they had that sad and bored look, the look that testified they'd seen all this before. The police hadn't arrived yet. It would be a long day for everyone involved, and Bart didn't want to be involved.

He heard honking behind him now and pivoted around to see. A car filled the space behind him, blocking the Isetta in tight. Other cars crowded in. And now the intersection he had just crossed was a tangled mess, too.

Bart eased himself back down through the sunroof into the Isetta and sat. What could he do? He only had so much time, not enough to wait out a traffic jam.

He glanced to his right. A young couple was sitting in a sedan parked at the curb with their windows closed. Maybe they were trying to wait out the traffic jam. The driver, about Bart's age when he'd married, was turned away from him, talking to the woman in the passenger seat. Bart couldn't hear what he was saying but watched anyway. The man kept talking. The longer the man spoke, the more his jaw and neck muscles tensed. His head bobbed and jerked, almost keeping time with each word. He was delivering a long, detailed speech to the woman. The woman was absorbing this speech without emotion. Her face was still, yet her worried eyes watched the man deliver each word.

Bart turned away. He didn't have any time for relationship entertainment today.

Though some people can't take their eyes away from traffic accidents, Bart could. But he couldn't take his eyes away from romance accidents. He returned to watching the couple.

The man was still talking. If they weren't married, they were living together. This was not their first date.

The man at last finished his monologue. He sat and waited for the woman to react. She held her worried look of concern about three seconds before her face flooded with tears. Ignoring the tears, she fixed the man with a stare that frightened Bart. Words followed the tears and stare and wouldn't stop. Whatever she was saying to the man was hitting home. His head snapped back as if he were just a welterweight in a heavyweight boxing match, absorbing a series of rights and lefts he had no chance of defending. She had taken his blows, stayed on her feet, and was now counterpunching him silly. She finished without a victor's smile, her face frozen with resolve. The man turned away from the woman's eyes and looked at the steering wheel.

"Yikes!" It was Bart's marriage all over again. Now he had even more reason to escape this scene, before he started feeling queasy again, thinking about Sonja.

His alarm at the scene in the parked car swung his head away to the opposite side of the street. He saw a possibility. If he could swing the Isetta around, he might avoid the traffic jam by going in the other direction, mostly on the sidewalk. Except the other cars, bumper-to-bumper, had locked him in.

He looked at the car in front, a woodie station wagon. Its gray-headed driver looked too frail to help Bart. When he looked past the Macy's bag of wet clothes on the package shelf behind him, he saw a determined old woman staring at him over her steering wheel. Her look said it was all Bart's fault. No hope moving these cars. Bart would have to find another way.

Across the street, four young men were standing around the engine compartment of a hot rod. Big men. They were looking at Bart. One of them said something he could not hear.

Bart slid open the Isetta's side window to listen.

The man stepped toward Bart. "What's your car, bud?"

Bart couldn't open the Isetta's door. It was too close to the woodie in front. He climbed out of the sunroof and down back over the luggage rack. The old woman glared at him. He walked over to the men.

"It's an Isetta — a BMW. Hey, I'm stuck, and I've got to be somewhere else, soon. Maybe you guys could help me move four or five cars, just enough to let me squeeze out and go in the opposite direction?"

One man walked over to the Isetta. He looked at both the front and rear bumper guards and then stood with his hands on his hips. The others came over to join the study.

"Sure is something," said the first man. "Rearrange some things and a Hemi could fit." He turned to Bart. "Is it for sale?"

"Sorry, not today. Maybe you could help me?"

Another came to the first man and put his face up to his ear. After a minute, he called the other two into a huddle. They talked. The first man broke the huddle and came to Bart.

"We think we can help."

Before Bart could ask how, the men moved toward the Isetta.

One man braced his hand on the woodie's roof as he tip-toed along its rear bumper to the pavement on the far side. Another man caught scowls from the old woman in the rear as he walked along her front bumper to the far side. Then the four big men each squatted and grabbed one of the four chromed-tube bumper guards protruding from the corners of the little car.

The first man coached the others. "Remember, save your back. Use your legs. On three, hop, hop. A one, a two, and a THREE! Up-sideways-down, and up-sideways-down . . . ."

The Isetta started moving, hopping, up, sideways, and down. It moved, again and again, as the four men grunted and laughed. In a few seconds, the men had bounced it clear of the other cars. The couple in the parked car watched as the old woman started her car and drove up to the woodie's bumper, filling the space Bart's Isetta had just left. She glared again at Bart and the men as the cars behind her moved forward, too.

"Wow. Beers for that!" Bart handed a twenty to the men and opened the Isetta's door.

The men crowded around as Bart climbed in.

"Isn't it something?" said one, opening and closing the door to see the steering wheel move, while another looked down through the sunroof. Another lifted the engine cover. "Maybe I could fit a three-fifty under there. Cool."

"Thanks, guys. But I've got to go." Bart pulled the big door shut and started the engine.

The men moved back, and Bart waved as he forced the Isetta over the curb and onto their sidewalk.

* * *

Part Three

Frank

32

Opening Doors

Drinking Again

"I'm back, Sid."

Bart settled onto a barstool in the Crystal Bay Yacht Club's public bar. He was, as before, Sid's only customer. "Want to talk some more, Sid?" Bart put a twenty on the bar.

"Mr. Lasiter. I almost didn't recognize you. Your clothes are — and what happened to your head?"

"Oh, long story. I'm okay."

"Okay, Mr. Lasiter. You know I do like to talk. But I also worry about someone seeing you paying me so much for a Coke. Better if we talk someplace else. If you don't mind?"

"Sure. Where to?"

"We could have dinner and talk across the road at Benny's." Sid nodded toward the front window and the road. "There. I'm off in a half-hour."

Bart turned to look out the window to the road. Across the road a green and gold neon sign said *Benny's*. As if on cue, the sign lit up.

"Okay, Sid. I'll see you at Benny's."

Bart left the Isetta in the Yacht Club parking lot and pushed his still-unfamiliar cowboy boots through the Club's deep gravel to the road, and across to *Benny's*. As soon as he'd pulled open the restaurant's glass-and-aluminum door, he could smell steak and onions, and coffee, and fresh pie. He found the pay phone and called Mrs. Concannon.

"Mr. Lasiter! How *are* you? When will I see you?"

"I'm okay. I still have a few things to check, and then I'll be there, at your house, later tonight."

"Good, very good. Is everything all right?"

"A lot of things have happened, Mrs. Concannon. We have to talk about what I've been learning, about the ransom delivery, about a lot of things."

"Certainly, Mr. Lasiter. We'll talk tonight. I'm anxious to see you. I'll be waiting for you."

"Okay, Mrs. Concannon. I'll see you in a — oh, oh! You know my car is still at your garage. Please tell Ramon I'll be in a different car, a little red one.

"I will tell him. Take care, Mr. Lasiter."

Bart hung up and looked around.

Benny's had likely changed hands a dozen times since its grand opening, probably soon after the end of WWII. It didn't have a single style you could name, but instead odd, occasional disconnects in the paint and fittings, as though each new owner had redecorated but kept something from the past that hadn't worn out yet.

What it did have was quiet, low lighting, older waitresses, and — based on the specials listed on a blackboard near the entrance — reasonable prices. Sid was probably a regular at *Benny's,* when he wanted to get away from the Yacht Club.

Bart selected a booth with a view of the highway and the Crystal Bay Yacht Club. A plastic-laminated menu showed *Benny's* was indeed a steak-and-drinks restaurant, with enough additional choices in meat and fowl to please most, along with some fish. Sadly, no Mexican food.

Bart wasn't hungry enough yet to feel disappointed. His late lunch from the *Juarez* was still fresh in his mind and stomach. A detective has to be flexible, ready to change plans at any time, and Bart had always been able to take in another meal.

A waitress on the tired side of forty arrived to take Bart's order. He told her he was waiting for an older gentleman to join him, the bartender from the Yacht Club.

"Sid? Of course. Can I get you something to drink while

you wait?"

"Just some water for now. I'll order when Sid gets here."

"Okay, Honey." The waitress stole another look at Bart's head bandage and clothes as she left.

Bart went through his wallet and pockets, counting his cash. Though he still had money in his Sacramento checking account, he was getting low on cash. Maybe, after this case, he'd switch to a different checking account, with one of those ATM cards.

He probably had enough cash left for Sid. When he saw Mrs. Concannon later, she would give him more expense money.

The waitress brought Bart's water. He read the labels on his pill bottles and took doses of antibiotics and pain killers.

He was thinking about what he had to do next when he saw an old man walking across the Yacht Club parking lot, smoking a cigarette. Sid. A different Sid. He looked a lot looser after he shed the bar apron.

"There you are, Mr. Lasiter." Sid forced his knees to bend enough to scoot into the booth across from Bart. He set a pack of cigarettes and a plastic lighter on the table. "Did you order yet?"

"Remember, Sid, it's 'Bart.' I told her I would order when you arrived. She seemed to know you."

"Ah, they all know me here." He turned toward the kitchen and raised his hand. Bart's waitress came over with her order pad in her hand.

"What'll be tonight, Sid? Do you want to hear the specials?"

"No. I'll have my steak. You know which one and how I like it, Doris. Remind Paul to go light on the onions. You know my stomach."

"New York, well done, light onions. Green peas, and the baked-with-skin, butter, and sour cream?"

"Yup."

"Separate checks?"

"One check. I'll take it," said Bart.

"All right, Honey. What can I gettcha?"

"I'll have a Guacamole Burger and Coke. Classic, please."

"Fries or potato salad?"

"Fries, please. Thanks, Doris."

Doris saw Sid's cigarettes and frowned. "You know, not in

here, Sid."

"I left a half-smoked one outside. Respect for *you*, Doris."
Sid showed a mischievous smile. "Nag, nag."

Before Doris could leave, Sid pulled at her apron string.

"Stop it now, Sid. Behave yourself."

"Doris?"

"Yes, Sid?"

"Tonight, hold the iced tea and bring me an Early Times over
ice — a double."

She stared at Sid.

"You heard me, Doris. Now, skee-daddle. My friend, Bart,
and I have some talkin' to do."

Doris went back to the kitchen and pushed their order slips
into one of the spring clips on a stainless-steel carousel hanging
over the pass-through counter. Then she began a conversation
with the cashier, an older woman. They stood with their hands
on their hips. They had a long, somber exchange, punctuated by
concerned glances toward Bart and Sid.

"Don't mind Doris. A drink now and then is good for you,
Bart, and it helps me remember and talk. So, what can I tell
you?"

"Just tell me whatever else you can remember about Drake
Concannon, what he was like, who he hung out with — that sort
of thing would be helpful to me. Wait — you said before some
of the Yacht Club people didn't like him. Why not start there?"

"Okay. Let's see. I used to hear members laughing about
Concannon behind his back. Some thought he was too dry and
technical, and humorless — a nerd, I think they say, these days.
One time I heard some at the Members Bar talking about him,
about Concannon being an engineer. They were laughing and
trading Concannon stories. One member says, 'You know the
difference between an engineer and an accountant?' The others
say, 'No, tell us,' and he says, 'An engineer, he's a guy who's
good with numbers, but he doesn't have enough personality to
make it as an accountant.'"

"Ouch."

Doris returned with their drinks.

"Thanks, Doris," said Sid.

"You're welcome, Honey. Your dinner is coming right up."

Sid broke his gaze from Doris swinging her hips back to the kitchen and turned to his whiskey. He rotated the glass slowly on the table, watching the light change as it passed through the thick tumbler's ribs, the ice, and the bourbon. Then he turned in the booth and held the drink up toward Benny's front window and the fading afternoon light. Again, he rotated the glass. The light passing through the lens of his drink colored his white hair amber. After a tilt of the glass to toast the day, he downed a third of the drink without pausing, sighed, and turned back to Bart.

"You know, Bart, staff never liked Concannon much, either. Concannon was rarely friendly. He'd only stop to talk to you if he wanted something, never just to be friendly. If I passed him in the Club hallways, or out on the Dining Room floor, I was invisible to him. Three feet away, I'd look right at him and say, smiling, 'How are you, Mr. Concannon?' He'd stare straight ahead and act like nobody was within two hundred feet of him. And, in a way, he was right. I, Sid, *was* nobody to him. Five minutes later he might be at the bar wanting a drink and it would be, 'Sid, how're you doing? Haven't seen you for a while.' If it was just an occasional once or twice, you might excuse him. Maybe he just had something on his mind. Except it was years' worth. He did it to all the staff. Unbelievable."

Bart sipped his Coke and nodded. He let Sid roll.

"Concannon was always cheap, too. Never tipped. Servers rely on tips. If Concannon opened his wallet, there'd be moths everywhere. I'd serve him, and he'd say, 'Catch you at the end of the month, Sid.' When he signed the check, his pen couldn't find the Tip line."

"Did he make it up at the end of the month?"

"Sort of. His problem, Concannon's calendar only has one month, and it's three-hundred-sixty-five days long. Lucky to get five dollars at Christmas. To see a man rich enough to be a member, and not tip . . . ." Sid slowly shook his head and looked for an explanation in his drink.

Doris interrupted, placing their orders on the table.

"Now, if you gentlemen need anything else, you just give me a wave."

"Bring me another E-T-rocks, Doris — another double."

Doris stared at him.

"Thanks, Doris," Bart said, and Doris left.

They didn't speak for a while and concentrated on their food.

"The food is good here," said Bart.

"I told you. Don't quote me, because I think it's better than the Yacht Club's."

"How's your drink, Sid? Bus driver's holiday?"

"Hah. No, it's good. I don't drink often. I used to . . . that reminds me. Another Concannon thing some members didn't like — his drinking." Sid threw back the rest of his first drink and pushed the glass, empty but for a little ice, to the edge of the table.

"What do you mean, Sid?"

"A place like the Yacht Club, there's always drinking. They drink and talk, mostly about their boats, the Lake, the weather, and the seasons. Sometimes it'll be about their kids, real estate, business, or politics. Or they gossip about other members and their wives — who's getting married, who's getting divorced, and why. They drink and talk and pass the time."

Doris brought Sid's drink and set it down in front of him. "How are you two getting along? Anything I can get you? Dessert, some pie — fresh peach today?"

Bart raised his eyebrows at Sid and saw no response. "No thanks, Doris."

"All right, Honey." Doris left the check on the table and returned to the cash register to speak with the cashier, who had been staring at Bart and Sid. She grabbed Doris's hand and dragged her behind the pass-through counter.

Now Bart could still see them, but not their faces, which were blocked by the order slip carousel. He could see their hands moving. Doris's hands were making calming gestures, but the cashier's hands were alternating between praying clasps and wild grabs at the air, trying to catch something slipping away. Doris took the cashier's hands in hers to stop the flailing and then gave her a consoling hug.

When Bart looked back at Sid, he was sipping his fresh drink.

"The senior members, what they really dislike is someone who can't hold his liquor. The Yacht Club is not some damned gas station with a refrigerator full of beer and two slot machines.

"Did you notice? No slot machines in the Club — even on the public side. On the Club side, the members run a tab and sign for everything, including tips. They think the direct display of money is unseemly, and that's just how they view any public drunkenness. They expect people to behave."

"What did Concannon do?"

"Some days something would bother him — who knows what? He'd be fall-down drunk before anyone noticed. Bad enough, but then I heard some members say Concannon would, with no warning, become argumentative in an ugly, insulting way, and sometimes grab another member's shirt or jacket lapel."

Bart nodded between bites of his burger. He noticed Sid paid more attention to his drink than his New York cut.

From a plastic squeeze bottle, Bart squirted ketchup in swirls on his fries. "When was the last time you saw him at the Club?"

"Let me think . . . about four years ago. I remember the last few times okay because, first, maybe five, six years ago, he came in with some blonde. I'd seen her in the Yacht Club a few times before, with other men. She was real different. Special. Older than his typical cocktail waitress dates."

Sid's talking slowed. He stared at the other diners and out the window between sentences, savoring his visit to the past.

"This blonde, the woman looked serious, like she had his number. Last time I saw her, they got into a brief fight about coming to the Yacht Club. I heard her complain it wasn't safe to cross Crystal Bay in his old runabout."

Sid swallowed a piece of steak and pushed some green peas onto his fork.

"She didn't like the Yacht Club much. Also, it looked to me like she wasn't comfortable around strangers. Anyway, you could see she really didn't want to be there. So, I didn't see her again, and Concannon came around only a few times after that. The last time, like I said, was maybe four years ago."

Sid looked like he wanted to talk more. He wasn't paying any attention to the twenty Bart had put on the table. Maybe Bart had unintentionally pried open a door long closed and now had to be ready for whatever came out.

Sid looked up from his drink straight at Bart. "I've been

holding something back, Mr. Lasiter . . . Bart. See, I first knew Concannon from the Lodge, the Cal-Neva."

"You knew him there, too?

"I worked at the Lodge long before I worked at the Yacht Club. I served Concannon in both places. It's just, I don't —"

"How far back?"

"Way back."

"When Frank owned it?"

"Yes."

"Wow. I'd be interested in hearing about the Cal-Neva."

"Done with your burger, Bart?"

"Yes, I guess I am. Sid, you haven't finished your food."

Sid gulped the rest of his drink.

"I'm not that hungry. Why don't we go next door to my motel room? We can talk there." He picked up the twenty.

"Okay," said Bart, leaving a tip.

At the register, Bart gave the check to the cashier. She rang it up without looking at Bart or Sid and gave Bart his change. Bart had turned to leave when Sid reached past Bart to put his hand on the cashier's arm.

"Martha — here." Sid held out the twenty with his other hand. "You know what I want, Martha."

She pulled her arm away, her face in pain. "Sidney, why? You were doing so well. Why now?" Her eyes turned to Bart.

Bart looked away.

Sid pushed the twenty toward her.

"Martha, just get it. You're not my mother, or my wife."

Martha's face said she *should be* his wife. Without another word, she took the twenty and brought a bottle of Early Times up from below the counter. She put the bottle into a paper bag and looked toward the floor when she handed it and change to Sid.

Sid took the bottle and his change without thanking her.

"C'mon, Bart."

He led Bart out of *Benny's* to his motel a few doors away.

* * *

33

The Wizard

Among My Souvenirs

Sid's motel suite was nice, compared to Bart's live-in office. The spacious main room featured a queen-sized bed, and the bed's headboard provided storage spaces and built-in lamps. Against the wall opposite the foot of the bed, the open doors of a wardrobe-entertainment complex showed Sid's big-screen TV and work clothes, cotton pants and white shirts, next to polyester track suits, all on hangers.

Near the entrance, a compact kitchen comprised overhead cabinets, a Formica counter with a stainless-steel sink, and a microwave. Sid kept the counter and sink as neat as his bar at the yacht club. Below the counter sat a half-size refrigerator. Bart saw through the open bathroom door a full tub with shower. In a separate living area, two soft armchairs and a coffee table rested near a desk and chair.

"Have a seat, Bart." Sid pointed toward the armchairs and set the bottle on the kitchen counter. *"Mi casa, es su casa."* Shaking some quarters from a jar, he said, "I'm going to get ice from the machines."

"Fine, Sid. I'll be right here."

"Back in a jiff." Sid stepped outside and pulled the door shut.

Bart recovered from comparing Sid's room to his own. He

noted Sid's home and furnishings were mostly impersonal, and
Bart's home didn't reek of tobacco. The room's only windows
faced the noisy highway. Bart guessed Sid always kept the
blinds shut.

Though he'd said he'd lived here for years, the place didn't
show much evidence of Sid. The only thing personal besides
Sid's slight wardrobe was an arranged display of objects on the
desk, spread out on a black and orange plastic tray. A gold tie
clip with a set of matching gold cufflinks sat near a gold cigarette
lighter. Each piece contained a single diamond. Nearby, several
heavy glass ashtrays, one filled with paper matchbooks, another
filled with boxes of wooden matches, sat next to tall stacks of
cocktail napkins and paper coasters. Each item was marked with
"Frank Sinatra," or "Frank Sinatra's Cal-Neva Lodge," in a hip,
happening, 60's, hockey-stick font. Looking down from above
the desk, a framed photograph of the entrance to the Cal-Neva,
dated 1961, guarded the tray.

Frank Heaven.

The door burst open. The traffic noise seemed to push Sid,
his arms full, into the room. He shouldered the door shut.

"I'm back. Got you some cold Cokes. Classic, like you
like." After handing Bart a can of Coke, Sid poured some of the
ice into the sink and put the rest of the ice and Cokes into the
refrigerator. "Want a glass and some ice? How about a little
whiskey?"

"Glass and ice, thanks. No whiskey." Bart hated cans.

"You don't drink alcohol much, do you, Bart?"

"Never got the habit."

"Don't mind if I do, do you?"

"Go right ahead."

Sid fixed himself a drink and set it on the coffee table. At
the desk he took a fresh pack of Camels from a drawer, and an
ashtray and the gold lighter from the black tray. He sat down
next to Bart and started a cigarette.

Bart admired the lighter. "Frank Sinatra, huh?"

Sid threw his head back against the seatback cushion and
slowly exhaled a cloud of smoke.

"Oh yeah. He gave these away when he owned the Lodge.
They say my little collection of Frank's souvenirs is worth a lot

these days. Anything from the Cal-Neva with Frank's name, even like those paper coasters, is collectible. I heard people make counterfeits to sell, copies of my ashtray here." He took a long draw on his cigarette and exhaled. "But I'd never sell."

"So, you *knew* Frank Sinatra?" Bart said, more a statement of fact than a question, like he was saying, "So, you *won* the lottery?"

"Yes, remember, I just worked for him, along with a lot of other people. Here, Bart."

Sid took a box of Cal-Neva wooden matches from the tray and offered it to Bart.

"Really?"

"Go ahead. I've got boxes of them."

Bart smiled and buttoned them into a chest pocket, behind the red dice.

"Want a pen?" Sid opened the desk drawer to show Bart a tray of orange and brown Frank Sinatra Cal-Neva ballpoint pens.

"Thanks, Sid. Gee, what was it like, working for Frank?"

"I wasn't exactly part of the Summit, you know."

"Summit?"

"The Summit, or the Clan. What most people call the Rat Pack, except Frank didn't like that name. He knew me by name, but we weren't buds."

"Sure." Bart frowned. "Then tell me about your time at the Cal-Neva. Tell me about Concannon."

"I worked at the Cal-Neva — we called it the Lodge mostly — eight years total, two with Frank. Best years I ever had, especially the Frank years. The North Shore was the place to be then.

"I did almost everything except deal cards. I washed dishes, cleaned rooms, I bussed tables, I took care of cabins, I served food, I served drinks — I did it all."

Sid stared at his drink and sank into his chair. "Everyone dressed up back then — classy. The music, the entertainers, the food — all first-rate. All the best people wanted to come to the Lodge. And the women, they were all just *sooo* beautiful.

"I was okay-looking then. Thank God for youth. On one of my days off, I might get lucky with a dancer or cocktail waitress, especially if I'd had a good night at the tables.

"I got to take care of some of the big stars. Frank — even Marilyn Monroe when she stayed there. She always stayed in Cabin 3, with the best view of Crystal Bay. I'd go to her cabin and say, 'What can I get for you, Miss Monroe,' and she'd say, 'Oh, you know what, Sid? Just bring me some champagne for now. It's so good to be back at the lake.' Like that. Sometimes she'd hardly be dressed. She'd walk around in front of me half-naked, like it was nothing. Judas priest! It was just the best job I ever had."

Bart let him talk. The customer at the bar was listening to the bartender get sentimental. Bart was patiently taking in all things Sinatra and waiting for Concannon things.

"Like I said, on my days off, I'd go to the tables, mostly at the other casinos around Crystal Bay. I'd wake up in my room late afternoon the next day, just in time to clean up and go back to work at the Lodge. I wouldn't remember much of the night before, but I could always tell if I had a good night. My clothes would be scattered across the floor and there'd be chips and crumpled cash on the floor and in my pants, with maybe a few girls' names and phone numbers on cocktail napkins. Then, if I had a bad night, my pockets would be turned inside-out, empty, except for scribbled notes I couldn't read about who I owed money. Later, there were more bad nights than good nights."

Bart still let him talk. Sid was smoking and drinking more, pausing longer between each recollection. As Sid drank, his Frank Sinatra's Cal-Neva Lodge ashtray was filling, and now held two lighted cigarettes.

"Drinking and gambling. Before I knew it, I owed people money, a lot of money. Then, I got kicked out and banned from the Crystal Bay Club, the Monte Carlo, the North Shore Club, the Nevada Club — all the clubs around the north shore. I drank more and more and started showing up later and later for my shift at the Lodge . . . sometimes not at all. I was on thin ice. Then they made Frank leave, and most of us got laid off. Frank's Lodge was over. When they started hiring back, they said they didn't want me — not reliable, they said. Some friends helped me dry out, and, after a while, they got me work washing dishes at the Yacht Club. Over time, I paid back what I owed."

Sid's eyes closed and his chin began to fall.

"And . . . Concannon?"

Sid's eyes snapped open. He looked lost for a second.

"Concannon? Oh, yeah. Him. The first time I saw Drake Concannon he was with The Captain, old George Whittell." He took a sip from his drink. "It was my first year working at the Lodge, the Cal-Neva. 1956. I didn't know at first who Whittell was, and Concannon was young like me. He looked like some college kid. I could tell right away, Whittell was a big deal, the way everybody treated him. Staff told me to be careful with Whittell, don't disappoint him. They said he's not mean. It's, if he wanted, he could buy the Cal-Neva like he was asking for ice cream on his pie."

Bart crossed his legs and sank back into his chair. He didn't want to interrupt, but he thought of something and leaned forward.

"With his big boat, the *Thunderbird*, was Whittell a member at the Yacht Club?"

"A founding member. Board of Directors' president from the beginning. As a matter of fact, there were stories that he saved Concannon's butt a few times, when other members had trouble with young Concannon and wanted him eighty-sixed from the membership. Only an oddball like Whittell could warm up to Concannon. They said Whittell kept a pet lion in his house.

"So, the *Thunderbird* . . . the Lodge had some piers for guests, inadequate for Whittell's battleship. But, when Whittell and his friends started the Yacht Club, The Captain made sure they put in a dock big enough for the *Thunderbird*. Of course, there was a custom space reserved for The Captain. But Captain Whittell mainly used the Yacht Club as a place to tie up his boat when he'd walk over to the Lodge."

"Makes sense if you have money."

"Oh, and he made sure the Yacht Club had gas available for members down at the piers, at wholesale. The fuel tanks on the *Thunderbird* — it was like filling a swimming pool."

"So Whittell and Concannon hung out together?"

"Yes. When I first saw Whittell with Concannon, I mistook Concannon for one of The Captain's gambler friends, one of his regular buddies. Whittell, he'd bring a buddy or two across Crystal Bay, tie up at the Yacht Club's piers, and walk over to the Lodge. They said Whittell would meet some people he liked, maybe celebrities or entertainers, and invite them and some girls back to his place on the east shore for some high-stakes poker. When I started at the Lodge, Whittell was already getting old, and soon would be in a wheelchair. Then he stopped coming to the Lodge."

"What did Concannon do then?"

"He kept coming, but by himself. As time passed, he seemed to have more money to throw around, and people treated him as someone important. Concannon tried the same thing Whittell did, taking people back across Crystal Bay. But he didn't have a big boat, and he wouldn't have been very successful, anyway. Concannon was no Captain Whittell. After he got divorced, he convinced a few girls to go back across the bay to his place. Most of them didn't find him likeable, and when they got back to the Lodge, they'd warn the other girls. They said he was rich, his waterfront house was grand, but he was dull and a handsy, mean drunk."

Bart sipped his Coke and listened patiently, measuring every word from Sid. As fascinating as Sid's stories were, he wasn't sure what good they would be on this case.

"And there's the lake. Not everybody likes water and boats. Some don't swim. Just a few hundred feet out from the Yacht Club's piers, the bottom drops off like it's going to China. The rough ride across the bay's deep blue water in Concannon's little runabout — it just scared the bejesus out of those girls. Later, I didn't see him taking girls to his boat. Concannon was just a wannabe who tried too hard to fit in. But he did have some connection with the casino people, especially the Italians, maybe Mob. Some of them seemed to know him very well."

Bart put down his Coke. "Jeez, Sid, it was his business, working with casino people."

"There was something special, something beyond normal business — something important."

The unknown gnawed at Bart's stomach. "Wait — what do you mean? How important?" His back stiffened.

"I remember this one night in sixty-three, Sinatra's last year at the Lodge. There was a fight — or disturbance, if you want. I remember it as the week right after Vince Edwards appeared there, early July. Frank worked that week. And, let me tell you, by itself, a fight wasn't unusual. Happened all the time.

"You know, everybody is eating dinner, enjoying the show, and drinking. Always drinking. Someone looks at someone's woman, or someone *thinks* someone looked at his woman, and they exchange words. Then someone moves to confront the offender, and they're already so drunk they fall down, just trying to get up from the table. Maybe a punch is thrown. Usually it misses, and most people don't see anything until it's over. Like a minor dogfight in the street, there's growling, a sudden burst of noise, a cloud of dust, and it's over — and nobody's hurt bad.

"Well, not this time. Concannon and Frank Sinatra himself almost got into a fight over a dancer, my friend Teresa."

Bart fidgeted and twitched in his chair while Sid took the time to light another cigarette and go to the kitchen counter for more ice and whiskey. The smoke was killing Bart. At first, he didn't mind Sid's drinking. He hoped it would relax and loosen Sid up, help him recall more, and speak freely. Now maybe too freely, and slower with each drink.

"You said Teresa?"

"Yes, my friend. She always tried to stay friendly with all of the customers, especially the wealthy ones. You were always living on the edge. The wealthy could tip big, or have you fired. Teresa didn't like Concannon much anyway, and that night he was drunk and had been bothering her for a while. Concannon was in love — that night, anyway. I was *really* in love with her. We used to sneak down to Frank's tunnel and . . . ."

Sid was gone again, and Bart had to reel him back in.

"Teresa and Concannon?"

Sid looked surprised to find Bart in his room. "Yes. Well, you can see why I didn't care for this soft, rich, wannabe, Drake Concannon."

Bart sat up. "But what happened?"

Sid took another long, slow drag on his cigarette. Bart was drowning in smoke.

"Frank had been going around, table-to-table, back-slapping old friends, catching up. And he would always say hello to new customers, too, asking them where they're from, are they having a good time, are they enjoying their food, enjoying the show?

When he was in a good mood, he was a great host.

"I was waiting on tables and not paying much attention to anything beyond my own responsibilities. While I was setting down two plates of Cal Neva Western T-Bone, I heard a shout, and then quiet, like the party just stopped. When I looked up, I saw Frank himself holding Teresa behind him while he talked to Concannon. I didn't see what was wrong, except Teresa looked afraid. Then Concannon grabbed for Frank's jacket collar. Big mistake."

Bart squirmed in his chair.

"There was shouting, then pushing and shoving, and I saw some Italians run over to break up it up — before it became a fight, before Frank and Concannon could throw punches. Didn't notice the Italians before, but they were there in an instant, like they dropped right out of the ceiling. The Italians separated Frank and Concannon, carefully but firmly. Frank would have hurt him if it had continued, because Concannon looked like he didn't fight much past grade school."

Bart was growing impatient. "So, they had a beef. Where's the mob connection?"

"Wait, I'm getting there. See, it was the way the Italians separated those two — that's what was strange. It was special. They treated young Concannon like he was Frank's equal, or better."

Now Bart's brain was locked on hold. He just waited and listened.

"There were three guys with Concannon. Two at his sides held him up and tried to calm him down. But they were very nice to him, like he was a big boss, and they were his employees. The third stood in front of Concannon, like a wall between him and Frank. And then there were two holding back Frank, a big guy, and a smaller guy who, even though he looked younger than the others, acted like he was their leader.

"I didn't understand it. Concannon was just another rich customer to me, like hundreds — just more obnoxious. Big deal if he didn't come back. There were lots more where he came from. Like, one time —"

"And?" Patience could be Bart's friend, but Sid's foot-dragging was driving him nuts.

Sid looked at Bart. "Oh. Then I and a few gawkers moved closer."

Bart leaned forward in his chair.

"The smaller Italian, the young guy near Frank, he grabbed Frank and said something to him. I only heard part of it, a few words in Italian which I didn't understand. Of course, in the casinos you got used to hearing some Italian now and then. I knew just simple phrases. It didn't matter much because I was watching them more than listening. Frank's eyes were scary, and his face tight and red. Frank could be really nice, even to complete strangers, but once you'd crossed him good, it was hard to cool him off."

"And?"

"Sorry. Frank was hot. He wanted to reach past the big guy holding him back and put his hands on Concannon.

"Whatever the young guy said to Frank, then *everything* changed, like night-to-day. Frank shook his shoulders loose, straightened his tie, smiled, and stepped forward to shake Concannon's hand. He told Concannon, for him, whatever he wanted was on the Lodge for the evening. All the Italians took Concannon to a table and sat down with him. Frank took Teresa away and brought a waiter and two of the best girls back to Concannon's table. Frank smiled at Concannon, gave the girls each a fat stack of hundred-dollar chips and told them to, 'Take good care of Mr. Concannon.'"

"Jeez, what did that guy say to Frank?"

"I didn't know until later that night when I had time to ask Teresa. She said Frank saw Concannon bothering her and tried to politely back the drunken slob off. Instead of him calming down, Concannon spit a stream of ugly insults at Frank, and then grabbed for him. Frank was about to sock him when the Italians arrived.

"Bart, I almost didn't believe her. Normally, someone who behaved like that to Frank would've been immediately thrown out and banned from the Lodge. I asked her what changed, what cooled Frank? She said one of the Italians, a young man with a big scar on his neck, said to Sinatra, '*Francesco, è il Mago — lo Stregone!*'"

"Yikes! What's that mean?"

"And when Frank still fought to get at Concannon, the man got right up in Frank's face —"

"But *Sid*, what did he SAY?"

"I'm *telling* you, Bart. He got up in Frank's face and said, 'Frank, Frank! It's *him*. He's the *Wizard* — Concannon's the *Wizard!*'"

* * *

34

Closing Doors

I'll Only Miss Her When I Think of Her

Bart stepped out into the night air, pulling the door to Sid's room shut. While he waited for the traffic on Highway 28 to let him cross to the Yacht Club parking lot, he ran a mental finger down his new, updated to-do-list. He'd better call Al Wexler first.

Looking to his right past the motel office toward *Benny's*, Bart paused. He didn't want to return to *Benny's*, where the cashier had given him the fisheye when Sid asked for the bottle. Bart noticed the motel office had a Pay Phone Here sign outside the door.

Entering the motel office, Bart ignored the desk man's look and went straight to the phone.

"Al? It's Bart. You aren't sleeping already?"

"Hey — naps are both privilege and necessity for the old and infirm. What's up?"

"Remember? I asked you about looking at Concannon's second marriage."

"Oh, yeah. Sorry, just waking up. Yes, the marriage. Wait, let me grab my notes."

Paper-rustling sounds at Al's end of the line kept Bart listening while he waited.

"Got'm. According to Washoe County's database, there *was* a second marriage. Concannon married again in August 2002, to a Rachel Wall. But get this. When I asked for a copy of the marriage license, the Washoe County people were surprised to find their copies of the license *and* the application missing. First I've heard of *that*. And I can't find anything on this Rachel Wall. Bart, she's a ghost."

"Hmmm. Probably a paperwork screw-up."

"Maybe. But it doesn't smell right. Something else — since I asked people about your Drake Concannon, I've been getting calls."

"About what?"

"Remember? I warned you this might happen. They ask, 'What are you working on, Al — who's it for?' Bart, you can't ask about Mob business without seeing some blowback. Be careful. And hey, how about that consulting fee? Maybe we should call it combat pay."

"Okay, Al. I'll try. Thanks. I owe you."

Stepping out into the dark shadows along the sidewalk, Bart caught a flash of movement to his right. Too late.

"Yikes!" Hit hard, Bart's foot caught on the sidewalk and his arms spread for balance as he crashed to the ground.

Bart looked up at the linebacker who'd hit him. It was Martha, the cashier from Benny's. Her face said she was on a mission.

Bart got up on one elbow. "Martha, are you okay?"

She stopped and leaned over Bart. "I just got off my shift. What did you say to Sidney? Why did he want alcohol? Is he all right?" She didn't wait for Bart's reply, hurrying past him to Sid's motel door.

"He's sleeping. I think he's all right," Bart called after her as he got up. He wasn't sure. Bart had left Sid snoring, after moving him onto the bed to sleep it off. He left a few more twenties — guilt money — on Sid's desk before leaving.

"Sidney? Sidney? Are you all right? It's Martha." She knocked hard and put her ear to his door.

Leaving Martha behind without a goodbye, Bart found a break in the traffic and crossed the road. The dimly lit Yacht Club parking lot was busy with people entering and leaving the Club.

After Sid's Wizard story, Bart had barely noticed the rest of what he'd said. Sid would nod off, wake, and then mumble about his time at the Cal-Neva. Mostly about Teresa. Bart had made the mistake of asking Sid, "So, what happened with you and Teresa?"

As he trudged across the parking lot, his shoulders burdened with guilt, Bart felt bad about steering Sid down memory lane. He hadn't thought that asking Sid about Concannon would open that sad door and wondered if Sid could close it again. It was probably a swinging door.

Sid's four-decades-long moan for his lost love, Teresa, had unnerved Bart. It reminded him of the aftermath of his marriage to Sonja. Sid had been drinking so much that maybe he wouldn't remember much in the morning, Bart hoped. Maybe, if Bart found the kidnappers, and brought Drake Concannon back home alive to Mrs. Concannon, maybe he would have at least saved the Concannons' marriage. Maybe.

Rather than help, Sid had added to Bart's problem. The problem Bart had with Drake Concannon was, both for his own and Mrs. Concannons' sake, he wanted to believe, better yet know, that Drake Concannon was a straight shooter, an innocent victim. But everything Bart had heard kept telling him Drake Concannon was connected to the Mob. He'd heard, but didn't want to accept, Al Wexler's description of Drake Concannon as a mechanic, a Mob super technician. Sid's Wizard story backed up the detailed story Al had told him and pushed Bart to accept Mr. Concannon as a Mob fixture.

What Sid said just piled more onto one side of the Drake Concannon scale in Bart's head. The Mob side of the scale was starting down, tilting the Snow-White side up. Now Bart was sure the Mob was connected to Drake Concannon's kidnapping.

Heading straight for the red Isetta, an egg-shaped lump in the Yacht Club parking lot shadows, Bart continued to muse.

Footsteps crunching through the Yacht Club gravel behind him froze Bart's musing. He stopped mid-stride. Something was jabbing him in the back. Certainly, a gun.

* * *

35

Tech Savvy

I'm Beginning to See the Light

"Hey, Dick — hold it right there and get your hands up high. Angie wants to see you." A young man's voice. He gave Bart's spine a sharp poke again.

Raising his hands high, Bart detected several of Angie's presumed friends standing behind him. He reached into his bag of snappy comebacks.

"Jeeez! A lot of dames want to see me, but there's only twenty-four hours in a day — what can I do? And who's this chick, Angie? I'm hoping you mean Angie Dickinson."

"I wouldn't work for no chick. Of course, Angie is a guy, smartass. You ever say that near Angie you're dead — take my advice. And who's Angie Dickson?"

"Dick-*in*-son. Ocean's Eleven with Frank?"

"Frank who?"

"Forget it."

"Hey, Dick, what's with your head. Does it hurt?"

"Only when I think."

"Funny. Maybe you shouldn't be thinking. You're already in trouble."

Angie's friend frisked Bart thoroughly. After he examined Bart's wallet, the friend stood still a moment.

"All right, Lasiter. Wait here and don't move. My friends, they got you covered. Hey, great clothes."

"Okay, okay." Bart stood in place, then slouched to one side and dropped his hands to half-mast. Tough guy. This is where the boss tells Rockford he shouldn't be working on this case, and then they rough him up to show they're serious. Rockford would always be okay, except for a tear in his sport coat. Bart was smart — he didn't own a sport coat.

The gunman, way too young for the suit he was wearing, approached a car angled sideways taking up three parking spaces at the side of the Yacht Club. A pristine, washed-and-waxed, black, '70s Cadillac sedan waited. A tinted backseat window lowered, and Bart's wallet was handed in. Bart didn't see the gun. The man spoke with someone inside the sedan for a minute and returned to Bart.

"Okay, Dick. He's waiting. Move."

They marched to the car with more sharp jabbing in Bart's back.

"Okay. Open it. In you go, Dick."

Bart opened the Cadillac's heavy rear door. It was dark inside — no interior lights. He sat down and closed the door. Bart detected a mixed scent of perfume, cigar, and bourbon. The perfume: A young babe looked back at him from the front passenger seat. The cigar and bourbon: Opposite Bart, a raspy voice came from the dark.

"Take a walk, Honey. Go get yourself a drink or something. I gotta talk to this man."

Without looking back, the babe exited the sedan and, in cocktail dress and high heels, slinked off toward the Club entrance.

In the broken shadows of the back seat, Bart saw a short round man in a dark suit, maybe in his late sixties. His face looked both soft and hard in the dim, strange mix of light from the Yacht Club — warm candlelight from the dining-room windows and ice-cold blue from the Club's neon sign.

"I'm Angie. Thanks for seeing me, Mr. Lasiter."

"What choice did I have, with a gun in my back?"

Angie waved a hand as though he were shooing a fly. An expensive watch and ring caught some light. "Oh, that. That's just Carlo. He's not serious."

"I'd say a gun is certainly serious."

"No, not Carlo. His uncle says we can't let him carry a gun. He's got a ticket for that already. The *gun* is Carlo's new iPhone. He likes to poke it into people's backs. Gives him a kick. Now let's you-n-me talk."

"Okay."

Angie paused, studying Bart's head bandage. "Hurt your head?"

"Naw. It's nothing."

"Okay. I hear you've been askin' around about a friend of ours, Drake Concannon."

"Maybe."

"What is your interest?"

"You have my wallet and, I'm sure, you saw my cards. I'm a private investigator. I do confidential investigations."

"That's good to know, Mr. Lasiter. I might hire you myself, sometime. But what I want to hear you tell me now is, What — Is — Your — *Interest?*"

Bart hesitated, then spit out, "This man hired me to do some background checking on Mr. Concannon . . . because . . . the man wants to open a new Indian casino in California."

The round man exhaled slowly in the darkness.

"Really . . . ."

"Yes," said Bart, gaining confidence. "He told me he heard Drake Concannon is the man, the expert to see for the best setup of gambling machines. But he's new at this and wants to know more before he spends all that money."

"I see. So . . . did you talk to Mr. Concannon?"

"No . . . not yet. I've just been doing research, so far . . . you know, gathering opinions."

"Do you know where he is?"

"No. I've been to his office in Sacramento, but he wasn't there."

"Funny . . . I've been trying to find him myself. Seems I can't. It used to be easy. His wife says he's on a trip. Doesn't tell her where he's going, she says. He always told *us* before."

They both were quiet for a moment.

"Gee, Angie. You never told me what's *your* interest in Mr. Concannon."

Angie grunted.

"A fair question, Mr. Lasiter." Angie exhaled another grunt as he leaned forward to open a compartment built into the front seatback. "A drink? Bourbon, grappa?"

When Angie leaned forward from the shadow, Bart studied his captor. Mostly bald, Angie had a solid, confident face. Also, an old, vicious scar starting under his ear and disappearing around the back of his neck.

"Nothing for me, thanks."

"Okay." Angie settled back into his seat. "I'll tell you, Mr. Lasiter. My interest is like yours, just a lot more personal and long-standing. I represent a private group of investors in the entertainment industry who have employed Mr. Concannon for decades. He does very special work for us. We're not only business associates, but we're also friends. I have known him since I was Carlo's age. Even then, he was a very important man. We're always concerned about his well-being."

"Well, how could I help you?"

"For now, just go on with your research. When we hear from him, I'll tell him you were asking."

"Oh, good. Thanks."

"Wait — there's more. I've decided to hire you now, instead of later."

"I'm kinda busy right now, Angie."

"This won't interfere with your regular work." Angie leaned forward and pulled a roll of bills from his pocket. He peeled off five hundreds and handed them to Bart. "A retainer, Mr. Lasiter. What I want is, when you hear from, or see Drake Concannon, or even just hear a rumor about where he is, you contact me right away, and collect your fee from me — *capisce*?"

"I'm not sure —"

"This is one of those jobs you can't refuse. It's important."

"Oh, okay . . . may I ask why?"

"Normally, I wouldn't waste my time explaining anything to you. You would do what I want without questions, believe me. But this is very different."

Bart listened and stopped thinking about snappy come backs.

"Mr. Lasiter, I'm just support staff for the people I represent. They, in turn, you could say, are support staff for our associates in the east. Our responsibility, my responsibility, is to take care of Drake Concannon. But we don't know where he is now, and all my people are looking for him. If we can't find him soon, our associates back east will learn he's missing, and they will be upset. Then my employers will be in trouble. And then I, and you, will be in trouble. See?"

"Yes."

"Here's my card."

Bart took the card and held it up near the window.

Angelo Stagnetti

775-555-0117

astagnetti@earthway.net

"You have email?"

"Carlo takes care of it for me." Angelo leaned across Bart to open the door. "Now, take your wallet and get back to your work, Mr. Lasiter. I'm going to hear from you, soon. *Capisce?*"

Bart's efficient dismissal reminded him of several first dates. He nodded to Angie as he exited.

Bart moved on autopilot back to the Isetta. He felt relieved to have escaped unharmed from an undefined danger, and with more cash, but his theories of the Concannon case had been tossed like a salad by Chef Angie.

When he got to the Isetta, he turned back in time to see Carlo sliding in behind the Cadillac's wheel. Carlo drove up to the Yacht Club entrance and honked twice.

The babe appeared and posed at the top of the steps. *I want to share this award with my fellow contestants. You are all so deserving. I will never forget you!* In no hurry coming down the steps, she worked her high heels, heel-to-toe, each stair-tread a pedestal, with her different parts moving in concert, as much side-to-side as straight ahead. Performance over, she slipped into the back seat. Carlo's two friends turned a new Mustang north onto Highway 28. The sedan followed. Bart was trying to start the Isetta when their red taillights winked goodbye.

* * *

36

Reckless Bart

It Worries Me

When the Isetta finally started, Bart tried to follow Angie and his friends. The Isetta's dim headlights swept over *Benny's* and Sid's motel as Bart turned onto the highway. There were lights across Crystal Bay on the Nevada shoreline, mostly from Incline Village. He let himself believe he could see lights at Eagle Cove, too.

After pushing the Isetta hard, Bart could see the Cadillac's taillights ahead. His hands gripped the steering wheel tighter. His reflection in the speedometer's glass worried him, the scant light from the Isetta's only instrument highlighting his locked jaw. He tried to catch up but remained far behind them until they turned onto Highway 431, northeast toward Reno. Good. They weren't continuing east on Highway 28 and then south to Eagle Cove.

But Bart's unfocused worrying increased and then peaked. He jammed a silver cowboy boot down on the soupspoon brake pedal, skidded to the side of the road, and switched off the engine.

Think, Bart, think! Angie had said, "He doesn't tell her where he is going, she said." Was Mrs. Concannon maintaining the secrecy she demanded about the kidnapping and therefore protecting her husband? Or was it something else? It was good Angie and his friends were driving toward Reno instead of Eagle

Cove. Bart didn't want Angie interfering with his investigation of the kidnapping, and he certainly did not want Angie to frighten his client. She had enough worry.

But then, had they already been to Eagle Cove? Had they already bothered her? *Would* they bother her?

Mrs. Concannon? Rachel Wall? Bart was stunned. He had never known, nor even missed knowing, her first name, never mind her maiden name.

This job was suddenly not so much fun. Bart's confidence was dissolving. He felt the weight of dread, responsibility, and the unknown, all crushing his narrow shoulders.

Well, that's why she was paying him beaucoup cash. She expected him to ignore his misgivings, wear his big-boy pants, and solve problems.

Bart Lasiter, *Detective*.

He would have to take charge and settle some issues, one way or another. He turned the ignition key, pushed it in, and turned it again to start the engine. He grabbed his sore ear when it hammered back to life and turned the red egg back onto the highway to Nevada. After traveling a mile, he whipped the steering wheel around. The little tires squealed in the night, answering his abrupt command.

Yikes! He hadn't checked for other cars before he U-turned. No one was there, and Bart lucked out again. Reckless Bart, now westbound on a mission, determined to get answers, close to solving this case. It could happen, with just a little more effort on his part. A push from Bart and this pirate house of cards would fall.

One more stop before he would see Mrs. Concannon, a stop for answers.

* * *

37

Vampire

A Lovely Way to Spend an Evening

Approaching O'Hara's, Bart saw light spilling from the windows of the single-wide pirate trailer. He turned right off North Lake Boulevard onto Carnelian Woods Avenue and forced the Isetta uphill. He did a quick U-ey and parked under a redwood tree. He sat in the Isetta thinking.

Could these ersatz pirates really be kidnappers? Scar looked like the ransom-note man, but how could Bart be sure? Who else was a suspect? No individual he could name. These three seemed too flakey and ridiculous to plan and then execute a five-million-dollar kidnapping.

But Bart knew, often crime doesn't make sense. Sometimes, criminals you think are smart are stupid, and those you think are stupid are smart, or at least lucky. Because the stupid ones don't know they're stupid and are expected to fail, they'll try anyway, and sometimes succeed. Bart had to incriminate his pirates or eliminate them as the kidnappers. How could he force the issue?

Bart pulled the Isetta's fabric sunroof closed, slid the side windows shut, and climbed out through the big front door. He locked the Isetta and walked down the hill, enjoying the fresh night air under the stars.

Before crossing North Lake Boulevard, Bart stopped to watch the trailer. The light from the trailer was a dull, multi-colored flickering. Pirates watching TV.

Crossing the street, Bart aimed for the shadow under trees near the bedroom end of the trailer. Up close, he could hear their voices commenting on the TV. Now sure his buccaneers were absorbed watching TV, he moved toward the old pier. He wanted to look under that tarp.

Slipping quietly past the trailer, Bart advanced toward the dock, stopping after a few paces to listen, and then taking a few paces more. He changed his mind again and detoured to the tin shed where they stored their motorcycles.

Bart found the shed unlocked. Lucky. He was not adept at lock-picking, like his friend and Berkeley Police partner, Marty Brooks. Bart slid the thin metal door open, hoping to find an uninjured Drake Concannon. No, just three motorcycles and shelves holding tools and supplies. For Mr. Bocco, Bart recorded the license plate numbers in his waterproof notebook. After closing the door, he started back toward the pier.

Halfway to the pier, a yell from inside the trailer froze Bart. After no one came out, he figured they were just exuberant pirate drunks enjoying their TV.

At the pier, Bart flipped off the light switch on the pole, darkening the pier, except for light from the street and distant buildings. Bart sat still in the shadows for five minutes, waiting for a reaction from the trailer to the pier light going dark. After no pirates left the trailer, Bart crept onto the pier, approached the boat, and lifted the tarp.

He saw a long, low, black, shiny fiberglass hull. This boat looked sleek and very fast. Also, expensive — a fuel guzzler, a rich man's boat. Where would they find the money for this boat, or even gas? Stolen? Halfway down the length of the hull, he saw large letters.

DONZI

Lifting the tarp further exposed a Jolly Roger flag clipped to a wooden pole, lying flat near a chromed socket on the boat's aft deck. After Bart's eyes adjusted to the darkness, he looked down at the boat's transom and saw black script formed by a scant, red outline over the black fiberglass:

VAMPIRE could have been the boat they used to view the red light in Mrs. Concannon's window Friday night, and attack Bart Saturday night. Thinking back to the ransom delivery, he touched the boat. His stomach turned. But, after a second, he felt better, because finding this boat answered a question.

Bart left the pier and sneaked past the trailer's living room, moving back to the bedroom end. He rejected looking through the trailer living room windows, right where they were watching TV, as foolish. So close to cracking this case, he wouldn't take unnecessary risks now. Mrs. Concannon was counting on him.

At the trailer's bedroom end, Bart listened. Listening wasn't enough. He had to see, too. The trailer's window was above his head. He had to get higher.

Looking for something to stand on, he saw a group of cement blocks spread on the ground where another trailer had rested. Gathering the blocks and stacking one on the other, he made a platform for himself. Standing on his pyramid of blocks, he could just see through the dirty back bedroom window into the trailer. The bedroom was empty except for an old mattress and wrinkled sheets. Through the hallway he could see Hook sitting in the living room at the trailer's far end, between Scar's boots and Stumpy's peg leg.

They were watching TV while they talked. Bart couldn't see the television. Hook was looking up, above the hallway door. Bart could hear only parts of their conversation, plus drunken mumbling, and some of the TV dialogue. The TV music and sounds reminded him of his childhood. There were many avasts, maties, and arrrghs, surrounding some talk of prisoners and hostages.

"Scar! Gimme that rum!"

"Hook, this is my rum. You done drunk yurs."

"Scar, an' rewind that part, so's I can sees it ag'in."

"Four times now, Hook."

"So? Go get the other bottle from the Donzi!"

"Hook, that's Patch's rum." We was savin' it to toast Patch on the high seas?"

"Look at Patch. Could he be sayin' something to us?" asked Stumpy.

"Yeah," said Scar. "He's sayin', 'Don't you drink my rum.'"

"The rum! Get it!" said Hook.

"Get it yourself, why dontcha!" said Stumpy. "I dint wanna watch this movie again, enyway. Yu seen it way too much, Hook. Yu promised we could watch *Escape from New York*. Snake Plissken with his eye patch. Yu make us watch what *yu* want, but yu won't watch what *we* want, Scar an' me. Scar an' me had to go down into Sacramento by arselves to see *Pirates of Penzance*, 'cause – *yu* – dint – want – to!"

"Wasn't what we 'spected," said Scar. "Fairies."

Bart frowned. Finding the Donzi was good, but this drunken pirate babble might go on for hours, and yet reveal nothing.

"Back that up. You talked over my fav'rit' part," said Hook.

"No — fast forward. Hook, we seen this twenny times," said Stumpy.

"Hey, I'm workin' the remote, but I ain't takin 'orders," said Scar.

They argued back and forth, still saying nothing interesting to Bart.

"What about the dick, whatever his name," said Stumpy. "He's lucky. But not for us, 'cause he's still out there. He could be a problem."

"You mean Las-i-terd?" said Hook.

"Las-i-terd — hah! That's it. What are we gonna do with him?"

Bart flinched. Not good.

"Yu just wait, Stumpy. Yur right about him bein' lucky, or he'd be smart-assin' Davy Jones right now. We got new plans for the great detective, but they ain't act-tee-vay-ted yet. Been waitin' since Cap'n Jack's to put 'im in his proper place. Yur gonna like what I got planned fur 'im. Boss says we can do it. The best part, we don't haf-ta go get'im — he's gonna come to *us*. When the boss calls, we go into action. Stump, yu just wait."

What? Hook said, "come to us." Bart was already there. Did they know? And who's the boss?

Then, just as Bart remembered the movie had to be *Treasure Island*, Scar jumped into view, and leaned toward Hook.

"It's always Wait. 'Wait, wait, WAIT!' I'm tired of *waitin'*! *WHEN* are we gonna be rid of that old fart Concannon and get our money?"

Hook jumped to his feet and screamed back, "I told yu never say that name!" Then Hook threw a big left into Scar's face, knocking him and the remote to the floor.

Teetering on his pyramid of cement blocks, Bart mumbled, "There's my answer. Now what am I going to do?"

The arguing stopped. Only the TV could be heard. The music swelled. Bart remembered the ending: Robert Newton, as the squinty-eyed, smiling pirate, Long John Silver, was taking the chest full of treasure away in a small boat, and young Jim Hawkins, a softy, was helping him at the end.

The music rose to a big finish.

Hook stood with his face fixed in a trance. Bart remembered the sunny blue sky behind Robert Newton in the final scene, now coloring Hook's face sky blue.

"Look . . . he's raisin' the sail," Hook said.

Scar sat up on the floor. "Stumpy — look! Hook's *cryin'!*"

Rage filled Hook's face as he focused all the strength he had left in his good arm to throw an empty Captain Morgan's rum bottle toward the TV.

He connected.

After an explosion of glass, sound, and light, like a dying star, the trailer went dark. It was quiet for a few seconds until one of the cement blocks under Bart's boots collapsed in pieces.

"Yikes!"

Bart's new boots, two silver, shiny, dogfighting airplanes slashing through the air, crashed like thunder into the trailer's metal siding as he fell butt-to-ground, hard.

He sat in sand, dirt, and silence, holding his breath, waiting for a reaction from the trailer. They surely heard him. His heart raced. Then a noise.

Inside the trailer, a telephone rang.

Bart got up — and ran like hell.

* * *

Part Four

Almost Like Being in Love

38

Vampires in the Night

It Gets Stranger in the Night

Bart stopped running after he had safely crossed North Lake Boulevard and saw no one following him. He speed-walked straight up Carnelian Woods Avenue and caught his breath just as he reached the Isetta. Before he climbed in, he heard a boat's big V-8s thundering awake down on the water.

With the Isetta's lights off, Bart released the handbrake and let the little car roll back down the hill, while he watched for any sign of his trailer rats. When he reached the edge of North Lake Boulevard, he stopped and watched. Seeing nothing, he started the engine and turned east toward Nevada. Passing the trailer, he saw the Donzi was gone. *Vampire* had disappeared into the night.

Bart turned on his lights and drove. It was time for a serious talk with Mrs. Concannon, if it weren't already too late.

Bart worried while he followed the highway to Eagle Cove. He was tired, his head hurt, and the Isetta's engine was thumping his brain into submission. He slid open the side windows, and then the sunroof again. The cool night air rushing in dampened some of the engine noise, the air rush being louder than the engine. The dose of cool oxygen would help him think. He was not ready to analyze and decide, but that was what he had to do.

Bart had left Sid's motel room certain the Mob planned the

kidnapping, and the few prospects for Drake Concannon's future were dim. Using Hook was typical Mob M.O. for jobs like this. The theory says that the Mob would hire outsiders to insulate themselves from suspicion. But the involvement of Hook and friends had been just a theory, until now. Scar's outburst in their trailer convinced Bart the three bogus pirates really were the kidnappers.

Bart had suspected the kidnappers were working for the Mob, but now he believed Angelo. He believed that the Mob was looking but couldn't find Drake Concannon, and, therefore, they weren't involved in his kidnapping.

Unless there was one part of the Mob that didn't know what the other part was doing. Or maybe there could be some other gangsters making their move on the Mob by grabbing one of the Mob's prized assets. Yikes. The tall muddy heap of possibilities put Bart's head into a fog. His bravado about being highly paid for a simple job was fleeing. Why did he ever think he could be a detective? This case was much bigger than anything he had investigated in Berkeley or Sacramento.

Bart was sure of only two things: First, Hook and his not-ready-for-Mensa helpers were not up to such an ambitious plan without a guiding hand, "The Boss." Second, Bart had not found Drake Concannon, dead or alive. But Scar's complaints to Hook implied Drake Concannon was still alive. Somewhere.

Then there were the puzzling differences between what Mrs. Concannon had told him about her husband, and what Bart had learned about him. Bart would talk to her about that tonight. Or maybe later, when the time was right. There might yet be a plausible explanation. Sometimes the wife just doesn't know everything about her man.

Because Bart assumed Drake Concannon might soon be dead, he had to tell the Sheriff everything — or as much as he could. By staying silent any longer, he might lose his license. Well, he wasn't sure. But, if the Mob or other criminal groups were behind the kidnapping, he might need the Sheriff's help and protection, despite Mrs. Concannon's wishes. He had to convince her reporting the kidnapping was essential, for both the Concannons' sake and his own. He would summon clear logic and whatever charm he had left to overcome her fear of law enforcement and earn her cooperation.

With his plan fixed in his mind, and worry about Mrs. Concannon's safety cramping his gut, Bart pushed the Isetta to its limits. Careful with the unfamiliar little car on curves, on the straights he exceeded the posted speed limits and hit 55 mph, at least according to the Isetta's speedometer, through Crystal Bay and Incline Village. Reckless, he pushed the needle into the red on every up-shift, exceeding the engine's rev-limit. Blowing the engine would be disastrous, but he couldn't keep his foot from mashing the throttle after every up shift. Before, he'd never fully appreciated the Klimo's quiet luxury. On every uphill grade, the Isetta's one-cylinder motor pounded his head. He sighed with relief when he let up on the throttle and turned off the highway onto Eagle Cove Road.

This night the outer chain-link gate was locked, and two big Rottweilers ran free behind it. When Bart stopped at the gate, the dogs rushed the chain-link gate, barking and snarling. What now? To them, the Isetta must look like a red hard-boiled Easter egg.

Bart honked, and a flashlight beam appeared from behind the trees. Ramon called the dogs away from the gate and, with a command in German, ordered them into a down-stay fifty feet back from the fence. Ramon looked over the Isetta closely until he could identify Bart. The dogs lay like Sphinxes and watched while Ramon opened the gate.

Bart drove through the gate and stopped, keeping one eye on the dogs. Ramon locked the gate and then walked to the front of the Isetta, where Bart had already pushed the door open. Ramon studied the Isetta's interior before deciding how to enter. After settling himself on the bench seat, he watched Bart grab the steering wheel and pull the big door closed. When Bart started the engine, Ramon's face wrinkled. His right hand reached for the grab bar on the door frame and held on.

As they drove toward the second gate, Ramon yelled more German out the Isetta's sunroof, sending the dogs away into the darkness. Ramon seemed at ease. It meant there had been no trouble here from Angie or anyone else.

When they stopped at the gatehouse, Bart opened the Isetta's door. Ramon got out and opened the iron gate. He waved Bart on through and stayed behind.

Bart drove on toward the house, now more confident Mrs. Concannon was safe. He began rehearsing what and how he would tell Mrs. Concannon, both so she would accept his advice, and to reduce her stress and worry about her husband.

When he reached the turnaround at the garages, he saw the Klimo where he had left it. He parked the Isetta next to it and started toward the stairs. He paused, then came back to close the Isetta's windows and sunroof. No mice, no squirrels. His pill bottles rattled in the deep pockets of his gambler's shirt as he walked.

It was different tonight than before. Walking down the stone path from the garages, the shadows seemed ominous, and he could smell burning wood, and hear music. The tall, wide stone chimney from the living room fireplace spit puffs of smoke and wild glowing orange and red embers into the gun-blue sky. And the lights in the house seemed lower than before.

Isabel greeted Bart at the door.

"Missus Cee 'spect you, Meester Bart. She wait big room."

"Thanks, Isabel."

"Wait. Meester Bart, you hurt your head?"

"It's okay."

Isabel finally noticed Bart's new clothes. Her face started another question, but she stopped. Instead, she asked, "What was the noises, like broken washing machine, by the garage?"

Bart said, "Nothing," over his shoulder and entered. Isabel followed as he moved toward the music.

It was Frank Sinatra's comeback hit, *Strangers in the Night*.

The big room was much darker than it had been on Friday or Saturday night and felt different. The same lights as before were on but dimmed to a third of their former brightness. There were candles, too, something Bart hadn't noticed on the nights before. In the massive fireplace, huge logs burned red, hissed, and popped, spitting little orange comets across the stone floor.

When he saw Mrs. Concannon, she was standing at the picture window looking out into the black over the lake. In the subdued lighting, her blond hair glowed gold against the back of her black floor-length dress. Her left arm stretched above, with her hand high on the window frame. Her hip rested against the window frame too, and her right leg extended a step out to the side. The dress was painted tight to her body, except for what looked like a light-colored stripe down the right side. This vision froze Bart before he could take another step. He was seeing a model, straight from the cover of some thick fashion magazine.

Bart be serious. You have a job to do. After a few sobering seconds, this vision at the window saddened Bart. As beautiful as it was, it made him feel sorry for her. The pain and loneliness she must be feeling. He felt driven to help and protect her.

A jolt of anxiety struck Bart deep in his gut. He remembered this drive to help and protect Mrs. Concannon was the very same feeling he'd had about his new wife-to-be, Sonja, just before he proposed. He remembered how a powerful cocktail of emotions stole his sobriety back then. It was the draw of both her beauty and innocent frailty, like Mrs. Concannon's, mixed with that urge to protect. He believed everything would be okay if he could just protect Mrs. Concannon. But now he had to be more aware and in control of his emotions and think clearly. Besides, Mrs. Concannon was already married.

He coughed loudly enough to be heard above the music.

Mrs. Concannon turned from the window.

Bart could see her hair had been hiding the high collar of her dress. Now the light-colored stripe in her dress had disappeared.

"Oh, Mr. Lasiter! I was so worried about you. Are you all right?"

Her composure changed when she noticed his thrift-store clothes. She looked puzzled, then recoiled when her eyes found his silver cowboy boots. What's happened to him trying to help the Concannons must worry and embarrass her,

She brought her eyes back up to his head. "And look at that bandage on your head. Are you in pain?"

"Oh, no — it's not so bad."

"Oh, you are just so, so brave. Please, allow me to at least get you something to eat."

"Well, yes, I am hungry."

"Good. What would you like, Mr. Lasiter?"

"A sandwich?"

"Of course. Isabel, will you please make a sandwich for Mr.

Lasiter?"

"*Por supuesto,* Missus Cee," Isabel said and left.

"And something to drink, too, Mr. Lasiter?"

"Oh, don't go to any trouble. I'll have some of whatever you've got. Thanks."

"Yes. Now, please sit down, Mr. Lasiter." She nodded toward the sofa facing the big picture window. "I want to hear what you've learned."

She walked toward the bookcases and went behind the bar. He noticed that what he had thought was a stripe on her dress, was a long slit from her hip to the floor. Every stride on her black high heels brought her naked leg in and out of the slit in the dress.

Behind the bar, she paused and looked up toward the ceiling. "Oh, why don't we wait for your drink? I'll fix you something nice later, Mr. Lasiter, when Isabel brings your sandwich." She reached under the bar, and the music volume went down.

"Sure, okay. Later."

Mrs. Concannon left the bar and sat on the sofa at Bart's left side. She stretched her long legs out to rest her feet on a thick glass plate covering a slab of driftwood. She was at least as beautiful as she had been at breakfast the morning before in the gazebo. Except, now she was wearing an anklet of black onyx beads. The beads' shape was as he remembered her earrings that morning in his office. Black hearts.

Her feet settled next to a glass dish of exotic flowers. "I'm exhausted, Mr. Lasiter, mostly with worry. Please forgive me."

"Don't apologize. I think you've held up well, really well."

Trying to change the subject, he said, "Tell me about these flowers?"

"Oh, yes. They're orchids. My florist in Reno flies them in from South America. The black one is *Schunke's Maxilleria,* and the black striped one is *Vampire's Dracula.* I just love them. Captivating, the black, aren't they?"

"I guess, but they're not really black, just almost black."

"They are black."

He nodded and fell silent. Yikes. He was beginning to feel uneasy about all her black things. When she'd first come to his office, he thought all of the black was really cool. Now, more important than colors, he had to steer her to thinking about the Sheriff.

"You know, before this trouble, my husband and I had really enjoyed our life together here at the lake." She moved her legs to stretch. The slit fell open. "It was paradise to us. The water and boating in the summer, the snow on the trees and mountains in the winter — it's all a paradise." Her eyes changed focus. "Snow — I grew up with snow, every winter. A new, white, snow is so . . . so *clean*, and pure. White, no red. A new snowfall would often begin at night. I remember as a child watching the snow late at night from my bedroom window. It has a gentle touch that covers the past, that covers everything. A new snow makes everything new and innocent. It's just so beautiful when you wake to it the next morning. It's like starting over . . . a true rebirth."

She returned from wherever she'd been and turned to Bart.

"What I mean, a kidnapping anywhere else would always be terrible, tragic. But here? That's why this awful kidnapping is so unthinkable, so out of place." She saw Bart looking at her legs and moved them to close the slit.

Bart blushed. He'd tried not to stare but had failed.

"All I can think about is my husband Drake's safe return."

"That's why we must talk about some things. Tonight, now, Mrs. Concannon."

She seemed to have not heard Bart and ran her hand slowly over her leg. Her long fingers with red-painted nails smoothed the dress. "You know, this dress is one of Drake's favorites. It's Chinese silk. It's from my dressmaker in Hong Kong."

Bart looked around the room, away from her legs. Burning candles in black-iron sconces on the walls flickered throughout the room. The fire in the walk-in-sized stone fireplace crackled and filled the room with shadows and heat. The entire scene suddenly reminded Bart of those old black-and-white vampire movies where a young, innocent man worries that his fiancé has fallen ill. The vampire silliness cheered him momentarily as he discounted the possibility of seeing Bela Lugosi this evening. A black boat somewhere in Carnelian Bay was the only vampire Bart knew. Maybe now an orchid, too.

When she saw him look at the fire, she said, "You know how

chilly it can be here in the evenings, even in the summer. All this stone."

Bart nodded, but he was warm.

"Now, why don't you tell me what you've learned in your investigation?"

"Okay, Mrs. Concannon. First, were you contacted by any casino people? Italians? Maybe an Italian guy named Angelo or Angie?"

"No, Mister Lasiter. I have told you before that I do not know any casino people. I have no reason to talk to them."

She denied talking to Angelo. So, he would have to —

"Now, Mr. Lasiter, you were going to tell me what you've learned."

She leaned toward him and stared into his eyes.

"Yes, Mrs. Concannon. To begin with, I've identified three local criminals as the kidnappers. They are outlaw bikers who have been in and out of trouble with the law for decades. Also, they see themselves as pirates, which would explain the ransom note's pirate symbols. They live in a trailer near O'Hara's Boat Yard, over on the California side in Carnelian Bay. But, from what I've been able to see, Mr. Concannon is not there."

"Splendid work. How did you ever find them?"

"Just my normal detective methods — following leads and hunches." That sounded better than Dumb Luck. "I first ran into them down in Sacramento."

"What are these people like, Mr. Lasiter? Do they seem reliable? Will they release my Drake, now that they have the ransom?"

"Sorry, Mrs. Concannon. I think they're neither reliable nor predictable. We followed their instructions exactly, to a T, but they shot at me anyway and left me to drown in the lake. They don't follow rules. Who knows what they might do?"

"And they are the only ones involved?"

"The only ones I have seen, but they don't look like they could normally take on a job this big. It's way beyond the petty theft they are used to. Worse, they don't look at all capable of planning something like this. I'm certain someone else planned this whole thing and then hired them."

As she slipped out of her shoes, he saw again her long

slender toes, and her toenails painted blood red. She drew her legs back from the table. After pivoting to face Bart, she folded her legs beneath her on the sofa cushion, opening the dress slit up to her hip. She leaned toward him and stared into his eyes. "Oh, they do sound like evil men. But, my goodness, who could be directing them?"

Her eyes were doing strange things to him. He looked away and tried to concentrate on what he had to say. "I'm sorry to say this, Mrs. Concannon. Maybe you didn't know enough about your husband's casino business. I'm sure he's had associates involved in organized crime, and I believe he, too, is connected. Maybe involved for years, decades before you met him."

"No. I don't believe it! I know in his job he is sometimes forced to deal with questionable casino people, but organized crime? I don't believe it. I'm sure he would have told me. We were always honest and open with each other."

"Sorry, Mrs. Concannon, but a husband doesn't always tell his wife everything. Possibly some faction of the Mob, or other criminals, ordered his kidnapping. Maybe some of them had some grievance with him and did it to teach him a lesson, or to get back some money they thought he owed them."

"Are you sure?"

"No, but it's likely."

"That's horrible, just horrible. Have you told anyone else this, or mentioned anything about Drake's kidnapping?"

"No. You asked me not to. No, only you, Mrs. Concannon." She smiled.

"This is unbelievable, Mr. Lasiter. What do we do now?"

"We have to go to the Sheriff. Now, tonight. It's no longer the simple kidnapping we started with."

She looked out at the lake while he explained.

"If it had gone the way we'd hoped, no one would know, and your husband would be home safe now. But it didn't. Now my license is at risk. They tried to kill me. And — this is an awful thing to say to you — I'm afraid, because they have the ransom, they have no incentive to leave your husband alive. Sorry."

"Oh, please don't say that." She looked down at the floor near the bookcase. "I'm sure that Drake is still alive."

"I hope you're right, Mrs. Concannon. But we're running

out of time. If he's still alive, we've got to act now. We've got to call the Sheriff and do it tonight. Now, here's what —"

"Oh, Isabel! It's you. I was so interested in what Mr. Lasiter was telling me that I didn't hear you arrive."

Bart saw Isabel standing behind the sofa holding a silver tray. The interruption upset him, but seeing the tray reminded him he was hungry. On the tray she'd plated a sandwich of thick slices of French bread, with black olives on the side.

Mrs. Concannon stood and examined the sandwich. "Oh, thank you, Isabel."

"White turkey and avocado with Provolone on the Pugliese bread. Okay, Missus Cee?"

"Will that do, Mr. Lasiter?"

"Thank you, Mrs. Concannon. It looks good. Thank you, Isabel."

Isabel rolled her eyes toward Mrs. Concannon and said to Bart, *"De nada,* Meester Bart."

"Isabel, I'll take that for him." She took the tray and smiled.

"Thank you, Isabel. We won't need any more help tonight. You may return to your bungalow. I'll be out on the lake early tomorrow morning, for most of the day. Please take tomorrow off for yourself. All right?"

"Yes, Missus Cee. Thank you." Isabel smiled and left the house.

"You're going boating tomorrow, Mrs. Concannon?"

"No, no. Isabel is such a sweetheart. She almost refuses to take a day off if she thinks I'll be here. It's a little white lie for her benefit."

"I see. Yes, she seems very dedicated."

"Oh, I could tell you stories about her."

"Yes, maybe later. Now, our call to the Sheriff. Where's your telephone?"

She took one hand off the silver tray to touch his arm, her fingertips smoothing the hair on his forearm, lingering over the old bullet-wound scar. Looking straight into his eyes, she said, "Let's have that drink first. You and I must think about what we will tell the Sheriff."

* * *

39

Black Magic

Like a leaf that's caught in the tide

Mrs. Concannon carried the tray to the bar. She reached behind, and the lights faded from dim to off, leaving only the fire and candles. While the candles flickered, the music came back up louder, louder than when Bart had arrived. It was still Sinatra.

After the tingling from her touch had left his arm, Bart called out from the sofa loud enough to be heard over the music, "For me, just Coke . . . or root beer is fine. Sprite's okay."

"Oh, all right, Coke it is Mr. Lasiter. Classic. But I think you need a real drink."

"Exactly. Classic. How did you know?"

After a minute, she brought a glass of Coke to Bart.

"Thank you." The coke tasted slightly off. Maybe she was out of Classic and mixed it with diet. He drank it all. "I was thirsty."

"Don't worry, there will be more. That was just a starter. I'm working on something better for you."

"Okay. Thank you. So, you like Sinatra?"

"Oh, yes. I'm a big fan. After a misunderstanding, Mister Sinatra sent Drake a crate of all his albums. He autographed each one to Drake."

"Wow. My father is a fan. And I am, sort of."

Bart listened to the music, short random selections from

Sinatra's sixties and earlier albums. He looked around the room, leaned back into the sofa cushions, and reflected on his good fortune. Money in the bank, a beautiful, wealthy client, and Bart Lasiter, *Private Detective,* right here, kicking back in a dream-worthy, classic, waterfront home on Lake Tahoe. Big-time Bart. Yes, it's true, he had been shot and almost drowned, but he'd survived. Feeling happy, he turned to her.

She was swinging a big ice pick at something in the bar sink.

"I'm preparing a special drink, especially for you."

"Oh . . . okay."

She set two heavy glasses filled with chunks of ice up on the bar and splashed dark amber liquid from a decanter over the ice. She came from behind the bar carrying the drinks and walked toward the big window. Her legs moved as if she had rehearsed every step. The slit in her dress alternately displayed and hid her leg, almost in rhythm with the music. And every step held Bart's attention.

She stood at the window and held a drink out to Bart. "Come to the window, Mr. Lasiter. Let's look at the lake together while we enjoy our drinks and talk. The lake calms me, centers me, and helps me think."

Water. She was exactly like Bart. The lake calmed her and helped her think. That pleased him. But could they see much of the lake at night? He stood up and joined her at the window. He accepted the drink she had prepared for him, and then backed off a respectable distance. Both of the drinks looked the same to Bart. Swirling the ice around in his drink, he asked, "What is it?"

"It's Jack Daniel's and ice. Unspoiled by water or soda, as my husband likes to say. It's Drake's favorite. Let's drink to him, my husband."

To Bart's taste, hard liquor was just too strong. But he was tired, and maybe it might help his sore head. He remembered Jack Daniel's was Frank Sinatra's favorite whiskey. He knew how stressed Mrs. Concannon had to be now. He wanted her to be comfortable and wondered if he could refuse her anything.

"To Drake," she said, facing him.

"To Mr. Concannon," he said.

He took a modest sip of his drink. It was strong and had a

thick taste of smoke, or charred wood. And the ice chunks made his upper lip cold. He sipped a little more.

She had a generous gulp of her drink and smiled at him. After another swallow, she kept her glass up near her mouth.

Bart's eyes were drawn to her fingers around the glass. They were long and delicate. Her fingers gripped the glass firmly, yet kept moving, slowly and fluidly, as if they had no bones. Her fingers reminded him of a picture of a Hindu goddess with many arms. But when he tried to fix the picture in his mind, the arms moved, and the goddess started changing colors, from bronze to dark green, to dark red, and then black, except the arms always ended with painted red nails. He forced himself to look away.

When Bart looked back at her face, he saw just her hand with the drink, and her eyes above the rim of the glass.

Bart was losing himself in her eyes. There was something familiar about that mesmerizing deep blue color, more intense than he remembered. Her eyes were too strong for him. Before he could decide what was familiar, he had to look away again.

He looked around the room. Something was different. The furniture was moving and changing shape.

When he looked back, her eyes seemed to be measuring him, as if she were waiting for something. From above the rim of the glass, her eyes spoke. "Have a big drink, Mr. Lasiter. Please relax. You've worked so hard for us."

Bart felt an unfamiliar tranquility, then took a mouthful of his drink. He felt it burn in his throat and he almost choked.

She lowered her drink away from her face and smiled. "It is so fortunate that I found you. I have a warm, comforting feeling of optimism and calm now that you are here. Somehow, I know this will all turn out well." She sipped more of her drink without moving her eyes from his. "Isn't it mysterious, the way life can change so dramatically in just a few days? Who could have imagined that we'd be here together tonight?"

Such a sudden and complete change in his circumstances was beyond Bart's imagination. But he still wanted to maintain his equilibrium and steer her back to their immediate problem with the Sheriff.

"Do you dance, Mr. Lasiter?"

"Oh, I knew a box step once. Wait . . . why?"

Her questions were distracting him. Bart wanted to talk about the Sheriff and what they had to do. She was probably doing this on purpose, asking questions to avoid the unpleasant facts confronting them tonight. He would have to take control and guide her down the right path.

"Because sometimes . . . like watching the lake, dancing calms me when I worry. Would you please dance with me?"

"Oh." He blushed again.

"I've embarrassed you, have I not? You needn't be. Even though Drake isn't back home yet, even though I would never do anything at all to dishonor my husband, I feel drawn to your strength, to your shield, to you, my knight. Mr. Lasiter, I feel I must be closer to you tonight."

The leg emerged from the slit and moved toward him.

He took a big gulp of his drink. Then another, the drink almost choking him as it warmed his throat. He wanted to say something, anything, but the whiskey had taken his voice.

"May I call you 'Bart'?"

He managed a raspy, "Okay."

She approved with a smile.

He had to look away again. Now the flames from all the candles were strange. The candle flames waved in concert as if one. The fireplace was no respite. It was like staring into her eyes, except the blue was only at the core of the fire burning the logs, surrounded by deep red from the embers. The outer yellow flames hissed and danced and moved like her fingers had on her drink. He was afraid the flames would dance out of the fireplace and across the floor to burn him. Shadows cast by the flames were crawling over the ceiling timbers.

He tore his gaze from the fire and found her eyes still on him.

"Oh . . . you want to dance?"

"Listen to the music, Bart. It's just for you. Listen."

He did. He now noticed that the same song had been playing again and again.

She moved closer to him, so close he could no longer see the slit or her leg. He found himself in a cloud of her perfume. Her perfume and the drink were doing something to him. Something like the flames. Something was happening he didn't understand. But now he could really hear Frank.

She absolutely did look like an angel now. If her Drake Concannon were dead, wouldn't she need a new man in her life? Someone to take care of her, protect her, and watch over her?

The music was filling his head.

"Do you hear the music now?" She smiled. "Let's dance, Bart."

"That old black magic has me in its spell . . ."

He heard the music, and it held him speechless.

"That old black magic that you weave so well . . ."

"Bart, I'd like to kiss you."

"Those icy fingers up and down my spine . . ."

She reached her hand around him and slowly slid her fingers up and down his spine.

"The same old witchcraft when your eyes meet mine . . ."

Her eyes met his and wouldn't let go.

"The same old tingle I feel inside . . ."

He felt a tingle inside.

"And then that elevator starts its ride . . ."

He felt his knees weakening.

"And down and down I go . . ."

His chin was dropping.

". . . and I'm aflame . . ."

He felt warm. His face was hot.

"Aflame with such a burning desire,

That only your kiss can put out that fire . . ."

He saw Mrs. Concannon's lips rising to kiss him.

" 'Cause you are the lover I have waited for,

The mate that fate had me created for . . ."

Suddenly, he felt an ancient bond with her.

". . . your lips meet mine . . ."

What was happening?

". . . down, down and down I go . . ."

Why hadn't he noticed the intricate carvings in the ceiling timbers before? He heard chunks of ice bouncing off the floor.

". . . round and round I go . . ."

The ceiling timbers began to rotate.

". . . In a spin . . ."

". . . Like a leaf that's caught in the tide . . ."

He saw his glass floating in the air above him. Then, like a truck from Hell, the cold stone floor raced up and slammed into the back of his head.

". . . I should stay away but what can I do? . . ."

Bart heard his own voice somewhere, singing:

"I should stay awake but what can I do?"

While Bart fought his fall into darkness, he dreamt he saw pirates standing over him and a blond woman in a black dress eating a sandwich.

* * *

Part Five

Davy Jones's Locker

40

Concannon's Mines

You Got the Best of Me

Bart woke inside a musty stone silo. He was being carried to the top. No, maybe it was a well, a dry well, and he was being carried to the bottom. His head wasn't right. He was upside down, and someone was carrying him *down*, not up, down a spiral iron staircase deep into the earth, the air growing colder as they descended.

As the pirates from his dream carried him down the spiral stairs, he'd woken to an unfamiliar version of consciousness. The alcohol, and his head hitting the floor, had done something strange to him. Bart was like one of those who wake up during surgery, and can see and hear and feel pain, but cannot move, and no one around them knows they are awake.

Something else about that strange dream bothered him. He remembered being on his back on the floor. From there, he had seen the bookcase behind the bar move. The Nancy Drew novel section swung into the wall and became a doorway. A familiar metal hook had pulled the bookcase back, the same hook now between Bart's belt and pants, next to his '57 Chevy buckle. The hook was holding him up while others carried and guided his head and feet down the stairs. It was making him dizzy, going around and around upside down.

"Drain, drain the bowl, each fearless soul," sang a pirate.

It wasn't a dream. It was a nightmare.

They reached the bottom and left the staircase through an arch lined with flat pieces of the same stone Bart had seen throughout the Concannon house. The arch was the beginning of a narrow, stone-walled hallway, gently winding downhill, further into the earth. Bare bulbs spaced along the plastered ceiling lit the hallway, highlighting the spider web of mortar between the flat stone pieces lining the walls and floor. The mortar spider webs seemed to move and taunt him. The light from each bulb left a trail in his eyes that only disappeared when he came to the next bulb. Something wasn't right.

Soon, he could see beneath him narrow-gage iron railroad tracks set into the hallway's stone floor. The pirates carrying him stopped and dumped him onto the floor between the rails. The floor was cold. He wanted to get up. He couldn't move. The boots near his head were too familiar. They belonged to Hook.

"Wait here. I gotta plan fur 'im." Hook walked away down the hallway, whistling a pirate ditty while he dragged his hook, screeching against the stone wall. Out of sight, around a bend in the hallway, Hook spoke with someone.

Bart couldn't make out what they said, or recognize the other person, but he learned he could swing his eyes around, even if his head didn't move much. He saw at the left side more stone hallway wall. On the right, he saw an arched doorway cut into the wall, leading to a large, glowing room.

Yikes! He looked through the doorway and saw wondrous things. Was he far away in Egypt, dreaming of Tutankhamen's tomb? Gambling devices of every kind, whole and in parts, lay everywhere about the room. At least fifty slot machines lined the walls, each machine a different design, all lighted, showering the floor, walls, and ceiling with a dancing rainbow of colors. Again, streaky trails followed when Bart moved his eyes.

A huge gaming table filled the center of the room. Bart couldn't see its top surface, but the bottom surface had about twenty holes, filled from above with roulette wheels.

Under the table, boxes overflowed with machine parts. Parts of slots, wheels, and what Bart guessed were coin and bill handlers. Bart imagined a casino after an 8.5 earthquake.

Hook came back, stood with his thumb and hook tucked

into his dirty jeans, and barked, "Pick up the Dick an' foller me."

They dragged Bart down the hallway to a wooden door in the left wall. Hook opened the door, and they carried Bart in.

In the center of the room, they let Bart fall to the stone floor. From another area, he heard music. It was still Frank Sinatra.

"Arrrrrrgh." Hook kicked Bart in the ribs. "Yu stay put, Romeo, if ya knows what's good fur-ya."

Hook and the others left the room, latching the door behind them. At least they didn't tie him up.

No window in the door, just a screened ventilation aperture above the door, but Bart could hear them out in the hall. He was distracted by the sound of violins.

Frank again, singing *Prisoner of Love*.

Bart lay on his side on the cold stone. Now he could move both his eyes and head. Maybe the rest would follow. He was in a workshop. Fluorescent tubes on the ceiling hurt his eyes. The long, cold-white tubes wouldn't stay straight for him. They looked like noodles, or worse, glowing worms. He tried to ignore the light worms and look around.

Machines dominated the middle of the room. Drill presses, metal lathes, and, right above him, a Bridgeport mill. He had seen machines like these before, in the basement garage of a Berkeley cop who was a part-time gunsmith.

Small-parts cabinets and engineering reference books rested on wooden-topped steel workbenches, set end to end along the stone walls. Some of the workbenches held labeled drawers and cabinets in their bases. Fitted below other benches, beehives of cardboard tubes held rolled blueprints. On the walls above the benches, panels of pegboard displayed a selection of hand tools, clamps, and jewelers magnifiers. Drawings, tables, sketches, and scribbled notes pinned to cork boards covered other walls. Grinders and vises of different sizes occupied the edges of some benches. A dentist's drill and fluorescent lamp sat attached to another bench.

Bart didn't know who else was down in the tunnels. He only knew Hook was there. The others must be Scar and Stumpy, but there might be more. He didn't know what happened to Mrs. Concannon, but did he detect her perfume in the hallway?

Bart heard voices from down the hallway, arguing. Hook

and another man.

A woman screamed — it was Mrs. Concannon!

Scream or not, her voice thrilled Bart. She was alive. But what was happening?

"Drake! *Believe me.* He'll kill us both if he must. Give him the code! Let them take the money. We'll still have the house and your income. *Stay alive!* Please, Drake, I want you safe!"

Bart heard some muffled conversation he didn't understand. Quiet conversation was hard for him to hear because of the stone walls and the music playing upstairs. Now Frank was singing *Night and Day.*

More low conversation, and then silence. Then mechanical noises, like a metal gate dragged open across the stone floor.

Hook yelled, "Got it! We got it!"

"Well, well, Mr. Cee. After holdin' out on us, that weren't so hard, were it? Finally, ya gave it up. Where'd a fat land rat like yu get all this cash? More than ya need, fur sure. Feel better now? Just think a it like yur doe-natin' to the old mariners' retirement fund. As their spokesman, I thanks ya."

"Untie me. You promised to let us go!"

"I'd like ta give ya something, in return fur-yur doe-nation. Howdja like a anchor, a big one? You could hold it tight to yur fat chest while yu go swimming in your lake. If it was up ta me, right now we'd be asking ya ta see fur us how deep is the lake. With the anchor, it won't take too long an' bore ya, gettin' ta the bottom."

"Where is my wife? Cut me loose. You promised to let us go if we gave you the money!"

"Now, now, Mr. Cee. I *did* say that, truly, I did. But really, who would trust a guy like me? I thunk ya was supposed to be a real *smart* guy. A *GENIUS!* But yur just another college boy, book-smart an' plain *STUPID!* Eagle Cove? Arrrrrrgh — now it's *PIRATE'S COVE!*

"You'd better let us go, right now. Before it's too late."

"Late fur what?"

"You'll see if you don't untie me."

"No chance, rich boy."

"What are you going to do with us?"

"Yu'll find out, real soon, Gramps. Me, I'd still like ta make you walk the plank. Don'tcha want ta tell me how deep is this lake? Deeper 'n whale shit, I'm sure. Ah, but first, I almost furgot. There's someone here ta see ya."

Bart heard some light footsteps, a few words he couldn't make out, and then Drake Concannon's rising voice:

"You . . . you . . . *La Strega!*"

BLAM, BLAM!

And then a woman's singing voice carried throughout the underground complex:

"Night and daaaaaay —" BLAM, BLAM! "Yoou arre —" BLAM! "All done!"

* * *

41

Bart's Dilemma

What'll I Do?

The gunshots and eerie singing echoed down the hallway, followed by complete silence, except for the percussion notes from an empty cartridge casing dancing across the stone floor.

The gunshots shocked Bart — he hadn't seen any guns but his own on this case, and his gun was in the Klimo. Then a spike of pain at the back of his head reminded him of *why* he fell into the lake. No guns, right? Duhh.

When the pain hit Bart, his body jerked. Surprised at the movement of muscles that he thought weren't working, he tested moving his arms and legs. They responded enough to give him hope. If he could get back on his feet, he'd have a chance to turn the tables on the buccaneers, or at least escape. Concannon's workshop was filled with potential weapons.

While Bart stretched his muscles, he visualized sneaking back down the hallway, up the spiral staircase, through the bookcase, and into the house. If he could find Mrs. Concannon's phone, he'd call the Sheriff. If he couldn't find the phone, he could take the Klimo, crash through the gate, and drive along the highway to the first phone he could find.

The Sheriff would take care of Hook's crew and free Mrs. Concannon. Bart didn't really have a personal stake in this. He wasn't Bogie's Sam Spade. He had no Archer. Maybe Aggie was his Archer. But no one had killed his partner.

Bart's dilemma was, if he left now, Mrs. Concannon would still be a prisoner down the hallway somewhere. How long would it take the Sheriff to arrive? After he had escaped from the workshop, it might be fifteen minutes before he could reach a house phone, and at least a half-hour before he'd find a phone down the road — if he could find his Klimo keys — and then more time to get the Sheriff to Eagle Cove. Two hours later? Could he take the chance Mrs. Concannon would still be alive?

What if he stayed to fight? If he got as far as the Klimo, he could retrieve his gun and come back down the spiral staircase. With a gun, he knew he could handle the three pirates.

But who else was down there? Who was the singing woman with the gun? He knew Mrs. Concannon was held in another room. Isabel? Did Hook have a girlfriend? Why didn't Hook know how Concannon earned his money?

Bart was, again, afraid of all he didn't know. What if they had taken his gun from the Klimo? What could he do back in the house and the tunnel without the gun?

He decided. He would go for the phone and the Sheriff and hope the Sheriff would be in time to save Mrs. Concannon.

Where were his pills? He rolled around and couldn't feel anything in his pockets. His pills were gone, his cash was gone, and the keys to the Klimo and the Isetta were gone.

Bart struggled to stand up on his feet. If he were to escape, he couldn't afford to wait any longer. He grabbed a hammer off a workbench and limped toward the door. He heard Hook yell.

"What good's a hostage what's all hurt?" Hook roared with gut-twisting laughter. "All right, Buccaneers. Just *look* at all that treasure! Ya knows whats-ta do. Step lively now!"

Hook ordered someone to start loading cash. Footsteps in the hallway said Hook's crew was now in action. Bart's chance to sneak down the hallway without notice was gone. He'd have to wait for something to change.

BOOM!

* * *

42

Hot Cash

It Happened in Monterey

"Ahhhhrgh! *Help* **me!"**

"Hook! Ramon's on fire."

"Get that fire stingwisher!" screamed Hook. "The cash is burning. Fur-get Ramon!"

"Where is it? Throw somethin' on him!" Scar yelled.

Bart heard pitiful moaning, and then the steady swoosh of a discharging fire extinguisher.

"Put that fire out!" yelled Hook.

"Oh, oh — Ramon's in bad shape," said Scar.

"Well, shit!" said Hook. "That tricky old fucker Concannon had one more booby trap. He said, 'You'll see.' Didn't think he had it in 'im. Ramon hardly stepped in there when somethin' blowed up, shootin' fire *all* over. It was just like Nam again."

"Hook! Will ya just look at Ramon!" yelled Scar.

"Looks like we lost at least ten grand. Scar! Get Ramon out-a-the way. We gotta get this cash loaded. We gotta *schedule* to keep! Stumpy, where ar ya? Come in here!"

"Yeah, Hook?"

Bart could hear Stumpy's peg-leg hitting the stone floor.

"Go in the money cage with this sack an' start loadin'."

"You sure it's safe, Hook? No more booby traps?"

"O' course it's safe. There was just that one. I checked."

"Okay, if you say, Hook."

"Hey, Stump. I'm goin' ta get the carts an' more sacks. Be right back."

Outside Bart's workshop door, Scar pressed Hook.

"How'd this happen, Hook? You told us you disarmed the booby traps. You gotta know what *I* think about fire!"

"Nuttin ta worry 'bout, Scar. Just a ac-cee-dent. How's Ramon?"

Scar cleared his throat and got his voice back under control. "Ramon . . . he won't be sailin' with us . . . enny-more."

"Sad, Scar, but more treasure for us. Now go help Stumpy load cash."

Hook waited in the hallway, probably for more explosions. Bart decided to hammer Hook if he came through the door.

After several minutes, Bart heard Hook clomp back down the hallway and yell, "Stumpy! Yur slowin' us down with yur leg. Take a timeout an' check the Dick. Keep a eye on 'im 'til I needs ya."

"Aye, aye, Hook. But I *like* handlin' cash!"

"Let's all of us do ar jobs, like a real team, an' yu'll soon be swimmin' in cash."

"Aye, aye, Hook."

Stumpy's slide-thump, slide-thump was coming up the hallway. Bart was afraid to move now, not knowing where the others were, especially Hook. Bart had always liked the cut-off-the-head-and-the-snake-dies theory, and Stumpy was at best the snake's tail. He quickly returned the hammer to its place and stretched out on the floor where they had left him. Maybe he could learn something from Stumpy.

The door flew open, propelled by Stumpy's peg leg, now pointed at Bart. Stumpy smiled and looked down at his wooden leg.

"How about that?"

Stumpy stood on his good leg while his hands gripped the door frame. He let go of the door frame, slide-thumped in, and closed the door.

"Say, Dick, what's happenin'? Awake now, huh?"

Bart looked up at Stumpy but didn't move.

"Well, Stumpy, I've been resting here making plans to use

all these tools to build a rocket ship to take me away from here, but I haven't finished because I ran out of coffee."

"Smart-ass, that's what Hook calls you. You're a wharf rat to me."

"Wasn't I a *bilge* rat before?"

"Maybe."

"Well, am I a wharf rat or a bilge rat? Decide."

"It's the same, Dick. A wharf rat is just a wharf rat, till he jumps from the wharf to the ship an' heads for the bilge. *Then* he's a bilge rat." Stumpy looked up and paused to think. "But if the bilge rat jumps ship back to the wharf . . . ."

"Very scien-terrific. But my head hurts. I still can't move. Where are my pills?"

Stumpy laughed and pulled a plastic bottle from his jeans, the antibiotics. Shaking the bottle near his ear showed a few pills remained. "These? What kinda pills are these? I ate the whole other bottle an' most of these, an' dint get no buzz.'

"They were antibiotics and pain killers, not the kind you get high on."

"Figured that out."

"Why are you here?"

"Hook says ta watchya."

"You guys did something to my legs. I don't know if I'll ever walk again."

"Good. Otherwise, I'd hav-ta tie you up."

Stumpy looked at the workbench-mounted tools. "Far as walkin' goes — hah! We got plans for your walkin' again, walkin' to Dee-Jay's locker, that's fur sure."

"Hey, how long am I going to be here?"

"'Til they're done sackin' up the cash." He pulled at some tools.

"Talk to me a bit."

"Why, Dick?"

"My head hurts and talking would take my mind off the pain."

"So? About what?"

"Your leg?"

"Oh." Stumpy stopped playing with the tool that looked like a dentist's drill. He stuck out his wooden leg and slid his back down the face of a cabinet door to sit on the floor a few feet from Bart. He lifted his right knee to straighten out his peg-leg.

"I was on my bike, ridin' the white line on I-5 near Los Banos, when I came up behind two panel trucks. One was tryin' ta pass t'other but couldn't do it."

"Los Banos, where people stop to eat and get gas?"

"What? Anyway, I dint want ta wait, an' was squeezin' 'tween them when this citizen decided *that* very second, he just *hadda* empty his ash tray out the winda. Blinded an' choked me awful, an' I musta caught my leg by his tire. Happened so fast. Trashed my bike. Later I had a ar-teee-fish-shal leg below my knee."

"Does it hurt?"

"Not in the summer."

Keeping Stumpy relaxed and talking was part of Bart's plan to overpower him, the slowest and weakest of the three pirates.

"Why don't tough guys like you pirates smoke cigs?"

"Hook taught us displin. In lockup, there's all this fussin' an' fightin' over smokes. 'Don't smoke an' yur free,' he said. Hook wanted us to sell our smokes an' pay him the money. For protectin' us."

"How come you guys don't wear swords or cutlasses?"

Stumpy slipped two fingers under his dirty red bandana and scratched. "We did, until burnin' a streak up the freeway on the way to Monterey, the tip a Hook's cutlass caught up in his drive chain. Bike blew up an' threw him good. No more good times on that bike. Hook had to ride double with Scar comin' home."

"That's when he lost his hand?"

"No. He lost his hand back in Nam . . . but I can't talk about that. Hook gets mad."

"Okay, but the sword-in-the-chain thing — he was hurt bad?"

"No. Hook's lucky. When the bike blew, Hook landed in a big patch of ice-plant near a offramp. Slid fifty feet. He said it was like high-speed belly-floppin' in guacamole. Dint get hurt none."

"And how did Scar get burned?"

"In Mule Creek. He was sleepin' when his cellmate set him on fire."

"So, you three served in Viet Nam together?"

"Naw. I tried the Marines after I quit high school. I dint pass their tests. The sergeant said, 'Sorry Son,' he wanted recruits bad, but my scores, and my juvi-record, they wouldn't let 'im take me. Later I got drafted, but the Army doc said my feet were no good."

"What about Scar and Hook?"

"Scar, he told me he was National Guard, going to summer camp and weekend squad meetin's. When he started skippin' the meetin's, they decided he'd done enough and wasn't worth keepin'. They kicked him out."

"And Hook?"

"Yeah, Hook was in the Army, an' he went to Nam. Cam Ranh Bay. Said he spent ten months in big warehouses drivin' a forklift, an' handin' out blankets an' boots, an' countin' C-rations."

"You said that's where he lost his hand."

"Now I told you, he don't like talkin' about that. I dunno, but —"

"What about his eye — the patch?"

"Ohhh! Really can't talk about *that*."

"Well, what happened?"

"Oh, heck, I'll tell you about the arm. He was in some bar in Nha Trang, just being Hook, *way* outta control. He liked to go there to find Army Lurps an' show 'em they wasn't so tuff. He reached behind the bar, tryin' to grab the owner's gun. Bar owner came down on his arm with a ma-chet-tee — cut the hand clean off."

"Ouch! They couldn't sew it back?"

"Bar owner threw it in the drainage ditch an' chased Hook away with the gun. Hook ran back to the base an' told the MPs some VC tried to kidnap him and take him into the jungle. Told them he, like a wolf, had to cut his own hand off to get away. Nobody believed 'im, but they doctored 'im up and sent 'im home. He can go to the vets' hospital when he needs. But they told him his purple heart got lost somewhere."

"Too bad for him. So, how's Hook lucky?"

"Cee Eye Dee was on Hook's case. They was close ta court-marshalin' 'im for stealin' Army property for his black-market sales. When he lost his hand, he got sent home before they could try him. No stockade. They just gave him a general discharge. Not honorable, not dishonorable. Hook don't care. He dint want no college on the GI Bill, dint want to be a cop or judge."

Every time Stumpy looked away, recalling something, Bart would try scooting closer. If he could keep Stumpy talking long enough, he would make his move.

"So, how long have you guys been riding together? Do you belong to a club?"

"Together fur years, but we don't join clubs no more. We rode with the Angels for a while."

"The Hell's Angels?"

"Who else?"

"What happened?"

"We were still probies, so they see if they like us enough to make us Angels, too. Almost a year we rode with 'em. Then Hook got in a fight with one of the old Angels an' they tossed us."

"Wow. That must have hurt."

"Hook was really pissed we was rejected. Worse, the Angels said the fight wasn't so bad. Hook was just 'too weird' for the Angels. Too weird! Hook wouldn't talk for a week."

"Bummer, huh?"

"Then he saw *Treasure Island* on TV."

"I did, too, but it didn't make me want to be a pirate."

"The flick dint. It was Hook's dream after. In his dream we was all pirates on a fine ship, fulla treasure, flying the Jolly Roger. We was rich-n-free. No cops, no paroly officers, no landlords. Hook made it sound real. Then he read every book he could find on pirates. He made me this leather an' wooden leg an' throwed away my plastic leg. We bin pirates ever since."

Bart was trying to slide his knees up to make a move when Stumpy caught him.

"I thought your legs dint work! Lay still an' quiet, Dick. You got me talkin' an' not payin' 'tention. You need tyin' up."

Embarrassed at being caught by pea-brain Stumpy, Bart said, "My name is Bart, Bart Lasiter. Not 'Dick'"

"That's what *you* say, Dick! Lasiter? *I* say it's Lose-i-ter. Loser Lose-i-ter, that's who you are, Dick! Or maybe it's Lassie-ter, you puppy doggy. I bet you play Frisbee. You're a college guy thinks Frisbee is the same as football. The Raiders versus the Frisbee Wimps — guess who wins!"

"It's *Bart Lasiter*, Stumpy. Lasiter, *with one S!*"

Stumpy was angry and red-faced. Using his hands to push himself up against the workbench, he inched up from the floor. When he was standing, he leaned back against the workbench while he caught his breath and puffed out his scrawny chest.

"Biff Jerky!" yelled Stumpy, "that's *yur* name." Stumpy leaned and sneered. "That's right, Dick. Don't look s'prised. 'Cause Hook told us."

Bart lunged at Stumpy and grabbed his wooden leg. He pulled on the leg with all his strength. As the leg came free of Stumpy, the little pirate fell, just missing the dentist tool, but hitting his head on the edge of the workbench. He landed flat on his back, knocked out cold.

Bart stood up. "It's Biff, *with two F's!*"

Bart took back his remaining pills and found all his keys and cash in Stumpy's jeans. One problem solved. Stumpy had his Sinatra Cal-Neva matchbox, too.

In one of the workbench drawers, Bart found rope and rags. He tied and gagged Stumpy. Keeping Stumpy from alerting the others would buy him some time to reach a phone.

It was quiet out in the hallway now. He went to the door, dry swallowing his remaining antibiotics.

* * *

43

Dental Plan

All the Way

Stumpy's eye was huge. It opened.

"Mmmmff!" Stumpy tried to speak. He jerked his ropes and tried to sit up.

"Hey, look. It's our friend, the Stumpster." Bart was on his knees, straddling Stumpy's chest. He had tied Stumpy's hands together behind his back, and they were now under pressure beneath the little pirate. Bart held the articulated medical lamp right up near Stumpy's face. He was looking through the big magnifying glass centered inside a circular fluorescent tube.

"Cat got your tongue?" He removed the gag from Stumpy's mouth.

"You scared me with the light. Git *off* me!"

Bart didn't move. "How's your head, pirate?"

"Owww. It hurts awful!"

"You'll get used to it. Hey, you might still have some of my pills working in you."

"Lemme go!" Stumpy wriggled and kicked.

"We can talk. It'll take your mind off the pain."

Hand frozen on the workshop door latch, Bart had changed his mind. The safe move would be to run and call the Sheriff, then let the Sheriff deal with Hook and his friends. As logical as his escape plan was, Bart didn't feel right about leaving Mrs. Concannon tied up somewhere down the hallway.

No, Bart would stay and fight. He was Mrs. Concannon's protector. Her shield, her knight. He would be with her all the way.

"Git that light outta my face!"

Bart swung the light away.

"Now, Mr. Stumpy. We're going to have a little talk, and you're going to tell me things, in a nice calm, quiet voice." Bart held Stumpy's detached peg-leg above his head and swung it in a circle. "Scream once more and I'll hit you with your peg leg so hard you'll never sail again."

"I ain't talkin'. Lemme go 'fore Hook comes back an' hurts you."

"Hurts me?" Bart leaned in to apply pressure.

"Owww! My hands."

"Worry about *me* now, not Hook. *I'm* your problem now."

"Ain't worried none about you, Lose-i-ter."

Bart reached back to grab the dentist's drill and swung its articulated arm down to where Stumpy could see the drill tip.

"Oh, look. This dentist's drill-thing already has a nasty-looking bit in it. Looks like it's probably tungsten carbide, or even diamond. Cut through anything." Zzzzzzt. Bart made it spin again. Zzzzzzt-zzzzzt.

Now he had Stumpy's attention.

"Stumpy, if you don't answer my questions, I'll be a failure. I'll have to quit the detective business and find a new trade."

"Yur a lousy detective. I ain't tellin' ya nothin'!"

"Then you've forced me to start a new career. I think I'll learn how to be a dentist. Want to help?"

"You wouldn't."

Zzzzzzt, zzzzzzzzzzzzzzt!

"Don't!"

"Ever see *Marathon Man*? Dustin Hoffman?"

"Now there's a question I *can* answer, Lose-i-ter. Yeah, I saw it. Why?"

"Remember what happened to Dustin Hoffman?"

"Yeah. He ran a lot, met this girl an' . . . Noooooo!"

"Yes! Zzzzzt, zzzzzzzzzzzzzzt! I'm going to see if you have nerve. Which room is Mrs. Concannon in? Is she still okay?"

"What?"

Zzzzzt. Bart brought the tool close to Stumpy's face.

"Answer the questions, or I drill. Where is she? Where are you pirates headed?"

Zzzzzt, zzzzzzzzzzzzzzt!

"Okay, I'll talk. Keep that thing away from me. I don't know where we're goin'. Neither does Scar. Hook says only the boss knows, an' the boss talks only to Hook."

"I might believe you. But where's Mrs. Concannon? How did you choose Drake Concannon to kidnap? Who's the boss? Who's the woman with the gun?"

"One question at a time! I can't tell you no more. Hook would —"

Zzzzzt, zzzzzzzzzzzzzzt.

"You keep that thing away from me!"

Bart, busy questioning Stumpy, forgot his back was to the door. He felt a change in the room's air and heard a noise behind him.

"Uh oh."

* * *

44

Life Coach

You Go to My Head

Too late, Bart ducked. Something hard glanced off his back and shoulders and hit the back of his head. His head again! Lights out, he fell onto Stumpy.

Bart dreamed he was surrounded by legs, legs arguing with each other.

The shouting woke him. Afraid of how his head would react to movement, he sat up slowly and carefully. He saw Hook and Scar wrestling with Stumpy.

"Lemme at 'im! Lemme at 'im! I'll drill all of this wharf rat's teeth — all of 'em!"

Stumpy was waving the drill with one arm while Scar used two hands on Stumpy's other arm to pull him away from Bart.

The big pirate's hook pulled on Stumpy's belt from behind. Hook shook his head, his face showing a doughy frown of disappointment.

"Don't got no time fur that, Stumpy. Put-chur leg back on an unlax. You knows we all got serious work ta do. And ya wouldn't be pissed an' hurtin' if'n ya'd done what I *tol'* ya ta do."

"What? What!" Stumpy was straining, trying to pull his arm free from Scar.

"I tol' ya," Hook whispered, leaning near Stumpy's ear, still pulling on his belt.

"Ya gots-ta . . . *CONTROL 'im*, Stumpy!" Hook yelled, spittle flying and his face turning red.

"He tricked me, Hook." Stumpy dropped the drill. His eyes sought forgiveness while he used his head band to wipe his ear.

"I guess. But us pirates ar sposed-ta *BE* the tricksters, not sposed-ta *GET* tricked, Stump."

"Yur right, Hook, just like always." Stumpy looked down at Bart.

Hook followed Stumpy's gaze and leaned down toward Bart.

"Lookie here, Buccaneers. We got arselves a land-lubber trickster, a Stranger-in-the-Night! Dooby, dooby, lover boy. How'd-ya like that taste of the belayin' pin, unsalty dude?"

"Hook, it ain't no belayin' pin, and you know it,' said Stumpy, still angry and scowling. "It's a vintage soo-va-neer Willy McCovey, thirty-five-ounce."

"Naw, thirty-*three*-ounce, thirty-five-*long*," said Scar.

"Shut up," said Hook. "Willie Mac weren't no sailin' man. Now, if I say somethin' is somethin', then, it's *somethin'!* Got that?"

"Okay Hook, if you say," Stumpy and Scar replied, as if one.

"I *do* say. Pull yurselfs together. An', Stumpy — this time, *Tie — Him — Up!"*

Bart followed Hook's advice and decided to pull *himself* together and not dwell on his failed escape. At least he had both car keys back, hidden in his silver boots. Maybe now he could retrieve his gun — if it were still in the Klimo, if he got another chance to escape.

Bart watched Stumpy re-attach his peg-leg, and then dress the short leg of his jeans down over the leather transition between flesh and peg. Finished, Stumpy pushed the groggy Bart back to the floor facedown. He tied Bart's hands behind his back, then tied his ankles together and ran the end of the ankle rope up through Bart's wrist ropes and pulled.

"Ow!"

"Quiet, dentist." He pulled the end of the rope tight, leaving Bart trussed up like a Thanksgiving turkey. "Shoulda done this before." Stumpy used his hands and good knee to stand up.

Hook smiled. "Good job, Stump."

Bart wasn't defeated yet. He rolled onto his side where he could see them.

Stumpy got an idea. Bart knew this because Stumpy smiled while looking above his head — he probably saw a flashing light bulb.

"Let's burn this place and be done with it."

Bart didn't like the sound of that.

Hook forced his face into a mean squint and cocked his head to one side.

Bart remembered his little dog, Bullets, would cock his head to one side when he listened.

"Listen-up, Stumpy. All the years we bin ta-gether, I tries my best ta learn ya. Learn ya *what?*"

"What?"

"I tries ta teach ya — The Pirate's *Lawr!*"

"What's that?"

"You *fur-got?*"

"Sorry."

Hook took in a big breath and his face turned red again. Then he bent down near Stumpy's ear.

"It's pillage . . . *THEN* burn!"

Stumpy flinched and rubbed his ear. "Sorry, Hook. You know I woulda answered right if I was more mellow. I bin needin' something to mellow me." He looked up again to the light bulb above his head. "What about rollin' a big one outa that fine Humboldt we got?"

"Hook!" Scar's eyes grew wide as he spit out, "I'm on that, too! We been on edge so long. This is way too much like work. Whatcha say, Hook?"

"No, no. Remember, Bucs, the Boss said, no weed a'fore the deed. Just maintain a little longer. We're done with this, ya can smoke yur lungs an' heads in-side-out. With a sailor's breeze, payday is just o'er the horizon."

Listening, Bart decided it would be a shame to die at the hands of Moe, Larry, and Curly playing their grade school version of *Treasure Island.*

Hook paused, working something out in his head. Ignoring Bart, he spoke to Scar and Stumpy quietly.

"Hey, you two — now listen to Hook. Bucs, the money'll

be good all right. You saw old Concannon's money cage? Just picture, like in *Treasure Island*, that big pirate's chest fulla gold kerns, sun shinin' an' sparklin' off-a-the gold — only more in good used foldin', *cash* money — sacks of it!

Scar and Stumpy sat on the floor and listened, as if Hook were their daddy on Christmas eve, playing Santa Claus.

"But more important, I wanna tell ya somethin'. The pirate's life is the best, the best we got, the best we *ever* had. Ya knows, we tried it all. The pannin' fur gold, the pirate bookstore —"

"We closed that too soon," said Stumpy.

"Amen. Before Johnny Depp," said Scar.

"I wanted to learn about dot coms," said Stumpy.

Bart rolled his eyes.

Hook was ready to explode. "HEY — I'm talkin' here!"

"Aye, aye, Hook," said Scar and Stumpy.

"I'm SAY-in', we fucked up at ever'thin' else. Ever'thin' else played out dry. Our *only* choice left is ta be *proud* pirates, pirates to the full — or *nothin'!*"

"Aye, aye, Hook."

Bart heard Frank again. More *Prisoner of Love.*

Hook looked at the door, and then the ceiling, doing a slow burn listening to the music. "I hate that skinny little dago." He turned back to Scar.

"Scar? You go back up there, the big room. See if we left anythin'. An, when ya leave, close that door tight into the bookcase, an' be sure it latches."

Scar started for the door. "Aye, aye, Hook."

"Hold steady, Scar. Before yur done up there, turn *off* that *goddamn music!*"

"Aye, aye, Hook." Scar left the room.

"Now Stump, leave the dick here an come help me with them carts."

Stumpy stood on Bart's hand with his peg leg. "Loser Lose-i-ter." He slide-thumped out after Hook and shut the door.

* * *

45

Choo-Choo Train

They All Laughed

Bart tried but couldn't loosen his ropes. He would have to observe and wait for his chance.

The noise of carts rolling in the hallway and an electric-motor puzzled Bart. After a half-hour listening, Bart had Hook's money-moving routine down pat. They would load maybe three carts full and then move them somewhere. Bart could hear the cartwheels screech, over-loaded and bearing down hard against the rails. Then quiet until he heard the carts come bouncing back empty.

Bart heard Scar return from upstairs. He had failed. Frank was still singing, *Prisoner of Love*.

"Scar! I tol-ya to kill that Dago-singin'."

"Sorry, Hook. I punched all those buttons, an' I tried. It stopped. But it's got a timer, a repeat, or somethin'. It's not like what's in ar trailer — ain't no eight-track, or cas-sette tape. It's got big reels a tape, an' a hun-nert buttons an' switches. Hook, yu shouldn't be blamin' me. Real pirates don't know no audio-video, and I ain't no rocket scientwist, either."

"All right — fur-get it."

"Aye, aye," said Stumpy.

"Hook?" said Scar.

"Yeah?"

"Speakin' a eight-track. You see what the Dick has in his

weirdo limo? I looked through the windas. *Two* radios! Both are real electronic tuning radios, and the one in the back seat has a cas-sette tape player, one of the first. Let's take'm, just like the old days."

"Scar, keep yur sails full and yur compass true. Dint you see those big shelfs fulla cash? No time to waste on car radios. We gotta job ta finish. But those *was* good days, wasn't they?"

"The best!"

"Okay, you two — enough sailin' round-n-round memory cove. Grab some sacks an' load 'em. We'll pile them sacks high, an' after this one, only one more trip!"

"Aye, aye, Hook."

Bart heard them singing pirate ditties while loading carts again.

"Okay Bucs, ready to roll. All aboard!"

"Aye, aye, Hook."

"Wait. Belay my last. Scar, I got a idea-er. Stump'n me will go with the carts. You get the Dick, bring 'im out in the hallway, an' wait for us."

"If you say, Hook."

Bart heard Hook order Stumpy to climb on a cart, followed by the sound of screeching wheels and that electric motor.

Scar entered the room and cut the rope tying Bart's ankles to his wrists. With a grunt, he hauled Bart up onto his feet.

"Steady now, Dick."

"Hey, Scar, aren't you going to at least untie my feet?"

"Nope. A smart detective like yu should know how-ta hop." Scar pushed Bart toward the open door. "Too bad Stumpy isn't here to see ya hoppin', like *he* was when you took his peg-leg."

"Awww, come on. I'd already forgotten. It's unhealthy to carry grudges."

Scar snorted and pushed Bart to the doorway.

Bart leaned into the doorframe for balance. He couldn't see anything, except the tracks went around a curve in the hallway, but he could hear the carts moving. He could see the track's iron rails moving in the floor, loose after so many years. Then the sounds and the track movement stopped. He and Scar waited about twenty minutes before hearing the carts move again. Bored Bart thought Scar was used to waiting for Hook.

The sounds grew louder. They were coming back.

"Whooo-eee!" sang Hook, appearing around the curve in the hallway, waving his hook through the air. When he saw Bart balancing against the wall, he smirked.

Bart laughed. "Look, Scar. Hook's got a choo-choo."

"I seen it before."

Hook was commanding a miniature industrial electric tractor with iron wheels riding the rails. It was pulling a train of three empty carts up a slight grade, with Stumpy riding the last cart, playing caboose tender. At least Hook wasn't wearing a striped engineer's hat.

When the train stopped, Hook jumped off and approached Bart.

"Whatcha think, Biff? Gramps Concannon hadda lotta toys, eh?"

Bart didn't answer. But he did think Concannon was the best candidate for a La Cosa Nostra version of Walt Disney.

"Now, Biff Jerky, we got somethin' fur-ya ta do, solve a problem yu could say."

"What?"

"The Bucs an' me want-ta see how smart ya are, smart-ass."

"Untie me and we'll see."

"Bring him closer, Scar."

Scar pushed Bart until he hopped along the wall closer to the train.

"That's it, hop like a cute fuzzy bunny," said Hook. "Now stand there, detective, do some detectin', an' tell us which cart ya like the best."

"What?"

"Go on. Tell us."

The three pirates stared at Bart and waited.

Bart pointed at the cart closest to the little tractor. "This one."

"A-Arrrrrgh!" All three pirates pointed at Bart and laughed and slapped high-fives.

"What? Did I pick the wrong one?"

That set them off laughing again, even harder.

"Okay Bucs, you heard the great detective. You see the one he picked. Load that-there cart!"

Scar ran and Stumpy slide-bumped to a room further down the hall and returned with fat, heavy sacks they piled onto the cart. After multiple trips down the hall and back, they had several layers of sacks packed tightly together on the cart.

Hook smiled. "That's nuff, Bucs. Bring the great detective over near his cart."

Scar and Stumpy pushed and jabbed Bart until he had hopped close to the loaded cart.

When Bart was in place, Hook held up his hand.

"Hold fast right there, Citizen." Then Hook filled his face with a big greasy smile.

Bart stared at him. "What?"

"Now we gots a black-bag job fur-ya, Mr. Jerky. Yur a sneaky guy, aren't-cha. A black-bag job is reglar detective work, no?"

While Bart tried to understand what he meant, Hook reached his good hand into his back pocket and, like a magician producing a silk handkerchief from nowhere, whipped out a black cloth bag. He used his hand and hook to jam it down over Bart's bandaged head. Bart felt a cord in the bag's opening tighten around his neck.

"If-in yur a good little detective, I won't have to tighten it on yur neck any tighter."

"Ow! I can barely breathe in here."

"When ya signed up ta be a detective, dint-cha figure there'd be days like this? Sounds like ya wasn't ment'ly pre-pared, it does ta me. Okay Bucs — *now*."

Yikes!"

* * *

46

The Black Bull

Deep in a Dream

They yanked black-bag-blinded Bart from his feet and tossed him high in the air. He landed on his back, face-up on his cart's sack pile. His feet were pointed downhill, and his head was toward the tractor, uphill from the sack destination.

"He ain't tuff," said Scar.

"Lose-i-ter," said Stumpy.

"Be loadin' them other carts, Bucs!"

Bart lay on his sore back, arched over the sacks, his hands tied beneath him. The three pirates left for more cash.

A strange, distinct odor surrounded Bart, maybe from the black cotton bag. After a time, he decided it was not the bag. He remembered this scent. He'd just left Peet's Coffee on Solano in North Berkeley with a hot cup of morning coffee, trying to fix the lid, dripping some latte on his winter uniform. Bart looked up to see a man running toward him.

"Os-si-fer, Os-si-fer!" He tugged Bart's arm, spilling the rest of his tall latte. The man's eyes were strange, and he was sweating heavily for a forty-degree morning in January.

"Os-si-fer, they're comin' to take it, they're comin' to take my munny!"

"Who?"

"Them!" He pointed down the street to an area devoid of two or four-legged beings.

Bart decided, having seen this before, the man was coked out of his gourd. "Sir, take me to your money, so I can help!"

"Right!" The man took Bart's hand and dragged him down the street to a parked car. When the man opened the trunk, the subtle perfume of eighty-seven-plus-thousand dollars in loose small bills filled Bart's nose.

Bart's bed of cash wasn't in a car's trunk, but it smelled the same. If he wanted, he could think he was protecting these sacks of cash for Mrs. Concannon, being right on top of them. But Bart couldn't move, and she was more important to him than her money.

When he swung his head side-to-side, he could see the ceiling's bare light bulb. With enough light, he could see through the black cloth. But, arched belly-up over the sacks, even if the bag were removed from his head, he could only see side-to-side, up, and a little back — upside down. And all the action seemed to be forward, not back.

The pirates ignored Bart and kept busy loading sacks onto the other carts. It gave him time to think. There had to be a way out of this mess.

Bart's heart sank when Hook shouted out, "Bucs, the deed is done! That's the last of 'em. Hop on yur carts — it's ar glory train ta Port Royal!"

"Aye-aye, Hook," two answered.

Bart watched upside-down while Hook squeezed into the tractor, threw a switch, and pushed a lever. The train started moving.

The train rolled along the track for minutes and then started down a shallow grade. The air became fresher and warmer. His back hurting, Bart hoped there would be a soft landing at the end of this ride.

Bart tried to notice and memorize everything around him, his way of fighting to stay alive. He wanted to know as much as possible before he would try another escape attempt. If he got the chance. He tried to keep track of how many people there were around him and where they were, but so far, it was just the same three.

The carts were picking up speed. As they moved further, Bart tasted fresher air, and the sound changed. They must be near the end of the tunnel, and maybe water.

Wham! Bart heard Stumpy's cart hit something and stop dead. Scar's cart took up the slack and slammed into Stumpy's, and then Bart's cart hammered Scar's. Hook's tractor took up the last of the slack and crashed into Bart's cart.

"End-a-the-line, Bucs."

They were still indoors, but Bart felt it was more open, and he heard water. Maybe an indoor swimming pool.

Bart heard electric whirring and a rush of moving air. Fans, then a muffled explosion as a large motor started. The smell of exhaust, maybe diesel, and the sound of water spitting followed. He remembered from the boat show, cool water is drawn from the lake and then circulated through the engine and exhaust manifolds for cooling, before returning to the lake through the exhaust tubes.

The engine settled down to idle. A second engine started. A big boat. The Donzi had two engines, but they were gasoline, not diesel. Bart decided they were in a boathouse, not an indoor swimming pool.

Because he had not heard the three pirates move, Bart was sure there was at least a fourth person there, on the boat.

New sounds interrupted Bart's thinking: chains stretching and sprockets turning, raising a heavy door. More air, fresher and cooler.

Bart straightened his back to lift his head and looked around, seeing what he could see through his black cloth bag. He saw an open, wooden staircase, probably access to the boathouse from the interior of the house, also separate folded-open steel double-doors for access to Drake's tracked tunnel from the boathouse. Hinged storage shelves on the boathouse side would conceal the double doors, like the living room bookcases. Bart was feeling better, confident he was figuring this all out, and would soon free himself and Mrs. Concannon.

He heard a noise behind him and turned his head to see.

WHAP!

"End-a-the-line, Citizen. Yur ticket's done bin punched!"

Bart saw a filmy picture of Hook tucking a leather sap into his belt, and then heard someone's body hit the stone floor. Hook had hit him and yanked him from his bed of sacks.

"Stow these sacks away on ar ship. Now! Step lively, Bucs. A risin' golden tide is ar bounty!"

As Bart was losing his fight to stay conscious, he looked from the floor out into the boathouse. He was afraid. Was it a bad dream again? He saw a massive black bull charging toward him. He could still hear Hook's booming voice on his trip to a lonely, dark place.

"I knew ya was fakin', Mr. Jerky. Trying to spy on ar op-a-ray-shun, weren't-cha, Citizen? Ya just don't know what's good fur-ya. Well, I gave ya a little lead sleepin' pill, so's we could go about proper pirate bizzness, without no inner-ference from dick-less private Dicks!

"Aye say this fur-ya, Citizen. Ya don't quit easy, but if'n I hav-ta take time out to stifle ya ag'in, yu won't like it none. It'll be Dee-Jay's locker fur-ya!

"Step lively now, Buccaneers. It's — Arrrrrrgh — all downwind from here!"

* * *

47

The Black Ship

Riding high in August, shot down in August

Oh, Look at Me Now

Bart woke, surprised to be standing up, but not on his own.

Where was he now? Was it another bad dream?

The black bag was gone. Now he could see. Wrapped in heavy rope holding him tight to the big, fist-thick redwood plank pressed against his back, Bart saw his arms bound at his sides along the edge of the plank. When he turned his head, the plank rubbed against his bullet-wound stitches.

Bart was on the small mid-ship deck of a cabin cruiser. His back was against a bulkhead between the door to the forward main cabin and the helm at the portside. He could see a shorter aft cabin, with a roof waist-high above the deck. A curtained window in the aft cabin's short door showed light but Bart could not see in.

From the glass in the doors leading down into each cabin, light spread over the deck and his feet. He saw he was standing on the footplate of a steel, rubber-tired moving dolly. A single canvas strap buckled across his belly held him and his plank to the dolly frame. Hannibal Lector without the leather mask or fava beans. On the roof of the aft cabin, lay a long, upholstered white pad, obviously for sunbathing. Pirates sunbathing?

This boat appeared just as perfect and polished as the black-sided Chris-Craft Corvette at the boat show, at least the parts he could see. If this were the same boat, Hook and his friends must have stolen it from O'Hara's for their pirate raid across the lake to Eagle Cove.

It made sense, pirate-wise. The three buccaneers were the only security guards at O'Hara's, with complete access to the workshop and the boat keys. Someone would notice the boat's absence and call the Sheriff, but not before morning. Bart wondered if he would be alive then.

Looking for a shoreline, Bart saw only the now familiar endless water and darkness, with occasional clouds of mist near the lake's surface. The water and darkness reminded him of the white boat, *Linda Lou.* He shuddered. Still, his present situation might be worse. Now he really wished he had chosen motel management instead of private investigations.

Bart's head was on the way to almost normal, but it still ached. He couldn't say it was a hangover because he'd had so few, but that must be part of it. There must be a limit to how many times your head could be hit before there was permanent damage.

Dissonance: Bart remembered his father carrying on about Erroll Garner. His father would play the *Concert by the Sea* album over and over, when the mood suited him. He'd force Bart to listen to the entire LP without interruption, not just one or two tunes. "It's all one, Bart, one piece of pure perfection, continuous pure genius, from beginning to end. Bart — the dissonance! Do you *hear* the dissonance?"

Bart could hear Erroll pounding the keys and grunting a lot. Some of it sounded off-key to Bart. He wasn't sure about the dissonance.

"The dissonance, the in-between, Bart, a very special place between the perfect and the flawed, but part of neither."

Now Bart should be enjoying his biggest, most lucrative case ever, but not with head injuries and bound up like a juicy pork tenderloin. Dissonance. Maybe he was in the dissonance now. Whatever it was, it was new and no fun to him.

And Frank, too. In all his years of listening to his father's Frank Sinatra music, he never would have imagined last night and now.

As he viewed Frank's LP Album covers fanning through his

memory — *In the Wee Small Hours, Songs for Swingin' Lovers, Songs for Young Lovers, Frank Sinatra Sings for Only the Lonely* — a new album cover appeared: *Frank Sinatra Sings Songs for Lonely Celibates in Unfortunate Circumstances.* Before he could see which songs Frank would sing on the new album, he heard noises from the forward cabin, laughing and celebration, like he was back at the trailer. *Déjà vu,* all over again.

The door to the forward cabin exploded open and banged into his knees.

"Ow!"

Hook stomped up onto the deck through the tiny doorway, his bulk temporarily blocking out the cabin's light behind him, followed by Scar and Stumpy — a shark and his two remoras. Now the little mid-ship deck was crowded. Somebody should leave. *Shut up, Bart.*

"Well, lookie here. Mr. Jerky is awake!" Hook threw his arms out wide, nearly smacking Scar and Stumpy. His chest expanded with satisfaction as he drew in a pirate captain's share of the night air.

"Ah-Arrrrrrrgh!" howled Hook, like a wolf to a full moon. Snapping his hook open and closed, he was full of himself, more than usual, if that were possible.

Bart felt complete defeat. It was one thing to think about Hook as a kidnapper or even a murderer. It was an entirely sad, different thing to see him standing right in front of tied-up-you, in complete control. The pirate clown had Bart's life hanging from his metal hook.

Hook flashed a big smile at Bart. He was wearing two fancy flintlock pistols, both cocked, tucked in cross draw fashion under his wide leather belt. Gold plating shined on the barrels. The grips were carved ivory. Much too fine and grand for a discount pirate. The only comforting news was he didn't have a cutlass, too.

"Arrrrrgh, I say again!"

Hook's face was scary. The scant light from the cabins and the helm instruments highlighted the hard bones of his face and jaw and covered his eye in dark shadow. He wiped dirty, gray hair back from his face. He could use a bandana.

"Well, tough guy Citizen, Biff Jerky, private *Dick*, un-salty dude, now yur finally a standup guy!"

Bart summoned what was left of his sad, casual demeanor. "Good one. Wassup, Hook?"

"Yur always a smart guy, ain't-cha? Not as much now." Hook tried to look like he felt sorry for Bart but gave up and laughed. His face switched to a huge, taunting grin. "Whatcha think, Biff? Now that I'm armed proper-like, an' got me a fast, black ship, I'm my full pirate self, as I were always meant to be. Oh, look at me now!"

"Whatever. Send pictures of yourself to *Pirate Magazine*. It'll scare the kiddies." Bart squirmed under the ropes.

Hook laughed deeply, as if Bart couldn't say anything that would bother him and pulled on Bart's ropes.

"Aw, don't worry none, Hook, I tied 'im up good."

"No ya dint, Scar." Stumpy clomped forward, his wooden leg thumping on the teak deck like a brass door knocker, and grabbed Bart's ropes. "Look! Ya dint use the bo'lin knot on this dentist, which *I* learnt, an' *you* dint. It makes it easy to untie. Just one yank and it's free."

Scar rolled his eyes for Hook. "Stumpy, I used good ole square knots on his ropes, cause, *duhhh*, there won't ever be no need to *un*-tie 'im!"

Bart didn't like that.

Hook scowled. "Stop squallin' you two, an' roll 'im over to the portside gate."

Scar and Stumpy wheeled Bart past the helm and captain's chair to the portside of the boat, positioning the dolly with Bart's back to the water.

"Open that handrail and gate, so's he can feel the sea's bite at his back," said Hook.

Scar flipped up and folded back a hinged section of the handrail, and then unlatched the port-side gate, swinging it out over the water.

Bart really worried now. Just one pirate mistake would tip him backwards through the gate and over the side. Evening swells were beginning to roll the boat like O'Hara's piers. He knew he wasn't Houdini and, even if he could free himself of the dolly and plank, he had never tried to swim in silver cowboy boots. Judging his '57 Chevy belt buckle probably weighed a pound all by itself, he suddenly missed Mrs. Concannon's life vest.

"Now, yu two get yurselfs outside a that rail and stand on that deck-ledge, on either side of 'im, so's he can't go nowheres. At least 'til I says. Arrrrrgh!"

Obedient, Scar and Stumpy carefully climbed over the aft cabin roof and slid along the narrow ledge that ran from the forward deck aft and encircled the cabin areas. Scar gripped the frame of the helm's side-glass on Bart's left and Stumpy gripped the aft-cabin-roof handrail on Bart's right. They stood balanced on their toes at Bart's elbows, ready to follow Hook's orders. Hook retreated to the starboard rail, shining his greasy smile at Bart.

"Poor Mr. Jerky thinks we're gonna make him walk the plank. Biff, we knows yur too super-speshal for ord-nary plank walkin'. Arghrrrrr! Yur takin' the plank *with-ya*!"

The three wannabe pirates laughed and stomped their feet, though, short of foot room, it was light tippy-toe taps for Scar and Stumpy, the narrow exterior deck affording only a toehold.

Bart interrupted their fun. "What about the steel dolly?"

"Don'tcha be worryin', Citizen. We'll make it sportin'-like, an' take the dolly away a'fore ya go o'er the side . . . maybe."

Hook filled his chest with fresh night air again and cocked his head to one side. "Ya *do* know, private detective — maybe I should call yu private de-*fect*-ive — it's a sorry thing we can't have this fun in the sunlight so's we could see ever'thin'. We could attach one of them white dinner plates to your chest, or maybe on top-pa yur head — a long screw right in the middle would hold it." Hook paused and again cocked his head to the side. "Ya knows about the speshal white plate, don'tcha — the white plate them scientwists use ta measure how clear the lake water is at certain depths? How 'bout instead, maybe ya can just swim back up from the bottom an tell us how clear an' deep this lake is. I'll bet deeper'n whale shit! Arrrrgh!"

While hoping Hook would pull a rib-cage muscle laughing, Bart mustered some bravado. "The white plate, it's called a Secchi disc. I read that in the library."

"Oooooo — the *lie-barry!*"

Scar and Stumpy nearly lost their footing laughing at Hook's humor.

"Laugh all you want, Hook, but I've heard you say all that before, in Concannon's basement. Old stuff, heard it before, and you know there aren't any whales in Lake Tahoe."

"OH!" Hook's eye got big, and his nostrils flared. He shook his head to clear the hair from his eye. "You *ARE* a smart-ass! Well, un-salty dude — it'll make fixin' you *ALL* the more fun!"

Maybe Bart's untethered smart mouth had gotten him into trouble again. For the last time? He stiffened under his ropes, waiting for Hook to give the order that would send him to a cold and, this time, fatal drowning. He took one last look at the stars and closed his eyes. When nothing happened, he opened them and saw Hook leaning back against the starboard rail. His mocking grin had been replaced by a doting schoolteacher's earnest smile.

"But first, Mr. Jerky, while yur prayin', think 'bout maybe yu'd rather be shot, an' not haff-ta go swimmin'?"

Bart really opened his eyes and glanced at Scar and Stumpy.

Scar and Stumpy gave each other a quick stare. *What?*

Hook flipped up his eye patch. "Hey, hold steady, you three." He used his good left hand to draw the flintlock pistol from his right side and brought his extended arm and the pistol to eye level. The muzzle pointed at Bart's face. Bart saw a big hole in the muzzle, dark and bottomless.

"Ah . . . Hook? What's the plan?" said Scar.

Frozen in place, not understanding, the three stared at Hook and the gun.

BOOM!

* * *

48

Increasing His Share

If a Pirate I Must Be

Hook made a big hole through the red bandana around Stumpy's forehead. Sporting a look of disbelief, Stumpy's head snapped backward, leading him over the side into the dark water.

"Ever since I done Patch, I bin dyin' to try them pistols ag'in, a pirate's proper tools."

Stumpy's departure rocked the boat and Bart's steel dolly and then splashed cold water on Bart's legs and his short-lived relief, relief that he wasn't the target. Yet. He felt unburned black powder and something warm and wet on his face on his right side where Stumpy had stood. What it was, he didn't want to know.

"There, ya see, detective? I wanted ta have a demon-stray-shun fur-ya, so yu'll know how ta go o'er the side, proper-like." Hook grinned while he blew smoke away from the pistol's muzzle. "See how Stumpy went over? *That's* how yu do it."

Bart waited for his vision to return after the muzzle flash. His ears were ringing while waves of orange and dark blue light pulsed in his eyes. He heard Scar grunt and turned his head as much as he could against the plank, only to see Scar's face twist and turn different colors. Poor Scar's forehead glistened with sweat, soaking through his purple bandana. He held his position standing firm at Bart's left side, but his hands gripping the wooden frame of the side glass showed white knuckles, and he he bounced on his toes, like he was late to the bathroom.

Hook set the spent pistol down onto the aft cabin's roof and switched the other pistol over to the right side of his belt.

"Dint mean fur-ya ta worry, Scar. Don'tcha worry yurself none — yur the smart one. Stumpy weren't too smart, and he bein' a cripple an' all, he was sa-veerly holdin' us able-bodied Pirates back. You-an'-me, Scar, we're a team. And Scar, now, *yur* share of the treasure is even bigger!"

Still twitching, Scar produced a limp smile.

Bart dropped his caution and butted in. "Don't believe him! Jump, Scar, jump. Swim for it. You believe Hook, and you're dead. Bank on it."

"Shut yur pie-hole, Citizen! Don't pay 'im no 'tention, Scar. Pirates' plans don't concern a taxpayer none. What's the great detective know 'bout anythin' anyway?"

Scar was acting, trying to look relieved. Bart was sure Scar didn't trust Hook any more than he did.

Scar fought to control his twitching. "Yu had me goin' there for a minute, Hook. Yu knows I always bin *helpin'* yu, bin *with* yu, bin on *yur* side, a hunnert-per-cent. Like yu said, Hook, we're a *team*."

Hook cracked a big smile and held it. Scar began to relax.

"Ooooops — I almost fur-got what the boss said. Sorry, Scar."

Hook drew the other pistol and fired — *BOOM!* — sending Scar to join Stumpy.

Bart twisted to look down at the water. In between muzzle-flash memories, he saw an empty purple bandana floating on the surface.

"Say hello to Da-*vy*, team-mate-*ty*." Hook's grieving lasted two seconds, and then his head swiveled to Bart. "Now there's even *MORE* treasure for me. Blimey! I'm a bad, *BAD* pirate." Shaking his head in triumph and waving the smoking pistol high in the air, he snarled, "Arrrrrrrgh!" into the night sky.

Again, Bart's ears were ringing, his eyes were flaring, and his nose was full of the smell of burned black powder. Now flecks of unburned black powder, and other warm, wet things, were stuck to both sides of his face. A miniscule discomfort compared to his big problem: Except for Bart himself, Hook had run out of people to shoot.

Hook's greasy grin returned, a faithful match for the grin of the skulls on their motorcycles. Flipping his eye patch back down into place, Hook tucked the empty pistol back under his belt. He approached Bart, held up his left hand, and made a fist. "'Member this?"

Bart saw **D E T H**. Hook's spelling bothered him less than the idea and the lunatic behind it.

"An', how 'bout looky this?" The big pirate raised his right arm and the hook up to Bart's face. The hook gripped a piece of white paper.

Bart saw a familiar spot of black ink — as if Hook had torn it from the ransom note.

Hook leaned into Bart's face. Bart recoiled at the stench of spiced rum, stale pepperoni and anchovy pizza, and one shower-a-month Hook.

"Here. Hold this, *detective*." Hook stuffed the paper black spot into a chest-pocket of Bart's gambler's shirt and grinned, completely satisfied.

Hook stepped back to the edge of the aft cabin's low roof and removed the second pistol from his belt. He laid it down on the roof next to the first pistol. From a leather pouch hanging from his belt, he retrieved two lead balls, patches of cloth, and a brass ramrod. He set them down next to the pistols and took a powder horn from his belt.

"We can't keep Davy Jones waitin', Biff. Now's yur turn. Like I said, I was thinkin' a makin' ya swim. But I liked shootin' so much, I think it best ta shoot-chya, Mr. Taxpayer. Maybe gut shoot-chya, *then* yur o'er the side. Don't wantchya ta miss any speriences!"

"Mr. Taxpayer" diverted Bart to thinking about his taxes and all the money from Mrs. Concannon, until he remembered he'd failed to earn the bonus money and wouldn't be alive to file a return.

"Watch now, while I reload these fine duelin' pistols. These pistols got a proud pirate's his-tory, I'd bet. Real his-torical ant-teeks. The citizen I stole 'em frum paid a lot of kerns fur-'em. They're dainty-small, but real hand cannons with n-gravin' and carvin' on ivry handles. Now, here's where I gots-ta pol-a-gize ta ya, Mr. Jerky. I only got these two pistols. Good ones like these duelers come in pairs. But my ole mates, Stumpy an' Scar, an' yu, Biff Jerky, makes more than two. Three tar-gits, two guns!"

Bart squirmed in his ropes. Jeeez — more math!

"I'll haf-ta reload. Yu just wait. Don't go no-wheres, an' don't-chu worry none. It'll be a learnin' 'sperience for ya."

Bart's mind was spinning, trying to see a way out. What would Captain Blood do?

"This reloadin', it's a chance I'm givin' ya fur-ya to learn how it was a'fore, when it was *real*, back in the good times." He poured powder from the horn into the muzzle of a pistol.

"The *good* times?"

"Yes, *good times,* Biff. Sailin' . . . *under the Black Flag.*"

As he said, "good times," Hook's eye glistened, and at *Black Flag,* it was wet. *Treasure Island,* all over again.

Hook stared into the night at waters yet to be sailed.

"Oh, God — *Yes!* Fine-ly, I'm livin' my dream. Yes, *yes,* how I *do* love the Pirate's Life!" Lost, living his dream, Hook carelessly let the pistol point to the deck, spilling the powder from the barrel. "Bilge!"

Yikes. Bart tried to think of something fast, to delay Hook, and extend his own life. He feared he'd be joining Stumpy and Scar, and never learn what they did with Mrs. Concannon.

After Hook recharged the pistol barrel with more powder, he concentrated on loading the lead ball and cloth patch pinched in his hook into the muzzle of the pistol in his left hand, then reached for the ramrod.

"While I'm doin' this loadin', you be sayin' yur detective prayers, Cupcake. Fate is bearin' down on ya, hard an' steady, tie-foon-like."

"Bilge!" Before he could use the ramrod, the lead ball fell from the barrel and rolled across the deck. Hook flipped his eye patch back up, and went to his knees, looking for the ball.

What could Bart do? Think, Bart, think! What could stall the mortal intentions of this un-hinged ersatz pirate?

Bart desperately searched his memory bank for movie pirate scenes. Not *Captain Blood.* Not *Treasure Island.* He found Rip Torn admonishing Kelsey Grammer in *Down Periscope*: Bart should *Think like a pirate!* Now or never, it was Old Town Bart's time to act.

"Wait a minute, Hook! Did you know my full name is *Black Bart?*"

"Hah! Biff Jerky, ya spent too much time in Old Town. I bin to the Wells Fargo Museum there. I read that pamphlet about the stagecoach robber, a'fore they tossed me for trying to borry a souvenir gold nugget from their display case. 'Black Bart,' the poet. Whoop-dee-doo, I'm scared even more stiffer!"

"No, not that Black Bart. Think of another."

Hook had found the ball and returned to trying to fit it and a patch into the muzzle of his pistol.

"What're yu goin' on about, Jerky?"

"I'm claiming *Pirate's Rights!*"

Hook looked up at Bart. "What?"

Bart had finally interrupted Hook's sacred pistol-loading demonstration.

"That's right, Hook. I'm a descendant of the greatest pirate, Black Bart Roberts. I'm the latest Bart in a long, long, proud line. The Pirate's Ways were passed down from him, the master, to his son, and from him to his son, and so on, Bart to every Bart in my family."

"Yu? Black Bart? Yu?"

"Yes. He was my great, great, great, great, great, great grandfather, on my mother's side. He was the king, the greatest of all the Caribbean pirates. You know who Black Bart was, don't you?"

Maybe Bart threw in several extra "greats," more than was chronologically correct, but he knew math was not Hook's strong suit.

"Well, yeah. O' course. Any good pirate knows Black Bart Roberts took four hunnert-sevendy ships in four years. But —"

"We Barts learned a captured pirate captain *always* has the right to demand a *Last Request* before he's forced to walk the plank. *Pirate's Rights.* Of course, *YOU* knew that. Didn't you, Hook?"

Hook, surprised and put off balance by the force of Bart's challenges, dropped the lead ball again and let the pistol hang from his hand, powder spilling to the deck. He fumbled for an answer, but Bart interrupted him again.

"Hook, you *are* the captain of this ship? *Captain* Hook? You *are* the Master here, are you not?"

Hook, again taken by surprise, hesitated.

"I . . . well . . . we —"

A small noise in the dark from the stern side of the aft cabin interrupted Black Bart's almost successful scuttling of Hook's confidence. Bart was still seeing spots in front of his eyes and couldn't see what or who had made the noise.

Hook turned to the sound and stood. He smiled. The smile left, followed by the color from his face.

Bart's eyes cleared. The woman's small hand held a large automatic, and it was pointed straight at Hook.

"No, no — not *meeee! Noooooooo* —"

BLAM, BLAM!

Bart's eyes shut down from the muzzle blast, then opened again as he watched traces of the shiny ejected cartridge cases bounce across the aft cabin roof, two fireflies leaving glowing contrails in the summer night.

Hook's knees buckled, his hand released the empty flintlock, and his hook pointed to the sky. He crashed at Bart's feet.

Hook's eyes appeared to be looking back up at him, except they were focused on something far beyond Bart. Wet Valhalla.

All was at peace now. She had saved Bart. For the first time that night, Bart was sure he would live to see the sunrise.

The woman went down into the aft cabin and came back up to the amidships deck through the cabin's forward door.

His savior.

She wore a tailored black nylon jumpsuit, black baseball cap, and black Sperry Top-Siders. Gathered by a black band into a ponytail, her blond hair extended through the opening above the cap's adjustable strap.

He thought she was perfect.

She looked down at Hook, smiled, and then set her smoking gun down on the cabin roof beside Hook's other pistol. After removing rubber plugs from her ears, she turned to look at Bart.

Bart, his ears ringing again, grinned. "You got here just in time, Mrs. Concannon. Another minute and I would have been back in that cold water."

She had saved him, again.

Standing straight and tall, she smiled at him and then turned to the gate at the starboard side. She left the handrail in place but opened the gate below. She grabbed Hook by his feet and pulled.

Surprised by her strength, Bart watched her drag Hook's body to the open gate and push his legs through. Holding his hook in the air so that it wouldn't scratch the deck, she planted a black Top-Sider on Hook's head and pushed the spent pirate through and into the water.

Bart laughed and said, "Hey, Hook, say hello to Stumpy and Scar, and Davy Jones for me."

After closing the gate, she gathered Hook's leather bag, powder horn, and pistols, and tossed them in after Hook.

Bart had been so happy to be alive, but now he worried.

"Mrs. Concannon, you're throwing evidence into the lake. The Sheriff would want the body and guns."

She turned to him and smiled. In a full and confident voice he had never heard from her before, she laughed without mercy.

"Some detective you are."

* * *

49

Captain Wall To the Helm

I Haven't the Time to be a Millionaire

"What?" Bart was confused.

She didn't answer. Instead, staring at Bart, she hopped up backwards to sit on the roof of the aft cabin. Gone was the frightened, fragile wife who had depended on Bart. This new Mrs. Concannon sat with her legs hanging spread in the posture of an athlete. Now, without her makeup, even in the soft light from the cabins and helm instruments, she appeared older than he had imagined.

"You never caught on, did you, Lasiter? Now there's just the two of us. I'm impressed. I'm not pleased — just impressed. You're lucky, if nothing else."

Bart saw his lucky pajamas.

She wiped her hands on a black towel and looked at Bart.

"I failed to control you. I underestimated you. I chose you because I thought you would stay out of my way until I needed you for the ransom Saturday night. I thought you would stay busy paying your bills, buying lottery tickets, and helping old ladies in the crosswalk. Or whatever Boy Scouts like you do to pass the time. I thought you'd do as little as possible."

"As little as possible . . . *Chinatown*," he mumbled.

"Don't drift off on me, Lasiter. Humor me. *Do* you buy lottery tickets?"

"I don't buy lottery tickets. I don't think I'd win."

"Just as well. You'd be one of those who's a millionaire one day and broke the next."

"You hired a detective. Detecting is what I do."

"So, it would seem. Because of you, I had to dance my way through several probing calls from Angelo Stagnetti. 'Where's Drake? There's some private investigator named Lasiter asking questions.' Well, letting you run around asking questions was a mistake I'll not make next time."

"It's what I do. Talk to people. Next time?"

"Well, with ten million dollars in cash in the forward cabin, you wouldn't think I'd need to marry again. But who knows?"

"Just ten? Sorry."

"Quiet. You were supposed to be dead Saturday night, an important part of my alibi. I was watching you with Drake's night vision video equipment. I expected to have a tape of you motoring across the lake to the white boat and disappearing in a gunfight. Then you showed up on the west shore, alive, because those incompetents couldn't shoot straight. I had to talk Hook out of using his dueling pistols instead of the M-16 and night scope. Viet Nam vet — really!"

Bart heard but didn't want to believe. His client, his Mrs. Concannon, had ordered him *shot*. He'd broken his own *Rule Two*. He'd become Bart Lasiter, Blunt Instrument. Worse, an expendable Blunt Instrument.

"The first job I gave them was to dock and maintain my Donzi at their trailer. They could barely do even that." She shook her head in disgust. "But they were what I had. A woman must learn to compromise and adapt to get what she wants. Hook did seem sufficiently ruthless. It made the unpleasant-but-necessary sex more tolerable, but not something I would want to remember. That trailer — it was . . . ."

She was ignoring Bart. He said, "I didn't go inside. Maybe it's in House Beautiful."

"Be quiet while I'm talking. I had a good plan, Lasiter, but you failed to cooperate. After you had died in the white-boat shootout, after I had taken care of the three morons and cleaned up, I, the terrified wife, would go to the Sheriff with the story of the kidnapping, and how unreliable Lasiter and the kidnappers had disappeared. You would have all died on the lake in a gun battle, one you started. Eventually, the bodies of you and them, and Drake, would float in to fill out the picture. That's why I insisted you wear a life vest.

"'Poor Drake,' I'd say. They were ready to exchange Drake for the money when Lasiter tried to keep the money for himself and started shooting. Low-budget Lasiter, shady detective.

"I needed this elaborate farce and your bodies for the Sheriff, yes. More important was backing off Drake's Italian friends. Of course, they'd have suspected me, just not enough to hurt. I'd have given them access to Drake's secret rooms after I had moved most of the cash. 'He never told me what he did down there, and I didn't look,' I'd say, and they'd be satisfied. And if not? I've always been good at staying a step ahead. But you've ruined all my carefully planned timing, and now it's Plan B."

Uh, oh. Finally waking up to the reality of his situation, Bart hoped he could keep her talking until he could make something happen. But what?

"Weren't you afraid when you shot Hook, you'd hit your boat?"

"Lasiter, I don't miss. And the two wonderfully engineered hollow points I used stayed inside the big pirate — no bullet holes in the mahogany, and no scratched varnish."

"Okay. Where to now?"

"Hah!" She dropped from the cabin roof to the deck and approached him. "You know that joke? If I tell you, then I'd have to kill you? Well, I *am* going to kill you."

The muscles around Bart's stomach clenched.

She turned away from him and went to the starboard rail. She looked down into the water.

"Is he still dead?"

She turned back to him. "Funny."

"Just making conversation."

"Ah, conversation. You know, detective, anyone who lives outside the law, anyone who keeps a few secrets, that person is someone who eventually will have to talk about it. It's too much to hold inside indefinitely. Some are even dumb enough to talk to the cops — not me. But I can tell *you*, Lasiter." She checked the huge black watch on her wrist. Satisfied, she leaned back against the rail. "We're ahead of schedule. Talking to you will be pleasant and harmless."

Relieved to hear his death would be delayed, Bart tried to look interested.

"Tonight, I'll take this boat on her last run down the length of the lake, pushing forty knots all the way. A shame, the last run, because this boat, this lake, and I were made for each other. It was our collective, holy destiny. Dramatic, you might say, but my whole life has been one long journey to this boat and this lake.

"I love to speed across this lake. When Drake and I were first married, before I had this boat, I'd wait until he had fallen asleep or was preoccupied down in his workshops late at night. After a few Martinis, I'd take my Donzi out and make a full throttle run down the lake to the Keys at the south end. On the way back, I'd buzz the length of the west shore, shaking piers and rattling windows all the way. I think old Nevada George Whittell would have approved.

"The speed and crisp night air were rejuvenating, and later I would enjoy the stories that would go around the lake about some inconsiderate fool in a fast black boat who was spoiling the tranquility and sleep of responsible second and third generation waterfront residents on the west shore. I always pictured someone like Drake, probably a banker or lawyer from San Francisco, stumbling out of bed in the middle of the night, throwing on an old plaid shirt, and hobbling out onto his deck, looking for the sonnofabitch who woke him. Some Nevada-side *nouveau riche*, he'd say. The morning after he'd complain that the lake wasn't as nice as years before."

Her mood was going dark. Bart didn't know this new Mrs. Concannon.

"You don't like the old lake people?"

"I guess they aren't bad people. And, to tell the truth, I've been with the moneyed old in one place or another for decades, right there among them. When I was young, I used to think that you could marry into respectability. Long before I'd met Drake, I learned you couldn't. I've never felt accepted. I always knew that I had come to the party by sneaking in under the tent. In the end, you are who you are."

She walked the compact deck, not looking at Bart.

"I know I'm sensitive. When you've been dismissed, taken for granted, ignored, it changes you, and you react to any slight, any hint of that for the rest of your life. You can't live long enough to forget."

Bart tried to calm her. "Look at the success you've become."

"You mean the success you thought I was before tonight, don't you?"

This kind of talk worried him. He wanted to change the subject. "So, you like to go fast?"

"Lasiter, they can take the girl out of the racer, but they can never take the racer out of the girl."

"What happens when you arrive at the Keys?"

"People will be waiting for my boat at the marina travel lift. She'll be hauled out and set down on a dedicated flatbed trailer. Then, trucked down the highway to the travel lift in Stockton, where other people will be waiting to set her back into the water. It's amazing what generous sums of cash can arrange, with no questions asked."

She stopped pacing and smiled.

"From there, it's a smooth run to San Francisco Bay. After a brief pause in Sausalito to top off the tanks, I'll be looking at a beautiful sunset as I pass under the Golden Gate Bridge and make that turn to port. In the morning I'll be safe in Mexican waters. Then one more day and a few stops for fuel before I'm home in the harbor at Cabo San Lucas.

"Can't you see me in old Spanish lace? Hah! And dollars are good-as-gold in Mexico, you know. Of course, I have gold and stones, too, mostly at my ranch near Cabo. And then there is the pure joy of numbered Swiss bank accounts. I've worked hard all my life, Lasiter, and my hard work has rewarded me."

"You have a house in Mexico?"

"Since my first husband died. I needed some place to go, and I had all that money. I found this forgotten land, acreage that had once been a fine ranch. Over the years, like my boat, I've restored and improved it. I've been going there for decades, to rest and get away from people, and reinvent, when I needed. It's very peaceful and private. No one knows much about it except the locals and the caretakers who live on the ranch.

They are all very loyal. I see to all their needs.

"And then there is the harbor, too. Cabo has a beautiful, sheltered harbor, with talented people to care for my boat. She'll be happy there."

"So, you have it all figured out?" Bart tried to stretch his ropes and maintain circulation in his limbs while he listened.

"I think so. Lasiter, did you know that since 2005, Mexico won't extradite someone who faces the death penalty? A real irony — the bigger the crime, the safer you are."

Mrs. Concannon was not looking at Bart when she asked the question. She was looking into the dark, at what Bart assumed was an uncertain future.

"Sorry, I don't want to rain on your parade, but all the Mexicans need to extradite you is a letter from your District Attorney saying they won't seek the death penalty."

She laughed. "Lasiter, whether it's city, county, or state, DAs are usually elected, which means they always fear public opinion. And they have big egos, sometimes huge egos. Try convincing the DAs from a half-dozen states to agree with each other to waive the death penalty for someone the press will call a serial killer."

"A half-dozen? Oh."

"And, failing that, there are countries that won't extradite under any circumstances. I've always been good at staying a step ahead."

Bart wanted to change the subject again, to lighten her mood before she turned lethal. "With all that cash on board, and just yourself, aren't you afraid of pirates?"

She stared at him for a long minute. "You're clever, more than you look, or I had thought." Then she relaxed and smiled. "Despite your research, you didn't know that the harbor at Cabo San Lucas was once the home of pirates? They attacked the Spanish Galleons returning from the Philippines to their home base in Acapulco. You could say that I belong in Cabo."

"I missed that."

"No, Lasiter, I'm not afraid. I have yet to meet a pirate I would fear. And I don't want any new crew members, including a descendant of Black Bart Roberts, if that's what you mean."

"You have to sleep on your way to Cabo."

"I rarely sleep. And I have some helpful stimulants."

"Does this mean I'm not getting paid anymore?"

Now she laughed freely. "You've *been* paid."

"What happened to the five million dollars?"

"Hah! There was no five million. What cash I had here went to you and expenses and the three clowns. Drake controlled the spending money. Most of the cash was down in that cage. Do you think I'd trust the three Mouseketeers with millions in cash? I wasn't sure they would take it, but I *was* sure they could lose it. I didn't want to hear that five million went to the bottom of the lake. It was old newspapers, of course. I told Hook that it was real money, and that they should store it safe in their trailer until we were done, when we'd split it. Hook was so well trained by then I knew he wouldn't even open the packages."

"Did Ramon know?"

"Ah, Ramon. Yes, he knew. He wrapped the newspaper. Ramon and I, well . . . we have a special relationship."

"*Had.* Remember?"

Her face flushed.

"I liked you better when you were funny, Lasiter. My better husbands could make me laugh, at first."

"I try to be funny, to lighten the load."

"Are you sure, Lasiter?"

"What?"

"If you look at professional comedians, a lot of them aren't trying to 'lighten the load.' Some of them are very depressed, tortured individuals. They crave laughter, applause, approval, and the attention of others. They never got any attention from their mothers when they were young. Have a Mommy Problem, detective?"

Bart didn't need any more abuse from her. He stayed silent, glaring at her.

She twisted her face in feigned concern. "Oh, hurt your feelings? Sorry."

"I'll *live.*"

"Good. You must learn to let go, Lasiter. Ramon didn't make it, but I did. Money and people come and go. Always be ready to move on. When it's time to go, you go. You go without hesitation to save yourself. If you're strong enough, you leave everything you have behind. Your dreams will always be with you."

"What happened to Mr. Concannon?"

"Drake never left the compound, locked in his workshop the whole time. I fixed his drink at the bar — same as yours — Wednesday evening, after I had hired you. The boys took him down below — same as you. The funny drink is a little trick I learned when I was a working girl."

"What was in the drink?"

"As I told you then, Jack Daniel's . . . with the traditional chloral hydrate. But I learned to set the stage with a dose of LSD. Your Coke. Classic. It's fun to watch a man who thinks he's in control become simultaneously bewildered and weak. The look on your face as you passed out was priceless."

"It's not as much fun on the receiving end."

"It wasn't meant to be *fun* for you, Lasiter. I'm not a cruise director."

"Hey, good one. So, he wasn't taken from his runabout."

"The boys used the Donzi to tow the runabout out after dark. They disconnected the bilge pumps and let it drift toward shore. It sank. I always asked Drake why he didn't have that boat restored. He was the original owner, and yet he let that boat, a true classic, fall to rot. It needed a new bottom at least ten years ago. He'd say, 'It's okay. It's got two bilge pumps and two batteries now. It'll soak up for one more season.'"

Anger tightened her face. "Drake was always clueless — clueless, boring, and — worst of all — *cheap!*

"I found out how cheap early in our marriage, when I asked him for a second-anniversary present, this very boat. A man in Chicago owned it. The man had for years refused to sell it. I visited him and tried to change his mind. He refused all my offers. And then . . . he died." She couldn't conceal a smirk. "He had no heirs. I knew that my boat would be available from his trust. And I knew the lawyer charged with liquidating the trust assets." She smiled. "I've been to a few barbeques."

"Drake had long ago built the second boat house down in the cove. He wanted to put a big boat there. I think he wanted to emulate his idol, George Whittell. But Drake's wife was long gone, and Captain George died. After that, Drake was in his workshop day and night and lost interest in another boat. So, *I* would use the big boat house.

"Drake had my boat shipped here by rail from Chicago to Carnelian Bay. He told the manager at O'Hara's to, 'Just clean it up, do whatever she wants, and send me the bill.'

"I told O'Hara's what I wanted. They liked it. Then I told them not to bother with estimates, just do the job and give us one bill when it was finished. And don't bother Mr. Concannon with any details. He's a very busy man.

"Everything was fine until Drake saw the bill. He looked like he was going to die on the spot — if only. He screamed, 'That's over ten thousand dollars a foot for cleaning up an old cruiser!' He paid, but he didn't talk to me for a week. After that, he put me on an allowance, as if I were his daughter! I enjoyed my boat, but I started to reconsider my future.

"He owned that stone mansion with its fifteen waterfront acres and another twenty acres inland. It's worth an easy fifty million, and he had millions in new and old bills down in the cage, plus residuals and retainers from his casino work bringing in another one-to-two million a year. But he didn't want to spend a cent. You could say it killed him to spend a cent."

Bart wondered if she was talking to him or herself. She seemed lost in the story, looking out into the darkness instead of to Bart.

"His divorce did something to him. Women can be cruel. I can say at least that I never left any of *my* husbands in pain.

"After the divorce, all he wanted was white cotton socks with black shoes, a white vinyl pocket protector in the pocket of a white polyester, drip-dry, short-sleeved shirt, gray pants, and a clip-on tie. And, of course, a technical problem to solve.

"And wine — he couldn't tell the difference between a foothills Old Vine Zinfandel and a three-dollar Merlot."

Her face took another strange turn as she spit out, "And black, black — he never liked *BLACK!*" Her head jerked toward Bart.

"Do you know what I said before I shot him? Happy anniversary, Honey."

* * *

50

Growing Up

The Way You Look Tonight

Bart's head still hurt, and he was fighting to keep his fingers, arms, and legs from going numb, but he wasn't going to discourage Mrs. Concannon from talking. He was not happy listening to her, but, so far, it beat a shooting or drowning.

"It looked like Drake was going to have a heart attack when he saw me with a gun. The heart attack would have deprived me of a long-anticipated pleasure."

"Why didn't you just divorce him?"

She laughed, looked over the starboard railing again, and shook her head, as if she were, yet again, forced to revisit a great unfairness.

"The one thing that he did right in his first marriage was use a prenuptial agreement — unusual foresight for such a young man. It saved him money and property, if nothing else. Today, all these single, wealthy, . . . *gentlemen* . . . they all know what prenups are. Some of them would spend more money on their lawyer writing a tight prenup than they ever would on a nice honeymoon. Anyway, Drake had a prenuptial agreement ready for me to sign, as though it were as normal as sleeping in a bed. 'Oh, sure Honey. You know best. Where do I sign?' Parents dead, no heirs — what did it matter?"

She turned back to Bart, looking past him toward the lights on the west shore, and tilted her head to the stars.

Bart couldn't resist. "You caught him like a fish."

"Yes, Lasiter, he was a fish, but not just any fish. He was like his fat Mackinaw."

"The one on the wall? Why?"

"That one. Tahoe trout grow large because, even though the lake is nutrient poor, they live longer here. They can hide in the deep, cold water, year after year. They grow old and fat, and careless. Catching that fish thrilled Drake — God knows I heard the story enough. But, like the Mackinaw, Drake hid at Tahoe, safe in Eagle Cove, year after year, growing old, fat, and careless. And then I caught him."

"You took advantage of him."

"No, Lasiter, you make it sound easy. Convincing Drake Concannon to marry me was my finest accomplishment, the result of everything I had learned since I left my father's house. Lasiter, some of my husbands *were* easy. But not Drake. He was still so gun-shy from his first marriage that I had to use every trick I knew, and then invent some new ones.

"And, of course, the best trick, the hardest trick, was making him think that our marriage was all *his* idea, and that *he* had to convince *me* that we should marry. 'Really, Drake? You're sure? Get married?'

"I will admit that it could have been worse. Drake didn't seem to have any friends — just business associates. When I first visited the Yacht Club, it didn't take long to see that they barely tolerated him there. They wouldn't interfere. And once I had signed the prenup, Drake relaxed and let me take care of the remaining details. A Reno lawyer I knew provided a no-questions-asked, completely legal Nevada marriage license — without Drake appearing for the application — and a minister to marry us at the small boathouse. Drake wanted our marriage to be at the Yacht Club. Can you imagine? I said, 'Oh, Drake, why not on your pier, by the water? Beautiful. Nice and quiet — just us at home. Okay, Honey?'"

"So, you were just after his money. You tricked him."

"Lasiter, you have no right to question me. You don't know what I have been through."

"What?"

"Let me shock you." She paused and looked at him. "I had

an unhappy childhood."

"Well, I *am* shocked."

She hopped back up to sit on the aft cabin roof and let her legs hang.

Bart thought, it's okay, don't worry about me — I'll stand.

"Look, Lasiter. The only mother I had was a wrinkled and whiskey-stained snapshot of a young woman who was gone before I knew I was supposed to have a mother. My father was a drunk. He bounced from job to job because he couldn't stay sober. He had even been a teacher and a cop. Teacher, cop, father — they're supposed to protect children. He beat me, a child, like they say about voting in Chicago — early and often. He said it would keep me from being a whore like my mother."

"Wasn't he ever good to you?"

"When he was sober was best, almost tolerable. And when he was drunk, if he could just focus on something besides my mother. Sometimes, when he was drunk, instead of hitting me, he'd become sentimental and start talking about the old days, when he was a kid, and later after he had been drafted. When I was young, he told me about his Army days.

"His unit had been assigned to northern Japan in 1951. At Camp Chitose, his day job was with the military police. He'd even drag out his army MP uniform with its leather harness and shoulder lanyards. 'See? Your father was somebody.' But after work, at night, he'd go off-base, to bar hop and walk the streets, enjoying the smells of restaurant food and the smoke from wood fires heating the tiny houses.

"Downtown one winter evening, crunching through the snow, his nose full of cold air, he was drawn to a Japanese movie theater by its colored posters displayed on gray wood, weathered old buildings. The posters were huge images of scowling men with swords and guns over brightly colored exclamations in Japanese characters. He bought a ticket and watched a gangster movie. No subtitles, just Japanese. He liked it, even though he mostly didn't understand what the actors were saying. He watched more and more of these gangster movies, and he understood more of what the actors were saying. Japanese movie fans who saw his interest helped him with the translation. He told me this story about the gangster movies dozens of times.

"Jabbing the air with his cigar, he told me how the most successful Japanese gangs drank only Scotch, Johnny Walker Red, which was about thirty dollars a fifth then in Japan. But the gang's leader, who was always the smartest, the toughest, the most ruthless and fearless, the one the gang members both loved and feared, he drank only the most expensive, the almost unaffordable Johnny Walker *Black*. Only the smartest, the toughest, the one who's always in charge, could have *Black*."

Black again, but Bart didn't stop her.

"When I was eleven in Milwaukee, I started ditching school to ride the bus down to Lake Michigan. I hated school. I felt so out of place, so alone, so unlike the other girls. They all had mothers. They smiled and laughed, and there was never any hint that they were being beaten by their fathers. The nuns were no help.

"I'd go to the beach for the day, at McKinley Park. On one of those trips, a day after he had beaten me again, I saw these people at the Yacht Club. They were near the most beautiful boat, a cabin cruiser. All that polished chrome and stained and varnished wood. And its sides were *BLACK*.

"I watched some of the people go aboard for a cruise on Lake Michigan. As the cruiser motored away from the Yacht Club's seawall, headed for the breakwater, some of the people stayed behind and waved goodbye to the people on the boat. I waved to them, too, and they waved back. The people standing on the seawall wore suits and dresses. The people who had boarded were well-dressed, too, but more casually, except for one. She was a beautiful blonde, wearing nothing but a trim black bathing suit. She was stretched out on the aft cabin roof, here, where I sit now. The blond woman lifted her sunglasses and looked at me, like she already knew me. She raised her drink to salute me. Her look said to me, Don't worry young lady, you belong on a boat like this. You *will* have a boat like this.

"I didn't know then that her black boat was already eight years old, because I had never seen anything like it before. I watched until that boat was past the breakwater and out of sight, and then went home a changed little girl. Now I had a picture to hold, a picture of my future.

"I knew then that I wanted to grow up fast, own a boat like

that, and be like those people, well-dressed, happy, respected, drinks in their hands, with not a care in the world — they could go *anywhere!*

"Later I found that I might have to have that very boat, that specific boat, because there were so few produced just like that. Lasiter, I dreamed. Every night I dreamed. I wanted that black boat, and all that went with it.

"Then, when I was fifteen, my father . . . ."

She looked away and became quiet and still.

"Well, you don't need to know the details, Lasiter. Let's just say it was a good time for me to leave home."

Bart remained silent, hoping to keep her talking.

"I ran away. I was always hungry, but I survived. I went to New York and worked the street, looking through restaurant windows at people inside eating and drinking. Then *I* moved inside. If you are pretty and smile, there is always a job serving food. When I had a driver's license that claimed I was old enough, I worked in bars. I tended bar at the catered parties of the wealthy.

"Then I became a wife, a wealthy wife. Because I chose them and then let them pick me, all my husbands had boats. But they weren't *my* boat. I paid a yacht broker to keep track of my boat, tell me where she was and who owned her." Her face twisted again. "I learned, and went after what *I* wanted, Lasiter — what I was *owed!*"

She frightened Bart, the way she looked tonight. Then her face and shoulders relaxed, and her mood lifted.

"It hasn't been *all* bad. Betty, the sad little girl who read children's mysteries and dreamed to escape the pain — she fought and grew to become a woman of the world. I've traveled and lived all over the world. I've eaten the best food. I've had the best of *everything.* Would you believe that this high school drop-out can converse in five languages?"

"Sure." Keep talking. Try all the languages.

"But I confuse you, Lasiter — with all the different voices I have — don't I?"

He didn't answer.

"You see, it's a matter of necessity, and personal history. When you can't stand who you are, you keep trying to be someone new. You create a new history. But the new you that you create will only last so long. Then you must invent another version of yourself. Life is easier when you have a role to play. You just focus on the job at hand. The job tells you who you will be.

"The most important thing is to never give up. Lasiter, they almost had me, several times, but good, thorough preparation for that possibility, and the strength to never give up, pulled me through, free to live another day, back home at my ranch in Mexico."

She looked at Bart, in his funny clothes, roped to a plank. "Don't worry, Lasiter. It won't be a problem for you much longer."

Though keeping her talking was his only hope, Bart began to wish she would just *shut up*. But there was more water behind the floodgates.

"I guess I'm on the run again. I'm good at that. Maybe this will be the last time. Maybe I'll settle down. I am older now. When I leave U.S. waters and the FBI behind, I'll be free like never before. Now that I have my boat and all this money, I should retire."

She looked at him and locked him in place with those blue eyes again, as if he were a judge and she were pleading before the Court of Bart. "I want you to know, Lasiter, that I did try to love my husbands, each one.

* * *

51

Love is Difficult

Something Wonderful Happens in Summer

"My first marriage was wonderful, in the beginning. I was serving drinks one spring in Brooklyn when he came through the door. He was handsome and wealthy. We went to Niagara Falls, and later lived on Lake George. I was full of happiness and optimism at the beginning. But I just couldn't hold on to that feeling.

"When I would marry again, at least the first several times, I always wanted us to honeymoon at Niagara Falls, trying to recapture that original, optimistic feeling. I tried."

"How many did you say there were?"

"Just accept that I tried. I did. It would have been better for everyone if I had been able to love them, even one of them. After a while, they would change. Or, maybe, I would change. Then it would be time for me to move on, often as the end of the boating season approached. The fall was always beautiful, but sad, the beginning of a death. The winters could be long, too long, and remind me of Milwaukee. But, believe me, I *did* try.

"Over time, you learn something that is very important. If you can't love someone, you must love some *thing*, a place, an idea — a boat. It is important for survival. What do you love, Lasiter?"

Bart couldn't answer. He thought of Aggie, Old Town, and food. He had to change the direction of this conversation.

"What about Isabel? Was she in on all this?"

"No. She is quite an innocent soul. I like her a lot. Drake told me that she didn't know about his secret workshops down below. He had to tell me early in our marriage. 'Where have you been all these hours?' I asked. He had a workshop near the big boathouse, but it was cover for the hidden tunnel. He told Isabel to just call him on the intercom when she needed him, and to stay out of his workshop.

"She, of course, knew about the big boathouse, and would help me on my boat. I took her all over the lake. Before that, she was always afraid to go out on the lake, because of Drake's runabout. No, she had no part in any of this."

"Hooray! One person who's not a disappointment."

"Lasiter, that's why I hired you — you're a Boy Scout."

"Better than a murderer."

"You're in no position to be arguing with me."

"If you say so."

"Now, we're almost done." She slid off the cabin roof and stood. "I had prepared a wonderfully nuanced speech for the Sheriff, but it's of no value in Plan B. So, as a gift to you before you die, I will perform for *you*, instead. Pretend that you're the Sheriff. Observe, Lasiter."

Bart watched as she sat on the deck. Closing her eyes, she slowly pulled her arms against her body, like she had that first day in his office. She brought her knees together and drew them up. Then her body began slow, rhythmic undulations from her feet to her head.

Method acting, thought Bart. She's visualizing a TV nature program with some python dressed in black nylon swallowing a monkey.

The dim light from the cabin doors showed tears forming. She opened her eyes and looked up to Sheriff Bart.

"Oh, Officer — I made a horrible mistake! I hired this Lasiter fellow to find my husband."

Bart was impressed. She was good, if a little over the top.

"I hate to admit this, Officer, but my husband Drake had left me before, for other women. He would be gone for a few days, or even a week at a time. I didn't like it, not at all, but in time I learned to accept it. He had always come back before.

"He was such a brilliant, dynamic man. I knew instinctively that there was no one woman who could ever satisfy him, though the Lord knows that this woman tried. I just wanted Mr. Lasiter to tell me where my husband was going, and that he was safe. I had never tried to interfere with his escapades, though it was difficult and painful for me."

She paused to wipe the tears that had run to her nose and mouth, using a black linen handkerchief from a zippered pocket in her jumpsuit.

"Then the ransom note arrived. I wanted to go straight to the law, but Mr. Lasiter insisted that it would be better for my husband if we avoided the authorities and let him handle it himself. And he took the ransom note and my copy of our contract and tore them up, saying there should be no paper trail. I *trusted* him!"

She paused for more eye and face wiping.

"Then I gave him all that money for the ransom, to get my husband back. He said he would wrap and deliver it to the kidnappers for me and return with my husband. I should have known he would want to take the money for himself. I wasn't thinking right. I felt lost and helpless. I was only thinking about getting my husband back home and safe.

"Something happened. They had guns. Someone killed my poor Drake. Officer, I was such a sad fool to have listened to Bart Lasiter, instead of trusting you and law enforcement. I lost my husband, and I lost the money. Now I am a *widow!*"

Her head bowed to her lap and her body shook as she sobbed. Her one-person audience, Sheriff Lasiter, was fully attentive, but uncomfortable in standing-room-only. Bart wiggled and flexed his toes. His legs were going to sleep.

After a minute, she composed herself and stood.

"What do you think, Lasiter? Good, no? Of course, it would've been better with the veil, and lots of makeup running down my face."

She was back to being herself — whoever that was.

"The drama classes at Northwestern were special. For a moment, I wanted to be an actress — I enjoyed it that much. But I like to be in control. You seem to pity me now, but you don't understand. No father, no husband to control me. Now, *I'm* in control — *of everything!"*

Bart worried. She was going full-tilt squirrely again.

"Were you in any films or plays I would know?"

"No. In the end, instead of Broadway, I chose to play on a smaller, private stage. And for a larger share of the box office."

She checked her black watch. "Well, now it's time to go. I still have to take my boat and those sacks of cash out of the country."

She stepped to the helm and flipped a switch. Bart heard fans begin to spin. Concentrating on her instruments, she started the two V-8s. She ran the port engine up for a moment, then let it settle back to idle. She repeated with the starboard engine. The quiet of the night was now cut by low rumbling, and exhaust spitting at the stern. Bart could smell the diesel exhaust.

She turned back to Bart. "It's a shame I'm forced to leave Eagle Cove behind. I had gotten used to the lake with my boat. I might have been very satisfied living as the wealthy widow Concannon, grieving in her stone castle on the Nevada shore of Lake Tahoe. Certainly, one could do worse. But moving instead to Mexico permanently may be for the best. Had I stayed here, I'd have always been looking over my shoulder."

Bart thought it hard, given his situation, to feel her pain.

"Well, you changed all that, Lasiter. You've ruined my plan, my chance of staying on Lake Tahoe."

"All that time, I thought I was helping you."

"That's your problem, Dudley Do-Right. You thought. No, you *felt.* Now I'm going to enjoy killing you. Surprised? It's not like one of your movies. No happy ending, for you."

She reached for her pistol.

"Would you like to have it over quickly?"

* * *

52

No Rehab for Ahab

A New Kind of Love

Over quickly? Bart wondered if she expected an answer. Stalling was not a great plan. It was his only plan.

"What are my choices?"

His bravado was fading. Even all roped up to the plank, his knees were sinking on their own. He visualized Frank singing *Five Minutes More.* Then she surprised him.

She set the pistol back down on the cabin roof.

"Pistol . . . or water?" she asked, as though it were a game show. "I think I'll just tip you over the side. I could almost do it with one finger. I *like* the idea of you being conscious every second of your drowning."

Nope. No choice for Bart.

"You're sadistic." Bart's disgust was displacing his fear.

"The question is, detective, with you tied to that plank, *One,* will you drown on the surface because the plank is floating on top, and your face is under the water? Or, *Two,* maybe, after you go over the side, you and your plank will spin and bob in and out of the water in my boat's wake as I leave. You'd be like Ahab tied to the White Whale — waterboarding out in the open. Or, better yet, *Three,* is your thick old plank waterlogged enough to carry you deeper?"

Bart had never tried to watch game shows, but if it would extend the time he had left, he was willing to play.

"What's behind door *Four?* I don't like those three choices. I wouldn't pick any of those."

She leaned back against the main cabin near the helm and played with the wheel. "You know the story about the lake and the ghost logs?"

"Ghost logs? No, but I like ghost stories. Please, tell me."

"The story goes that the lake is so deep in places, like right where we are now, that the thermocline is at least a hundred feet down. In a lesser big lake, maybe Wisconsin's Geneva Lake, in the summer the thermocline might be less than thirty feet deep. You know what the thermocline is, don't you, Lasiter?"

"Maybe. Maybe not. Tell me." Take all night.

"That's the demarcation line, where the denser, always cold, still water below is separated from the lighter, warmer, active water above. The demarcation is so distinct that it's like a membrane that you can stick your arm through. Your hand would be cold and your elbow warm. Cold below, warm above. Understand?"

"Go on. But if I don't understand, I might ask you to tell me all over again."

"That's the spirit. You'll understand. I know you're smart. Sometimes."

"Try me."

"Long ago, logs they cut on the lake's west shore were dragged across the lake's surface to the east shore, to the mills at Glenbrook, where they were cut up for the shoring lumber in the Nevada silver mines. On the trip across the lake, some of those logs absorbed so much water that they could no longer float. They sank. But some couldn't absorb enough water to sink through the thermocline and go all the way to the bottom."

"So, what's the point?" Bart was suddenly tired of games.

"Don't be impatient. Now, if you went down there below us, to the thermocline, you could still see those old ghost logs floating on top of the denser water, like abandoned ships in space. Forever. Lasiter, maybe you'll wind up there with those ghost logs, preserved and floating on the thermocline a hundred feet below the surface, roped to your plank. Tahoe's Ahab."

The image left him speechless.

"That would be okay with me. You spoiled my plan and

alibi. I don't need your body now."

Bart lost hope. His back hurt and his head had returned to throbbing, keeping time with her never-ending chatter. He was so tired, and his arms and legs were numb under the ropes.

She moved closer to him and released the canvas strap holding him and the plank to the dolly.

"There. Now when you go into the lake, the dolly will fall free, and won't weigh you down. It will take longer for you to drown."

Bart remembered Hook calling that *sportin'*.

With the rope forcing the plank against his back and pinning his arms to his sides, he still couldn't go anywhere, or stop her.

"Bart, how tall are you?"

She had used his first name and asked a question that seemed so out of the situation's context. It gave him a flash of renewed spirit. He tried to use it.

"With the dolly?"

"No, without."

"About six-two."

"That's about right. I do confess, I've always thought you are a handsome man. Perhaps a bit of a clown, or doofus. But, from our first meeting in your office, you really have cared about me, and you have been charming — of course, all in a manner, well, unpolished. Your problem is simply that you don't know your place."

"So, that morning, when you hired me, you assumed I would do what you planned?"

She opened a cabinet near the wheel and brought out a black towel and a bottle of *Evian* water. She wet the towel and dabbed at the black powder residue around Bart's mouth. Very gently.

Bart wondered, could she be changing her mind?

"When I saw your ad in the Yellow Pages, I knew you were a good candidate. *Lasiter Investigations — I'm ready to help.* Really. A little research told me you were a Berkeley ex-copper, accused of beating up street mimes."

"Those charges were dropped."

She smiled. "Then, when I phoned, and your line was out of service, I worried that I was too late. But I didn't have anyone else, so I climbed those stairs and found your door unlocked.

As soon as I saw you, I couldn't believe my luck."

Her eyes flashed. "I thought you were perfect."

Bart gulped.

"That minute, I knew who you were. I knew you were mine. My plan was off to a perfect start."

Bart had never imagined himself as a pawn, but she wouldn't be giving him time to dwell on it.

She spread the ropes encircling his chest, using the slack to expose the buttons in his gambler's shirt. She slowly unfastened the buttons, pausing after each one.

Yikes.

Smiling, she looked into his eyes. Her hands grabbed the shirt and jerked it wide open, exposing his bare chest.

An eerie illustration of a bare-chested Bart the Pirate and Mrs. Concannon embracing on the cover of a romantic thriller novel appeared to him. He could see the back-cover tease for *Pirates and Lust*:

Denied love and respect on land, she satisfied her needs at sea, seizing men and treasure at will. His heaving man-chest was cruelly bound and restrained by ropes as coarse as barbed wire, ropes that could not stop her from kissing the pain away.

Now he was being tortured by his own sense of humor.

What was she going to do?

She stood back to look at him, the bare-chested Fabio-lite. Then she returned and slowly traced her finger over the edges of what muscles showed on Bart's cold chest, again watching for his reaction.

He wanted to deny her any reaction, but failed, his skin jumping under her electric touch.

Amused, she smiled and leaned back against the aft cabin.

"Bart, now it's your turn — your chance to answer the question."

Relieved for the moment, he said, "More questions? Which question?"

"The same question I asked some of my husbands."

"Maybe that's a compliment. Ask away."

"Okay. If you knew that you were about to have sex for the last time, the last time of your life, would it make the sex better?"

Bart thought. Last time. Last time Classic Coke. Last time

burrito. Last time sex —

"What?"

She took off her black cap and removed the black hair band. She brought her face near Bart's and shook her hair loose, some of it whipping across his lips. Wearing a frightening smile boasting both sexual promise and sadistic pleasure, she leaned her breasts into his bare chest.

He felt the nylon move across his skin. The thickness of her black jump suit didn't prevent his blood pressure from spiking. She looked up into his eyes, studying his reaction. Now he could feel her breath on his face and neck and smell her hair. And that perfume again.

It brought him back to their last night together at the stone house but without the Sinatra and Jack Daniel's. He could use both, now that he had that same old tingle inside again. He saw a brand-new album cover from Frank:

Sex and Death for Swinging Lovers

Backing away a step, she planted her feet and put her left palm flat on his chest. She watched his face and applied a little pressure.

Bart was sure she was finally going to push him through the open gate into the water. It surprised him, how quickly he could feel sick.

When she saw his reaction, she pushed harder, and then let off. Again. And again. She laughed, watching his face as his dolly rocked back and forth.

Now he knew. She had done it. *She had made him dig his own grave.* The grave was right behind him, wet, and sixteen-hundred-feet deep. Now he would *lick the shovel clean.*

With her left hand again applying steady pressure on his chest, she moved her right hand toward his face. She put one finger on his lips, paused while she searched his eyes, and then pushed her finger through his lips and teeth to touch his tongue. His body stiffened against the ropes. She smiled immediately. Keeping the pressure on his chest, all the while watching his eyes, she withdrew her wet finger and slowly dragged it down his chin, neck, and chest until the ropes stopped her. Every flicker of Bart's eyes reacting to her finger made her smile.

Bart was panicking. He didn't know if he liked this kind of attention right now. He wanted his total focus to be on staying alive.

She kneeled and tugged at the ropes around his waist until she had uncovered his '57 Chevy belt buckle.

He looked down on her hair. What would she do to him, and how did he wind up here? His despair was as intense as the gold of her hair.

"Wait! What about my choice? And don't you want me to answer the question?"

She yanked the buckle open.

Yikes!

He felt her fingers pulling at his Brooks Brothers pants zipper.

Yikes! Nothing to protect him in full commando-mode.

His zipper was almost down when her blond hair burst into flames of white light.

Searchlights blinded his eyes.

"*FREEZE!* HANDS UP! FBI!"

"Shit!" Then Mrs. Concannon pretended to faint, and fell to the deck, her sleeve landing in a puddle of Hook's congealed blood. "Shit, shit!"

A different bull-horn voice followed the FBI's.

"NOBODY MOVE! Is that you, Bart?"

"Marty?"

* * *

Part Six

Returning to Earth

53

Strike the Black Flag

He's Been a Poet, a Pauper, a King,
And Yes — a Puppet, and a Pawn

Marty Brooks? Bart was as confused as blinded. The bullhorn voices in the night preceded the sounds of boats racing up to the big Chris-Craft. His eyes cleared in time to see Marty Brooks in a Sheriff's uniform holding the foredeck railing of the Placer County Sheriff's *Marine 6* aluminum patrol boat, the same craft Bart had seen at the boat show. Two men in camo FBI SWAT fatigues stood right behind Marty. They held on as their boat brushed into the starboard side of Mrs. Concannon's black Corvette.

The collision set Bart's dolly in motion rolling across the deck toward Marty.

"Yikes!" yelled Bart, before holding his breath.

Once the dolly started rolling, Bart didn't know if it would tip forward or backward. If the dolly went backward, the back of his already damaged head would slam against the plank when it hit the deck. If the dolly tipped forward, Bart's face would be the first thing to hit the deck. Instead, like a unicycle balanced by unknown forces and Bart's terror, the dolly remained upright, slowly rolling forward. The dolly stopped rolling when it hit Mrs. Concannon, who pretended not to notice. The dolly and Bart then tipped forward, sending Bart's face on a collision course with the deck.

When Marty saw Bart rolling, he dropped his megaphone,

leaped from his boat onto the Corvette and caught Bart on the way down. The FBI men followed Marty and went straight to Mrs. Concannon. They picked up her gun, handcuffed her, and searched her for other weapons, while she still pretended to be unconscious.

Washoe County Sheriff's deputies from Incline Village boarded the Chris-Craft's port side from their boat, *Marine 9*, and secured the cabins. After the Sheriffs' boats, a white fiberglass runabout drew alongside carrying two passengers in blue FBI jackets. They climbed aboard and joined the other FBI men near Mrs. Concannon and stood over her. The little deck was crowded again, but this time Bart would be happy to leave.

"Elizabeth Lombowski, we have a Federal warrant for your arrest for the murders of Jacob Crandall, Martin Whittaker, Harold Swanson, Robert . . . ."

Marty Brooks steadied Bart and the dolly with one hand while he pulled a folding knife from his back pocket and flicked it open with his thumb. He put the long black serrated blade between Bart and the plank and cut through the rope, freeing Bart.

"Bart, you look like Ted Kaczynski when they dragged him out of his shack. What happened to your face?"

"Yikes. Wait a minute." Bart reached into one of the helm cabinets for a fresh black towel and bottle of Evian. He scrubbed his face clean.

Mrs. Concannon, still on the deck, but with one eye open, forgot she was unconscious and tried to move her sleeve out of Hook's blood. The FBI agents noticed and looked at each other. After receiving no response to their offer to provide an attorney, they picked her up and strapped her into an orange life preserver before taking her to the white runabout.

Ted Watson and Hank Delaney from O'Hara's handled the white runabout for the FBI. Mrs. Concannon looked confused. Bart had seen her distressed before — at least acting distressed — but never like this. She sat on the upholstered bench seat at the back of the white boat's cockpit, her head darting back and forth. She was looking for something. A way out, Bart was sure. He wondered if the life preserver was preventing her from jumping overboard to end it.

With his legs still partly asleep, Bart leaned against the Corvette's helm while he zipped up and buckled his pants.

"What happened to Hook and his pals?" asked Marty.

Bart buttoned his shirt. "They're in the lake. They're not coming back."

"Feed the Mackinaw," said Marty, while he helped Bart onto *Marine 6*, still under the control of Marty's crewmate deputy.

Bart was happy now that he knew he would live but was strangely more concerned about Mrs. Concannon than himself. Her bizarre life story and network of excuses held together until you remembered it involved killing a lot of men who he assumed meant her no harm.

But now she was acting out in a way that surprised him even more. She's coming un-glued. Her life's front door is swinging on one failing hinge in the strong, cruel wind of reality. They had finally caught her.

They all waited while the Sheriff's deputies from Nevada rigged a towing harness through the chocks at the bow to the mooring bit on the deck of Mrs. Concannon's beloved, black-hulled Chris-Craft Corvette. Hank Delaney came aboard and went to the Corvette's helm.

Marty Brooks and Bart watched the big Chris-Craft swing around under tow, bringing its broad transom under the Sheriffs' lights.

Hanging proudly from a bleached and varnished teak mast at the cruiser's stern, fluttering in the bright lights, Captain Edward England's black flag mocked Bart with crossed bones below a white skull. Low on the transom, four polished copper exhaust tubes protruded through chromed bronze rings. The engines, still at idle, spit low rumbling salutes through the tubes.

Above the exhaust tubes, gold leaf lettering outlined in black formed – **1954** – on the port side, and – **Lake Tahoe** – on the starboard side. And higher, black script outlined by a narrow band of gold leaf flowed across the bourbon-colored mahogany transom to display the Corvette's name, the name Bart, while falling into the water at O'Hara's, had missed:

Coeur de Noir

One of the FBI agents yelled to Hank, "Kill those engines. For all we know, she's got it booby-trapped. We'll tow it in into Carnelian Bay and impound it at O'Hara's."

Mrs. Concannon had turned red and angry. She sat sulking on the back bench of the white runabout. Except for her orange life preserver, she was all black in a world of white plastic.

She came to life when she heard the engines die, and saw her proud and beloved Bullnose, resisting like a roped calf, being dragged away by *Marine 9*. Mrs. Concannon jumped up to stand on the white vinyl seat, her blond hair swinging as her head jerked from her Corvette to the men trying to restrain her. Her eyes were wild and frantic, her face crimson. She swung her arms, pulling against her handcuffs and the two FBI agents trying to control her. Bart was sure she was going to jump into the water until they got her under control.

Finally held tight by the agents, she sobbed and stared at her boat. Tears washed down her face. Like a mother having her child torn from her arms, Mrs. Concannon yelled, "You've done enough to her. Don't let those lines touch the varnish!"

* * *

54

Weak Heart

Love and Marriage

Bart was still trying to understand Mrs. Concannon during his ride back to Carnelian Bay. Maybe it would all be clearer after he warmed up.

The steady drumming of twin V-8s pushing the Sheriff's aluminum-hulled patrol boat remained in the background while Bart enjoyed *Marine 6*'s warm cabin. The heat helped him rub some circulation back into his cold limbs.

Marty Brooks smiled at Bart and put his arm around the shoulder of the man at the helm. "Bart, this is my crewmate, Eddie Walsh. He's been with Placer County his whole career."

"Marty told me you two go back some," said Eddie, without diverting his eyes from the water ahead.

"We do."

While Eddie kept the boat on course to O'Hara's, Marty Brooks laid out his side of the story to Bart, who hadn't heard from him since they'd left the Berkeley Police Department five years before, each for different reasons.

Marty had been Bart's best friend in Berkeley. They'd met in their rookie class, shared a room while they went through Berkeley's police academy up in Sacramento, and competed against each other during training. Marty had been a three-sport athlete in high school, and at Humboldt State, and won most of the firsts in the physical tests the training academy had thrown at their class. Bart was better with some of the written tests and always finished ahead of Marty on the shooting range. Accurate shooting requires physical skills, but more, it requires a Zen-like concentration that allows the shooter to conquer distraction and slow time itself. Bart could usually call on that, at least when the targets were paper.

"Bart, when I left Berkeley for Florida, I lost track of you. I'm sorry, but I admit I was too busy with my new life to stay in touch."

"No harm, Marty."

"Cool, Bart."

"So, what happened?"

"After a few months of enjoying Florida's beaches, I hooked up with the Miami-Dade County Sheriff. I went to Florida to see something different, something different than Berkeley. I wanted some real action instead of babysitting protesters and chasing bums and butt-ugly naked people off Telegraph. I'd seen way too much of the Hey-hey, ho-ho, fill-in-the-blank-has-*GOT*-to-go crap, and the sooo-scary stilts-and-cardboard-coffin crowd. Naturally, I got more in Miami than I'd asked for.

"When I wasn't inside doing *paperwork* —"

"THE LAWMAN'S BURDEN!" Bart yelled, then laughed.

"— I spent my time on the water rescuing wealthy numb-nuts boaters. And chasing pirates. Not the Long John Silver kind, in tall boots swinging a cutlass, but Armando, Veek-tor, and Shawn-tay in Nikes and Gucci's swinging AK47's."

"Don't hold back — you didn't like Florida?"

"Bart, I'll take rattlesnakes and black bears over pythons and gators any day, or sharks and barracudas. Two years of that and I'd had more than enough. Please, fly me back to California. Because of my Florida water experience, the Placer County Sheriff found a spot for me here."

Bart rubbed his legs and smiled. "Remember, Marty, you left Berkeley right in the middle of those mime attacks? Six months of beatings and robberies targeting the *Gold Mimes*?"

"How about the attack at their silent auction? Frustrating."

Simultaneously, Bart and Marty sang out, "CAN'T HELP PEOPLE IF THEY *WON'T TALK!*"

They high fived and laughed. Eddie just smiled and shook his head. He'd never worked in Berkeley.

Bart realized he was beginning to feel like his old joking self again, as if emerging from a spell. It felt good, though his head and back hurt when he yelled and laughed. Still, it was a joy to be alive and back with Marty Brooks again.

"Okay Marty, now tell me, how did you get involved in this Concannon thing, and wind up saving my butt?"

"Sorry Bart, mostly coincidence. I built up my Tahoe watch-list of informants, probationers, and parolees, and one day I'm watching Hook and friends when I see my old Berkeley bud, Bart Lasiter, tailing them. I couldn't believe it! Bart, where did you find that car?"

"The Klimo — it's a long story."

"I call beers first on that story, Bart. Anyway, it was a shock to see someone tailing my pirate kids, and then a double shock to see it was you. I was just about to get your plate number when a truck cut me off and I lost you. I didn't know where you lived or how to contact you."

"You should have called Fred."

"Ah, Fred. Of course."

"But then I don't have a cell phone, Marty. You might've had trouble contacting me, anyway. So, what put you onto Mrs. Concannon?"

"Last year, the FBI guys in Sacramento asked the Sheriff for help with this woman the Feds have been tracking for over ten years. They hoped we might run into her around Lake Tahoe. They didn't know then that her name, her new name, was Concannon.

"They called her 'Betty' — the Betty project — because that's the name they picked. They had *more* names — too many. But after a while, they concluded all the names belonged to just one woman, 'Betty.'"

"Betty? I heard what the FBI guys called her on her boat, but I thought her name was Rachel Wall."

Marty shook his head. "No, Bart. Rachel Wall is one of her bogus names. Another phony name she had used was Jackie Delahaye, short for Jacquotte Delahaye. Know what Rachel and Jacquotte have in common?"

"No clue."

"They were both female pirates hundreds of years ago."

"Yikes. Female pirates?"

"There were more than you would guess."

"But Betty or Elizabeth is her real name, right?"

"As far as they know. But think about this. Queen Elizabeth the First? They called her The Pirate Queen."

Bart looked out at the water and shook his head. "Marty, I'm really tired of pirates. So, she's been bad for a long time."

"Really bad. Bad for the Law, but she's been really good at covering her tracks. It took a long time to find her. Every year local and state agencies around the country would come to the various FBI seminars with their cold cases, including suspicious husband deaths and outright husband murders. The Feds saw a pattern. Maybe one woman could be responsible for a certain group of dead husbands, even though the victims were spread across the country. They checked what fingerprints they had and found some case-to-case matches, confirming the connection, but no match to a person, a known identity in the FBI fingerprint database."

"The prints — why didn't they see the connection sooner?"

"Again, she was really good. The sudden deaths of her early husbands were not initially suspicious. Many of the back-water coroners don't have the scientific training to determine the exact cause of death. Their whole thing is more baggem-and-taggem than CSI. Looks like a heart attack, it *is* a heart attack.

"Each time one of Betty's husbands died, usually at their lakeside home, she widowed-out clean. She would hang around after each husband's funeral just long enough to collect and cash out her earnings, and then quietly disappear. By the time people began to ask questions, she'd be gone. Into thin air. The houses were already cleaned, repainted, sold, and filled with the new owners long before there was any reason to collect prints.

"After the first few, if she learned someone suspected her before she could carry out her organized plan and could perform her weeping-widow routine, she'd grab what she could, kill the husband, and quickly disappear. And because she was in a hurry, there'd be prints, and maybe DNA. But, like the coroners, the local law enforcement people in these three-man lakeside agencies weren't that sharp. Sometimes they didn't submit what prints they had to the FBI, and the computer database didn't exist until '95. And most of this was before we knew what to do with DNA."

"What about IDs?"

"Twice the Feds got excited when they found a driver's license record under the name she was using during a particular marriage, a driver's license from a state that required a thumb print. But the thumb prints belonged to people who couldn't possibly be her."

Bart mused, "It sounds like she paid people inside state DMVs to get the IDs she wanted. No Kinko's, no Photoshop."

"First class, all the way."

"Where did they get 'Betty'?"

"When the Feds looked at what they suspected were her early marriages, a few neighbors or yacht club members they interviewed said the woman was called, "Betty." Betty became a serious ViCAP project."

"Oh, Marty, wait — ViCAP, the FBI's Violent Criminal Apprehension Program, right?"

"Bart, you haven't forgotten."

"Sometimes I'm good. Keep going."

"The Feds think she met her first husband in the late sixties, when she was a barmaid in Brooklyn. They concluded Betty moved her new black-widow career from Brooklyn to upstate New York on Lake George, New Hampshire on Lake Winnipesaukee, and then back to New York in the Thousand Islands."

"Where they make the salad dressing?"

"Bart, the joker. After the Thousand Islands, they thought they knew who she was, but they were too far behind her to help the dead husbands she left in Florida's Lake Dora, Miami, up north in Chicago on Lake Michigan, and then in Wisconsin in Lake Geneva."

"Yikes!"

"Yes, busy Betty."

"So, always boats and waterfront?"

"That was her hunting ground. In time, the Feds' theory became she was going to yacht clubs and classic boat shows to find her later husbands — these guys like Drake Concannon that lived on the waterfront. Wood boat, gray hair, strong wallet, weak heart — her specialty. And these guys are *not* smart around women. Each one she married was richer than the last."

Had Fred Clifford been right, that Bart really wasn't smart around women? Bart listened while Marty told the story of the woman who almost closed *Lasiter Investigations*.

"The Feds lost her again seven years ago. They had her nailed down in Idaho on Lake Coeur d'Alene. She was living in a huge log and stone house on the waterfront. Stone houses for a stone-cold killer. Just hours before the Feds moved in, she fled, leaving them to clean up another dead husband. But this death was an obvious homicide, and because she left in such a hurry, they worked the crime scene hard and found some good prints and DNA. Now they had her complete ID package, minus the mugshot. All they had to do was find her."

Bart had few doubts about his Mrs. Concannon, both from listening to her and Marty Brooks, but it was all still hard for him to admit. Mrs. Concannon, a cold killer. How did it happen to *him?*

First, he had to admit that it *did* happen. Like years ago, in Berkeley, when he'd been shot. It was summer, and he was in short sleeves. He remembered watching the blood pouring from the hole in his bare forearm, spreading over his wrist. Though he gripped his arm tightly above the wound, blood continued to drip onto his uniform pants. He watched the red soak into the dark blue. He saw it all. And yet, even as he fainted, he still couldn't believe that he'd been shot — it just couldn't have happened. Not to *him.*

"A real setback, Bart. After Idaho, the Feds had to start over. Then another husband turned up dead near Seattle, on Lake Washington. No house this time — they'd been living on a 52-foot Chris-Craft.

After that, the Feds began to watch *all* the classic boat shows across the country. Membership at the Antique and Classic Boat Society swelled with Feds. They were confident that sooner or later they'd find her again, maybe here at Tahoe during the big classic boat show, a target-rich environment for gold-diggers."

"There is a lot of money here."

"More than we'll ever see, Bart."

"Even so, after all that time, why was it so hard to find her?"

"Bart, the Feds only had a few descriptions of her, different descriptions. You knew her as a blonde. She was a brunette in Idaho, a redhead in Chicago. As soon as she decided which man she wanted, she'd cut him out of the herd, isolate him, and take over his life. You've seen those documentaries where a female lion picks one antelope from a thousand and runs it down?"

"Yes. I always feel sorry for the antelope, even though I know the lion is hungry."

"Hungry, but smart. She avoided people who would ask too many questions, and cameras. She hated cameras like vampires hate the sun. They'd lose her trail for months at a time because she convinced some of her new husbands to travel. They'd be out of the country — Europe, South America, the Far East. Some called her 'Black Betty,' because the sketchy descriptions usually mentioned black, some black clothes, black cars, black boats. Her Lake Geneva husband had a waterfront mansion near — of course — Black Point. And you saw, she named her boat, *Coeur de Noir* — Black Heart."

"Black — I think I've seen enough of it."

"After a while, some of the Feds started calling her '*Pioneer Betty*,' because, as she traveled west — probably always to Tahoe — she was leaving behind a trail of discarded household goods and bodies. Not a bad call, because — except for the detour to Seattle — she finished a few miles from Donner Pass. Our Betty progressed from little Betty Lombowski to Woman of the World, and number six on the FBI's Most Wanted list."

"So, Marty, how did you become part of this?"

"Like I said, I was just watching Hook, a crime waiting to happen. One day I see him meet with this blonde. She sure didn't look like Hook's type, but she and Hook shared some serious conversations. And she kept looking over her shoulder, always searching. Now she was the antelope, her nose in the air, watching for the lion. She looked different than the one the Feds had described until I watched her for a while. My gut said she could be Betty. On my own time, I followed her into Nevada to Eagle Cove. When I saw her stone-walled acreage, I had a hunch she was our girl.

"I was obsessed. I took notes and photos, but my big break came one day when she stopped for gas in Kings Beach. She threw a plastic water bottle into a trash barrel from the window of her black Mercedes. As soon as she cleared the gas station, I carefully transferred that bottle into a paper evidence bag and raced back to the barn.

"I showed my boss all I had, and the Sheriff told the FBI guys in South Lake Tahoe what we thought. They sent the bottle to the FBI lab at Quantico. A week later, the South Lake Tahoe FBI guys called us. The water bottle was gold. We had a match on the prints, and a preliminary match on the DNA. Their bosses in Sacramento came up here to meet. They built a team with us and the Washoe County Sheriff from the Nevada side of the lake."

"You did good, Marty. I wish I'd known."

"You contributed more than you know. After I saw you tailing my pirates, I started asking about you at their favorite hangouts. At Bill Meyer's, Captain Jack's, and O'Hara's, they each told me you'd been there and what you said and the questions you were asking. It made me want to stay even closer to Hook, to find you and find out why you were after Hook. When Eddie and I were at the boat show, I thought I saw you, but you disappeared."

"I did disappear. I fell in. No, Marty, you guys saved me."

Marty looked at Bart. "Sorry, Bart, we were almost too late to help you. We hit the stone compound last night with search warrants and an entry team. I followed the Washoe guys in, but only the housekeeper was there. It was really weird. There was a big sound system with a tape loop playing Sinatra tunes over and over."

"Ah, one of the few good things."

"Sinatra, huh? Bart, I would've put you down as a Beach Boys, *In My Room* kinda guy.

"Not really. Maybe. So, what did Isabel say?"

"'No Meester Cee. Missus Cee go big boat.'"

"I don't think she knows much."

"The Feds will find out what she knows."

"Until you found me, I was a goner."

"Sorry, but we were really just looking for Betty. We didn't know you were with her. Even with the housekeeper telling us she was out on a big boat, we had the entire lake to cover.

Twenty-two miles long and twelve miles wide, a lake that big can hold a lot of boats. Using all our night vision gear and radar, we still had trouble finding you. We were moving toward you when we heard shots."

"Marty, I'm not complaining."

"Hey, Bart, I *am* complaining. Here I left Florida to get away from pirates, and California gives me Hook and Betty! I *hate* pirates. And now, everywhere you turn, you're hit with all that *Pirates of the Caribbean* crap.

"Pirates with eye makeup. Did you know there's supposed to be a new pirate movie where all the pirates are vegetables?"

"I'm not surprised. What kind of veggie would Hook be?"

"Eggplant, undoubtedly," said Bart.

Marty laughed. "Now we have to find Drake Concannon."

"You didn't go into the basement?"

"We did. The housekeeper showed us two basements. The one under the kitchen just had food and a lot of wine. The one under the living room just had gardening tools. No Concannon."

"There's another, secret basement. Down there you'll find Concannon's body and prototypes of secret casino equipment."

Bart explained the hidden staircase behind the bookcase and described as much as he remembered of the layout of Drake's workshops. Then he told his side of the rest of the story, leaving out the most embarrassing parts.

Marty mouthed a cigarette and looked for matches.

Bart handed Marty his Frank Sinatra Cal-Neva matches.

"Cool matches. Do you still like burritos?"

Bart smiled. "I'll buy."

* * *

55

Deep Blue

Elizabeth

The advancing early light from a salmon-pink sky followed Bart, Marty, and Eddie in *Marine 6* toward Lake Tahoe's Carnelian Bay, tracking the wake and running lights of the FBI's white plastic runabout carrying Mrs. Concannon. This white boat was not dead in the water, but far out in front on the way to O'Hara's.

The Sheriff's aluminum boat gave Bart a smooth ride and a hint of what boating on the great Lake of the Sky might be like without kidnapping and shooting. He was feeling better.

When would Dr. Gupta open his office? Bart would have him look at his head again. The FBI medic checked his head but said he should see a doctor. Then he'd catch a ride back to Sacramento, maybe with some of the Sac-Town FBI guys, to check on Aggie, and maybe make a used clothing donation, including silver boots, to St. Vincent's. The Klimo would be okay at One Eagle Cove for a few days.

When they reached O'Hara's, Marty jumped off *Marine 6* to the pier and helped Eddie tie up. But Bart was cautious with his first step to the pier. He had a way to go before his legs would feel normal again.

The FBI agents had already brought Mrs. Concannon onto the pier. She was still in handcuffs, her head hanging — no longer the proud Lady of the Lake. They were a short distance away up the pier with a graying man in a dark suit. Bart guessed he was the FBI agents' supervisor. The man removed Mrs. Concannon's orange life vest while he questioned her. He was waiting for her to respond.

She turned away from the man and saw Bart on the pier, standing free. Her face lightened for a second, then she looked sad and pained — even remorseful. Most of it came from her eyes. Her eyes pleaded with him, and she mouthed the words, *Help me.*

Miss Wonderly, undone.

Certain she had gone into her never-give-up survival mode, Bart didn't move, or even change his facial expression in response, though he still felt an irrational urge to protect her. This was new and difficult for him, but he gave her nothing.

Bart could hear his Bogart delivering the bad news to his very own Miss Wonderly — O'Shaughnessy. *"Don't be silly, Mrs. Concannon — you're taking the fall."*

When Mrs. Concannon saw Bart would not respond, the look of remorse disappeared, and those blue eyes drilled into him with an accusing stare. Even after all he'd been through, and all he knew about her, he could still feel those eyes bore deep into him, setting hooks to pull him in, to somewhere he could no longer afford to go.

When Bart still didn't respond, her body stiffened. She looked angry — as if she would explode. Then she seemed to calm herself and began to look resigned. Her face and body slowly relaxed. No fight left in her now. As she herself had recommended, she was letting go. She was leaving him and their brief shared history behind now, like so many before.

Mrs. Concannon turned from Bart to the man in the suit, her whole body completely transformed. The tiger had left, making way for the sleepy kitten. The kitten looked up into the man's eyes. Bart knew she would be crying. He heard her begin.

"Oh, Officer, I made a horrible mistake! I hired this Lasiter fellow . . . ."

For the first time, Bart got it. He didn't think about it. He *saw* it. He saw what he could not or would not see before. He saw *her.*

Like the *Elizabeth* in Frank's *Watertown* song, she'd been dressed in Bart's dreams and became what he wanted to see.

Bart was waking from the dream that had been a nightmare. A chess game where he was an innocent, colorless pawn, and the White King — the Wizard himself — was tricked, mated, and killed by the Black Queen.

Now he saw his former employer, Mrs. Drake Concannon, or Rachel, Jackie, Elizabeth, Betty, whoever she was — he saw her eyes were the same deep blue as the deep water of Lake Tahoe.

Until you looked deeper. Until, if you weren't afraid, you could look beneath the Tahoe Blue in her eyes. Then you could see her eyes were — her favorite — *Black*.

Black as Lake Tahoe's deepest underwater canyon.

Black as the ink spot on the ransom note.

Black as the hull sides of her cherished boat.

Black as the flag flying from its stern mast.

The same Black Flag under which naïve Bart Lasiter had been sailing from the moment she walked into his office.

* * *

56

A New Day

Too Close for Comfort

Bart had screwed up again. He'd forgotten the hot plate for his coffee and the microwave for his Pop-Tart could not be used together without blowing a fuse. A spare glass-bodied fuse and a jog down the hall to the fuse box near the toilet fixed it. Now done with meal prep and breakfast, he could turn on the ceiling fan and report to Mr. Bocco.

Bart sat at his desk listening to Mr. Bocco. He used a piece of paper towel to wipe sticky Pop-Tart residue from the corners of his mouth. Leaning back to watch the fan turn above him, he pulled open a top corner desk drawer and swiveled in his chair to rest his feet on the extended drawer. Aggie had the center of the desk, curled up and purring on the green blotter.

"That's right, Mr. Bocco," Bart said, sipping his coffee. "I can give you the *Lasiter Investigations* Service Guarantee. Your pirate motorcycle bums, at least those three, will never visit your Ristorante Positano again. . . . You're welcome. Now, about my fee, 'Eat for free on Mondays,' you said, right? . . . just me, I understand. How long can I eat for free? . . . well, you're very generous, Mr. Bocco. We'll call it a retainer. You just call if you need anything. See you next Monday. Goodbye."

Bart had other calls to make, including one he dreaded. He got out the card and dialed using the eraser end of one of his new promotional *Lasiter Investigations* Number Two pencils.

"Angelo? Mr. Stagnetti?"

"It's Angie. Mr. Lasiter?"

"Okay. Sorry, Angie. Yes, it's Bart Lasiter. I'm calling to tell you I've found Mr. Concannon. Like you asked."

"You took your time calling, Mr. Lasiter."

Bart watched the fan turn and drummed the eraser end of his pencil on the desk.

"Sorry, Angie. I did. I was tied up. And, anyway, Mr. Concannon couldn't talk."

"Yes. I heard, from other sources."

Aggie threw a left hook at the bouncing pencil and knocked it from Bart's hand to the floor. Bart barely noticed.

"Angie, are you angry with me?"

"No, Mr. Lasiter. Sometimes these things happen, no matter what you do. We told him not to get married again. At least wait a bit until we could check her out. We never got a handle on her history, but he said he was going to marry her anyway. I never trusted that woman."

"Are you going to be okay, with your employers?"

"Yes, I think so. There is always speculation surrounding a death like his. His passing is a great loss for us. We'll adapt. We'll be okay. We usually are."

"Good, good."

"Mr. Lasiter, I'm a man of my word. Late or not, you did what I hired you to do. Carlo will be in Sacramento in a few days. I'll have him drop off an envelope at your office. We'll do business again at another time. Goodbye."

"Goodbye, Angie."

Bart set the telephone hand piece gently back onto its cradle. He felt a lot better. He didn't feel great about being friends with the Mob, but any source is a valuable source. And now he had one fewer potential enemy and more cash in the pipeline.

Bart's new answering machine had several messages on the tape, all from Al Wexler. "You owe me Bart. This is a big story in Nevada. Consulting fee. Remember? Call me."

He'd call Al later that day. He wasn't in the mood yet to discuss Eagle Cove. Maybe just send Al a check. Behind his bed screens, he turned on the TV. He wanted something to listen to while he straightened up his office. Maybe he'd look in the thrift stores for a radio, or a second TV, one of those thirteen-inchers. Now it was too much trouble to move the heavy pink TV from behind the screen to the top of the green file cabinet where he could see it. Moving the folding screens was out, in case an unexpected new client came through the door. Besides, the oriental waterfalls calmed him.

Looking for spilled laundromat quarters, he found more shreds of paper strewn under his bed. A large, brown-paper-wrapped package had arrived yesterday, and before Bart got a chance to open it, Aggie had used it for a scratching pad, obliterating the return address and kicking it out of sight under Bart's bed. Bart opened the remaining wrapping and found two shrink-wrapped items: The first, a Deluxe Junior Pirate Kit, contained a black vinyl eye patch and gold-colored metal earrings, along with a rubber knife and self-sticking silicone rubber scars. The second was a Junior Detective Kit comprising a magnifying glass, plastic handcuffs, and an official Private Investigator's ID card. There was a note with a phone number,

Heal and deal! See you soon — Marty

Bart laughed. He was happy to be back in contact with his old friend. After turning down the TV, he dialed Marty.

"Bart, you got my package?"

"Sure did. It will be a big help to me."

"That's what I thought. How's your head now?"

"Better. How are you doing? Wrapping up the case with the Feds?"

"We went into the trailer . . . did you get a look inside?"

"I just looked through the trailer's bedroom window at night. What did you find?"

"To begin with, we found your bales of newspaper wrapped in plastic bags and duct tape, and a typewriter — like these clowns did a lot of typing. But you did okay to get away from this bunch, Bart — alive."

"They did try to kill me, and I almost drowned — twice."

"Did you know there was a fourth guy? Old Patch? John 'Patch' Emerson? He rode with them for years. He wore a real eye patch — lost the eye in a fight at Folsom."

No, I didn't know. A real eye patch? I'll bet Hook was as jealous as a fake pirate could be."

"No doubt. Well, I didn't see the Patch-man anymore with the other three and heard rumors Hook and Patch got into an argument back in the spring, to settle who would be top seadog. Appears Patch lost the argument. We found him, old one-eye, hanging off the trailer wall, like a mounted deer head, alongside their TV. He's in the morgue now, at least his boiled and sun-dried skull and crossed femur bones are. There was a hole in his skull's forehead, about .50 caliber, and a lead ball rolling around inside. They're trying for a DNA match to his sister. We think the rest of Patch was fish food in the lake."

Bart's stomach took a turn. "I think I saw more than enough of the trailer, Marty."

Bart was feeling a little queasy again. His head was better physically, but not psychologically.

"Marty, I've got some things to do. I'll call you next week. Maybe you can come to Old Town for dinner. I'll buy. I know a nice Italian place, if we eat on a Monday."

"Cool, Bart. Later."

Bart shook his head, trying to forget. He went behind the screen and turned up the TV volume.

". . . in other news, a food interest group is calling for stricter measures to tighten industry safety standards for cheese," said a news reader.

"A good thing, Aggie — I once cut myself on a piece of sharp cheddar." Bart loved TV news.

". . . and while cleaning his gun, it suddenly went off and hit his television set. After an interview with police officers, Mr. Rayburn said —"

Bart mimicked the serious tone of the news reader: "Deep into his second six-pack, Mr. Rayburn got his gun to help Jim Rockford . . . ."

Pleased with his own entertainment, Bart felt he was now in a better mood. He would call Al Wexler. He had turned down the TV again and was on the way back to the desk when the phone rang.

"Hey Bart. I'm going to Reno this morning. Why don't you ride with me? I could use the company on the drive, and you could retrieve the Klimo."

"Okay. Thanks, Fred."

He'd call Al when he got back.

Bart wanted the Klimo back home in its garage, but he had mixed feelings about returning to One Eagle Cove.

After he finished his coffee and filled Aggie's cat-face dish with some chicken and tuna, and another dish with crunchy dry food, he placed them on the floor in the hallway outside his door. Aggie followed him to the dishes.

"Aggie, I'm going to be gone all day, with Uncle Fred. You can take care of yourself. I'll be back later."

* * *

57

Nevada Lasiter

Oh! What It Seemed To Be

Sitting on his building's front steps, Bart saw Fred pull up across the street behind the wheel of a shiny black hardtop, waving through the windshield. He stopped at Teddy Judah's statue as Bart crossed the street.

Bart slid into the front seat. "Okay, let's go."

Those were the last words Bart spoke for a while.

Fred drove north on Second Street to I Street, then east under I-5 and down J Street. A turn north on 16th Street took them onto freeway, the Highway 160 connector to Business 80.

When they were finally on I-80 East, Bart said, "This car is old, isn't it?"

After Bart's initial silence, Fred was happy to talk.

"It's a sixty-one Buick, the Electra, with the big V8. They call it a Bubbletop. It was one of my dad's. He hardly drove it and always kept it tuned and garaged. He loved it — better than any Cadillac, he used to say. It's barely got sixty thousand miles on it."

"It's just like it's new." Bart slid his hand over the padded dashboard.

"Well, none of us are new. But it is a keeper."

"I'll bet this car would have drawn some attention in Reno last week."

"Hot August Nights?"

"Sure."

"That's why I'm going today, instead of last week. You tire of saying, 'No, it's not for sale.'"

On I-80, Bart had trouble believing this same drive he had made in the Klimo just a few days ago had really happened. Though his big bandage was gone, the remaining discomfort from his head wounds said it all really did happen.

Once past Auburn, Fred's big Buick coupe climbed I-80 toward Donner Pass, seemingly without effort. It would have left the Klimo far behind, panting. Bart sank back deep into the seat padding.

"What are you going to do in Reno?"

"First, I'm going to check on a property in Incline Village, after I drop you off at the Klimo. Then I'm going into Reno, to see an old lady friend. She and I, we've known each other for years. I want her, finally, to agree to move to Sacramento and live with me. She keeps saying, 'No.' So, we'll spend a little time together, have some good fun, and I'll make another pitch for her to live with me. She'll probably turn me down again, and then I'll go back to Sacramento, maybe lonelier than when I left."

"You don't sound optimistic."

"Bart, optimism is for young people, who don't know any better. Regardless of what she says, I need a good woman, a woman who wants to share my cottage on the river with me. I'm getting too old to live by myself."

Bart pondered what "too old" meant and couldn't picture himself there.

"Speaking of women, Bart, what about those stitches on the back of your head?"

Bart just shook his head and studied the thick carpeting at his feet.

"So, you missed the big payoff?"

"Yes. But I got five thousand dollars. A lot of that is gone, but I'll be okay financially for a while. It was all cash — no paperwork — so, no one will want it back."

"A no-paper-work job, huh?"

Of course, Fred had read the newspapers. Plus, Fred still had law enforcement contacts, and what Fred didn't know, he would have, knowing Bart, accurately surmised.

They passed through Truckee and left I-80 at Highway 267, driving southeast until the highway ended near Kings Beach, awarding visitors a grand view of Lake Tahoe. A left turn put them on Highway 28 along the lake shore. While the big Buick rolled by the Cal-Neva, the Crystal Bay Yacht Club, *Benny's,* and Sid's motel, Bart watched without comment. He was becoming uneasy about going all the way to One Eagle Cove with Fred.

When they arrived in Incline Village, Bart said, "Fred, I really appreciate the ride, but you've done enough. Why don't you let me out here? I can catch a cab easy."

"Are you sure? I admit the sooner I see my lady friend, the happier I'll be."

"I'll be fine. You go on with your day."

"Okay, Bart. Thanks."

Fred stopped on Tahoe Boulevard and let Bart out.

"I'll see you back in the Capital in a few days, Bart, probably alone."

"Optimist."

"Right back at you."

* * *

58

Return to the Scene of the Crime

When No One Cares

As Bart walked along the road, he saw other people walking, or riding in their cars, all moving freely, all untouched by what he had experienced last week. They were all unaware that lives and fortunes had been lost.

The Concannon estate's value, and Betty's hidden, yet-to-be-found-and-counted fortune, were immeasurable. Bart's unearned, fifty-thousand-dollar bonus was a fortune to him.

These strangers didn't know, so they didn't have any reason to care. Bart felt separated from them, and everyone else. No one cares. He hoped he would get over it.

A cab turned the corner. When the driver saw Bart walking, he slowed.

Bart waved to the cabbie.

"Can you take me to Eagle Cove — down highway 28?"

"You have the money, I'll take you anywhere."

Once Bart had given him the Concannon address, the driver started talking and didn't stop. Bart kept quiet, just looking out the window and thinking. Along Highway 28, his thinking was interrupted only once, when he saw that kid, Tyler, in his red truck coming from the direction of Eagle Cove. The magnetic plastic Reno Messenger sign on the truck's door had been replaced with one that said, *Holy Pizza!*, with the top of the exclamation point covered by a chef's hat.

When the cabbie turned off the highway onto Eagle Cove Road, Bart's gut tightened. Today, Eagle Cove felt strange.

"Wow, what a place. I've never been here before. Does this road go all the way down to the lake? Is the house waterfront? Any big boats?"

The driver's chatter slid right past Bart's ears.

Until they saw the gatehouse, and the cabbie asked, "Hey, isn't this the place the FBI raided, and somebody died? I think I saw this place in a picture in the newspaper."

Bart looked out to the side, looking for the end of the stone wall. "I didn't read the paper."

A bright blue sky threw bolts of sunlight down through the sugar pines, making the stone wall's concertina wire glow hot white. How different it all felt. In the gatehouse, instead of the late, lamented Ramon, there was a man in a blue nylon FBI jacket watching their approach. He stepped out of the gatehouse and held up his hand to stop the cab. When the FBI agent raised his hand, his jacket fell open, exposing a holstered pistol next to a badge attached to his belt. Bart got out and retrieved his wallet from his jeans while the cab idled. He could see a second man in a white shirt and tie inside the gatehouse, sitting behind a desk eating a slice of pizza and reading a newspaper.

After examining Bart's ID, the agent asked, "What do you want?"

"I was with Placer County Deputy Sheriff Marty Brooks during the arrest, and I'm here to pick up my car."

"Which car?"

"The silver one — the Chrysler limo. Who do I see about it?"

"See Special Agent Einhorn. He's in charge."

"Oh, Einhorn. I met him at the debriefing a few days ago."

"You'll find him in the main house." Then he called back to the man in the gatehouse. "Hey, Phil — it's the K-car."

Phil looked up from his newspaper and laughed.

Bart ignored the agents and told the cabbie to take him through the gate.

Phil dropped his slice and newspaper, jumped to the door, and leaned out. "Stop him, Pete. Wait a minute, detective. No cabbie." He wasn't laughing now.

"Oh?"

Phil's face turned hard. "I heard about you, Lasiter. This isn't a PI hospitality house. We aren't here to service you. Do you know how to walk, gumshoe? Walk." Without waiting for a reply, Phil returned to his pizza in the gatehouse.

Bart rolled his eyes at Pete and paid the cab driver.

The cabbie whispered, "I guess he don't like you." He spun the cab in a tight circle through the sand and pine needles back onto the paving to the highway. Bart walked a few paces and turned. He saw Pete enter the gatehouse to join Phil, who had already picked up the telephone.

Bart's walk downhill was pleasant. The fresh air, scented with pinecones and needles and decaying earth, was unlike his average day in Old Town. Squirrels and birds flitting through the trees and over the boulders took his mind off his problems. The pleasant diversion ended when he rounded a tall boulder and saw the turnaround at the end of the driveway.

There all the wooden garage doors were folded open, and unmarked cars and vans crowded the turnaround. The big tailfins of a dusty white Cadillac convertible protruded from under a tarp in one of the garages, and in the next space another tarp partially covered a faded red sports car. In the end garage, near the steps, a new black Mercedes coupe sat perfectly parked with the nose pointing out, ready to go.

Bart saw the Klimo. He had parked it off to the side that night, and the Klimo hadn't been moved. It looked forlorn, wearing a coating of road dust and pine needles. The Isetta, also covered in needles, sat next to it under a sugar pine.

When Bart reached the bottom of the stone stairs, he noticed something ahead at a bungalow. Isabel was coming out the front door, carrying a cardboard box toward an old sedan. When she saw Bart, her face went from sorrow to joy and back in a few seconds. He walked over.

"Meester Bart! *Ese hombre, Agente Unicornio*, he say Missus Cee gone, then make me go in Meester Cee's secret tunnel." She began to cry. "He make me look at Meester Cee, and then Ramon. *Muertos!* And so many questions, over and over until I can't think. This morning, he make me sign papers about what I said. Then he say I must go now. I say I can stay and cook for them, like for Meester Cee, but he say no, I must go, stay here no more. Now I have no home and no job! What to do? Where will I go?"

She fell to her knees, sobbing. Bart knelt next to her and put his arm around her shoulder.

"Don't you have relatives, or at least some friends who could help you?"

"No. My whole life has been here. I left my family in Mexico when I was seventeen. A friend told me I could work at a restaurant in Reno, Rosalita's. I worked there a year. Then my friend said a regular customer needed someone like me at his new house by the lake — Meester Cee. I have been here ever since. I have some old friends in Reno, but I couldn't stay with them long."

"Do you have some money to go to a motel?"

"I have a little money saved, but it won't last long."

"Try to be optimistic. Maybe something good will happen."

Bart picked up her box and went to put it into the back seat of her car. When he opened the car door, he froze. One of the big fence-patrol Rottweilers was staring at him from the front seat.

"Isabel?"

"Oh, sorry, Meester Bart. He won't hurt you. Zeus is a good boy. He's just a big puppy."

"Okay."

Bart slowly leaned into the back seat. "Hey, Zeus, how-ya doing there, big fella? Want to sniff my hand? I knew some of your cousins, when they worked for the PD."

Bart curled his fingers down safely into his palm and slowly extended his hand across the seatback to the dog.

The dog watched and then leaned forward to sniff the top of Bart's hand. Then he dragged a half-foot of wet tongue across Bart's hand and wrist. *Friends.* He put his big paw up onto the seatback.

Bart took his paw and shook it. "Hey, Zeus, good doggie. Good to meet you. I'd stay and talk, but I gotta go now."

Zeus watched Bart put a hundred dollars into the box under some of Isabel's things. Outside the car, while keeping one eye on the dog, Bart wiped his hand on his jeans and returned to

Isabel.

She smiled. "See? I told you he's okay."

"What happened to the other dog?"

"Hera? My friends in Reno took her in. They couldn't take both dogs."

"They should've taken you and both dogs."

She started crying again. "I can't bother my friends. I have to find my own job and place to live."

"I have an idea. When you're ready, call this man and tell him I sent you." He bent down and handed her a business card. "He might have work for you."

The card read Clifford Properties, with Fred's name and a telephone number.

Her sobbing ebbed while she looked at the card. She stood, her eyes still wet, looked at Bart, and nodded a thank-you.

Bart smiled and turned to the main house, where he saw more vans parked near the side of the house. They had driven around on the service road. Agents were loading boxes into the vans. He approached one man and asked where he could find Agent Einhorn.

"He's inside, probably still down in the tunnel."

Bart approached the entrance. He fought off an image of Mrs. Concannon holding the door open for him, her blue eyes inviting him in. Instead, the heavy wooden door was held open by a rubber wedge. Bart entered the foyer and then the big room.

Light from the lake sky poured through the immense picture window and washed over the room and labeled packing boxes stacked in groups around the stone floor. Pine needles and sand and dirt tracked in from the agents coated the floor. Bart walked between the boxes to the sofa where he'd sat with Mrs. Concannon that last strange night. Then he looked to the picture window where she had stood. For a second, he could see her there, leaning against the window frame. He walked to the window and looked at the boathouse and pier, and Lake Tahoe. His trip at night out on the lake from that pier seemed ancient history, or maybe it never happened.

Bart turned toward the bar and the wall of bookcases. Scattered on the bar were several thermoses and a dozen empty soft drink cans. Behind the bar, in the now-empty bookcase, the section that normally concealed the circular staircase was wide open. He could see the stair railing and the stone silo walls. He closed his eyes and jerked his head down. When he opened his eyes, he saw a wide smear of dried blood on the floor where his head had landed that night.

Without warning, his stomach rolled, and he felt queasy, as if the big room were closing in and crushing him. He felt his throat tightening. He was sure he would faint if he didn't leave. He hurried to one of the doors leading out to the lake, yanked it open, and bolted out into the sun. He stopped on the stone patio, breathing deeply. After a few minutes, his intake of fresh lake air returned him to almost normal.

Bart followed the stone path toward the gazebo. He walked until he could see the gazebo, where he had eaten breakfast with Mrs. Concannon a few days, or maybe a lifetime ago. Would he see the white china settings on the blue cloth, and her repose at the table? Instead, he saw four FBI agents sitting in the gazebo, their talking and laughing mocking Bart's memory of that day. The wooden tabletop in front of them was naked, the blue cloth replaced by soft drink cans and open cardboard pizza boxes.

Beyond the gazebo, charging toward him, a big mahogany runabout cut through the cobalt blue, leaving a wide V-shaped wake tipped with white foam. Eight revelers in bathing suits were waving their hands in the air. They were waving to the agents and enjoying a close look at the stone estate as they sped past. Then they saw Bart and waved to him, too. A postcard from the fifties.

Bart didn't wave back. There was something wrong with them waving to him. The normalcy of the scene made him want to jump out of his skin. The boat's transom stung him, boasting *No Cares*. Bart watched them disappear around a bend to the south, until just the wake from their boat remained.

Taking in a deep breath of fresh air, as though it were a stiff drink, Bart braced himself for a return to the big room. He went straight to the bookcase, stepped through, and leaned out over the railing above the spiral stairs. The air choked him.

* * *

59

Vertigo

Just an Old Stone House

Bart could smell the same old stone and iron, and now, maybe old blood and burned things. Bending out over the railing, he remembered cleaner dry air and the closed-in feeling from that night. Looking down the spiral stairs was inducing vertigo. He fought it and pulled himself together before he and the stairs could spin out of control.

"Agent Einhorn? Yo?" he called down.

"Yeah? Oh, it's you, Lasiter. Phil called. Down here."

One cautious step after another, Bart descended the spiral staircase, two hands gripping the iron handrail all the way down. The air got cooler, and he got hotter, descending toward the scene of his recent nightmare. Stepping around the spot in the hallway where he was first dumped to the stone floor, Bart found Special Agent Einhorn in the room that had held all the slot machines and roulette wheels. The room was now two-thirds empty.

"Ah, Lasiter. You missed a real mess down here, going from O'Hara's straight back to Sacramento after the debriefing."

"I had to get back."

"Burned cash, burned Ramon, and old Concannon shot up dead. A real mess."

"I had obligations."

"We heard. How's your cat?"

"Oh . . . he's fine. What's going to happen to this place?"

"Uncle Sam is the caretaker until Treasury and the Courts have sorted it all out. Much of it is still considered evidence."

Einhorn used a reel of clear packing tape to seal a box and then applied a bar-coded and numbered label. He wrote something on the label, and then next to a matching barcode on a sheet of paper on a clipboard.

"We found some interesting devices and plans here, many unknown to us. We may visit some casinos soon."

"Who gets what's left?"

"Concannon didn't have any heirs, if you don't count Betty. Not legal heirs anyway, and we're barely cordial with his other, Italian, family. I'll bet when the IRS accountants sort through what paper there is, all of this will belong to The People for back taxes, especially when you consider penalties and interest going back over four decades."

Bart leaned against the wooden door frame. "What about the Chris-Craft?"

"Which one?"

"The big one — the Corvette."

"I was in it at O'Hara's yesterday. Both the Sacramento and South Lake Tahoe offices tell us all the boat nuts keep calling, wanting to know if the 'Black Bullnose' is for sale. We've been through it to our satisfaction. O'Hara's could sell it for us, but that boat is too expensive just to dump on the market. You see inside?"

"Not inside."

"Talk about spare-no-expense. It will probably wait with the house for an outcome. Soon, before the weather turns, we'll bring it back here to its boathouse. It's expensive to keep a boat that big under cover at O'Hara's. I'm told the water in the boathouse here doesn't freeze in the winter, and there are slings to pick it up out of the water. Who knows how long the lawyers and bean-counters will take to decide? We know a few of us will live here until then. I've lived in worse places."

"When you said, 'Which one?' about the Chris-Craft, I had to think, because I never saw the runabout, except in pictures. She told me it was on the lake bottom."

"*Em-Eye-Tee*? Real shallow water. We pumped some air

into it to lift it off the bottom enough to drag it the short distance to the beach. But it's in bad shape. He never maintained it — so much for higher learning. The people at O'Hara's say it still has significant value as-is. They'll buy it for future restoration."

"For a smart guy, Drake Concannon had some blind spots, enough to get himself killed."

"Lasiter, that's one place where I have to agree with you. But, before you decide exactly how smart he wasn't, come look at something." Einhorn tossed his clipboard, marker pen, and reel of tape onto a box and led Bart down the hall.

They stopped at the room where Drake Concannon died, and Ramon burned. Bart never saw the room that night. Now the floor had dried blood stains and blackened burn marks. Einhorn coaxed him toward the back of the room while Bart tried to step around the blood stains.

At the back of the room, Concannon had carved a caged area out of the granite. It had to be where he'd kept his cash. The steel-framed and cross-barred heavy wire-mesh door, scorched and twisted from the same flames that fried Ramon, hung wide open. The metal keypad on the door frame was blackened and its plastic number keys had melted into gooey, colored drips.

Behind the wire mesh, the cash room was at least the size of a small bank vault, with the three inside walls covered by wooden bookcases. In the center of the room, a metal table had escaped most of the flames. The table and shelves were empty now, but Bart guessed they once held millions of dollars in cash.

"What do you think, Lasiter?"

"I don't know. What *should* I think?"

"Look." Einhorn stepped to the back-wall bookcase and reached under a shelf. The bookcase swung into an empty room, again lined with wooden bookcases. "We found it by accident."

"Wow, cool. What was in there?"

"A nice selection of guns, Viet-Nam-era grenades in cloth carry-pouches, and two suitcases."

"Yikes."

"Each of the suitcases held several changes of clothes, some cash and traveler's checks, and a different false identity with Drake Concannon's picture. Passport, driver's license — the works, and all up to date. Oh, and the lining of each case held several hundred-K in large bills, and four more identities."

"Boy Scout's motto. So, he was looking over his shoulder, too."

"Lasiter, when you work for the Mob, they offer you only one retirement plan."

"The fake IDs and escape plans — he and his wife were more alike than they knew."

"Made for each other."

Bart stepped into the little room and looked around. "What was on the shelves?"

"More cash, if you can believe it. Treasury is happy."

"So, she and her pirates missed some of Drake Concannon's cash?"

Einhorn laughed. "They were in a hurry and probably so happy with what was on the shelves in the cage they didn't think about trick bookcases."

Bart tried to picture Concannon with the suitcases. "Okay, he had an escape kit. But why in there?"

"The way we figure is he knew one day someone would have a gun to his head trying to get into his cash cage. Tied up, he'd give them the disaster code. Like the normal code, it unlocked the cage door, but it also started a slow fuse rigged to a grenade he'd hidden in the cage ceiling. A white-phosphorous grenade. *Willie Pete Dishes the Heat.* Boom and burn. Go ask Ramon. But, if Concannon was still on his feet, then he'd pretend to cooperate, open the cage with the disaster code, and head for the getaway room. See this?" Einhorn pointed to the backside of the secret door. "One-inch-thick steel plate. And look at the closing mechanism. Once he hit the close button, big hydraulics slammed the door shut. You wouldn't want to stop the door from closing with your hand or foot. Once he was in this room, they couldn't touch him."

Bart looked around the secret room again. "Okay, but how is it a getaway room? He's trapped in here. Does he just wait for everyone to burn up outside and then peek out?"

Einhorn smiled. "Well, maybe, or . . . ."

"Oh." Bart's fingers felt around under the shelves of the back-wall bookcase.

Einhorn laughed again. "No Lasiter, it's just a wall. But

look at this." He went to the left wall bookcase, reached under a shelf, and pushed a section in.

Bart was staring, open-mouthed, at another tunnel. "Oh, wow. Where to?"

"North, and then splits into three branches. One ends near the lakeshore, past the cove, and the other two come out in different areas of the woods. Try that one, Lasiter." Einhorn pointed to a shelf in the opposite-wall bookcase.

Bart found a metal lever inset into the shelf bottom. He pressed it and the section swung in. Bart inhaled the cool, musty air from another tunnel.

"Wow, it's like those nesting dolls, Matryoshka dolls, that they sell at the Russian gift shop near my office in Old Town. Open one and there's always another one inside."

"If you say so. Phil and I came straight from Buffalo. The other guys in northern California and Nevada are spread too thin. We haven't had time to go sight-seeing in Sacramento."

"I could take you."

Einhorn just stared.

"Where does this tunnel go?"

"South, with two branches ending in the woods. Another branch comes up into a supply closet in one of the garages through another trick storage shelf. And each of these tunnels has several false turns that take you nowhere, either dead end, or they circle back. Can you imagine, if you went in there, trying to follow Concannon through one of these tunnels while he's dropping grenades behind like Easter eggs at every turn?"

"No, for sure *I* wouldn't try it. But if he went into the woods, how does he get over the wall?"

"You didn't walk the grounds the way we had to. Way out away from the gatehouse, the stone walls have arched openings filled with locked steel doors. A tunnel from here on each end comes up in the woods near one of these doors. We found the keys to the steel doors in the suitcases. All-in-all, well planned. If she hadn't tricked and drugged him, he might have beaten them. Concannon must have worn out a few miners here."

"Pharaoh Concannon. He had true tunnel-vision."

Einhorn didn't laugh. Bart was beginning to feel Einhorn didn't like him.

"Okay, Lasiter. End of the tour. I have work." He led Bart back to the hallway and down to Tut's slot machine room.

Fine with Bart. He'd seen enough tunnels and secret rooms to last for a while. Maybe he'd seen too many. Bart was afraid later that night he might have that dream again, the one where something is inside of something, which is inside of something, which is inside of something else.

Like the Matryoshka dolls. Or the tunnels. Or Betty.

* * *

60

Mustard on That

Nothing in Common

Einhorn stopped outside the slot machine room. "I've got work to do, Lasiter. Anything else?"

"Well, Agent Einhorn, now I'd like to take my car and go back to Sacramento. Okay with you?"

"Which car?"

"Oh . . . the Chrysler limo."

"The housekeeper told us the K-car was yours, but what about the red egg-car?"

"The BMW?"

"If you say so. Whose is it?"

Bart wanted to disclaim the egg-car, but they would soon check with the California DMV and find Bart's name on the paperwork Larry King would have filed with the state.

"Let me ask you a question, Agent Einhorn."

"Okay."

"You're hauling a lot of stuff out of here, aren't you?"

"Yes . . .?"

Bart dug into a back pocket of his jeans. "Here — take this."

Bart handed him the paperwork for the Isetta. "Maybe you can have one of those charities pick it up or take it to a car dealer for me." Bart reached into his front pocket for the Isetta keys. "I don't need it now."

Einhorn's lips curled into a frown of disgust while he read

through the paperwork. "The egg car is yours, too?"

"Yes."

"Lasiter, you have really weird taste in transportation. Do I *look* like I have time to dispose of cars for you?"

"So, you mean, no?"

"Good detective work, Lasiter. You take both your vehicles, soon as you can. You need jumper cables or a push, the guys will help you. You have gas in them, right? The government might give you some gas, just to be rid of them. Or, maybe, you just use a big key to wind up the egg-car?"

"Ha, ha. I'll be okay. Thanks."

Bart didn't like Einhorn's mood turning dark. The earlier Einhorn was bad enough.

"We never saw your vehicles as something Betty would ride in, let alone drive or *own*. Be glad to have them out of our way."

Bart had reached his fill of Einhorn's disapproval. It had become excessive. His head still hurt, and he just didn't have the patience to think or calm himself. He grabbed the first thing that came to mind and lashed out.

"Okay. So, what about some of you FBI guys not helping, being slow on the up take?"

Einhorn's face twisted. *"What?"*

"I saw on a DVD — several DVDs — the FBI has an 'Anti-Piracy' program. *Piracy is not a victimless crime.* So, where were *YOU* when Hook and his pirate friends were committing piracy, huh?"

Einhorn's eyes narrowed. He stared at Bart a long time before answering.

"That refers to the illegal copying of videos, Lasiter."

"Oh . . . I knew that."

"Maybe I'm being too hard on you, detective. Maybe you need counseling, someone to hold your hand. Maybe you're missing your pirate buds. You could visit them in the morgue. They floated into the path of some water-skiers on the west shore near Homewood while you were gone. Bad news, hitting a puffed-up pirate sausage with your water ski, don't you think?

"But maybe you just need a friend, Lasiter. The FBI has a Victim Specialist down in the Sacramento office. Are you a Vic? I could arrange an appointment."

"No. No thanks. I'll be fine."

But Einhorn, really steaming now, wasn't done.

"Lasiter, I like my job, and I'm proud of what I do. But we have way too many people looking over our shoulders, from Congress at the top down to Joe Citizen, and those people often have questions or complaints about our work. And local law enforcement — sometimes, no matter what we do to help, some think we're taking over *their* cases. And, after all of that, way down at the bottom of the barrel, we find *private detectives.* Do we have to put up with private richards and junior Sam Spades, too? Lasiter, a private detective is *nothing* — no, *less* than nothing."

"Hey, I was a cop."

"*Was.* And then, *only* a Berkeley cop."

"I have a license."

"A license? A license! Yeah, from Consumer Affairs. They tell me California thinks so little of you private dicks they make you stand in line with people opening a wig salon, barbershop, or maybe a hot dog stand. Want mustard on your license?"

"Very funny. Sorry you feel that way, *Agent* Einhorn."

"Feel? *Feel!* Lasiter, even in California, FBI agents don't '*feel.*' They *think!* They *think,* you *feel.* And it's *Special* Agent. *Special!* I'm busy now. If you need anything else, one of the other Special Agents will help you. Tell them *I Feel* it's time you got your clunkers out of here, and to give you anything that will help you go away. They all know your story." Einhorn laughed as he returned to labeling boxes.

"Okay. Message received. Bye." Bart, biting his tongue, started back toward the spiral staircase.

He heard Einhorn calling out from the room, still laughing.

"One more thing, Lasiter. The guys think, they —"

His laughing increased.

"They *feel* they saw *mice* in the back seat of the K-car."

Einhorn's laughing was now robbing him of his ability to speak. Bart heard him take a deep breath and sigh.

"Maybe . . . maybe the mice are members of your *staff,* or your *Secret Operatives.*"

Bart had one foot on the first step of the stone silo's spiral staircase, and his hand on the iron railing. He thought about going back. He thought about keeping his license. He gripped the railing so tightly his fingers hurt.

Relaxing his grip, he began the climb back to the surface. "Thanks."

* * *

61

One Less Egg

I'll See You Again

Bart swung open the big front door of the Isetta, dumping pine needles onto and into his shoes. He shook them off and started to climb in but saw his plastic bag of damp clothes still on the Isetta's package shelf. He took the bag to the Klimo's trunk and put it in next to a box of road flares and duct tape. He longed to be driving the Klimo again, but he had to deal with the Isetta first.

Whack! A heavy pinecone bounced off the Isetta door, right where Bart's head had been a moment before. "Yikes."

After he flopped back into the Isetta and pulled the door closed, his back hurt where it had grazed the cinder blocks during his fall at the trailer, and where later it had been tagged with the Willie Mac belayin' pin.

It took a bit of running the Isetta's starter motor before the engine would fire. When it started, the noise hurt his head again, and drove two wrestling squirrels off a nearby boulder into the trees. With his now dry, size eleven Nike Air lowcuts working the tiny pedals and left hand working the gear shift, Bart backed the Isetta away from the Klimo and started up the driveway toward the gatehouse.

Bart prayed the gate would be open when he arrived. He didn't want to stop and suffer more not-so-subtle ridicule from Pete and Phil. Keeping the speed up as much as the narrow, twisty, driveway would allow, Bart drove, alternating between watching the pavement and looking down at the speedometer, until he could see the stone wall through the trees.

As he came around a cluster of boulders and sugar pines, he saw the gate was wide open. He downshifted and floored it. Even though it was daylight, he switched the headlights on to high beam. He was hoping the lights and speed would keep the agents from seeing who was driving. He still had to come back for the Klimo, but he hoped to limit his suffering from these disapproving Feds.

Wrong again, the bright lights and noise from the Isetta's screaming engine alerted the agents. Passing through the gate at better than thirty miles per hour, Bart let go of the steering wheel, covered his face with one hand and waved at the agents with the other.

The agents, who were standing outside the gatehouse, looked fooled for a second, but then laughed and yelled, "See you later, Lasiter!"

Bart got both hands back on the wheel in time to avoid a boulder. He made it to the highway and turned toward Incline Village.

He measured Drake Concannon as he drove, suffering a mixed feeling of reluctant awe. Even though he was a criminal, and had been tricked and murdered, Drake Concannon had been formidable. Bart viewed the impressive and numerous skills and accomplishments of Drake Concannon in a mirror, where he could see Concannon's accomplishments next to his own, where Concannon's admirable strengths contrasted with Bart's glaring inadequacies. Concannon was dead, Bart was alive. But . . . .

Bart was feeling bad again. Einhorn hadn't helped. Bart better return to his to-do list and stop moping. In Incline Village, he stopped at the first used-car lot he saw.

"None of my Village customers would be caught dead in this thing. You gotta give me some money, at least, say a hundred dollars, for the paperwork, and taking it to the junkyard in Reno. Almost zero chance I find a buyer."

Bart looked around at the dealer's stock, a lot of expensive American and foreign cars. He might be right.

"What if you do find a buyer? Will you send my money

back to me?"

The man just grinned and held out his hand.

Bart sighed, and handed over the keys, paperwork, and a hundred-dollar bill. Except for a few dollars and the retainer Angie had given him, he was broke until he got home and could access his checking account.

The man held the hundred up to the sky and then looked at the sales paperwork. "You bought this only a few days ago. Deep Blue . . . Lepkowitz — it figures."

"What figures?"

"Nothing. You know, Lasiter, if this egg-car only had big tires, maybe a V-8 crammed into the back, then you could sell it to one of those hot-rod nuts in Reno."

"You too, huh? But you don't *see* big tires, or a V-8, *do* you?"

"No, just an idea." He chewed gum while using a yellow highlighter to mark the places on a form for Bart's signature.

"Well, it's weird enough that maybe I can sell it. Last week a lady came in here looking for a car for her side business. She said birthday party clowns and balloons — something like that. I'll call her. I know she said she wanted a funny car."

Bart finished signing and handed back the paper. "Call me a cab?"

"Hey, you're a cab."

Bart, feeling down, left the used car lot and walked along Tahoe Blvd., hoping for a cab to take him back to Eagle Cove. He heard a car behind him turning his way from a side street. It had already passed him when he saw it was a cab.

"Hey!" Bart waved his arms at the cab and jumped up and down. It made his head throb. He chased it until it stopped.

"Wow, I didn't think you saw me." He opened the cab's front-passenger door.

They locked eyes.

"It's you. Déjà vu all over again!" The cabbie flipped the meter flag. "Where to this time?"

"All over again." Bart climbed in. "You know the way."

* * *

62

Surf's Up

My Way

While Bart paid and released the cabbie near the gatehouse, Pete approached.

"Where's the egg-car?"

"What egg-car?" Bart smiled.

Pete smiled. "See you later, Lasiter."

Walking past the gatehouse, Bart saw polished wingtips up on the desk, below two hands holding up a newspaper.

"Hope it's all bad news, Phil," Bart muttered, and kicked a pinecone from his path. A big salary to sit on his butt reading the paper. Combat pay.

This time, his walk from Pete and Phil's gatehouse to the garages was faster and more deliberate. Tired of Eagle Cove, he avoided looking at the stone buildings, especially the main house.

When Bart saw the Klimo, he felt better. He'd be going home. Soon it would all be over. He opened the driver's door, took in the familiar Klimo smell, and sighed. He got in and sank down into old K-limo luxury. Revived, he swung his legs back outside and removed his Nikes. He held them outside and gave each a good shaking. The pine needles from the Isetta had been irritating his feet, and he wanted to return the needles to the Federal Government.

Shoes back on and tied, he assumed his driving position and

pressed the buttons to lower the Klimo's electric front windows. He leaned back into the seat with caution. No back pain from the Klimo — pillow-top seat padding. He found his gun still in the center console, undisturbed.

The Klimo started with the first turn of the key. Thank you, Tony. Approaching the gatehouse for the last time, Bart found Special Agent Pete waiting outside. Pete waved him to a stop, approached, and rested his blue-sleeved elbows on the Klimo's passenger-side windowsill while Bart let the engine idle. He smiled at Bart.

"All done, Lasiter?"

"Yeah. Where's Phil?"

"Just left for lunch."

"So, what's up?"

"I just wanted to talk to you before you left, without Phil around."

"What about?"

"You shouldn't worry about what some of these guys think. Einhorn and my partner, Phil — they're hopeless hard-asses. They don't think there's enough room on the planet for them and local law enforcement. And private dicks? Don't ask."

"Einhorn told me. Thanks, Pete. Is it because you guys are from back east? The Sacramento Feds seem more easy-going, friendly."

"Back east? Maybe just ball-crushing cold, mixed with ice and dirty snow versus bright sunny beaches and bikinis. Back east, it tortures you. You don't want to hear about someone else enjoying warm weather."

"Surf's up." Bart smiled. "Anyway, I'm not going to let it bother me."

"Smart. Oh, wait. Phil brought up a box for you, a present from Einhorn." Pete went into the gatehouse and came back out carrying a cardboard box, less than a foot square, and passed it to Bart.

No tape. No bar-coded label. Scrawled in marker pen across the box's lid was,

— Lasiter —

"What's this?"

"Phil said Einhorn just laughed."

Bart shook the box. "Maybe it's some doughnuts, or an autographed picture of J. Edgar Hoover at Pimlico, standing at the two-dollar window."

"I don't think so. Einhorn doesn't have a sense of humor."

"Maybe. I've heard him laugh. I'll open it later." He set it down next to him on the passenger seat. "Pete, I have a question."

"Sure. What?"

"Any word on Mrs. Concannon? Betty?"

"Okay. What I know, she hasn't waived her rights, but she hasn't acknowledged them either. She says hello and talks about the weather, while feigning ignorance about why she's behind bars, or even that she *is* behind bars. They'd like some help from her, clearing old cases. But she mostly just stares at the wall. It's like she's off in her own little world and entertains visitors now and then. And each time they go to see her, she behaves and sounds like a different woman, like she's revisiting each of her past identities."

"What's going to happen to her?"

"Hard to say. They got her a public defender for now, but Betty doesn't want to talk to her. She might have money she could use for her own legal defense, but any money she has could be connected to a murder somewhere, not to mention she hasn't filed an income tax return for decades, except as the wife of Mr. Next Victim. The Feds and Mexicans are looking for the ranch in Mexico you described, but who knows what name she used? And then, after the Feds, which state AGs will want her? Looks like she's not going anywhere for a while."

Bart studied his dashboard instruments.

"One more thing, Lasiter. Me, I think you did all right, all things considered, especially with you working alone. Yeah, maybe this woman had your number for a while. But she was a real pro, the best of the worst. And while you were gone, word came in they're going to add another count to Betty's murder indictment."

Bart wheeled his head back to Pete. "What?"

"One of her early husbands had a brother who didn't like her. When the husband died mysteriously, the brother hired a private investigator to get close to her. Later, the brother told local law enforcement the PI disappeared without telling him anything or collecting a fee. Well, the PI turned up, in the house Betty shared with that husband, bricked up behind a crumbling false wall in the basement. He — his remains — didn't look happy. One in the loss column for you PIs."

"Ugh."

"You know, the guys, they argued over pizza about you. 'Was Lasiter extremely lucky, or really smart?' Were you saved by dumb luck, or by your clever manipulation of Betty, keeping her talking until help arrived? They just couldn't decide." Pete watched Bart's face. "One of them claimed you fell for her."

Bart turned his head back to the Klimo's instrument panel. The voltage gauge still wasn't working. Maybe he'd have Tony look at it when he got back. He looked up and out the windshield toward the highway and then turned back to Pete.

"Pete, I'll take dumb luck over bad luck, anytime. And no, I didn't . . . she was . . . just a client."

"Well, *I* didn't have trouble deciding about you. Many men fell before you, and you're the only man left alive to talk about it. She needed to kill you, but you're still alive. No matter how you did it, you're the only one who beat her.

"I'd say, you did it your way."

∗   ∗   ∗

63

Stone Walls

I've Grown Accustomed to this Case

Bart said goodbye to Pete and guided the Klimo past the boulders and sugar pines guarding the asphalt pavement back to the highway. He felt fine until he came to the highway and turned north. It suddenly stabbed him, the thought that he would never return to Eagle Cove. Something seemed wrong. Something was left behind in the big stone house. He fought an irrational urge to turn back. He barely won and drove on.

Did she, his client, the supposed Mrs. Concannon, really have his number? Logically, *she* wasn't a real person. *She* was only a clever illusion. *She* was Betty, playing a role, like Miss Wonderly, a woman who also had more than one name. If Mrs. Concannon wasn't real, then there was nothing for Bart to regret.

Logically.

No, the source of his bad feelings was not Mrs. Concannon, but that while on this case he'd felt really needed, special, even important. While it lasted.

Now, it was over. The stone wall he last saw in his rear-view mirror was now history. Now, once again, he was just another nobody on the outside of that stone wall, on the outside of all of Lake Tahoe's stone walls, a nobody who had briefly trespassed in the playground of gods.

He had to shake it off and move forward.

Approaching Incline Village, Bart decided to call Fred about

Isabel. Bart telling her to call Fred was probably okay, but he wasn't sure.

Looking for a phone booth, Bart was distracted by noises in the back seat. "Yikes, my staff." The Klimo's power-operated divider glass still worked. He raised the glass, sealing off the back seat. Maybe he'd have Tony put José to work back there again.

Bart saw a phone booth and stopped. He got out one of Fred's cards and called the number.

"Fred Clifford, hello?"

"It's Bart. This number, it sounds like you're driving."

"It's my cell, Bart, for my tenants and business. I don't give out my home phone much. I'm driving, and alone. What's up?"

"I gave your card to this woman, and —"

"Isabel?"

"Yeah."

"She called. She's coming to my house tomorrow to talk. I might hire her as a live-in. She says she has a big dog, but that might be okay. We'll see."

"Good, Fred. I think she's really okay. The dog, too."

"Did you get the Klimo?"

"Yes. I just stopped at a phone booth in Incline Village to call you. The Klimo's fine."

"Bet you're glad to have the Klimo back."

"Yes, I am. I like it a lot — even more now. I had to buy another car for a few days and then got rid of it. Terrible car."

"What kind?"

"A little funny car — looked like an egg. It was a BMW — but not a real BMW. It was an Isetta."

"Really? An Isetta? I have a car-nut friend who has two of them."

"Why? A dealer in Incline Village told me nobody in Incline would want it."

"I can believe that Bart — that's Incline. But Isettas are collector items now. They call the type Micro-Cars. An Isetta wreck is worth at least five hundred dollars just for parts. Any running Isetta should bring over two thousand dollars."

"Oh. Fred, I've got to go now. Someone's waiting to use the phone."

"Okay, Bart. See you back in the Capital."

Back in the Klimo, Bart sat and stewed about the Isetta. Should he go back to the dealer and say he changed his mind? Maybe Fred's car-nut friend would give him fifteen hundred, or more, for it. Maybe he'd go talk to the dealer right now, while he was close. He noticed the box from Einhorn. He'd take a minute first to see what's in the box. Bart found a note and books.

Hey Lasiter —
We don't need these anymore, but they might help you solve crimes, you claiming to be a "detective." Hope I don't see you soon.
Special Agent Dale Einhorn FBI

The books were all Nancy Drew mysteries. Shuffling down through the stack, he saw *Trouble at Lake Tahoe, The Mystery of the Missing Millionairess, The Black Widow,* and *Into Thin Air,* among others. Further down, at the bottom of the box, he found some older Nancy Drew hardbacks: *The Clue of the Black Flower, The Clue of the Dancing Puppet, The Clue in the Crumbling Wall,* and *The Hidden Staircase.*

"Yikes." The hardbacks' pages were all dog-eared and had turned yellow at the edges. Each book had a name written on the inside cover, in a young girl's careful script:

Betty

After more pointless musing, Bart set the box down next to him and started the Klimo.

"Hope I don't see you soon, either, *Dale*."

Ready to pull out into traffic, Bart looked to the left. Then the right.

"Yikes!"

He saw it, racing down Tahoe Boulevard, straight at him. It was the red egg car. *The Isetta.* It had to be *his* Isetta. He felt sick, like he was at the mall again, where he'd stumbled into an old girlfriend, one of those who'd dumped him.

As the Isetta got closer, he saw a sign fastened across the

front door, and a fat, smiling woman in clown makeup behind the wheel.

He read the sign as the egg-car blew by, the motor once again hammering his sore ear and head.

BALLOON PARTY!

* * *

64

Going Home at Last

Long Ago and Far Away

It was mid-afternoon when Bart left Incline Village and his last glimpse of the Isetta behind. Bart eased the Klimo through Crystal Bay to Kings Beach and took highway 267 to Interstate 80 West, where he headed down the mountain, back toward Sacramento and home. Old cars, trucks, and hot rods returning from Reno's Hot August Nights dotted the highway. Bart closed his windows tight and tried to discourage the Klimo-curious by avoiding eye contact. He wanted to think in peace as he drove, without the attention of strangers.

Bart remembered his client, Mrs. Drake Concannon, Betty, Elizabeth, handcuffed, and what she'd said about letting go, leaving everything behind to escape and live free another day. If she'd let go and left everything behind in Eagle Cove, she might have been free by now, safe on her ranch in Mexico. She had broken her own rules by becoming too attached to her boat, unwilling to abandon it in Eagle Cove.

"When it's time to go, you go."

According to her principles, if she'd left earlier, she'd be free and still have her dreams, if not her boat.

But the black Corvette *was* her dream, her *Black Bird*.

The big black boat was young Betty's foothold in her own future. She had dreamed a dream. The dream of acquiring the boat was the beginning, the first focused dream of her youth, representing escape, freedom, and status.

Leaving her boat behind would have destroyed her. In the end, her black boat did destroy her.

Bart couldn't waste time and emotion feeling sorry for her. Bart had reason to feel sorry for himself. But wasn't the way it turned out his fault? Didn't he break his own rules, at least *Rule Two*, the rule about not being part of a scheme, about not being a Blunt Instrument?

Self-pity was not a Bart vice. Whatever happened to him, happened to him. He was used to having limited control. His teenage mother had been in constant motion before he was born, and she didn't slow down after he was born. He had grown up being dragged from one place to another. Bart went along.

Which was worse? That he was tricked and used by a serial killer? Or that, once again, he'd let a woman become his focus while he threw all caution into the wind? Near Roseville, after avoiding another cluster of car nuts, Bart decided the woman thing was worse. It opened all the doors for manipulation and deception. Keep those doors closed, and he'll be all right.

Bart could have escaped and let the sheriff and FBI save her. Instead, brave-but-blind Bart stared down danger to protect her. He almost died learning, like his ex-wife Sonja, Mrs. Concannon didn't need protection. *He* was the one who needed protection.

Being deceived in the future would be less likely after he had thoroughly studied each of his mistakes on this case. Yes, a logical examination of his moves would show what he should have done. Logic would do it.

But logic hadn't been a big help so far. The woman thing just laughed at logic. Bart didn't know what he would do in the future if there were another woman like Betty. He didn't have a plan. He had a problem. Emotions drove him, like winds that changed direction and intensity without warning or explanation. Or apology. And if a woman was involved? Double all that.

Music, especially the songs of Frank Sinatra, also affected Bart's emotions. The Frank Sinatra song book worked for Bart the way the Bible worked for some other people: There was always a title, or phrase, or complete song appropriate for any occasion. He often thought Frank lived just above him, right behind his shoulder, ready to whisper a title into his ear, flash an album cover by his eyes, or sing whatever fit Bart's need that moment. But lately, the song Frank picked, or just that song's title or lyrics, seemed to mean something different than before, yet the words had not changed. This left him doubtful about certainties in life.

As he drove on, Bart noticed he had been unconsciously humming a tune, one of Sinatra's. Immediately, he knew which song, and the lyrics.

Sinatra sometimes changed the words of songs to suit his mood or the occasion, like a jazz musician taking an old standard and creating a personal version. His dad explained this once, when Bart was a cop.

"Hear that, Bart? Do you hear it? Frank's doing with his voice what Erroll Garner does with his piano!" He gestured toward Bart's uniform. "Bart, I hope you don't worry too much about who's good and who's bad. No one is *all* bad or *all* good. Life isn't black and white. Frank, Ray Charles, Nat Cole — they weren't perfect men. Take what they gave you — the love and art in their music. Take it for what it is — a gift! Heck, if there were any real justice, we'd all be in jail."

Bart knew that wasn't right. But he remembered what his father had said about Frank changing the lyrics.

His father praised Sinatra's deletion of both the introduction and the ending of this song to focus on the heart of its message. But Bart's father wasn't there now. So, Bart didn't have to play it, and, not feeling great, he decided he didn't want to hear it or sing it.

Or feel it. The song used to give him a light, almost ethereal feeling. It was a feeling that said, *It's bad, but it could be worse, and it might get better — but, given who you are, be cautious. Optimism is not your friend.*

The feeling walked the surface of his skin, from head to toe, musical acupuncture that reached the hidden pain. He'd sink down into it and float. The feeling and Frank's song were one together. Bart reluctantly admitted this song could be his theme song. Bart's song.

Entering Sacramento, he chose to forget the song. Now almost home, he drove through downtown Sacramento, west on I Street, toward the river. When he turned left out from the shadow underneath Interstate 5, into the sun warming Second Street and Old Town, he lowered the Klimo's windows to let it all in. In the angle of the late afternoon sun, he saw a hint of autumn.

South on Second Street, he passed the Wells Fargo Museum and The Firehouse restaurant. He had to slow down for a horse-drawn carriage ahead, showing tourists through Old Town. He didn't mind. The sun felt good.

Anticipating the turn at L Street, around back to Firehouse Alley and his garage, he heard his father's voice.

Play it one more time. Play it for me. Bart, play it for yourself.

He couldn't stop it now. He heard Frank's voice, singing his song:

What is this thing, called love?

This funny thing, ca-alled love?

Just whooo, can solve, its mys-ter-ryyy?

And, why, should it make, a fooool of me?

Turning into Firehouse Alley, he saw the doors to his garage in deep shadow. Across the Alley, he saw the faded white boards of his building's backside painted gold by the setting sun.

Home.

He stopped by his garage, the Klimo idling, and got out. He heard a cat's meow.

Up on the balcony of his building's second floor, on the round table, Aggie yawned and stretched, savoring the last of the sun.

The End

Addenda

About this story

Notes for *Under the Black Flag:*

This novel started as a short story. It was to be one of five short stories, each starting with my 2006 Bulwer-Lytton Fiction Contest winning sentence, each featuring a different woman. It soon grew into novella size and kept growing. The other stories, except for *Bad News for a Ghost,* are yet to be written.

As a novel, my vision for it was that it would be a *respectful* parody of PI stories, visiting the great themes of classic Private Detective stories: dramatic events and scenes, violence, wealth vs poverty, unfulfilled dreams, and unrequited love. Sacrifice, trust, and faith contrasted with greed, deception, and murder, the unknowns overwhelming the detective's assumptions and skills.

Also, a personal favorite, cars and boats in some detail. In that respect, a Cozy for guys.

After a while, the book was too big (near 120k words) for most publishers looking at a first-time author (I assumed). Since then, I have tried to cut it, but not gut it, and quicken the pace.

The Chapter Titles and sub-titles are sometimes Sinatra song titles or parodies of his titles and lyrics.

My reference for Bart Lasiter is Robert Parker's Spenser. Bart is the opposite of Spenser — no three-beer lunches, no tasseled polished loafers, no psychologist girlfriend, or friendly brute to help him. *A Man Alone.*

Why the '54 Corvette? In my youth I dreamed about many things, including Chris-Crafts of all sizes. My father bought one of the first Chris-Craft kit boats, a 14' outboard-powered open runabout. I "helped" him build it in our basement in Chicago. I would have been in 3rd or 4th grade at the time. We would go to the annual winter Boat Show in Chicago, and I would go into the cruisers on display and imagine what it would be like to have one. Even then, I valued both speed and luxury. The Corvette had size but was not so big as to be slow. All boats are a compromise.

Other Bart Lasiter stories

Bad News for a Ghost –with– *Bart's First Arrest*
Bart goes underground to help an attractive TV reporter find a ghost, and Bart saves Berkeley from nuclear proliferation.
(Kindle Novelette 2013)

Looking for Mishka
Rock and a Hard Place Magazine Issue Seven
Bart helps an old woman search for her missing boy.
(Short Story 2022)

Always Rings Twice
Bart learns will power.
(Unpublished Short Story 2019)

Blood on the Stairs
Crimeucopia: We'll Be Right Back - - After This
Bart attends a Crime Writers Conference and pencils in a murder.
(Short Story January 2023)

Cane Mutiny
Pulp Modern Flash
[http://www.pulpmodernflash.com/2022/05/12/cane-mutiny-by-jim-guigli/]
Bart travels to San Francisco to help an old cop friend who became an assault victim and lost his cane.
(Flash Fiction May 2022)

Other stories by Jim Guigli

Listen to the Gunsmith
Guilty Crime Magazine
[https://www.guiltycrimemag.com/flash/listen-to-the-gunsmith-by-jim-guigli]
He didn't listen to the gunsmith.
(Flash Fiction July 2022)

Ben Hurt
Guilty Crime Story Magazine
[https://www.guiltycrimemag.com/flash/ben-hurt-by-jim-guigli]
Ben hurts at High-Tech.
(Flash Fiction) January 2023

Not Funny
Guilty Crime Story Magazine
A Sacramento comedian borrows trouble.
(Short Story Winter 2023)

Just a Dream
Crimeucopia: Strictly Off The Record
John Moss travels to Bicentennial San Francisco to find his missing sister.
(Short Story April 2023)

Supply and Demand
Crimeucopia: Let Me Tell You About…
Spies go to the movies. (Prequel to *Gold Digger*)
(Short Story September 2024)

About the Author

Jim Guigli read a lot, mostly crime and spy fiction, before he started to write. In 2005, he began writing single sentences for the Bulwer-Lytton Fiction Contest. The contest was created at San Jose State University in 1982 to gather and celebrate bad opening sentences, like Bulwer-Lytton's "It was a dark and stormy night . . . ."

One of Jim's 63 entries was bad enough to win. As someone said, the rest is history.

A favorite quote:

"It's not what it's about, it's how it's about it."
Roger Ebert reviewing *Boogie Nights*

Next: Read the first three chapters of Gold Digger, a future Bart Lasiter novel.

Gold Digger

Jim Guigli

a
Bart Lasiter
mystery

1

Karl

Northern Japan, Hokkaido, Chitose
12th U.S. Army Security Agency Field Station
November 1965

U.S. Navy Petty Officer 2nd Class Robert Metcalf
was watching the clock on the wall. With less than an hour to
go, it looked like nothing would happen before his mid-shift
ended.

Mid-Day-Swing — the three shifts that filled a 24-hour day.
"Mid" for midnight — midnight to 0700. The best shift, and not
just because it was the shortest of the three shifts. When the
Mid-shift ended, you came out of the windowless Ops Center
into the early light of a new day, just in time for a nice breakfast
at the mess hall or EM Club, even if it was just Army chow,
nowhere near as good as the Navy chow he'd had on a nuke sub
off the Kamchatka Peninsula.

And then you had the whole day to yourself until you had to
sleep — *if* you slept —before you went back to work at the Ops
Center again that night. If you hadn't spent the evening in
Chitose's many bars, four- or five-hours' sleep was enough for
a twenty-four-year-old, especially because you knew nothing
much happened on the mid-shift. You could coast through the
shift or use the time to sober up. Some even caught up on their
sleep. For Metcalf, this night would be different.

With his non-issue Wellington leather boots resting on one

of the lower crossbars of his G.I. aluminum typing table, Metcalf leaned back in his chair, his ears isolated deep in the comfort of the suede leather-covered, foam doughnuts of his headset, and listened to the sounds of the world.

He slowly turned the tuning knob on the huge rack-mounted R-390A radio at his side, running up and down the frequencies from below 1000 to above 6000 kilocycles, back and forth, searching for unusual naval traffic, usually Russian, and sampling radio signals of all kinds from transmitters all over the world, as long as they were powerful enough to reach Hokkaido, Japan's northernmost island, and the Army's vast wire antennas, strung on towers set in sand and scrub brush behind the Ops center.

Metcalf was one of what the Army Russian-linguist pukes called "ditty-boppers." Ditty-dah, ditty-dash, Metcalf found and copied manual Morse-code radio messages for the National Security Agency. Like his Army Security Agency linguist co-workers across the aisle, he was cheap labor for NSA.

Metcalf's "mill," resting solidly on his table, was a heavy military typewriter with sprockets at each end of the rubber platen roller, designed to pull up from the cardboard box on the floor between his feet, a continuous ribbon of edge-perforated six-ply flat-fold paper sandwiched with carbons. He had to hit the mill's keys hard to be sure that the type printed through the colored layers of paper and carbon to the last sheet, but he never had to stop to change paper until the box was empty.

He liked dial twirling, random searching. That's what you did at night on the Mid-shift. Specific targets and scheduled intercepts — like they had on the Day-shift — could make the time pass, but he preferred the freedom from routine tasks that the Mid-shift offered. You listened with one part of your brain while you turned the dial searching, but the rest of your mind was free to think and wander.

The problem with this work, thought Metcalf, was that it was too much like flying, at least as one pilot had described it. That pilot said flying was hours of boredom, interrupted by minutes of sheer terror. That's what this Morse intercept work was to Metcalf: hours of boredom, interrupted by that sudden, really important message. But you'd usually find it after it had started, and then you had to start typing immediately, all the while choosing the best antenna, fine-tuning the signal, taking pencil notes, yet never missing a radioed letter. You were it — there was no back-up.

The Army Russian-linguist pukes had it made. They had tape recorders. Just press a button and you copied everything. But the Army transcribers had to erase several reels of tape each evening that one of the lesser pukes would copy — garbled shouting from Japanese or Korean commercial fisherman the linguist puke had mistaken for Russian military exercises.

Metcalf had passed the last hour of fruitless dial twirling plotting revenge on the Army pukes.

Earlier, while he'd been concentrating on banging out an interesting unidentified message he'd found, one of the Army pukes distracted him while another puke used a Zippo lighter with a DLI Monterey Language School emblem to set fire to his ribbon of paper as it came up out of the box. He had just finished copying the last of the message when flames appeared over the roller of his mill. Shit. The pukes laughed and danced.

He knew he'd have to retaliate, soon. Make them pay. Must adhere to the Law of the Jungle, if you wanted to survive.

Maybe he'd start a rumor that NSA wanted more Russian Voice Intercept Operators in Shemya, Alaska, freezing far west of nowhere in the Aleutians — or Sinop, Turkey, on the shore of the Black Sea, very close to nowhere, and that, *to fill the need*, NSA was willing to pull people out of choice assignments like Germany . . . *or Japan.* The Army pukes feared both Shemya and Sinop. You could suffer frostbite in Shemya, from the cold or the boredom, and there were rumors of *mutiny* at Sinop, plus the Turks would slice you up if you even tried to date the wrong Turkish woman. Even for a short assignment, the Army pukes considered either place fit only for bottom-feeding anti-social recluses. Unless it guaranteed a promotion, even Army lifers dreaded such an assignment.

No, not strong enough, Metcalf thought. The smarter linguists — and many of the linguists *were* smart — had learned to ignore rumors.

Okay, the hat trick. He'd steal their covers — OD baseball caps — and roll them tight and wrap them in masking tape, like mummies. Or maybe staple them tight — use a whole box of staples. Or maybe both staple *and* tape — and then soak them in the toilet down the hall and turn them into solid ice in the freezer compartment of the Ops Snack Bar refrigerator.

The beauty of the frozen-cover trick was that, since you didn't wear it indoors, most people wouldn't notice that their cover was missing until they looked for it near the end of the shift. That's when you told the victim to look in the Snack Bar. The expression on the victim's face was worth all of the effort. He'd suddenly remember that the MPs wouldn't let him leave the Ops Center's fenced compound through the gate without his cover. "You're OUT OF UNIFORM!" The victim would be frantic trying to thaw his cover — or steal one from someone else —but it would be too late. He'd miss the Ops bus waiting to take him and his friends back to the barracks, breakfast, and a warm bed. He'd have to walk back two miles in the cold. Metcalf decided that stealing covers was exactly the right thing to do, but he would have to wait until tomorrow night — there wasn't enough time left to freeze a cover on this shift.

He smiled. When he was done, the Army pukes would leave him alone for a while. But, maybe, just in case, he'd better bring an extra cover for himself tomorrow. He'd hide it in his console rack under the antenna selector. After he'd beaten them, maybe he'd spend a day off racing his new Honda motorcycle through the sands of the Ops antenna field.

He continued to turn the dial and search while he planned and reviewed all the moves for tomorrow night. He had the rest of the shift to think about it.

Oh, Holy Jesus-Shit — there it was! He sat up straight, put his boots flat on the floor, and started typing. It wasn't just that he knew the call sign he'd just heard, the sender also had an unusual, heavy hand on the Morse key, so different that Metcalf recognized it immediately.

When the Army pukes across the aisle noticed Metcalf's excitement, he gave them a look that said, Now is not the time to fuck with me — *this is important!*

The signal was weak, but Metcalf was sure he had found *Baikal* again, the second time this month. Metcalf, like all the other Navy and Army ditty-boppers, had been warned when he he came on the job that any traffic to or, especially, from *Baikal,* was a very high priority. If he heard *Baikal,* he was to drop everything, run up the flag, and start copying.

He waved to his Trick Chief at the front of the room and listened while the sender kept repeating his call sign, *Baikal,* and his target contact's call sign, *Volga.* Metcalf already knew that *Volga* was Moscow, but he didn't know as much as he'd like about *Baikal.*

There was no message yet. *Baikal* kept repeating the call signs, giving Moscow plenty of time to find and fine tune his signal before he started his message. Metcalf adjusted his radio knobs and switched between different antennas until *Baikal's* signal was at its clearest and strongest.

After he'd typed in his Zulu (Greenwich Mean) time of intercept, the radio frequency, antenna, and the call signs *Baikal* and *Volga,* Metcalf waited for *Baikal* to start the message.

Trick Chief Petty Officer 1st Class Frank Davidson, hustled down the aisle and stood at his shoulder, watching the keys hit the blue six-ply as Metcalf recorded every letter he heard. Davidson noted the frequency, the antenna Metcalf had chosen, and the call signs.

"*Baikal.* Shit, it's reckless Karl again. I'll get the DF guys on it. Karl is taking chances. We're going to find him. Sooner or later," Davidson said over his shoulder, as he headed back to his desk at the front of the room.

After he had re-upped for his second tour on the job, Metcalf had asked Davidson about *Baikal.* How did they know the guy's name was Karl, and what was the big deal? The TC gave him a look that said he shouldn't be asking questions. Then he thought about his young Morse Intercept man for a moment.

"You know how to keep your mouth shut, Metcalf — you'd better — and you're my best man, so I'll tell you. What I know, Karl is a newbie spy, somewhere in California, north of San Francisco. Normally, someone like Karl would deliver his messages to a regional handler — not directly to Moscow, and not by radio. Maybe on hand-delivered paper to the Russian Consulate in San Francisco, and then by diplomatic pouch from there to Moscow."

"Why do they let him?"

"Because there's something special about Karl. So special that they'd let him communicate directly with Moscow, and then let him transmit long enough to risk that we could triangulate his signal and locate him."

"But we haven't located him."

"No, we haven't. Yet. He's reckless, but still plenty smart. They're thinking he's got to be moving his transmitter around." Davidson shrugged. "No luck, so far."

"How do we know his name?"

"They told me that 'Karl' was just a name they'd made up for him, to give him some flesh. But would they really tell me?"

New dots and dashes in Metcalf's ears jolted him back to the keys on his mill. Metcalf typed.

Karl had started the message. One group of numbers after another, page after page.

By the time Metcalf left the Ops Center, he'd missed his bus.

* * *

2

Requiem for Glasnost

Sacramento
Thursday, the day after Christmas, 1991

Karl parked his truck this morning, as he had so many times before, in the lot behind the Tower Theatre. The Theatre's marquee advertised the show times for the current features, *JFK, High Heels,* and *Madam Bovary*. He slapped his folded newspaper against his leg as he walked by.

JFK, he thought, what total capitalist crap. *High Heels* — Pedro Almodóvar, that Spanish pig. *Madam Bovary*, French, but too Russian. He wouldn't see any of them if he could help it.

Past the ticket booth, he headed to a wooden table on the outdoor patio of the adjacent Tower Café. He waved to his favorite waitress, Betty. She brought him a mug of hot black coffee, no menu, and left to take his regular breakfast order to the kitchen.

He sipped his coffee and thought about his life in California. Life was good. Karl was happy.

It was cold outside on the patio, even in the sun, but not cold enough to prevent someone who had grown up in a much colder climate from enjoying the crisp air and solitude. Except for the sparrows, the only birds around at this time of year, he was alone outside, the other customers preferring the warm tables inside.

The sparrows kept busy cleaning the ground at his feet. As long as he didn't make any sudden moves, they continued to search and eat.

Soon, Betty returned with his breakfast, three over-easy eggs with bacon, home-fried potatoes and onions, and thick slices of grilled and buttered French bread.

"Here we are," she said, setting the plate in front of him. "Enjoy."

As usual, he methodically devoured his breakfast. Now he would linger over his coffee and his capitalist newspaper, *The Sacramento Bee*. He removed the rubber band and unfolded the paper. His coffee had cooled enough for him now to take in a mouthful. He was about to swallow when he read the headline:

Gorbachev out; arms under Yeltsin
U.S. recognizes republics

By Leo Rennert
Bee Washington Bureau Chief

WASHINGTON — President Bush saluted Mikhail Gorbachev on Wednesday for his "sustained commitment to world peace" and — with the Soviet Union at an end — recognized its former 12 Republics as independent states.

The old scar that wormed its way from below his left eye down his cheek and across his lips squirmed while his face turned red. *It was all over.*

He leaned to one side and bent down until his head was below the table. The sparrows fled. He spat his coffee onto the ground and retched an oath:

"That focking Gorbachev!"

Betty, approaching with a fresh pot of coffee in her hand, stopped cold.

"Is there something wrong with your food, Karl?"

* * *

3

Will Work for Food

Lasiter Investigations, Old Town Sacramento
April 2008

"When are you going to stop eating those cheap burritos, Bart?" she said, stepping into his office and closing the door behind her.

"When you lower the price on yours, Mrs. Estrella. How *are* you?" He didn't stand but waved his free hand toward the blond oak swivel chair on her side of his desk. "Have a seat."

She examined the chair closely before sitting. While she was studying the chair, Bart slipped his burrito into a desk drawer among some bills.

After she'd settled into the chair, she noticed wrapping paper and toys spread across his desk. Bart had just opened another package from Marty Brooks, his old friend and co-worker from the Berkeley PD, and currently a Deputy for the Placer County Sheriff. A box labeled Little Buccaneer's Fun Kit lay next to a child-size plastic cutlass, a few gold-foil-covered chocolate doubloons, a plastic gold earring, and a vinyl imitation leather eye patch. He saw her staring at the display of pirate essentials.

"It's a joke gift from a friend. What brings you to my office?"

Her eyes left the pirate gear and focused on Bart.

"Do you have work now?"

"Well, even if I didn't have a little window in my schedule at the moment, I'd make time for you."

"You don't have a job, do you?"

He offered her a chocolate doubloon.

"I'd always find time for *you*, Mrs. Estrella. My policy is to serve my Old Town neighbors whenever they need help."

She ignored the doubloon and his dissembling and pushed on.

"I've got a job for you, but I won't pay you cash, because it's not a serious thing, except it really bugs me. If you do this thing for me, you can come to my restaurant and eat once a week, free, but only on a Monday or Tuesday."

Bart didn't answer. He was thinking about Mrs. Estrella, a divorced woman, not that much older than himself, and how every time he saw her, usually entering or leaving her Second Street restaurant, she always looked so nice, so together. He was thinking about how angelic her face was when he saw it turn angry.

"Are you listening to me?" she said, forcing him awake with her eyes.

"Oh, yes. Estrella's, eat for free, if I help you."

"And I'll take care of the tip — once a week. But, only on a Monday or Tuesday."

"Anything I want on the menu?"

Nodding, she said, "For the rest of the year."

"Why are you being so nice to me, Mrs. Estrella?"

"Don't you look at me that way, Bart Lasiter. I don't need any pets."

"I'm not giving Aggie away," he said, pretending that he hadn't recognized her dismissal. "What do you mean?"

"Aggie?" she asked.

"My cat. And, no, I didn't name him."

Aggie, a big orange tabby, jumped to the desk and rolled over for Mrs. Estrella. She stroked his belly and he purred, completely at home with her.

"So, that's your name, Boy? Aggie."

"I'm surprised. He doesn't do that for just anyone."

"What do you mean, 'just anyone'?"

"You're a stranger to him, aren't you?"

"No. I've been calling him, Boy. He comes in the back door of my restaurant, begging for food. I feed him every day. Why don't *you* feed him?"

"I *do*. Of course, I feed him. But I'm sorry — I didn't know he came to you for food, too."

"Not just me. I saw him coming out the back door of the *Firehouse* yesterday. That's what I mean about you, Bart. You're just like Boy, or Aggie — clueless, supposedly innocent, and helpless. I know men just like you, like my last husband. You're trouble. No thank you."

"Whatever you say, Mrs. Estrella."

"Monday or Tuesday — pick one."

"Oh." Monday was covered. He'd already earned a free meal every Monday at the Ristorante Positano on Front Street.

"Tuesday." He leaned forward. "Now, what did you want me to do for you?"

"Find my bug man."

Bart's mind spun while he tried to get a handle on *bug man*.

"Bug man? You think your phone is tapped?"

"No, no. Bugs. Bug-bugs. Ladybugs."

"Ladybugs?"

"Yes. Butch. He brings me ladybugs. He's my bug man. Butch the bug man. He sells me ladybugs for my roses. Early spring, every year."

"Why ladybugs?"

"They eat aphids. Can't have roses without ladybugs, if you're organic. And I have almost a quarter-acre of organic roses behind my house in Orangevale. Some of those roses were planted by my grandmother."

"Can't you buy the bugs from someone else?"

She rolled her eyes and looked up at the black-iron fan hanging from the ceiling. She found some spider webs up there.

"Do you ever clean this office? What a dump."

"The cleaning staff is on vacation. And it's a good office. Through my window you can see the tip of the Capitol dome."

She turned and stared at the window, finally standing up.

"Where?"

"Almost," he said. "Anyway, you could, before they put up that new building. So, what about another source for your bugs?"

"You don't understand. You're trying find bugs for me,

when I want you find my bug *man* — not bugs. Yes, I can buy the ladybugs at a nursery. But they cost more in those little packages, and they aren't as healthy. I've been buying ladybugs from Butch for more than twenty years, and now I can't get him to answer the phone. I told you — *it bugs me!"*

"All right. Tell me everything you know about him."

"We — my family — we've always known Butch. He sold bugs to my mother until she died, and then to me. But I don't know if we ever knew his last name — just Butch the bug man, and a phone number on a card." She handed the card to Bart.

He knew that the area code, 530, covered a vast area east and north of the Sacramento suburbs, all the way to the Nevada and Oregon borders. He made a quick mental review of the last time he looked at his car's gas gauge.

"I never had to call him before. He'd always call us. In the early spring he'd say he was coming down the hill in the next week or two, did we need bugs? Then we'd agree on a date and he'd show up at the appointed time in his old pickup. He'd have sacks of ladybugs in the bed. It was always cash, thank you ma'am, and see you next year. Very friendly, except the one time I asked him where he found his bugs. He gave me a lecture about how his skills and bug knowledge were not for sharing, or for sale. He said he was the best ladybug hunter in Northern California, and he intended to keep it that way. Except for that, everything was good and worked like a clock."

"You *hunt* ladybugs?"

"You find them up in the mountains all bunched up together under branches, in stumps, and by streams, under the snow — you have to know where to look."

"What happened this year?"

"No phone call from Butch. I called the number on his card a dozen times, but no answer. He doesn't have an answering machine or voicemail. I called the phone company to see if the number was still good. They said yes, still in service. I've been calling every day since."

"So, you don't know where he lives?" Bart asked.

"My mother told me somewhere up in the foothills, near Auburn, she thought, but I don't know. I've never needed to know before."

"I can get the address from the telephone number. Do you know any of his other customers?"

"I think he must have a lot of customers. When he came to my house, the bed of his pickup was always loaded with sacks of ladybugs, but he never mentioned his other customers to me."

"You said you and your mother were customers for decades. How old is Butch?"

"Oh, he must be somewhere in his sixties. Why?"

"Maybe he died on you."

"No, Bart. That's the strange thing I wanted to tell you about Butch. I saw him a week or so ago, in Old Town. I was in my car one afternoon, late, taking some things to the restaurant when he passed me by. After I recognized him, I pulled over but there wasn't room to turn around. There was a bunch of tourists in the street blocking the way, standing around one of the horse-drawn carriages. I watched Butch from my car, and then he left."

"You didn't get out and walk over to him?"

"I should have, but, you know, I was stunned. I just couldn't believe it was really my Butch."

"Why?"

"Because he was so different than the Butch I was used to. I saw him stepping off the wooden sidewalk, all dressed up in an expensive western suit and hat, and new handmade boots, like he was a rich cowboy on a date. I've never seen him in anything but a sweatshirt, old jeans, and work boots before, maybe the same sweatshirt for several years. That's why I didn't recognize him at first, and that's why I just stared. He was with a young woman I've seen in Old Town before. She looks a little like a hooker, though these days that doesn't mean much. I think she's Russian."

"How old?"

"The older I get the harder it is to say — late teens, early twenties. Like Butch's granddaughter. But she wasn't behaving like his granddaughter. More like his date."

"What were they doing?"

"They were getting into a brand-new red Cadillac, the little XLR Roadster, the one where the hard top disappears into the trunk. I looked at one last year, but I couldn't afford it. Butch held the door for her like they were going to the prom, and then got in. Had to take his hat off to squeeze in. Once he was in, he lowered the top for her, put his hat back on, and smiled, like he was back in high school. Then he did a U-turn and left. It still had that new-car sticker on the window from the factory. "

"Get the plate number?"

"Of course not."

"What about the woman?"

"I don't know where you'd find her. If you do, she should be able to tell you where to find Butch. When she was in the car, Butch gave her a necklace. She put it on. It was a thin gold chain suspending a single odd-shaped lump. It looked like a raw gold nugget."

After a moment of pondering what he had just heard, Bart said, "Okay, I'm on it. I'll get back to you. Mrs. Estrella, how about maybe a twenty for gas?"

After she'd left, Bart called Butch's number several times, but got no answer. Then he got Butch's address using the phone number. After he'd fed Aggie, Bart searched through his maps. He selected one map and did a quick study. He found Butch's address, at least his road, on the map. It was as Mrs. Estrella had said, in the foothills near Auburn. *Ophir.* What used to be Gold Country.

After saying hello to one of his third-floor neighbors in the hallway, Bart skipped down the back stairs of his building and sprinted through his backyard to Firehouse Alley. The weeds in his yard were a subtle green hint of what would follow.

Across the Alley he folded open the wooden doors to his landlord's garage and started his car, the '86 Chrysler K-framed limo he affectionately called, the *Klimo.* It started right away and idled smoothly and quietly. Backing out into the alley, Bart thought it was nice to have a car that ran well, when he had gas.

Before he could get out to close the garage door, he heard the screech of his back fence gate hinges.

"Mr. Bart?"

Bart stuck his head out the Klimo's window, twisting to look over his shoulder.

"Anton?"

The man stepped from Bart's back yard and approached the Klimo. A tall, muscled, hard-featured Slavic, Anton was the Ukrainian immigrant janitor Bart had met on the Concannon case. Anton and his brothers worked on cars. Maybe Anton was here looking for auto-repair work.

"Anton, what are you doing here?"

"I want see you, but your office locked. Office neighbor say come down to Alley before you liv."

"Okay, but what do you want?"

"I nid in-westigation. Mr. Bart, find my cousin."

Bart was stunned.

Two jobs in one day!

* * *

To be continued . . . .

(Gorbachev headline & Leo Rennert story courtesy of and copyright by, *The Sacramento Bee* 1991)

Printed in the USA
CPSIA information can be obtained
at www.ICGtesting.com
JSHW022300051224
74826JS00001B/1

9 798989 333714